THE
SECRET WIFE
OF
AARON BURR

Books by Susan Holloway Scott

I, Eliza Hamilton

The Secret Wife of Aaron Burr

Published by Kensington Publishing Corporation

THE
SECRET WIFE
OF
AARON BURR

SUSAN
HOLLOWAY
SCOTT

KENSINGTON BOOKS
www.kensingtonbooks.com

KENSINGTON BOOKS are published by

Kensington Publishing Corp.
119 West 40th Street
New York, NY 10018

All Kensington titles, imprints, and distributed lines are available at special quantity discounts for bulk purchases for sales promotion, premiums, fundraising, educational, or institutional use.

Special book excerpts or customized printings can also be created to fit specific needs. For details, write or phone the office of the Kensington Sales Manager: Kensington Publishing Corp., 119 West 40th Street, New York, NY 10018. Attn. Sales Department. Phone: 1-800-221-2647.

Kensington and the K logo Reg. U.S. Pat. & TM Off.

ISBN-13: 978-1-4967-1919-5 (ebook)
ISBN-10: 1-4967-1919-0 (ebook)
Kensington Electronic Edition: October 2019

ISBN-13: 978-1-4967-1918-8
ISBN-10: 1-4967-1918-2
First Kensington Trade Paperback Edition: October 2019

10 9 8 7 6 5 4 3 2 1

Printed in the United States of America

For all the American women
whose forgotten stories are waiting
to be remembered and told

PROLOGUE

Philadelphia
July 1829

I sit toward the back of the church, on a bench to one side where no one will take notice of me. No one does, either. Few things in this fine world are more invisible than a small and wizened old woman with dark skin.

Besides, today belongs to Jean-Pierre, not me. I watch him walk slowly to the pulpit, his shoulders squared and his steps measured. His forehead is broad and wise, his jaw firm with resolve, but it is his eyes that no one forgets, a gaze so filled with fire and courage that other men cease to speak in his presence, awed into silence before he says a word. He is my son, and so handsome that my heart aches with it.

"How fine Jean-Pierre looks today, Louisa," I whisper proudly to my daughter. "He's the very image of your father."

Louisa's brows are sharp and neat inside the curving brim of her bonnet. Despite my years, I am not sufficiently feeble that I require a keeper to guard me from mischief, but Louisa insists, and now sits so close beside me that her skirts spill over mine like a rustling wave of parrot-green cotton.

"John is nothing like the Colonel, Mama," she whispers back, using the English version of her brother's name as well as their father's rank. "Nothing."

I smile and nod, although I know better.

"Then you forget," I say. "I marvel that any father and son could be so much alike."

"Don't say that before John, Mama," Louisa warns. "You know his opinion of the Colonel."

Still I smile, though sorrow hides behind it. How did my little family come to this?

"Your father loved you and your brother both, Louisa," I say softly. "I expect he loves you still."

"But he doesn't love you, Mama." Even whispered, the words still wound, more than Louisa will ever understand. "Not as he should. Not as you deserve."

"He did when it mattered," I say, as I always do. "Now hush, and heed your brother."

Jean-Pierre stands in the pulpit, his head bowed as he composes himself. Sunlight from the arched windows streams around him. The congregation is content to wait, expectant and eager. My son is here in St. Thomas's by special invitation to discourse upon the subject of freedom. Jean-Pierre seldom speaks of anything else, so dear is freedom to him, and to all those who have come to hear him.

Freedom: a powerful word, with more meanings than there are wildflowers in a summer field. If I were standing in my son's place, I'd tell things differently. I'd speak of war and deceit and betrayals, of promises sworn yet broken and suffering that was nearly beyond bearing. But I'd also tell of trust and hope and love, a cautious finger on the balance against loss and sorrow. I'd tell of the girl that I was and the woman I became, both now so long ago. All of it would be the story—and the cost—of freedom. *My* freedom.

But that can wait for another time. Today belongs to Jean-Pierre. He begins, and I smile proudly as a mother does. Yet his voice, rich and deep, so much echoes his father's that the old memories begin to return again, and this time they refuse to fade away. I close my eyes, determined to listen more closely, but that only draws me deeper into the past, and away from the present.

And here I am again.

Here I am.

Veeja

CHAPTER 1

Pondicherry, India
August 1768

It was in my eighth summer, when the monsoon rains drummed at their heaviest, that my uncle Rahul sold me to Madame Beauharnais for two rupees.

How easily the thing was done! My uncle, a weaver of fine cotton muslin, had come to fetch my three cousins and me from the house where we were employed as thread spinners. The summer months were best for spinning, when the rains made the air wet and the thread swell, and we worked as long as the sunlight would permit. Each evening my back ached and the tips of my fingers burned from the hours spent with my spindle, twisting the thread as fine as a spider's web.

I didn't dare complain. Since the British soldiers had left Pondicherry and the French again had power over us, work was scarce, especially for Tamils like us. I was neither the youngest nor the most nimble at spinning, and if I were to lose my place Uncle Rahul had vowed to cast me out from our family. As long as my grandmother, my *ammatti,* had still lived, I'd known my uncle's threats were empty, but since she'd died of a winter fever last December, I'd lost the one person who had loved and protected me. Despite my every effort to please, my uncle's dislike of me had only increased. Now he struck me whenever he wished, and I woke each day fearful of what he might do next.

The spinning and weaving houses where my family worked and

the warehouse nearby were all owned by Monsieur Beauharnais, a French gentleman who seldom troubled his workers with his presence. Yet on this evening, as my uncle and cousins hurried through the murky late-day rains, the Beauharnais carriage with its matched gray horses stood waiting by the front door of the warehouse. The carriage's glass-paned lanterns shone bright through the rain, their dancing little flames reflected in the puddles around us.

Snapping his fingers with impatience, Uncle Rahul motioned for us to keep by the wall in the narrow street and to walk with more haste, so as to cause no possible inconvenience to Monsieur by our presence. But as I quickened my steps to keep pace with the others and not be left behind, my bare feet slipped in the muddy street. I pitched forward onto my hands and knees, and slid into the glow of the carriage's lanterns.

"Veeya!" My uncle grabbed me by the back of my blouse and jerked me upright. "Why must you be so clumsy?"

I scrambled to find my footing among the puddles, and from ill humor alone Uncle Rahul wrapped his hand around my long braid and snapped it hard, so hard that I cried out.

With a scrape of glass and metal, one of the windows of the carriage slid open, and a woman's face—ghostlike through the rain, pale and white-haired—appeared from the shadows within. She spoke in French, a language I did not then know, and at once one of the footmen hopped down from the back to stand beneath the carriage window.

"Madame desires to know if this child is your daughter," the footman said to my uncle, translating the lady's words into Tamil. Despite the footman's French livery, he was Indian, most likely a higher caste than we were. As the rain dripped from his laced cocked hat, he gazed down upon us as if we were the basest creatures imaginable.

At once my uncle released my braid and bowed low from the waist toward the carriage window.

"She is not mine, oh, most esteemed madame," he said in the wheedling voice he used with foreigners. "She is the bastard of my dead sister. Yet I keep her with me from charity, in the holy name of Krishna."

I stared down at my mud-spattered clothing. My uncle might

speak of charity, but from my birth he had treated me as an irredeemable stain upon our family. My poor mother had been no more than a girl when a party of British soldiers had fallen upon her one night as she'd walked home. With tears in her eyes, Ammatti had told me how these foreign men had used my mother like ravening wolves, and afterward discarded her broken and bloodied beside the road. She hadn't died then, as she'd longed to do, but nine months later at my birth. I alone had lived on, unwanted and despised by my uncle for the sins of my unknown father.

Madame Beauharnais spoke again, and the footman nodded.

"Madame desires the girl to step forward," he said, "so that Madame may see her face."

Uncertain, I hung back. I was the ugly one among my cousins and friends, the one who wasn't pure Tamil, and I was always mocked for the light golden-brown color of my eyes and skin and for my ill-shaped nose, both marks of my tainted blood.

"Do as he says, Veeya," my uncle ordered.

I'd little choice but to step forward into the light of the carriage's lanterns and raise my face for the French lady's scrutiny. Mud daubed my hands and clothes and the rain dripped from the *dupatta* that had slipped from my head to my shoulders.

I didn't flinch or look away, but met her gaze evenly, as if I'd every right to do so. At that time, I did. She stared down her long, quivering nose at me, considering, judging, like some terrifying deity. I had never before seen a Frenchwoman this close. I didn't realize that her face was dusted white with powder, or that the glowing red circles on her cheeks were painted with carmine, or that there were tiny pillows stuffed into her hair to make it stand so high and straight from her brow. All I knew then was what I saw, and if smoke had next puffed from her nostrils I would have accepted that as well.

Within a few moments, my courage began to slip away, and I scuttled back from the carriage and to my uncle's side. The Frenchwoman scowled, and flicked her beringed hand upward like sparks as she spoke again.

The footman nodded, though he did not hide his surprise or his disgust at the message he was to relay.

"Madame fancies the girl," he said. "Madame offers two rupees for her purchase."

I shook my head, not wanting any of this. Two rupees was more than my uncle could earn in a season of labor, more than I would earn in three years' time. My uncle refused to look at me and I began to inch away.

But my uncle was faster. He caught me by the wrist even as he thrust his other hand forward toward the carriage, his palm open and stained blue with indigo. The footman dropped the coins into it, and my uncle's fingers closed tight over them. Without a word to me, my uncle then shoved me forward.

This time it was the footman who caught me, and with his arm around my waist he lifted me high onto the box on the back of the carriage, at least six feet above the street, and sat me there as if I were a doll upon a shelf.

"Stay," he said sharply. "Madame orders it."

I twisted around to look to where I'd last stood with my uncle and cousins, hoping against reason that my uncle might change his mind. But already the four figures were hurrying away with their heads and shoulders bent against the rain.

The carriage swayed beneath me, and I realized that Monsieur Beauharnais had climbed inside to join his wife. I heard the footman close and latch the door, and then he clambered onto a small ledge at the back of the carriage, standing so that his face was nearly level with mine. He'd a nose hooked like a parrot's beak, curving over his upper lip, and he scared me, doubtless as he intended.

"Hold on, bastard," he warned, placing my hand on a leather strap designed for the purpose. "If you fall, you will be crushed by the carriage wheels, and the driver will not stop."

My perch was precarious on account of the box's painted board being slick with rain, and as the carriage lurched forward I clung to the strap with all my strength to preserve myself. We traveled very fast through the now-dark and narrow streets, farther and farther from Black Town, the part of Pondicherry where I'd always lived, and into White Town, where I had never dared venture.

When at last the carriage stopped, I still held fast to the strap, fearing what would happen if I didn't. The house before me was enormous and grand, and in the dreary rain it seemed to glow like a giant paper lantern lit from within.

The hook-nosed footman jumped down to open the carriage's door, and I could hear Madame and Monsieur quarreling. Other servants hurried from inside the house with wide umbrellas to shelter Madame and Monsieur from the rain as they climbed from the carriage and entered the grand arched doorway to their house. I huddled on my high perch until at last the footman recalled my presence, and returned to lift me down. With his fingers gripping my shoulder, he led me through a gate and into a covered courtyard, where we were met by other servants who gathered about us. They spoke over me in jabbering French, and prodded at me with their fingers. One man came forward with a length of rope and, seizing my arm, began briskly to bind the rope around my wrist, as if I were no more than a little beast to be tethered into submission.

But as soon as I felt the rope across my skin, I howled with panic and wrenched my arm free. Surprised at my boldness, the others stopped their talk to stare, and I took that opportunity to run away toward the gate.

I did not go far.

Instead, I was grabbed and pushed facedown against the puddled paving stones, with a knee pressed to my back to hold me there. Still I flailed and fought, sobbing as they jerked my wrists together behind my waist and bound them together. Then I was pulled to my feet to be led stumbling across the courtyard, and thrust into a small shed that was scarce more than a box. The door was slammed tight and bolted closed, and the footsteps and voices faded away.

I curled on my side where I lay on the damp dirt, my eyes squeezed shut against the darkness. I'd cut my lip when I'd fallen, and over and over I licked at my own salty blood. I wanted to cry again, but now the tears wouldn't come. Instead I lay there, listening to the racing of my heart and the beating of the rain overhead.

And yet somehow I did sleep, only awakening when the door to the shed opened and let in the pale light of morning.

"Fah, look at you," the woman said, addressing me in clipped Hindi. She was tall, with shoulders as broad as many men possessed, and wide enough to block the sun with her shadow. She was dressed in a patterned yellow cotton saree with brass bangles along her arms, strands of red beads around her throat and rings in her ears, a white French apron with red strings tied around her waist, and a ruffled white cap with a red bow on her head.

"What a filthy little beast you are!" she said. "You must be made decent before you are presented to Madame."

Awkwardly I rose to my feet. "Forgive me if I am filthy, mistress," I said as politely as I could. "It's not my own doing, but because others have made me so."

"You're a bold piece, to blame others for your disgusting dirt." The woman frowned as she saw that my hands were still bound, and briskly untied the rope. I whimpered as I tried to flex the soreness from my wrists and arms, but she'd no patience for that, and instead led me across the yard and ordered me to sit on a small bench. There she handed me a dish of rice and lentils, which I devoured without shame, it being my first meal since yesterday morning.

As soon as I was done, she took me to a large basin beneath a cistern that stood in one corner of the courtyard. She bid me strip away my clothing, and when my still-numb fingers did not move fast enough for her she ripped away the worn cotton of my blouse and *pavada* and tossed them aside. I began to protest, for I'd no other garments, but she cut my words short.

"Rags," she said as she ladled water over my head. "Madame has provided others for you."

"But I wish to keep my own clothes, mistress," I said, huddled in my nakedness. However ragged they might seem to her, my clothes were my only belongings, and I was loathe to part with them.

"Your wishes mean nothing," the woman said. "Your only desire must be to obey Madame."

"But, mistress—"

"No more addressing me like that, either," she said, scrubbing me hard with a rough cloth. "You will call me Orianne, the name that Madame calls me. You will learn to speak French, so you may better serve Madame."

"How?" I asked, bewildered. To me French sounded like so much harsh-sounding gibberish, impossible to decipher, let alone speak.

"If you are clever and listen, you will learn," Orianne said. "But take care. Although Madame will not speak Hindi or Tamil herself, she knows enough to catch you out if you're impudent to her in those tongues. Always recall that French is the language of this house, and spare yourself a whipping."

"But you are not French."

"Listen to me," she said sharply. "This is the house of Madame and Monsieur Beauharnais. They are French, and we are their property, which makes us French as well. If you wish things to go easily for you here, you will learn to listen and obey, and not to speak unless to reply."

Because of my uncle's temper, I'd long ago learned that there could be considerable safety to be found in silence. Thus I nodded, and kept quiet as I'd been bidden.

I shivered as Orianne sluiced last night's rainwater over my shoulders. When she judged me sufficiently clean, she handed me a bundle of clothes. These garments surprised me, and pleased me, too, for everything was of brightly colored silk. I'd never in my life worn silk, and the fabric slipped over my skin in a way that cotton never had. There were loose green trousers, gathered into cuffs at the ankles like *salwars,* a long blouse with a deep neckline, and a short sleeveless pink jacket with shining golden sequins sewn along the hems. Being a child, I was awed by the splendor of these garments, and thought of how much my cousins would envy me, if only I could show them.

Orianne frowned as she helped me dress, pulling the drawstrings on the blouse and trousers more tightly around me.

"These clothes belonged to another, and another before her," she explained briskly. "But those girls grew, and ceased to please Madame, and then they were sold away. You are small. Pray that you remain so."

"I can spin," I said, hoping that my single skill would make me sufficiently useful. "I can—"

"Do you believe Madame cares for that?" Orianne said scornfully. "That's not why she bought you. No, no! You are to be her new *poupée.*"

"Her *poupée?*"

"A doll, a toy, a poppet." Orianne drew a comb from her pocket and began to smooth and braid my hair. "All the French ladies keep young slaves—some girls, some boys—to wait upon them.

It amuses them. You will accompany Madame wherever she goes about the town, and stand behind her chair at meals, and oblige her in every way she wishes, whether at home or abroad. Do you understand, little one?"

I didn't, though I nodded anyway. "My name is Veeya, Orianne."

Orianne's mouth tightened. "Your name is whatever Madame chooses to call you. Now come."

She took me firmly by the hand, her skirts brushing against my arm as she led me across the courtyard. In this unfamiliar new world, I drew comfort from her large hand around mine, our palms pressed together and our fingers linked. The linen of her apron smelled of the kitchen, of turmeric and cumin and the other spices she'd been using.

By daylight the main house where Madame and Monsieur lived was even grander than I'd realized in last night's rain. Painted pale yellow with delicate white columns circled with carved flowers and vines, the house was still new, having been built with the rest of the new White Town after the British had burned the old one. A row of arched doorways were screened by shutters with woven cane to permit fresh air from the sea to pass into the house, a rare luxury in Pondicherry, especially in the seasons of rain. Even now a male servant stood at the far end of the veranda, tugging the rope that swung a large punkah back and forth to create a sluggish breeze through the house.

The black-and-white stone of the veranda's floor was smooth and cool beneath my bare feet, and as we passed inside beneath one arched doorway I tipped my head back and marveled at how high the ceiling was above our heads. There were other wonders, too, paintings in gilded frames, tables and chairs with legs carved like the feet of animals, and gleaming candlesticks of precious silver, and I would have lingered had Orianne not pulled me along beside her.

"Recall what I have told you," she whispered fiercely when we finally stopped before the door of one of the rooms. "Obey Madame in all things, else you shall be punished."

She entered the room, and I followed. At the far end was the woman from the carriage: Madame Beauharnais herself, sitting before a large dressing table. I could now see how Madame's skin was painted chalky white, with pink circles on her cheeks and black rings around her watery blue eyes. To me her eyes were those of a demon, lashless and staring, and her thin, sand-colored hair, in untamed disarray about her shoulders, was fit for a demon as well. Beside her a woman much like Orianne was combing and pinning Madame's hair into place, and against the far wall stood a footman, a darker-skinned African, yet dressed in the same French livery as the footman had worn last night.

Beside me Orianne bowed low, her skirts fanning around her on the polished stone floor. Not knowing better, I had remained upright. Too late I realized my error, and sank down as well, so low that my forehead pressed against the floor.

But I wasn't fast enough to please Madame. She spoke crossly in French, her displeasure clear to me even if her language was not.

"*Non, madame.*" Orianne's voice had become so unexpectedly meek that I would not have recognized it. Although she rose slowly, carefully looking downward, I remained on my knees, uncertain of what was expected. Before me were Madame's bare ankles and feet, swollen and crossed with blue-patterned veins, and thrust into heeled, backless slippers that were too small for her.

"'You are to be called Eugénie,'" Orianne said, repeating Madame's reply into Tamil. "That is the name Madame has chosen for you. Eugénie."

To my dismay, Orianne was then sent back to the kitchen. I'd thought her my ally, and yet here she was as powerless against Madame's orders as I was myself. I was told to remain, and ordered to stand to one side where Madame pointed. When at last Madame was done dressing, I was taken to her carriage with her, and made to crouch on the floor at her feet as we rode to another house.

Here we were greeted by a group of chattering French friends, dressed like Madame and equally idle. At first these women exclaimed over me, and patted my cheek and stroked my hair as if I were only another of the small dogs that yipped and yapped around their skirts. Soon enough, however, they forgot my presence, and for the rest of the afternoon Madame bid me stand behind her chair while she and the others gossiped and played and wagered at cards, long and tedious hours for any child. If I dared to sigh or wriggle, Madame would swiftly reach around and slap my arm, my shoulder, my cheek, whichever part of me was most convenient to her: sharp, stinging reminders of my place and purpose.

Nor was I excused when we returned to the Beauharnais house. Again I was ordered to stand behind Madame while she dined with Monsieur, neither of them speaking during a meal that seemed to stretch without end. My legs ached from standing, and my stomach growled and rumbled pitifully from hunger. I watched as dish after dish of rich, fragrant food was brought for Madame and Monsieur, while I had been given nothing since morning.

When their meal was finally done, the skies were dark and the cicadas buzzed and sang in the trees around the house. Monsieur's hookah was brought for him. I was made to follow Madame to her rooms, and again to stand while her maid undressed her for bed. I was so hungry and tired that I swayed on my feet, and only the dread of punishment kept me awake.

On Madame's dressing table sat a silver salver of sweetmeats, little cakes with candied fruits dusted all over with sugar. Although they'd been brought from the kitchen for Madame, she ignored them, and little wonder, too, considering all she'd eaten earlier.

But I looked at the little cakes with the greatest longing as my empty stomach gnawed at itself. I'd never before seen such cakes, let alone eaten one, and the longer I stared at them, the more alluring they became. Finally, as the maid began to snuff the candles for the night, Madame recalled my presence, and languidly ordered me through one of the other women to take the salver with the unwanted cakes back to the kitchen.

I bowed low and backed from the room as I'd been instructed. The footman closed the door after me, and there in the shadow-filled hallway I was alone for the first time all day. I looked down at the salver in my hands, and with no other thought beyond my hunger, I swiftly stuffed one of the cakes into my mouth.

Such supreme sweetness, such tenderness upon my tongue, such unimagined flavors of fruit and cream! In that moment both my hunger and my misery were forgotten, and I stopped chewing, the better to savor the pleasure of the cake upon my tongue.

I heard the door behind me open, and candlelight spilled into the hall. I gasped and turned quickly about, so quickly that I dropped the salver with a clatter, scattering the cakes that I hadn't eaten. Before me stood Madame in her nightdress, with the footman beside her.

There was no hiding my guilt. Madame saw it at once, how my cheeks bulged with half-eaten cake and my fingers glistened with sugar, and I in turn saw the fury that now lit her pale eyes. She barked an order at the footman, who caught me and pinned my arms over my head against the wall. I fought him in fear and panic, dreading what would follow, but he held me fast until Madame returned, a rattan cane clenched in her hand.

She grabbed a fistful of my silk blouse and yanked it upward, uncovering my bare back. As soon as the rattan snapped across my nakedness, I cried out, and jerked forward. The pain of that first blow only increased with the next, and the next after that. Eight in all: I counted each one, one small way to concentrate on anything other than the searing lines that now crisscrossed my back.

The footman twisted me around to face Madame, and released my hands. Madame's breath was coming in harsh, ragged gasps, and the rattan in her hand twitched through the air with a muted hiss like a cobra's.

"'Gather up that rubbish, Eugénie,'" the footman said sharply, translating Madame's orders. "You have proved yourself to be a thief, and Madame will never forget. Now go. *Go.*"

With trembling hands I collected the salver and the broken cakes, and backed from Madame's presence until the end of the hall. Then I fled from the house and across the courtyard toward the kitchen, where, in the manner of that place, Orianne and the others had already heard of what I'd done, and how I'd been punished.

Orianne took the salver from me and lifted the back of my blouse, clicking her tongue. Madame's rattan had not broken the skin as a whip would, but it had left marks that were already rising into welts as hot as burns across my back. I was crying now, too, heavy tears of shame and guilt and pain and despair together that slid freely down my cheeks.

"You must learn to obey Madame, little one," Orianne said softly. "She owns you now. You can never forget that. You are her property."

With a shuddering sob, I bent over, and vomited up all the pink, sugary cake that had cost me so dearly.

Eugénie

CHAPTER 2

Pondicherry, India
1768

I first tried to run away in earnest a week after I was beaten for eating Madame's cake.

I watched and waited for the time early in the morning when the kitchen gate opened and goods from the market were brought inside. Being small, I tried to slip through unnoticed amidst the bustle, but one of Monsieur's men caught me before I'd ducked through the gate, and pulled me back.

For my trouble I was beaten again, not with Madame's rattan cane, but with a thicker rod of bamboo, which, being more stiff, battered me severely across my ribs. Afterward I was tied to a post in the yard, with the others forbidden to come succor me. I was kept there for the rest of the day in the sun and through the night that followed as a cure for what Madame called my obstinacy. For the next fortnight my ribs ached so badly that I could only breathe in shallow little pants, and I'd have to pause on the landing whenever I climbed the stairs to Madame's bedchamber.

Two months passed before I dared to try again. This time I decided to be bolder, and when I accompanied Madame to a perfume shop that she favored I hung back near the carriage as the footman helped her through the shop's door. Instead of following, I darted beneath the stopped carriage and between the wheels to the other side, believing I would be safe among the passersby who thronged the narrow street.

But from his box atop the carriage, Madame's driver spotted me as I fled in my bright silk clothes, and shouted that I must be stopped. This time it was a stranger who seized me, and claimed the small reward the driver had promised for my capture. Madame was furious, and declared that if I attempted to flee again she would sell me to a brothel for sailors near the water. She ordered me whipped, six lashes across my bare back with a leather strap that left me bloody and faint.

After that, I did not try again to flee. It wasn't Madame's threats or punishments that kept me from attempting another escape. If that had been all, then I would have made another attempt, and another after that, until I succeeded. What kept me as Madame's *poupée* was the collar she ordered clapped around my narrow throat.

It was cunningly wrought, that collar, and fashioned by a jeweler so as to appear an ornament rather than the cruel device that it was. Made of some shining golden metal, the collar was inlaid with bits of glass that sparkled in the sun, and bedecked with tiny, dangling bells that jingled at any movement. Engraved on the band were words that said I was the property of Madame Beauharnais, and that if found I must be returned to her. Both the upper and lower edges of the collar were cut in a pattern of sharp little triangles like a jackal's pointed teeth, and every bit as biting.

Two footmen held me still when they fastened the collar around my throat. Although I clawed at every inch of the band, I could find no latch to remove it, nor could I find a way to cushion the sharp edges that nipped into my skin.

From that night onward, Madame herself slipped a chain through the loop at the back of the collar, and fastened the chain to another loop on the heavy post of her bedstead. With Madame in bed, I'd no choice but to curl up on the thin mat I'd been given on the stone floor, listening to her wheeze and cough in her sleep above me.

I soon learned to raise my chin and hold my neck straight to keep the little teeth of the collar from my throat, yet at the same time to keep my eyes lowered the way I'd been ordered. It entertained Madame to see me this way, and she claimed I looked as if I were raising my chin to beg for forgiveness from God—her God— as if any truly merciful god would ever be pleased by such cruelty toward a helpless child.

I learned to answer to *Eugénie* as if it had always been my name, though before I slept each night I'd softly chant my true name—*Veeya, Veeya, Veeya*—striving to remember it.

I learned to be more cunning when I took food from Madame's tray as I carried it back to the kitchen. I picked apart a hem in my blouse to make a tiny secret pocket, and squirreled away small bites of fruit and other sweetmeats that she'd left uneaten. Only when I was sure she was asleep in the big bed above me would I nibble at my plunder, finding comfort in the stolen sweetness one tiny bite at a time.

Perhaps most importantly, I learned the French language, as Orianne had advised when I'd first arrived. It was not a conscious act, but a skill acquired through daily use, one word at a time. At first I knew only the phrases of servitude, Madame's commands and the responses she expected. But in time other words followed as well, and with French came all the secrets of the Beauharnais household.

Madame and Monsieur spoke freely before us, as if we were mere deaf ghosts in their service. In this way, I came to understand that Monsieur had inherited the company that employed my family, and that he had little interest in its factories beyond what profits he could wrest from the labor of others. I saw, too, how little regard Monsieur had for Madame, and how unhappy their marriage appeared to be.

"It's on account of their sons, the young gentlemen," Orianne explained to me one morning while I waited for Madame's tea to be readied. Since I'd been fitted with the collar, I was permitted to visit the courtyard and kitchen on errands for Madame, and I would linger there as long as I could. "Years ago, Monsieur sent them away to Paris for their schooling, and Madame still refuses to forgive him."

"Do they ever come here to visit?" I asked. Paris was so often spoken of among the French—a rare and wondrous place that they all longed to visit like some magnificent holy shrine, far away across the seas—that I couldn't imagine any of them leaving it for Pondicherry.

"They have never returned," Orianne said, carefully measuring out the fine white sugar Madame demanded into a porcelain bowl. "They never will. They are grown men now, with affairs of their own, and no reason for coming back to Pondicherry. Haven't you heard Madame's laments?"

"She cries when she prays, but I never knew why," I said, devouring this rare gossip.

"You mean she wails and weeps as if her sons had only left yesterday, instead of years and years ago." Orianne made a grumbling sound of disgust, without a morsel of sympathy to it. "Of course Madame faults Monsieur for sending away her angels. Angels, hah. More demons they were. Now go, take the tray. Madame waits."

I hurried away with the silver tray in my hands and my head full of thoughts. Madame seemed far too old and too selfish to be a mother, and as much as I tried, I couldn't imagine the Beauharnais sons. But I did realize then that with a little guile I might turn Madame's unhappiness to my own advantage. It would not be so difficult. There was part of me that had always wanted to please others, even such a woman as Madame.

Thus the next time I witnessed her weeping, I feigned a silent show of sympathy (for of course I was forbidden to speak to her directly). She noticed, and found my performance most pleasing, rewarding me with a sliver of golden mango from her own plate. After that, I made sure to look especially sorrowful, or even to force tears of my own to slide down my cheek whenever she cried.

When I'd been younger and still Veeya, Ammatti would have scolded me for such deceitful behavior, but now it became a necessary part of my life. The more I pretended to be what Madame wished, the less harsh and more indulgent she became. She found fewer instances to strike me, and when she did she used only her hand, not a rod or cane. The flat of her hand still hurt, of course, but the pain faded faster, and I could bear it, or perhaps I simply grew accustomed to it, as I did with everything else.

In time Madame began to trust me with small tasks that were more personal and intended by her as marks of favor. I could also see that they were tasks that her lady's maid, an aloof light-skinned woman named Estelle who was dressed in French clothes, believed were beneath her.

I was given an ivory fan, carved with entwined elephants, to carry at all times, so that I might be ready to flutter it over Madame's face. I rubbed her wrists and knobbled ankles with perfumed oil when she complained that her bones ached with stiffness. I fastened the clasps on her jeweled bracelets and necklaces, and I pressed little circles across her forehead with my fingertips when she suffered from the migraine.

As my usefulness increased, Madame praised me extravagantly to her friends. She boasted of how I was her jewel, and how she had delivered me from a terrible past, as if buying me from my kin had been a remarkable act of charity. My place was always beside her chair, crouching so she could stroke my long hair for her own comfort, as if I were a cosseted pet.

And as with a pet, the collar remained around my throat, and each night the chain was clipped to it, and then to Madame's bed-stead. I was given only a single bowl of rice, lentils, or other mean food in the mornings, and a cup of the cooking water that remained in the pot in the evening. Because I was small, Madame believed that was all I required for sustenance. More food would be a need-less luxury, she declared, and one that would only spoil me for use-ful service.

No wonder, then, that whatever natural cheerfulness I might once have had shriveled away like a flower denied rain, and my childhood passed away with it. I dreamed of scraps of my old life, of how I'd plaited wreathes of flowers that my cousins and I had picked wild in the fields, of how I'd sit on my knees while Ammatti combed coconut oil through my hair to make it shine, of how I'd tried to catch raindrops on my tongue, but when I was awake, I no longer laughed, or sang, or danced for the pleasure of it.

These changes did not happen in a day, of course, or even in a single turn of the seasons. But by the time I was eleven and had served Madame for three years, I had become watchful and wary and solemn, with an owlish gaze that often made others uneasy. I seldom thought of myself now as Veeya; it was easier and less pain-ful to let one day follow the next, and neither recall the past, nor consider the future.

Yet before that summer was done, changes came to our lives that could never be undone, no matter how hard we might wish otherwise.

It began in an unremarkable fashion. Madame and Monsieur were joined at dinner by a guest, a younger French gentleman new arrived in Pondicherry. The evening was cool for the season, and although the windows in the dining room all stood open, there was no need for punkahs overhead, nor for the men who waved them. There were only three servants in attendance at the table, two footmen to bear and clear away the plates, and me.

That the newcomer had been long at sea was evident by the ruddiness of his complexion as well as by the loudness of his conversation, something I'd always observed among French gentlemen who wished all to take notice of them whether they merited the attention or not. The lavishness of the embroidery on his clothes and the white powder in his hair also showed that he was a gentleman, a member of a higher caste of French people.

As was to be expected, I was not presented to him, nor he to me, and whatever I learned was gleaned from what I overheard. He was Monsieur's nephew, the son of Monsieur's older brother, and leader of the family's trading company. Monsieur deferred to this nephew as if he were a prince. It was an amusing thing for me to watch, seeing the haughty Monsieur grin and grovel before another man half his age, and Madame no better in her fawning. But because it was late and I was weary and only half-listening, I didn't at first comprehend the news this young man had brought with him, or its importance to Madame and Monsieur.

"You know how happy this prospect makes me, Henri," Madame was saying. "But I must beg you to understand what it shall entail for me. To secure and pack all our belongings, to bid farewell to our acquaintance, to close up this house that has been our home for so many years—why, I cannot possibly do that in less than six months' time."

Henri finished the last bite of the roasted fowl on his plate, deliberately delaying before he answered Madame. He had eaten only the French-style food, and pointedly left untouched the Indian delicacies that included Monsieur's favorite curries. He blotted the grease from his mouth with his napkin and sighed, a drawn-out sigh of sympathy so false that even I could sense it.

"I regret the inconvenience to you, Aunt," he said as the footmen began to clear the table. "To place such demands upon a lady like yourself—ahh, it is insupportable! Yet you must understand that I have no say in the matter. The shipmaster desires to make his voyage to Saint-Domingue in a season that is safest for his vessel, his cargo, and his company. He insists that he must clear Pondicherry by the end of this month, before the monsoons begin in earnest."

"The end of this month!" Madame repeated with dismay. "However can I manage?"

Henri shrugged. "Perhaps you would prefer to remain behind, Aunt. Uncle Pierre can leave you here to conclude your affairs, and you may join him at your further convenience in another ship."

"No, no, I will not remain another day longer in this place than is necessary." Madame was shifting back and forth in her chair beside me, the wood creaking as her agitation grew. "I wish to be closer to my sons. I cannot be left behind."

Without turning toward me, she flicked her fingers, a sign I well understood. I stepped forward and swiftly opened her ivory fan, and began to flutter it to one side of her face to calm her.

"My dear, you realize my brother is sending us to Saint-Domingue." Monsieur wasn't looking at either Madame or his nephew, but was instead running one forefinger around and around the polished bowl of his spoon. "We are not returning to Paris."

"Did you not hear what Henri has said?" Madame said, her voice rising shrill. "If you may make a fresh start to your career in the Caribbean, then we may be reunited once again with our sons."

Monsieur's expression darkened. "That's what you wish to hear, not what has been said. Our sons will no more come to Saint-Domingue than they will here to Pondicherry."

"But what she says does have truth in it, Uncle." Henri sipped his brandy. "Your successes here have been mixed, yes, but fortunes can be made with great ease in the sugar trade by those who apply themselves."

"My brother forgets that neither he nor I are young men." Monsieur did not bother to hide his bitterness. "While he sits beside his fire and counts his money, I am expected to embark on a perilous voyage to this wretched island, and begin my life again."

"Not at all, Uncle." Henri smiled, a slow smile too full of teeth. "Consider it instead a kind of leisurely amusement for your dotage."

Monsieur snorted in disgust. "Do not mistake me for a fool, Henri."

"I would never underestimate you, Uncle," said Henri with an empty heartiness. "The sugar plantations at Belle Vallée will require little effort from you, and the house is the perfect jewel for a gentleman's estate. My father has expended considerable funds upon it, making improvements to the mills as well as to the living quarters. The overseer—Malet—is both trustworthy and firm, exactly as is necessary."

Monsieur nodded, mollified, or pretending to be.

"I've never found such a man to oversee the people in the factories here," he said slowly. "None that deserved my trust."

"You will trust Malet," Henri said. "Besides, the actual labor of the place is done by the slaves. They're the most valuable commodity of the plantation. By last count, I believe there were over two hundred working the cane fields. That does change, of course, due to deaths and sickness among the ones new arrived and unaccustomed to toil, but they shall be Malet's responsibility, not yours. All you must do is watch over the Beauharnais interests in the town, see that the sugar is sold for the highest price, and collect the profits that result."

I began to wave the fan more briskly. While this Saint-Domingue was an unfamiliar place to me, I did know how sugarcane was grown and harvested for its sugar. Many Tamils were employed in its cultivation on farms not far from Pondicherry, and the possibility of being returned to a place filled with my own people was exciting.

But what if Madame chose not to take me with her? What if I were sent to the market, and sold away to the sailors' brothels, Madame's most terrifying threat to me? What if—

"Eugénie!" Madame slapped my cheek, the quick, sharp blow that she employed whenever she judged me inattentive. "Mind me when I speak to you, you lazy little chit. Fetch my shawl from my room at once. Go, go, run, and return directly."

I bowed low and backed from the room, and only rose and turned once I was in the hall and out of Madame's sight. Only then, too, did I place my palm over the place where she'd struck me, and cup my cheek in my palm to try to ease the pain that her slap had left.

I trotted down the hallway as she'd ordered, my bare feet padding over the cool stone tiles. I always hurried down this hall when I was alone at night on some errand for Madame. The hall was lit only by two hanging lanterns, one at either end, and in the hazy half-light in between the painted faces in the pictures on the walls seemed to come alive, watching me. My trot quickened to a run, and the little bells on my collar jingled against my throat.

I darted around the corner that led to the stairs, the last corner of shadows before the next lantern's light. My foot was on the first step when a man's hand covered my mouth to silence me, and his arm circled around my waist and pulled me to one side. Terrified, I fought wildly, my arms flailing and my feet kicking. He stood behind me, and I couldn't see his face or who he was.

As hard as I could, I bit his hand, my teeth cutting into the fleshy palm.

He swore, and let me go.

Yet another hand grabbed my arm, pulling me to one side.

"Quiet, Eugénie, else they'll hear you," Orianne whispered urgently. She stood before me, the apron at her waist billowing like a ghostly white sail in the shadows. Beside her, still swearing and shaking the hand that I'd bitten, was Marc, one of the footmen who'd attended the table at dinner. "We have only a moment."

"I can't wait," I said uneasily, wishing she'd release me. Marc must have brought her here from the kitchen when he'd carried dirty plates from the table. I couldn't guess what they now wanted from me, and I'd no wish to be punished for being slow because of them. "Madame desires her shawl."

"Madame desires the world," Orianne said, leaning closer and blocking my escape. "Marc says they're being sent away from Pondicherry."

I nodded, my eyes wide.

"That's what the younger Monsieur said," I whispered. "That's why he's come here, to tell Monsieur and Madame that they must go on orders from Monsieur's brother in Paris."

Marc swore, his bitten hand forgotten. "I told you, Orianne," he said. "I didn't lie."

"I never thought you did," said Orianne.

"But if they—"

"Hush." She and Marc exchanged glances that had no meaning to me. "Tell me, Eugénie. Did they agree? Will they go?"

I nodded, and swallowed. "They must go," I said. "Monsieur Henri said so."

Orianne sucked in her breath so hard her cheeks hollowed. "Did they say where they are going? Calcutta, Madras, Bangalore?"

"Saint-Domingue," I said. "They said it many times."

"Saint-Domingue," repeated Orianne, as if testing the word like a new spice on her tongue. "Where is that, eh?"

"I do not know," I said, the truth.

"Try harder to remember, Eugénie." Orianne's fingers dug into my arm. "You heard them. Where is this Saint-Domingue?"

"I do not know." I jerked my arm free. "They didn't say, else I would tell you."

"You'd better," Marc said, glowering down at me, and warning enough. "You're the only one who has been with them all the night long."

"I'm always with Madame," I said defensively, and took a step backward, poised to run if I had to. "All I heard was that they were going to Saint-Domingue, and that Monsieur was supposed to sell the sugarcane that was raised there."

Marc bent forward as if he'd been struck, and he groaned, a deep rumble of despair.

"A sugar plantation!" Orianne's whispered voice was shrill with anguish. "Oh, little one, I pray that you are wrong. I pray that you have misheard!"

"They're already making plans," I said. "Monsieur Henri says they must sail by the end of the month."

But this only made her sag forward with an anguished cry. Marc caught her in his arms and she rested her chin against his shoulder. Forgetting me, the two of them began to weep as if the very world was ending, and perhaps it was.

"I must fetch Madame's shawl," I mumbled, and fled to Madame's rooms. They didn't follow me, and when I returned, first peeking over the top of the stairs, they were gone.

I brought Madame's shawl back to the room where Madame and Monsieur and the nephew still sat at the table, with the two men now puffing away on hookahs. Their conversation had turned to how much the French peoples despised the English, and whether or not they would soon again be at war, an old and well-worn topic to be worried over among Frenchmen. Nothing more was said of Saint-Domingue.

But the next day it became clear that preparations were already being made to leave Pondicherry. The house was soon filled with crates and chests that swiftly swallowed up paintings and furnishings, silver and porcelains, and all the rest of the Beauharnaises' rich belongings. The emptying house became oddly hollow, filled only with echoes and French-speaking ghosts.

I was kept so busy that I'd no opportunity to visit the kitchen to speak with Orianne. Madame embarked on a final round of visits and calls to her acquaintances to bid them all farewell. I accompanied her, of course, but to my disappointment there was never any real substance discussed among these vain and foolish women: only what clothing would be required for the voyage, and how large the new house would be, and whether the sailors in the ship's crew would be handsome, or not.

It was not until the final day before Monsieur and Madame were to sail that I learned my fate. As was the morning custom, I was with Madame as she made her toilette for the day. My role was to stand beside her dressing table, and hand wire hairpins, one by one, to Estelle as she brushed and powdered Madame's hair into its customary tortuous arrangement. The day was already warm, and the doors and windows were open to catch whatever breeze might come our way from the sea.

Suddenly a dreadful high-pitched wailing arose from the courtyard on the other side of the house. The sound held the mixture of terror and resignation of brute animals in the moment before they are slaughtered, except the wordless cry was from a human throat. My hand froze with a hairpin in my fingers, and Estelle, too, stopped her brushing to listen. It seemed impossible not to feel the pain in these cries, nor to be affected by them.

And yet Madame was. "Continue, Estelle; do not make me late," she said curtly. "I am expected at Madame Gibault's house on the hour."

"Forgive me, madame," Estelle murmured, but still she faltered, the silver brush dropping from her hand to the floor with a clatter.

"How clumsy you are!" Madame said sharply, cuffing Estelle's ear as she bent to retrieve the brush. "That racketing outside has nothing to do with you. It's only the slave traders come to collect the people Monsieur has decided to leave behind."

"*Only the slave traders.*" Cold words, callous words, unfeeling and without heart, enough to make me tremble where I stood. Would they come for me next?

"We can't take everyone with us, you know," Madame continued. "Surely you must realize that."

Another round of wailing underscored her explanation. It seemed the very birds in the trees had stilled in silent sympathy.

Tears slid down Estelle's face, and she crumpled to her knees with the silver hairbrush cradled in her hands.

"Oh, Madame!" she cried piteously, crawling on the floor at Madame's feet. "I beg you, please, please, do not send me away with the others!"

Madame recoiled and frowned.

"No more of this, Estelle, else I *will* have you taken," she said with brisk disgust. "Whatever makes you think I would embark on a long voyage without a lady's maid to tend to me?"

Estelle raised her teary face. "Then I am preserved, Madame? I am among your chosen?"

"What you are is a sniveling little slattern," Madame snapped. "I am taking you and Orianne and Eugénie, and Monsieur will have Gabriel to look after him. The others were no longer of use to us, and have been sold."

She turned in her chair so the back of her head now faced us, pointedly expecting us to finish dressing her hair. Estelle gulped, and scrambled to her feet, and together we completed the task that was expected of us, as if nothing else was any different.

It wasn't. Unlike Estelle, who seemed genuinely pleased to be accompanying Madame, I didn't know whether I, too, should rejoice, or be fearful, or something else entirely. I had longed to leave this house, and now I was.

I didn't care that Estelle had been spared, but I was grateful that Orianne would also be coming to Saint-Domingue. Yet when I remembered the last time I'd seen her with Marc by the staircase, I doubted very much that she would likewise be happy this day. While I was still too young to understand the powerful bonds that love created between men and women, I knew the cruel finality of what had happened today, and how Marc had been among those sold to slave traders while Orianne remained.

I went with Madame to make her final calls, and continued with her and Monsieur to a dinner in their honor. I watched, and listened, and thought of how much more fortunate Madame was to be able to bid such tender farewells to her friends than the slaves she had sold away earlier this same day. Some of those people had been in her household since she'd first come to India thirty years before, and yet she'd discarded them with as little emotion as if they'd been a broken bowl or teacup, with no further use or purpose to her.

It was long past nightfall when we returned to the house for the last time, and I was acutely aware of how silent the house was now without the others. It was not as if the footmen and housemaids and cooks-maids and laundresses and grooms and coachmen and all the rest had made so much noise as they'd followed the orders of Madame and Monsieur. But their presence had given life to the rooms and halls, and now that they were gone the house was like an empty tomb, bereft of warmth and heart.

While we had been out, the remainder of Madame's furnishings had been taken away to the ship, including her great heavy bed of mahogany. For this last night she was forced to make do with a plump mattress and pillows spread upon the floor.

"How I shall sleep on such a mean little pallet I do not know," she said peevishly as Estelle and I tried to arrange her comfortably. "I'll be covered with a thousand bruises by dawn, and by all the saints it will be a holy miracle if I'm not completely crippled."

I thought of how much more comfortable her well-stuffed mattress was than the mat that had been my bed for the past three years. I kept those thoughts to myself as I plumped yet another pillow to place behind her head.

"You know I must trust you tonight, Eugénie," Madame said, her face nearly as pale as the pillow she lay upon. "With my bed gone, there is no place for me to chain your collar. Instead I must trust you not to run away, but to remain here with me. Do you understand what trust means, Eugénie?"

"Yes, Madame," I murmured. She could speak all she wished of trust, but I'd already seen how every door and window and gate to the house had been closed and locked, on account of there no longer being any male slaves to guard us. The house would be as adept at keeping me locked inside as it was at keeping villains and thieves without.

But no matter how much Madame fussed, she had drunk enough wine at dinner that she was soon fast asleep. When I was sure, I left her, and hurried downstairs and across the courtyard to the kitchen to look for Orianne.

I thought at first she wasn't there. Usually a place full of voices and activity and temptations, the kitchen was now dark and silent. The shelves and cupboards and baskets that once had held such bounty were empty, the tables scrubbed bare. Only a few coals glowed in the hearth, kept alive to heat Madame's morning tea one last time.

"Orianne?" I called into the shadows. I heard a shuffling sound and what might have been a groan, and stepped closer. "Are you here, Orianne?"

"What do you want of me, Eugénie?" She startled me, a shadow huddled on the floor to one side of the fireplace. Her voice was rough and ragged, and I guessed she'd been weeping. "How does Madame wish to torment me now?"

"She didn't send me," I said. "She's asleep. I've come on my own."

Orianne didn't answer. The silence stretched longer and longer between us. I'd intended to offer comfort to her as she'd often done to me, but now that I was here, I'd no notion of what to say.

Finally I dared to step closer. "I wanted to see if you were—if you were well."

"Haven't you learned anything?" she demanded abruptly, and with a ferocity I hadn't expected. "What you want, what I want— none of that matters before what *they* want, and what *they* will have."

"I know that," I said defensively.

"Do you?" she asked. "What else do you know? Why did they decide to keep you today, and not sell you away like the others?"

Again I'd no idea how to reply, and I longed to see her face to be able to answer her in the way that would please her most.

"I'm sorry your—your friends were taken today," I said in a small voice. "I'm sorry it wasn't me instead."

She groaned, and pressed her hands to her forehead. "That's

nothing for you to be sorry for, little one. *They* did it and now it cannot be undone, no matter how much I cry tears that are torn from my heart."

I didn't answer. There wasn't more that needed saying. I sat on the floor across from her in the dark kitchen until the first dawn began to show through the windows, and then I crept back to my mat beside Madame, and was there when she woke.

The rest of the morning passed in the rush of our departure, with both Madame and Monsieur in disagreeable humor and short temper, and quick as always to fault others for it. But finally we were aboard the vessel that would carry us to Saint-Domingue, and sailing with the evening tide as the captain had wished.

Our ship was called the *Céleste*. To me who had never before been in a vessel of any kind, she seemed at once both very large and fine, and yet very small when placed against the enormity of the sea. I hadn't expected the ship to move so much beneath my feet, as if the waves had given it life. I felt clumsy and unsure, and watched with envy as the sailors skipped with ease across the slanting deck and through the rigging overhead.

As the sun set, I stood on the deck in my usual place at Madame's side while she and Monsieur bid their farewells to Pondicherry. For the sake of impressing the captain, Madame made a great show of pretending to cry while waving her lace-edged handkerchief, as if she weren't overjoyed to be leaving this place that she claimed to despise. Monsieur paid her no attention, and instead peered through a small spyglass that he'd purchased especially for the journey.

As for me, I gazed out at the city where I'd been born, turned golden by the setting sun. At a distance like this, it was little more than a jumble of buildings scattered around the old fort. Somewhere in the middle of those buildings my family must still live and work, bicker and laugh, and love one another as they hadn't loved me.

I thought of the crack, jagged like lightning, that had always marked the wall of our small quarters, and how my cousins and I would lie rolled in our blankets beneath it, whispering together when we were supposed to be asleep.

I remembered how Ammatti would take me with her to the market at the end of our street, and how proud I'd been when I was old enough to carry her purchases for her. She'd smiled so widely with approval that her eyes had nearly disappeared, and she'd called me her fine little pigeon as she'd slowly walked with one hand on my shoulder to steady herself. I would have done anything to make her happy, and I believe she would have done the same for me.

"This sea air chills me to the bone," Madame was saying, supported on one side by Estelle, and the other by Gabriel. "I don't know how I shall bear it. Where is my shawl, Eugénie? Why don't you have it when I am clearly chilled and suffering so? At once, Eugénie, don't dawdle!"

Reluctantly I turned away from the rail, and from Pondicherry, and all that it had meant to me.

I pulled my *dupatta* more closely over my head and shoulders against the wind, and followed Madame to her cabin.

CHAPTER 3

The Indian Ocean
1771

As could only be expected, neither the sea nor the voyage agreed with Madame, nor did she agree with them. No one could discover ill-usage like Madame. With Pondicherry scarcely from our sight, she had begun to howl at the meanness of her accommodations, and the disrespect she believed was being shown by the ship's company toward her.

It is true that for a French lady such as Madame, accustomed only to the luxury of a fine home, the cabins—tiny compartments scarcely bigger than closets—given to her and Monsieur on board the *Céleste* must have seemed disagreeable. Behind a louvered door for privacy, each cabin contained a narrow shelflike bed built into the bulkhead, a pewter bowl for washing and a looking glass pinned to a beam, and only space for a single chest of belongings.

Two of these cabins belonged to Madame and Monsieur, while a third was occupied by an elderly French cleric, Révérend Père Noyer, a long-faced holy man in black who kept to himself and his prayers. The fourth cabin had been converted to storage of the belongings of Madame and Monsieur.

No quarters were provided for Orianne, Estelle, Gabriel, or me. This, too, was cause for Madame to complain to the captain: not because of the slight to us, but because of the inconvenience to her, accustomed as she was to having us all nearby. It was decided that

Estelle would sleep on a pallet on the floor—that is, the deck—of Madame's cabin, while Gabriel would stay near Monsieur. Orianne and I were likewise given pallets, and told by the first mate, Roussel, to sleep on the deck in the common area outside the cabins.

"But that will not do, Roussel, not at all," Madame protested. "It's far too much liberty for Eugénie. You see the collar I've had put round her neck. It's my custom each night to clip a chain to it, and then to a post of my bed, to make certain she does not run from me while I sleep."

"And I ask you, ma'am: where would your little creature dare run?" Roussel was broad-shouldered and brutish in the way of many Frenchmen, and he spoke so loudly that his words echoed between the decks. "Recall that we are at sea, ma'am. I've yet to see a Negress who won't shudder and quake at the very sight of so much water. They haven't the sense to swim, you know, but sink like black stones into the deep."

He laughed, and Madame laughed with him.

"How reassuring you are, Roussel." Madame placed her hand familiarly on the mate's sleeve, a gesture she would not have dared make if Monsieur had been in sight. "I should hate to lose my little Eugénie."

"I shall take every effort to keep your property safe, ma'am." Roussel bent over me and spoke foolishly loud and slow, as if I were deaf or half-witted. "Do as you're ordered, you little monkey. Don't vex your mistress."

He raised his fist as if to strike me. I couldn't tell if this was simply more of his bluster or if he did intend to strike me, but by instinct I stepped back away from him. I'd long ago learned to judge the exact distance necessary to preserve myself from a blow from Madame, yet remain near enough that she believed it still were possible, if only she bothered to exert herself. So it was now with Roussel; he glared at me in warning, then dropped his hand and turned back toward Madame, waiting to preen and fuss further over him.

"I saw what you did, little one," Orianne murmured beside me as they left us to arranging Madame's belongings. "You put yourself in danger with tricks like that."

I shrugged with the unconcern of my age. "It spared me from harm."

"You've only been struck by an old woman," Orianne said. "A blow or a whipping from a grown man is different."

I shrugged again. "My uncle punished me if I was slow to obey him."

Orianne frowned. "Your uncle was your kin," she said. "He wouldn't kill you. But that man Roussel is different. If you make him look like a fool again, his pride will see that you pay with your blood."

I didn't answer. I suspected that she was right, though I was too stubborn to admit it to her. I'd already sensed that about Roussel, and how I'd be wise to avoid him as best I could during the voyage. What mattered more to me was that I was at last free of the chain to the back of my collar that had linked me each evening to Madame. Yet that first night aboard the ship, I slept on my side as if the heavy chain bound me still, a ghostly presence I could not shake.

I awoke to feel the ship pitching and rocking beneath me. The lanterns that hung from the beams overhead swung wildly and cast shadows that danced like demons across the bulkheads. I squeezed my eyes shut and clutched at my mattress, certain we all would soon be cast into the sea to drown.

"Wake, Eugénie, and be of some use!"

I opened my eyes to see Estelle crouching beside me. She had a shawl wrapped over her nightgown and her usually neat single braid was frayed over her shoulder. By the lantern's light, her face was greenish pale, with dark patches of distress beneath her eyes.

"Madame has been ill," she said. "Go above, and empty this."

She shoved the pewter washbowl from Madame's cabin across the deck toward me. The bowl was nearly filled with vomit and bile, and I covered my nose and face to keep from gagging myself at the stench.

"Hurry," Estelle said sharply. "Madame may require it again."

I rolled from the mattress, struggling to find my footing on the rocking deck. I braced myself against the bulkheads, moving from one handhold to the next as I held the reeking bowl in the crook of my elbow. My heart was pounding as I slowly climbed the steps of the companionway, and I dreaded what manner of nightmarish scene would await me.

But instead of the storm that I was certain must be raging, all I saw was the first light of day, and the pink of dawn along the horizon. Overhead the canvas sails snapped and cracked with the wind, a wind that tore at my hair and clothes like a wild beast. I clung to the rail, terrified of being blown from the slanting deck over the side, and into the white-tipped waves.

"What are you about?" shouted one of the sailors into the wind, coming toward me across the lurching deck as easily as if it were his parlor at home. "Come to toss that bilge overboard, eh?"

I looked down at the bowl in my hand, unsure of how I was to dispose of the unsavory contents. I was afraid to venture any closer to the rail, yet it seemed I had no choice. Slowly I began across the deck, gripping every handhold I could find.

"Not that side, damn you," the sailor said. "You'll foul the deck with your filth if you try to throw it into the wind."

With an oath, he grabbed the bowl from me and emptied it over the railing, then swiped it through a half hogshead of seawater that sat on the deck.

"There," he said as he handed it back to me. "Take care you don't come empty your puke when the captain's on deck, else he'll have you tossed over, too."

Beside the door to Madame's cabin, Estelle was squatting on the deck, her back braced against the bulkhead and a white cloth pressed to her mouth. Beside her was a small bucket, and I saw that she, too, had been ill.

"Where have you been?" she croaked at me. "You've kept Madame—Ah, my God!"

Abruptly she leaned over the bucket beside her and retched again. At the same time, I heard Madame call for me from within her cabin, and the sound of her, too, gagging.

So it would be for the next week, or perhaps it was a fortnight. One day seemed much like the next, and I cannot be certain. I ate only dried sea biscuits broken into watery cold tea, for no one offered me anything else. Of our entire party, I was the only one unafflicted. The ship's cook, who also served as the surgeon, came to peer at them each in turn, diagnosed it as no more than common seasickness, offered cinnamon bark to chew, and abandoned them to their misery. I tended to them all as best I could. Even Orianne was poorly, and lay curled in groaning misery on her pallet to one side of the deck.

I became adept at scrambling to the deck with full buckets and bowls. I learned to keep my knees bent and to walk with the roll of the deck rather than against it, and how to use the ship's movements to help carry me up the ladders and through the hatch. I'd found my sea legs, as the sailors called it, and it soon became second nature to me.

Madame gradually improved, and though she continued to keep to her bunk and play the invalid, Estelle could now tend to her demands well enough. When Monsieur recovered, he began taking his dinner with Captain Gagnon and Père Noyer in the captain's cabin, and seemed content to spend as little time as he could in his wife's company. Although Monsieur was the captain's guest at these dinners, he expected Orianne to prepare her customary curries for him; like most Frenchmen, he called all the wide range of Indian food by that single name. This she did in the ship's galley, and I nearly wept with longing as the familiar spicy aromas of Pondicherry wafted between the decks.

But Orianne and I were also given other tasks to perform, including scrubbing away with rough square blocks called holystones at the passageway decks between the cabins and where Orianne and I slept. Roussel himself had ordered us to do this every day, to keep the weather deck from smelling not from seasickness, but from our own persons. The *Céleste* was not a slaver, he declared, and he wouldn't have his vessel stinking like one on account of us.

"I was not brought from Pondicherry for this," Orianne muttered beside me as we scrubbed the deck on our hands and knees. "I am a cook, a keeper of the house for my master and mistress."

I nodded in agreement, wincing as I plunged my holystone once again into the bucket of chilly water. My hands were chapped from the seawater, the salt stinging and burning my fingers and my knees, and I'd no doubt Orianne's were, too. I'd worked harder in these last weeks on board the *Céleste* than I had in all the years combined that I'd belonged to Madame, yet Orianne would not dare complain to anyone but me. We'd both seen Roussel take a knotted rope to his own sailors, white-skinned Frenchmen, if they didn't obey orders as swiftly as he believed they should, his thick arm flailing the rope against their backs and buttocks until they jumped and swore with pain. I was sure he'd do much worse to us if we gave him reason.

"At least another ten days of this before we reach Mauritius," Orianne continued. "That is what the sailors say. And yet that will be only the beginning of this nightmare."

I paused, the dripping holystone in my hand. "Isle de France? Is that a city on Saint-Domingue?"

"I told you, that is only the beginning," Orianne said. Unlike me, she hadn't stopped toiling but continued to scrub, stretching out her arms with the stone in her hands, then pulling backward in a rhythm much like rowing a boat. Her brass bangles slid up and down her wrists with the same rhythm, and the hooped rings in her ears struck against her cheeks.

"Isle de France is another island," she continued, "and Port Louis is its greatest city. We'll stop there long enough to take on freshwater and provisions, and then off we'll be again to the next port, and the next after that."

"But what of Saint-Domingue?"

"It's a hundred and twenty days away," she answered grimly. "That is what the sailors say. A hundred and twenty days, or more."

A hundred and twenty days! I'd already grown impatient with this voyage of three weeks. Another hundred was too many for me to imagine, and silently I wondered if perhaps the sailors had lied to Orianne.

But exactly as she (and they) had predicted, on the tenth morning the lookout spied the green island of Isle de France on the horizon, and the *Céleste* dropped her anchor in the harbor of Port Louis that evening. I knew because Roussel sent word below to Madame and Monsieur and then Madame sent me to the deck to bring her further word. I was eager to accompany them ashore as her *poupée,* and be rid of the ship for even a day.

Madame, however, had other plans.

"You shall remain here, Eugénie," she said, frowning critically at her reflection in the looking glass. "While Monsieur and I are ashore, you and Orianne will do whatever Roussel requires. Only Estelle will accompany me."

"Yes, Madame," I murmured. My face must have betrayed the disappointment I'd no right to feel, for Madame scowled, and cuffed my ear.

"Impudent little monkey," she said, borrowing the name that the sailors called me by. "Did you really believe I'd take you ashore, too? You're far too shabby to be seen with me."

I bowed my head, ashamed. My once-fine silk costume had in fact become shabby and worn from my labors and from the wind and salt water. It didn't matter that Madame had provided my clothing and thus it was her doing that I'd come to more resemble a street beggar than her pampered *poupée*. I was the one who had offended her.

It was the same at the next port we put into for provisioning, and the next after that. I was always left behind, and the days of being a cosseted favorite seemed over. The more scullery work I was given to do, the more bedraggled and dirty my garments became, and the more faults Madame discovered in me as well.

One afternoon she accused me wrongly of leaving off the stopper of her scent bottle, when I knew she'd done this herself. In her rage, she struck the side of my face with the flat side of her hairbrush. The heavy silver hit me so hard that I fell dazed to my knees on the deck. She'd never hit me like this before, not with the brush instead of her hand. I'd always been quick enough to avoid such a blow, and the fact that I'd been caught unawares was almost as shocking to me as the blow itself. I felt doubly vulnerable. Somehow I struggled back to my feet and finished my task, fighting to keep back tears that I knew from experience would only make Madame strike me again.

When I finally saw Orianne, after the midday meal, she gasped with shock, but not surprise, and brought me a cold cloth to press against my face. By evening my left eye was swollen shut and my cheek in constant pain from the bruise. I'd no choice but to turn my head to see with my right eye alone, and I could tell from the way other people drew back that my face must indeed have been dreadful to behold.

Madame, however, acted as if nothing were amiss. The next morning, she set me to polishing that same hairbrush and the rest of the dressing set, by way of making sure I'd remember my punishment. I sat in a corner between the decks and rubbed away the tarnish that salty air had blackened into the flowery whorls of silver. It was not easy work, not with my one eye blurred and weeping, or with fingers clumsy with cold.

Orianne found me there, her apron a bright square of white linen in the murky light between decks.

"I have need of you, Eugénie," she said with her usual brusque manner. "Come with me."

I looked down at the dressing set, with half the pieces still to be polished. "I cannot, Orianne," I said with regret. "Madame—"

"We will finish the task together," she said. "With a spot of vinegar on the cloth, the tarnish will wipe away in no time. Now come."

I followed Orianne between decks to the ship's kitchen, called the galley, and a place I'd never before been permitted to visit. The galley was directly beneath the *Céleste*'s weather deck, with a metal funnel to carry the smoke and sparks upward and safely into the sky overhead. The cooking fire made the galley the warmest place on the entire ship. The heat was a luxury I hadn't expected, and slowly I felt my always-chilled limbs begin to lose their tension, and relax.

"Heed what I do," Orianne said, speaking to me in Tamil so that the ship's French cook—who was watching us closely—wouldn't understand. "This is the stove for cooking, called a camboose."

The camboose was a large, square box that sat in a shallow tray filled with sand to prevent stray sparks or excessive heat from igniting a fire, the greatest fear on board a vessel made of dry timbers. The cooking fires were contained within the camboose, and round-bottomed pots sat nestled in circular cutouts in the camboose's iron top. Already the day's ration of chunks of salted pork and onions that the crew favored were boiling away, an unpleasantly sour stench, and every few minutes the cook jabbed at the bobbing meat with a long-handled fork.

Orianne was granted one pot for Monsieur's dinner, off to the far side of the camboose. In a basket to one side were dried lentils and rice, and a newly caught fish with staring flat eyes. Even more important was the large round bronze box with pierced sides and a thick ring on the top of its lid: her treasured *masala dabba* that I recognized from the old kitchen in Pondicherry. The box was filled with little dishes and compartments for nuts, seeds, roots, barks, and ground powdered spices, each with its own tiny spoon of carved horn.

I thought of Ammatti's *masala dabba,* carved of wood and far more humble than this one, but guarded as fiercely as if it held pure silver and gold. I'd stood as close to the fire as I could whenever she had cooked, breathing in the spicy aroma that gathered and rose with the steam. Ammatti had hummed and swayed gently in time to the slow, wide circles she made with her big spoon through the fragrant mixture, while the trailing end of her saree and her long gray braid swung in matching rhythm. Sometimes she'd sing to amuse me, too, making a nonsense song of the names of the spices she was using. I'd sing with her, and it wasn't until later that I'd realized it had been her way of making me learn and remember the spices she'd liked best.

Now I watched Orianne move with the same kind of graceful efficiency, her movements reduced but not hindered by the galley's small space. It had been many years since I'd helped Ammatti cook, and I tried hard to obey Orianne's brisk orders to assist her as best I could. As soon as everything was in the pot and simmering, however, it became clear that Orianne had another reason for bringing me here.

"Madame has wearied of you, Eugénie," she said, continuing in Tamil as she'd delivered her earlier orders, again so the cook wouldn't understand.

"But I have done everything Madame desires," I said anxiously. "I've never given her cause to tire of me."

"She would never have struck you if she weren't," Orianne said, giving words to what I'd already begun to realize myself. "I've seen it before. She craves a new plaything. You are how old now? Ten years?"

"Eleven." I understood. From the first day that I'd been bought, I'd heard of how Madame sold away *poupées* who'd dared to follow nature and grow. I was still childish in my stature, but already my body was beginning to round into womanhood. Many girls my age were already promised as wives. If my uncle ever thought of me still, he doubtless congratulated himself on being spared the cost of my dowry.

"Nearly twelve, then," Orianne said. "Too old to be Madame's tiny doll. You must know more to remain of value to her and to Monsieur. That is always their greatest concern: how much you are worth to them. Otherwise, you will soon be sold."

She crouched down on the deck with the *masala dabba* on her knees, her long hands curved to hold the rounded sides.

"They kept me because I can cook to please Monsieur," she continued, motioning for me to join her. "Anyone can learn to cook that dull French rubbish. To choose and toast and blend the spices for a perfect curry—ah, that is art; that is mystery. But before a cook can do that, she must know every spice like an old friend."

She took the merest golden-orange pinch from one of the tiny bowls of ground spices, and held it out before me.

"Smell it," she ordered. "Taste it. Consider the color. Tell me which it is."

Obediently I opened my mouth, and she touched her fingertip on my tongue. I gasped, overwhelmed. For years my meals had been bland and largely without seasoning of any kind, spiced food being another luxury that Madame deemed too costly to squander on servants. But this tiny taste was enough to draw me instantly back to Ammatti's cook fire, so keenly that I could almost hear her humming beside me. I blinked back the tears that stung my eyes, but not before Orianne noticed.

"Fah, is your tongue blind?" Orianne exclaimed. "Must you weep over nothing? Here, try again, and no idle guesses, either."

She touched the spice to my tongue one more time, and I tried to focus entirely on the speck of flavor: a curious mix, orange sweetness turning to a half-bitter pungency.

"Turmeric," I said.

Orianne nodded, grudgingly. "Turmeric, yes."

I smiled, thinking of how Ammatti would have scolded me if I'd been wrong. "Please, let me try another."

"Not now." Deliberately Orianne closed the lid of the *masala dabba,* and latched it shut. "We shall have plenty of time for such lessons on the voyage. Becoming a cook cannot be rushed."

With a small sigh of disappointment, I sat back on my heels. Being young, I had never pictured myself as a cook, but now I could think of little else. Perhaps in some way, my *ammatti* was still looking after me. Perhaps within me was her gift for cooking, a way to save myself as well. Orianne was the most valuable and valued of any of the Beauharnais servants. I'd never once seen her beaten or whipped, or even corrected by Madame or Monsieur. To learn from Orianne would not only train me for a new role, but also preserve me from Madame's temper.

"My *ammatti* had a *masala dabba,* too, though not nearly so fine as yours," I said shyly, for I never spoke of my past, not even to Orianne. "That's how I knew the turmeric. I'm sure I can guess more."

"I don't want you to guess," Orianne said firmly. "I want you to know, by taste and by color as well. That is what your *ammatti* would have expected from you, too."

Orianne gave the round box of spices a final, fond pat, as if it were a living creature.

"Once I had an *ammatti* with a *masala dabba,* too," she continued quietly, and I realized from her expression that she was also slipping back to the comfort of her past, just as I had done. "So did her *ammatti* and her *ammatti* before her. The women in my family were always the best cooks in our village, for weddings, for feasts. Then the French soldiers came. . . ."

Her voice drifted off, yet I understood.

"Our grandmothers are part of us," she said finally. "They remain in our blood and in our memories, and so are the spices they favored."

As soon as I'd seen Orianne's spice box, I'd thought of my *ammatti.* Perhaps that was the real reason I'd been able to identify the turmeric: the memory, the taste, was in my blood, just as Orianne said.

Lightly Orianne touched her fingertips to my swollen cheek.

"This bruise will fade, little one," she said. "You are strong, and you will heal. Recall that no matter what Madame does to you or to any of us, she cannot steal our memory away. Remember that and you will never forget who you are."

The farther south the *Céleste* sailed, and the farther away from balmy Pondicherry, the colder the sea air became. The waves grew rougher, with a wind that howled and worried our ship like a ravening wild beast. From her well-cushioned bunk, Madame wailed as well, convinced that we would all perish, and begged Père Noyer to come say prayers for salvation over her. The sailors called the nearest landfall the Cape of Good Hope, and said that the wildness came from this being the place where two oceans met. To me there seemed nothing either good or hopeful about it. I shivered in near-constant misery from the cold, pulling my sleeves over my hands and huddling my shoulders against the never-ending chill that had burrowed into my spine.

And yet, in time, our vessel turned to the north. The seas became more calm, the winds more fair, the sun so warm that I was once again at ease in my tattered silk costume. We put into another harbor for provisioning, a city called Saint-Louis that appeared like all the others on our voyage, with a fortress and a cluster of French ships in the harbor. Again, I was left behind with Orianne on board the *Céleste,* while the others went ashore. We lingered here nearly a fortnight, shifting cargo as well as taking on water and fresh provisions, and then began the final leg of our voyage, across the Atlantic Ocean to Saint-Domingue.

I overheard all this, yes, but none of it meant anything to me. I'd no sense of geography, or the pattern of the ocean's currents. I couldn't comprehend how we'd sailed from one season to the next and back again. I'd lost count of how many days had passed since I'd last felt solid earth beneath my feet, and I hadn't any notion of how many more days at sea still lay ahead. All I wished was for this endless voyage to be done.

Five days after the *Céleste* had cleared Saint-Louis, the weather turned rough, rough enough that once again Madame was groaning and seasick, and soon Estelle was ill as well. Dutifully Orianne and I tended to their needs, but after a few days they seemed to worsen, their skin hot with fever. Roussel ordered us to take Estelle to the lower deck, where we tried to make her as comfortable as we could.

But Madame was much the sicker. Her pale skin was blotched with an angry rash, her breathing fluttered, and she didn't recognize us. Orianne summoned the cook in his role as surgeon, who took one look at Madame's spotted face and backed from the cabin.

Hastily Monsieur, Roussel, even the great Captain Gagnon were brought together in a solemn consultation before Madame's cabin door, while Orianne and I were told to stand away.

"They believe Madame will die," Orianne said darkly. "Look at them, the cowards. Men can never hide their fear of death."

I remembered the night my *ammatti* had died from winter fever. I'd sat on the floor beside her pallet and held her hand, my little fingers working restlessly into hers as if somehow I could keep her with me. Her skin seemed as hot as fire, and she fought for every breath, a labored, strangled sound that had terrified me. Near the end, Uncle Raul had sent me away to the front room, claiming that I was distressing everyone else with my whimpering. When at last I could creep again to her side, she was gone, cold and stiff with the staring eyes of death.

"Do you think Madame will die?" I asked Orianne.

"Perhaps." She gave the merest disdainful shrug of her shoulders. "If she does, she will at once take her place in her Christian Hell."

But as I stood beside Madame's bunk, I was terrified of how close death seemed to be in that small, hot cabin. I feared not only the presence of death itself, but also that somehow I'd be blamed for it. The cook came to bleed Madame, as was the French practice. He cut into her white arm with a thin-bladed knife while his mate had held a bowl beneath, and her blood had come thick and slow, as if it somehow had already died.

I was ordered to stay with her, and to wipe her face and limbs to try to cool the fever that burned her. Again and again I dipped her prized lace-edged handkerchiefs into water of violets, yet still the fever wasted her body, and her flesh sank deeper into her bones. Madame did not know me, and I was so tired that I scarcely knew her. Monsieur never came once to Madame. She had none who'd loved her at her side as she died. All she had was me.

At the very end, when the tips of Madame's fingers and toes began to blacken, Père Noyer came and wrapped his beads and cross around Madame's bony fingers. He read aloud from his holy book in words I didn't understand, and the instant Madame had stopped her breathing he stopped his reading as well. He was the one who briskly told Orianne and me how to dress the corpse in fine clothes, and stitch her into the bedsheets that became her shroud, with a rusted ball of shot tucked beneath her feet to carry her body to the bottom of the sea.

The entire crew was summoned to the deck. Monsieur stood between Roussel and Captain Gagnon while Père Noyer recited more prayers. Orianne, Gabriel, and I stood back behind them. Exhausted from my vigil, I clutched Orianne's hand to keep my feet on the pitching deck, and squinted into sun that seemed far too bright.

"You have triumphed, little one," Orianne whispered. "Madame will never again strike you."

I tried to feel that triumph, tried to focus on the white bundle with Madame's corpse, small and ordinary. Four sailors raised the board on which their burden lay, and as they solemnly tipped it over the side and into the waves I sank, too, my head spinning into darkness as I toppled to the deck.

I cannot say how many days I was ill, or why the fever did not kill me as it did the others. I'd strange and wandering dreams, and glimpses of Orianne tending me as I'd tended Madame. I remembered the soft murmur of Orianne's voice, and how gentle her hands had been upon me, but mostly I'd felt nothing but heat and darkness. All I know for certain is that the voices of the sailors finally roused me.

"Be quick about it," one sailor was saying. "Captain wants the carcasses gone at once, and I've no wish to be touching their poison any longer than I must."

I was lying on my old pallet, but on a lower deck murky with shadows, and I was so weak that it took all my strength simply to open my eyes. Not far from me, two sailors were bent over another figure, trying to pull the arms free from a printed cotton jacket. To my horror, I recognized the jacket, and the woman wearing it as Orianne. Uncertain of what I was witnessing, I gasped aloud, then pressed my hand over my mouth.

But the sailor in a striped cap had heard me, and quickly turned my way.

"Hah, the little monkey's still alive," he said. "I thought they'd all died."

"She looks more dead than otherwise," said the other man. Now I could see Orianne's face: waxy and stiff, her eyes half-closed and unseeing, her face and chest covered with the same red spots that had marked Madame. Orianne was dead, too, and I cried out with anguish and sorrow.

"None would be the wiser if we tossed the girl over the side as well," said Striped Cap. He yanked the hoops from Orianne's ears and the silk scarf from around her throat and stuffed them into his pocket. "Roussel would thank us. You know how he hates having this kind on board."

"The girl belongs to Beauharnais," the other man said. "She's his property. Harm her and you'll be the one to pay."

Striped Cap didn't answer, and together they quickly peeled away the rest of Orianne's clothing and put it in a bag, doubtless to sell or trade at the next port. When they were done, they roughly grabbed her stiffened limbs and hauled her up the companionway. I glanced quickly around the shadows, searching for the one thing I prayed the sailors had overlooked. There it was, tucked between the beams where Orianne herself must have hidden it: her precious spice box, the greatest single treasure she could have shared with me. Knowing it was safe, I followed the sailors as best I could, stumbling weakly up the steps.

I reached the deck as the sailors were awkwardly lifting Orianne's naked body over the rail, her long braid swinging in the wind like a black rope. The other sailors jeered lewdly, and whistled as her body finally toppled over the rail and splashed into the sea. Unlike Madame, there was no solemn service, no holy man to say prayers to ease her path into death, no fine white shroud or burial clothes.

From the rail I watched Orianne's unclothed body sink, then

rise up again, bobbing and twisting in the creamy churn of the ship's wake. I watched as long as I could, my cheeks wet with tears. I cried not for Orianne, who now was free, but for myself, who was not.

"Eugénie!"

Startled to hear my name, I turned quickly to see Monsieur beckoning to me from the quarterdeck where he often walked beside the captain. Now he was with Père Noyer, the priest's long cloak and robe whipping in the breeze. Quickly I wiped away my tears with my sleeve, and hurried toward the two men.

I bowed low, filled with dread. Had they, too, watched Orianne drop into the sea? Would I now be punished for being here on deck to mourn her?

"You're the last one, Eugénie," Monsieur said, an even-voiced proclamation. "First Estelle, then Gabriel, and now Orianne. This has been a very costly voyage for me."

He paused and frowned down at the deck, and Père Noyer laid a hand on his arm in silent consolation. At first I marveled that Monsieur hadn't included his wife in this grim tally, before I remembered that to him, being French, these deaths were entirely different. He had never outwardly shown much love for Madame, but she had been his wife, a white-skinned French lady. Orianne and others had been mere slaves from Pondicherry, and their deaths were the same as the loss of any other cargo that had been destroyed in the course of the voyage. They were a costly monetary loss, no more, significant enough to merit that comforting hand from the priest.

"The cook says Orianne taught you to make my curries," he said, still not looking me in the eye. "Is that true?"

"Yes, Monsieur," I said with as much confidence as I could muster. "It is the truth."

It wasn't, not entirely. There was so much more of cooking and curries that I hadn't had time to learn from Orianne, and now never would. But Monsieur didn't know that.

"Then you will take Orianne's place, and wait upon me at table," Monsieur said. "I will be dining as usual this afternoon with Captain Gagnon."

"Yes, Monsieur," I murmured. When I'd followed Orianne's

body to the deck, I'd been so weak that I'd swayed on my feet. Now purpose had given me fresh strength, and I resolved to be stronger still and prove my worth, not only to Monsieur, but for the memory of Orianne and Ammatti who'd helped make me that way.

I was alone, yes, but I'd survived. I'd come this far in my life, and I was determined to go further. I *would* be strong.

I was twelve.

CHAPTER 4

Belle Vallée
Saint-Domingue
1772

I'd had many months on board the *Céleste* to imagine the Isle de Saint-Domingue. I needed only three days to see how false those imaginings had been, and wish with all my heart that I'd been carried to any other place on earth than the sugar plantation called Belle Vallée.

I was treated like the rest of the Beauharnais belongings, and unceremoniously unloaded from the *Céleste* on the morning after we'd tied up in the harbor. The plantation lay some miles inland from the port city of Saint-Domingue, and four ox-drawn wagons were required to convey all the barrels, trunks, and crates. There wasn't room for me to ride. I was expected to walk. Once again a chain was linked to my collar and thus to the back of the last wagon so I wouldn't try to run away.

I wondered where they thought I'd run. On either side of the road were bright green walls of sugarcane, the canes and leaves towering high over my head and blocking all else from my sight. My legs were unsteady from being so long at sea, and I felt light-headed from thirst and the hot sun overhead as we climbed up the hills. Still I trudged between the ruts in the road carved by the wheels, one step after another. If I'd faltered, if I'd tried to pause, I would simply have been dragged along the road by the collar around my neck.

The sun had begun to set when at last we arrived at the plantation. Surrounded by palm trees, the main house was smaller than the Beauharnais home had been in Pondicherry, a two-story block painted white that looked more like a graceless fortress than a Frenchman's fine estate.

I was unchained from the wagon, and sent at once to the kitchen in the back. The cook was a dark-skinned, round-faced man called Perroquet who had little use or desire for a new slave in his kitchen, especially not in the middle of preparing the first meal for the new master. Perroquet barely glanced my way, and I was soon set to work scrubbing pans. I was given no food, for slaves at Belle Vallée were fed only in the mornings and at noon. Finally Perroquet declared the day's work was done, and I collapsed into exhausted sleep upon a grass-filled mat in one corner of the kitchen.

The next morning, Perroquet woke me by kicking my ribs.

"Lazy little bitch," he said as a greeting. "I need you to work, not sleep. Fill this bucket at the well."

The sky was just growing pale with dawn, yet as I stumbled sleepily from the house I could see that dozens of other people— the field slaves—were already leaving for their day's work.

The men and women wore clothes that were little more than rags, and the children with them were naked. Despite how quickly these people moved, other men with large dogs shouted and cracked whips at them as if they were no more than cattle to be herded. Sitting on a horse and watching was a tall Frenchman, ominously still in the middle of so much activity. This man I learned later was Malet, the plantation's overseer, and the one man who controlled the fates of us all.

Most of the slaves moved as quickly as they could to avoid the lash and the dogs, but others were either too weak or too infirm to move faster and received merciless attention from the drivers' whips by way of encouragement. Sunrise should be a moment of hope to mark the beginning of a new day, but the sense of despair and fear that I felt at this moment (and at every other dawn while I was in this place) fair threatened to overwhelm me.

Swiftly I looked away, and tried to concentrate on filling the bucket instead of what I'd just witnessed. None of the Beauharnais slaves in Pondicherry had ever been treated with this degree of cruelty. This could have been my life, too, if Orianne had not shown me how to use her spices. Because I had done well enough preparing Monsieur's curry each day for the rest of the voyage, I'd been told that for the present I would work in his house, not his fields.

The French called us all Negroes, but we'd each been brought here against our will from many different places. Guinea, Senegal, Ghana, Madagascar, and others besides, and we spoke different tongues as well. The very nature of the plantation under Malet's rule (for truly it was he, and not Monsieur, who ruled here as any monarch rules his kingdom) was to encourage distrust in one another. There were far more slaves and free blacks than white French on the island, and instilling fear and intimidation was the only way to keep those who toiled and suffered from fighting back.

For me it had begun that first day. The faded silk costume that Madame had long ago provided was taken from me, and the bundle with my other few belongings vanished as well. Instead, I was given the kind of clothing worn by all women who worked in the house: a loose-fitting jacket and petticoat, an apron, and a length of cloth to tie about my head to cover my hair. Everything was of coarse linen that had been stained and worn by other slaves before me. All that was left to me from my past was my collar, the one thing I would have gladly given up. I was seldom called by name; I was instead only another "girl," one more Negress, no different from any other.

Although I was considered a house servant, I was told that if I erred in any way I'd be whipped and sent to the fields, and that Monsieur's protection would last only so long. We toiled from before dawn until long after dark on the nights when Monsieur had guests to dine and play cards. Each morning I was put to work in a different way, from scrubbing floors to plucking chickens to hoeing and weeding the kitchen gardens, all things I'd never before done, and feared I'd somehow do wrong. Even while I prepared Monsieur's curries I was forced to guard myself from the small jealous rages of the cook, Perroquet, who disliked me for being able to please our master in a way he couldn't.

I was a constant target for his temper and for the long-handled ladle that he'd often use as a weapon to strike me. He'd endless reasons for punishing me, too: for ignorance of his wishes, for taking too long at a task, for having lighter skin, for speaking French as was done in Pondicherry and not Saint-Domingue. I tried my best to dodge his blows as I had with Madame, and because I was small and nimble, most times I did.

Yet I was also determined to learn his manner of French cooking. It wasn't easy, for here we were forbidden to taste any of the food we prepared. To take so much as a spoonful of a sauce or soup to our lips was considered stealing, and merited a whipping. Instead, all preparations were done by sight and scent and careful measuring of spices and herbs. It was a difficult way to cook, and one that went against all my instincts. Yet I recalled Orianne's advice, how knowing more would make me of greater value, and I studiously watched and learned and did exactly as Perroquet said. Orianne's precious *masala dabba* had joined me in the kitchen, but one day those spices from Pondicherry would be exhausted, and the more I knew of other kinds of cookery, the better.

As quick as I had to be in the kitchen to avoid Perroquet's ladle, working outside the house was far more hazardous, particularly in the kitchen garden. There were lizards and snakes hiding beneath every green leaf, and spiders called tarantulas, as large as a man's fist and covered with fur like rats.

But the greatest menace wasn't from the wild creatures of the island. I soon understood that all the slave women were expected to oblige any of the men at any time, for the purpose of breeding more slaves and increasing the value of the estate. I witnessed the drivers coupling roughly with women as if they both were beasts, bending them over benches or against walls, or shoving them to the ground to take them there. The women who'd dare try to fight back were still raped and then whipped. We were forced to witness their punishment as well as a cautionary deterrent.

For the first months that I was at Belle Vallée, I foolishly believed myself safe because I was a house slave. That all changed one gray morning when the air was heavy and still and clouds shrouded the tops of the mountains to the north. I'd entered the kitchen with a basket of eggs, which I expected to hand to Perroquet for a custard. I smelled the milk for the custard burning over the fire, and without a thought hurried forward to take the pot away from the coals. As I did, I saw too late that the kitchen wasn't empty. Instead, the overseer Malet was with one of the other house slaves, a young woman not much older than I named Fleur.

Fleur had been shoved onto the edge of one of the tables with her petticoat pushed around her waist. Her eyes were squeezed shut as she braced herself against the table. Malet stood between her outstretched legs with his thumbs digging deep into the fleshy part of her thighs to keep them spread wide. His breeches were unfastened and hanging from his hips as he jerked and worked between her legs. With each thrust Malet grunted loudly, while Fleur made a sad little cry of suffering, her feet flopping awkwardly behind his back.

Young as I was, I knew what Malet was doing to her, just as I knew she'd had no choice but to let him. I fled from the room and hid behind a fence until Malet came striding from the house, still buttoning the fall on his breeches. Inside, Fleur was squatting beside the fireplace and the pan of now-scorched milk, furiously stirring it as if that would be enough to make the brown, burned flecks disappear.

"Cursed milk," she muttered without looking up at me. Her face was flushed and her eyes furious as she stared down at the pot. "Perroquet's going to beat me good for this."

"But if you told him—"

"Told him what?" she demanded. "Told him *what?*"

I faltered. "About—about—"

"There is nothing to tell," she said bitterly. "Perroquet knows. Whether it is Malet or Monsieur or any of the others, they are all men, and they are all the same when they have the itch. We have no say. We are nothing to them, except—except this. We must let them do what they want, else it will go much worse for us. Now break six of those eggs and begin to whip them to a froth, else Perroquet shall beat you as well."

After that I took more notice of things I'd not seen before, or perhaps had purposefully ignored. When Monsieur invited his new friends from the town to Belle Vallée, white gentlemen who were French, English, or Dutch, the parties never included any wives, sisters, or daughters. On those nights, Fleur and others were told to put aside their ordinary clothing, and given the kind of dresses that Frenchwomen wore instead. Long after the meal was done and the cloth drawn, they remained in the front part of the house with Monsieur and the other gentlemen. I was asleep by the time they returned to the kitchen, if they returned at all. The following day, Perroquet favored them, and instead gave me the brunt of their work.

I'd always thought I'd been considered too inexperienced at service to wait upon Monsieur and his guests. Instead, I'd been simply considered too young and unattractive to be included in his entertainments.

And how had I not realized that Bette, another of the house slaves, was already with child? She worked as hard as anyone even as the swell of her belly became increasingly visible beneath her apron. She never spoke, not to anyone, and I'd wondered before if she'd all her wits. Now I wondered if she knew the name of her child's father, or if, like me with my mother, that child would be cursed to know only his or her mother's name, and no other.

As the weeks passed and the days grew longer, the dry season gave way to rain that reminded me of monsoons. In Saint-Domingue, the rain meant that a fresh crop of sugarcane was ripe and ready for harvest. A good harvest meant a profit for Monsieur and the rest of the Beauharnais family in France, and the fortune that he'd left India to discover.

While we slaves never profited from a good crop, we suffered from a bad one. Several years before, a great storm called a hurricane had destroyed a season's worth of cane juice, and ruined the fields besides, while slaves had drowned, starved, and been sold away.

Not that Monsieur cared for this, any more than he cared who labored to earn his fortune. His life of ease and pleasure continued much as it had through the sugar season, while Malet and his drivers forced the Beauharnais slaves to work even harder. Because I was good at listening, I learned of how the harvest was done, more than enough to be certain I never wanted any part of it. Men harvested the tall canes in the field, using a special knife with a curving, deadly blade called a machete, while the women and children bundled the cut canes in their arms and carried them to waiting carts drawn by donkeys. This needed to be done as swiftly as possible, for once the canes were cut, the day's heat could cause the juice to ferment and sour, and the crop was lost.

From there the canes were taken to the plantation's sugar works, and the wind-driven mills that crushed the canes and extracted the sweet juice. The mills were dangerous places, the site of terrible accidents for men and women already exhausted by overwork. Finally the juice was boiled in huge kettle-shaped coppers and refined until it became either golden-brown molasses or crystallized sugar shaped in special molds. This, too, was work for slaves, who were believed to better withstand the great heat from the fires and boiling sugar juice.

Mind you, I only know this from others' talk. Being a house slave meant I was never sent into the fields, let alone into the mills or boiling houses. But during sugar season, the news from those places came to us each day in the early morning, when Malet reported the day's tallies and events to Monsieur in the parlor. Always accompanying him were one or two of the overseer's drivers, who'd stand about the kitchen door and banter with Perroquet, Fleur, and the others.

One of these was a great bear of a man named Jupiter. His forearms and left cheek were carved with deep, curving scars left by an attack by another slave with a machete. Despite his size, he kept his chin low to his chest and gazed up at the world from beneath his brows, giving him a baleful glower. He was a quiet man, without the bluster of the other drivers, but his silent, looming presence made me wary. He watched me as closely as a great cat with a little mouse, and I soon learned to contrive to be elsewhere in the house and out of his sight whenever he was about.

One morning I stood peeling a basket of onions beside the open window. The scent of the onion skins burned my eyes and made me weep and snuffle, yet I knew Perroquet would take no excuses, and I still had most of the basket left to peel. Blinking back tears, I slipped the knife's blade against the bulb by feel rather than sight to free the paper-thin skins.

I was concentrating so on the knife and onion and not cutting myself that I didn't realize that Fleur and Bette had gone outside with Perroquet, or that I was now alone in the kitchen. I tossed another newly peeled onion into the second basket and paused to wipe my eyes with my sleeve.

It was in that instant that Jupiter came behind me. He trapped me against the table with his body, and reached around to squeeze my nascent breasts in his hands, his scent heavy and stale. He was more than twice my size, and as he ground against me my single thought was that he would tear me apart if he raped me. He *would* kill me, and I did not want to die, not like that.

I raised the paring knife and raked it across his forearm. He swore with shock and pain and drew back just enough so that I could struggle free. With the bloody knife still in my hand, I skittered away from him.

Yet I'd no path for escape. Jupiter blocked my way to the kitchen's door and the yard. Blood streamed from the cut in his arm, bright crimson against his dark skin, and more blood splattered across my jacket and petticoat.

"No girl's going to treat me like that," he said furiously. "No little yellow girl's going to cut me and run."

He lunged for me, his big arm scooping through the air. Again I darted back out of reach, my panic rising by the second. I could shout for help, but no one would come, not for me, and not against Jupiter.

I danced backward. The paring knife seemed like a sad little weapon now, yet still I clutched it tightly in my hand as if it were a soldier's sword. The kitchen wasn't large, and it was only a matter of time before Jupiter would catch me.

I couldn't let that happen. Instead, I turned and ran into the passage that led to the front of Monsieur's house. Slaves were strictly forbidden to pass through the grand front entrance, meant only for Monsieur and his white guests, yet my one thought was to escape Jupiter.

The very door was before me, my hand outstretched to throw the heavy bolt on the lock, when to my horror Monsieur and Malet appeared from the parlor. There was no hope for me now, no hope at all, and with a catch in my throat I made a shaky bow to Monsieur.

"What is the meaning of this, Eugénie?" he demanded, more in confusion than anger. He frowned down at my clothes, and the knife in my hand. "You're covered with blood. Has there been an accident in the kitchen? Why didn't Perroquet tend to you there?"

"Yes, Monsieur," I said quickly, considering what manner of lie might save me still. "I was peeling onions when—"

But then Jupiter himself charged into the passageway, and there was no use dissembling. Monsieur might have been fooled, but Malet was not.

"What is this, Jupiter?" he said sharply. "Fighting over some wench? You're of no use to me if you can't lift your arm."

He whistled, loud and shrill, and two other drivers joined us. Jupiter's expression darkened as soon as he saw them, and he began to shake his head.

"I'm not hurt, M'sieur Malet, I swear it." Despite the bloody cut, he raised his arm high over his head as proof that he could do so. "The girl tried to tempt me, then stuck me with her knife."

"No!" I cried without thinking. "That's not—"

Malet's hand struck me so hard across my mouth that I staggered to one side before he grabbed me by the arm to haul me back.

"You have the devil in you, bitch," he said grimly, half-dragging me toward the passage. "My leather will take the fire out of you."

I cried out with dread and fear. I'd lived at Belle Vallée long enough to understood exactly what his words meant, and even though from desperation I struggled to break free, I knew there was no escape from what would come next.

Jupiter and I were both taken to be whipped, to a place on the plantation far enough from the house so Monsieur wouldn't be troubled by the screams of his slaves. Jupiter was first stripped and tied to a log that was kept specially for the purpose. I was forced to watch.

Malet himself whipped Jupiter, and when his arm tired he had another of the drivers take his place. Even as Jupiter's back was slashed to raw and bloody ribbons, he kept his silence, without so much as a groan. When at last they were done and cut him down, he stared directly at me with a hatred that was worse than any words, and I knew he was considering his own private punishment for me—a punishment that next time would be impossible for me to avoid.

But I'd scarce time to consider that. I was next stripped with my hands and legs tied tight around a rough-barked palm so that I could not move. On the occasions when Madame had ordered me to be caned, she'd always specified the number of blows, and being able to count them had somehow made it easier to bear.

Malet didn't do that, and I soon lost track of how many times the whip cut into my back. By the time he finally stopped, I was faint with pain, shock, and lost blood, and when they took me down my legs were at first too weak to support me. Instead, I lay curled on my side, shaking and whimpering as a woman I didn't know washed my back with brine, a stinging thick paste of salt that was meant to keep the raw flesh from putrefying in the island's heat and damp, and to keep away the worms as well. The brine burned my poor tattered back, and in the agony of my pain I lost my senses, until salt water was thrown in my face to rouse me so that I might stagger back to Monsieur's house.

I was still expected to work in the kitchen that afternoon, and also expected to prepare a curry for Monsieur. Monsieur had invited a party of gentlemen to dine, and he wished to entertain them with an Indian dish. Perroquet did let me sit on a small stool to sort and soak the dried lentils, but it took all my strength not to topple over from dizziness. Because of the brine, the cuts in my back had already glazed over, but even the tiniest of motions made the rough linen of my jacket catch painfully on the tatters of my skin.

But as the final preparations were being made, Monsieur sent word that, for the first time, he wished me to be among the women serving at table tonight, and I wondered with despair if this were some further level of torment that he'd devised for me. I had no choice but to obey, and when the hour came I changed into one of the special dresses. In a small mercy, the dress was too big for my slight body, and therefore only barely brushed against my wounded back.

With the silver serving bowl of curry in my hands, I slowly followed Fleur and Bette up the stairs. Monsieur preferred to dine in a room on the upper floor, with the tall windows thrown open wide to catch whatever breezes might rise above the trees from the sea beyond. Even so, the room was warm, made warmer still by a blaze of candles burning in silver candlesticks on the table.

The three other men besides Monsieur were already seated. Perroquet had told us the guests were officers; he'd neglected to say that they weren't French, but British, in bright red uniform coats instead of blue. In truth, to me they looked no different from Frenchmen, with their stiff white-powdered hair and ruddy bluff faces that gleamed with sweat because they insisted on dressing too warmly.

It had been an English soldier who had sired me in an act of violence that had destroyed my mother's life, a fact that, tonight of all nights, I could neither ignore nor forget. I poured their wine; I cleared away their plates; I watched as they ate the curry I'd prepared. As I did, the knowledge of what my mother had endured and what had happened to me earlier in the day blurred with the scent of turmeric and coriander, of male sweat in wool uniforms, and the bright candle flames reflecting in polished silver: a feverish dream peopled by the three red-coated men before me.

Like all French meals, this one seemed interminable, and when at last Monsieur waved for the final dishes to be cleared and the cloth drawn I dared to hope I'd be spared. But when I began to retreat with a pile of plates toward the stairs, Monsieur waved impatiently for me to stay and, worse, to step forward.

"This is the girl I mentioned," he said. "The only one of all my servants to survive the voyage."

The three officers studied me as if I were some rare curiosity. Perhaps to them I was. They had all shed their coats by the end of the meal and pushed their chairs more comfortably away from the table. Now as they continued to drink, they were taking tobacco in long-stemmed white pipes, the pungent smoke stinging my eyes.

"Is she so fearsome a little wench that she must be collared?" asked one of the men, laughing at his own wit.

Monsieur chuckled. "No, that was my late wife's doing," he said. "Eugénie was a favorite pet of hers, yet she was forced to chain her each night to keep her from running away."

"So she is like every other little bitch," said the first man again. "Always in heat, and sniffing for the next mongrel who'll mount her."

Monsieur and two of the men laughed, but the third officer did not. Instead, he set his wineglass down on the table and frowned as he considered me more closely.

"How old is she, Beauharnais?" this man asked. He'd a full,

heavy jaw and pale blue eyes, while beads of sweat glistened across his forehead. The extra amount of gold lace on his uniform marked him as the most senior officer of the three. "She looks to be still a child."

"Do not be fooled by her size, Prevost," said one of the other officers. "Calcutta wenches are all like little dolls, on account of eating no meat. I'll wager she's eighteen if she's a day, and as hot a little strumpet as any of them."

I longed to correct him, and say I'd been born in Pondicherry, not Calcutta, that I was only twelve years in age, not eighteen, and that I wasn't a strumpet. But I was Monsieur's slave, and could say nothing without his permission.

"She could be twenty for all I know, Major," Monsieur said, enjoying his role as the genial host. "I told you, she was my wife's Negress, not mine, and as spoiled as can be because of it. The sum of her usefulness is that she knows the spices of India, but I wonder if that is worth the price of her trouble. Why, this very day, in her idleness, she offered herself to one of my best drivers, then turned fickle, and stabbed him with a knife."

Since I'd been brought to this place, I'd worked so hard in Monsieur's name that I often cried myself to sleep at midnight from hopeless exhaustion. Yet here all my toil and tears were now reduced to spices, and a knife.

"It's always the quiet ones that cause the most mischief, isn't it?" said the first man, looking me up and down with fresh appreciation. "Let me tame her for you. Come here, girl."

He patted his thigh in encouragement, clearly expecting me to come settle there.

I didn't. I couldn't.

"Come along now." Irritation crept into his voice. "Playing coy may work among the bucks in the fields, but I don't like being made to wait."

Still I stood, frozen in place.

"Obey me, girl," he said, and before I could react he'd grabbed me by the arm and pulled me onto his leg. He curled one arm around my waist and pressed directly against the raw wounds beneath my dress. I cried out and jerked forward, struggling to escape the pressure of his arm. He pulled me back and squeezed me more tightly to make me cry again.

"Don't fight me, bitch." He hooked his thumb into the back of my collar to keep me from pulling away. "I said I'd tame you, and so I will."

"Let her go, Hillarie," ordered the man called Prevost. "She's bleeding through the back of her clothes."

Hillarie ignored him, and held me fast. I was trembling from fear, revulsion, and pain.

"What of it, Major?" Monsieur said easily, motioning to Fleur to refill his glass. "My overseer gave the jade the lashing she deserved this morning. It's the only way for her to learn the price of making trouble."

Major Prevost's expression did not change. "I know the difference between discipline and cruelty, Monsieur."

Finally Hillarie took his arm away from me, and I quickly eased away to stand beside Major Prevost.

Smiling, Monsieur glanced at me. "You are my guest, Major, but Eugénie is my Negress, my property, and I must ask you not to interfere in her discipline."

"What is her price?" the Major asked curtly.

Monsieur's smile faded. "Forgive me, but I did not say she was for sale."

"Everything in this world is for sale," the Major said bluntly. "You've said yourself that she is idle and of little value to you."

"Seven hundred *livres*," Monsieur said quickly, his expression sly. "She was much beloved by my wife."

The Major didn't flinch. "Three hundred and fifty, and not a *sou* more," he said. "By your own admission, you keep this girl for no greater purpose than to service your guests. No whore in Saint-Domingue is worth one hundred *livres*, let alone seven."

I flushed with shame, and bowed my head.

Monsieur scowled at his glass, then slowly raised it toward the Major.

"Very well, then," he said. "She is yours. But you must take her with you tonight. I don't want her here to poison my other people another minute longer than is necessary."

* * *

I left Belle Vallée that night with Major Prevost, sitting on the floor of the hired carriage at the feet of the three officers. I made no farewells, and I carried nothing with me, for I owned nothing.

We soon arrived at an inn near the water, a region roiling with drunken sailors, soldiers, and other ne'er-do-wells. While the other two officers retreated to the taproom, the Major led me upstairs to the room they shared in common.

He'd brought a candlestick to show the way, and now that single flame was our only wavering light in this room. With a sigh, he sat on the edge of one of the beds, his hands resting on his knees as he looked at me, and I at him.

I stood with my hands clasped before me at my waist, as Madame had taught me. This way, too, he could not see how much my hands were shaking.

"Do you speak French?" he asked at last.

"Yes, sir, I do," I replied in that language.

"At least we have that," he said, and sighed. Among other Frenchmen, I guessed he'd be considered a handsome man, thickset and strong, about thirty-five years old.

"Those accusations that Beauharnais made of you," he continued. "How much of that was true?"

How was I to answer that? I didn't dare tell the truth, the real truth. To fault and question the words of the old white master to a new one seemed willfully (and perilously) unwise, and so I remained silent.

He waited for a long moment, his expression growing increasingly perplexed. "Do you not understand me?"

I nodded, my heart racing in my breast. Oh, I understood. Monsieur and the others had called me a whore, and this man must have bought me for that purpose. What other reason could he have? I remembered what Fleur had told me about obliging men with "the itch," whether we wished to or not. I hoped that he would be quick, and not hurt me too much. I swallowed hard, and bent to lift the hem of my petticoat for him.

He caught my wrist to stop me.

"No," he said quickly. "I didn't intend to—to do that. I am a married man, and I would never lower myself to use a servant of mine in such a fashion."

Relief washed over me, and I looked down at his hand still grasping my wrist. Beyond the close white linen cuff of his shirt, his skin was peppered with old scars from battles and black dots of gunpowder. Self-consciously he released me, and my petticoat fell back to cover my bare calves.

"I have never believed in the merits of whipping or other such West Indies measures," he said. "I intend to take you with me to New Jersey, a colony to the north, where you will serve my wife on our property there. So long as you obey her wishes, you shall find her a fair and just mistress."

I heard voices on the stairs outside, especially that of Hillarie, the officer who'd grabbed me earlier. I started instinctively, ready to flee.

"Don't be frightened of Hillarie," Prevost said firmly. "He won't touch you again, nor shall any other man. I'll make sure of that."

I remained unconvinced. He was an English soldier, and accustomed to violence as part of his trade. He'd bought me on a whim, after a long dinner with which he'd drunk much wine. What would he say when he awoke in the morning to find me on the floor beside his bed?

But what I soon learned about Major Jacques-Marc Prevost was that he was in fact that rarest of men, a man of his word. He never did expect me to share his bed, nor did he permit any of the other men in the inn to address me for that purpose.

The next morning, he took me to a blacksmith, and with one clip of the man's shears the collar that had circled my throat for years sprang away, and dropped to the ground at my feet: an ugly, tarnished, misshapen thing, with all but a few of the glass beads and bells that once adorned it gone. I ran my fingertips up and down over my now-bare neck, and across the thin, jagged scar that the collar's teeth had worn into my skin. The smith plucked the collar from where it had fallen to the ground and tossed it into a bin of scrap without a thought, and just like that, it was gone. Yet I would always remember how Madame had ordered it put around my neck, and how Major Prevost had ordered it removed.

I was the one left with the scars.

* * *

Two days later, the Major, his manservant Allen, and I boarded a small merchant vessel bound for the British colonies to the north, and a port city called New York.

After the voyage that I had endured from Pondicherry, this one seemed easy indeed. The Major had begun to address me in English, the most commonly spoken language of the colonies, so that I might learn it. Being young, I was an apt pupil, and soon could understand both his orders, and the conversations of others around me.

I learned one word in particular on this voyage. I had grown accustomed to being called a Negress, since the white French saw only the darker color of my skin, and no other difference between me and a woman who had been born in Ghana or Benin. The English sailors, however, called me a mulatto. It was not a compliment, but a judgment upon my mixed blood, and one I'd heard all too often. In Pondicherry I had been despised by my uncle and others for being too white, yet these Englishmen considered me too black, an inferior creature fit only for enslavement and low labor.

Little wonder, then, that I felt no eagerness to arrive in yet another country that was new to me. As we sailed into port, I could see that New York was unlike any place I had been. At the very tip of the city there was a large, spreading fortress for defense, but behind that lay a scattering of peaked-roof houses painted various colors, as well as warehouses and other buildings made of reddish-pink brick. Most notable were the pointed towers, or spires, that rose up along the sky from the numerous churches. The harbor was filled with vessels with flags from various countries, and among them were English warships.

Even as we docked beside a long wharf, the air of the city was a confusion of new scents to me: of fires from chimneys, of cooking food I didn't recognize, of the horses and oxen that drew the many carts and carriages, of low tide and tar. Fearful of becoming lost, I stayed close beside Major Prevost once we'd disembarked. The streets weren't dirt or mud, but paved with rounded stones that made walking perilous beneath my bare feet, and it was difficult for me to keep pace with him. The shops and houses on either side of us were small but neat, of brick or stone or painted boards. Instead of being left open to the weather, the windows in these houses here were covered by sheets of divided glass that shone in the sunlight.

The streets were crowded with people, and these New Yorkers seemed to rush about in a great hurry, as if they'd important business that must be addressed immediately. Although I kept near to Major Prevost, several times I was forced to dart from the path of a carriage that was going too fast and from men who were so engaged in their conversations that they'd nearly walked over me. They all spoke quickly, too, their speech so loud and fast that it sounded like clattering nonsense to me.

That same day, Major Prevost took me to a shop that sold used clothing, and had me dressed like an English bondservant: a linen shift that stank of its last owner, a rough gray jacket of linsey woolsey that laced up the front, a coarse osnaburg petticoat, shoes, woolen stockings, a plain cap, and a faded printed kerchief. The shopkeeper's assistant laced me into the stays, the first I'd ever worn. She told me I must be grateful to the Major for buying me these clothes and for making me decent. I did not agree. Before this my body had always been lithe and free, but now I was encased in rigid boning and stiff linen that constricted my every movement and chaffed my sides. The heavy shoes made me clumsy and awkward, and dragged at my feet with each step. Even my long braid had been twisted and pinned so tightly into a knot beneath the cap that my head ached.

Nor was Major Prevost entirely done with my transformation. He didn't tell me then, but waited until the following evening, after we had left New York by way of Cortlandt Street. We'd taken the Paulus Hook ferry and crossed the North River to New Jersey, and driven in a stage across what seemed to me to be endless farms and fields and hills, and then in a hired chaise.

"There," he said at last, proudly pointing toward a small cluster of roofs and brick chimneys over the treetops. "That's the Hermitage. That's my home."

Dutifully I looked, while he cleared his throat in that momentous way that all men do before they say things they wished they didn't have to.

"I do not know how much, if any, of what Beauharnais said of your past was true," he said. "I'm willing to forget those tales if you serve me and my wife well, and with loyalty. Nor will I mention any of it to my wife. This shall be a fresh beginning for you, if you are wise enough to see it as such."

I wasn't surprised that he'd keep my past from his wife. I was most likely thirteen now, a grown woman. What mistress would wish a new slave to arrive into her house with a reputation for wantonness and violence, however ill founded?

"Yes, sir," I said: the only two words that masters wanted to hear.

"Good," he said. "Good. There is one other thing. Since my wife and her family are English, as are these colonies, it would be best if you were called by a sensible English name rather than a French one. Mary. That's easy enough, isn't it, Mary?"

Veeya, my true name, would have been easy, too.

"Yes, sir," I said softly.

And Mary I became.

Mary

CHAPTER 5

The Hermitage
Hopperstown, Province of New Jersey
1773

Dusk had fallen by the time we drew up before the house, and lanterns had been lit in anticipation of our arrival. Even in this half-light, the house was unlike any I'd yet known: wide and squat and built of a reddish stone, with a long, sloping roof that extended over a deep porch running the width of the house's front.

On this porch to greet us stood Major Prevost's wife. With her were two young boys darting back and forth between two other ladies, as well as servants busy at their tasks, but she alone stood still and unmoving amidst all this swirling confusion. She was simply but elegantly dressed in a dark blue gown with a red shawl over her shoulders against the evening's chill, and she stood beside one of the lanterns so that her face was dramatically half in light and half in shadow.

The Major unceremoniously clambered down from the chaise before the horses had even stopped, the scabbard of his sword slapping awkwardly against his thigh as he went striding toward the porch. The boys bounded toward him, hanging on his legs and arms, and he warmly embraced each one in turn, calling them silly names of endearment to make them laugh.

Finally the Major went to his wife. Smiling, she held one hand out to him to kiss. He did so with great ardor, and then drew her slowly forward and into his arms, where at last she let him hold her close and kiss her as a husband should.

While all of this was transpiring, a groom had come to hold the horses and the Major's manservant had begun to take his trunk and other belongings into the house. With no responsibilities of my own, I climbed down and stood unnoticed and uncertain beside the chaise.

It was over the Major's shoulder that Mrs. Prevost's gaze first met mine, the surprise in her expression unmistakable. She eased back away from her husband, deftly turning them both to face me while keeping his arm around her waist.

"Tell me, James," she said. "Who is this?"

"This is Mary," he said, a bit too heartily. "I found her in Saint-Domingue for you. I remembered how you'd told me Chloe could use more help about the house and kitchen."

I was acutely aware of every eye on that porch studying me. From respect I bowed low from the waist to Mrs. Prevost, as I always had to Madame.

Someone laughed, a small laugh quickly smothered.

"You brought her all the way from Saint-Domingue?" Mrs. Prevost asked wryly.

"She came much farther than that," Major Prevost said. "She's from Calcutta, in the East Indies."

"Cal-*cut*-ta?" repeated Mrs. Prevost, placing an additional incredulous accent in the middle of the word. "Truly, Marcus. Wouldn't it have been much easier to purchase a Negress in New York, and perhaps obtain a larger one at that?"

"I believe Mary will prove her worth," the Major said firmly. "Chloe? Chloe, here. Take Mary with you to the kitchen, and show her about."

An older servingwoman in an apron appeared from one side of the porch, and beckoned to me to follow her to the back. There the kitchen door was open, and lingering aromas from the evening meal drifted from it into the yard.

I followed Chloe inside, and blinked to hurry my eyes to accustom to the half-light in the kitchen. Another woman was scrubbing the plates and pans from dinner in a large tub near the fire, and a man in a worn blue coat sat on a low stool mending the woven bottom of an overturned wooden chair.

All three paused to look up at me. Not to smile in welcome, but to look, and make their first judgment of me. I could hardly fault them for it, for I was doing the same. In my time at Belle Vallée, I'd come to think of the kitchen as a grim battlefield, a place where I could learn, but where I must always be on my guard. Already this kitchen seemed different, but I wasn't about to let down that protective guard.

"That's Hetty with the red kerchief," my guide announced, her hands settling at her waist over her apron strings, "and that's Caesar. I'm Chloe, Mrs. Prevost's cook."

Her face was as round as the full moon in the sky, and when she sighed her full cheeks puffed and her lips blew out that sigh with weary resignation.

"And you. You are Mary," she said. "What are you good for, a little thing like you?"

I raised my chin, determined not to be cowed even as I took care with my English words. "I will do what I be told."

She heard that foreignness, and her expression softened. "You're new arrived, then?"

I flushed. "Forgive me if I say wrong."

"You said it just right." She patted my arm. "I'll show you where you're to sleep. Hetty, go see if the Major'll be wanting anything to eat."

With a rush lamp in her hand, she led me up a back staircase with precarious wedge-shaped steps to the attic tucked beneath the house's slanting roof. Stuffed pallets were arranged on the floor along the walls, with a pitcher, a washbowl, and a chamber pot in one corner. Several small boxes and worn baskets held additional clothes and belongings. The only light came from the rush lamp, and from a narrow window at one end of the eaves.

"These are our quarters," Chloe said. "Those pallets, there, those are extras from when Mrs. Prevost has guests who bring their own people. Take whichever one you want and make it yours."

I nodded. I'd never lived in a place with a separate, private space set aside for servants to sleep.

"At planting and harvest, there'll be hired men sleeping over the stable," Chloe continued, speaking so quickly that I'd trouble following her. "Hetty stays here, too, when Mrs. DeVisme at the Hermitage doesn't have as much need of her as does Mistress. Mistress will call this house the Little Hermitage, on account of it being newer, though most people call both houses the same. So there's just the four of us here. Five, counting you."

Thoroughly confused, I nodded anyway. "I can help you now," I said turning back toward the stairs. "I can wash."

"You rest yourself here tonight while you can, Mary," Chloe said. "Tomorrow you'll be set to work about the house. This'll likely be the last night ever that Mrs. Prevost will let you be idle."

"Mrs. Prevost," I said carefully. "What kind of mistress is she?"

"Mrs. Prevost?" Chloe sighed again, and lowered her voice, even though we were alone. "She'd say herself that she's the best of mistresses. They all say that, don't they? But if Mrs. Prevost weren't hearing me, I'd say she's not the worst, and no more than that. You sleep now, Mary. We'll all be up soon enough."

She left me, the light of her little lamp flickering after her on the stairs. I *was* tired, and after the voyage and the traveling I was eager for a night's rest anywhere that didn't move beneath me. I was also glad to shed my clothes for the night. I'd welts beneath my arms from where the stays had rubbed my unfamiliar flesh, and blisters on my toes from the shoes, but once I wore nothing more than my shift, I realized that my thoughts were still too agitated for sleep.

I pushed the little window open to gaze up at the quarter moon, and the stars around it. I always marveled that no matter where I'd been taken, from Pondicherry to the limitless oceans to the West Indies and now here, the night sky never changed. Nothing else in my life was so constant as that silvery moon, and the mere sight of it calmed me.

But as I sat curled beside the window, I heard voices from below. At first I thought it was Chloe and the others cleaning the kitchen for the night, but then I realized the window was at the other end of the house. The voices I was hearing belonged to Major and Mrs. Prevost, and I was directly over their bedchamber.

"I thought you'd be pleased with my little gift, Theo," the Major was saying. "You've been writing to me that you wanted another woman to help Chloe, and now you have her."

"But that's exactly it, James," his wife answered. "I said I required another *woman,* not this little waif."

"Because she is young, you can train her as you please," he said. "She'll have no unfortunate habits for you to undo. Besides, if you had seen the situation in which the poor creature was forced to live, flogged like a common seaman for every imagined slight, when—"

"I am not without a heart, James," she said more gently. "You know that of me. Mary's lot as you describe it must indeed have been unspeakably cruel. But she's a young woman, not a stray puppy. We cannot give her a home simply because she has none of her own."

"I'd never call you heartless, my love, not you," he said, and the way he said it, followed by a long silence, made me suspect he'd chosen to reinforce his argument by kissing or otherwise dawdling with her.

I curled my arms tightly around my knees as I sat on the floor beside the window, wishing the conversation had concluded in a way that was more satisfying to me. How could she want to be rid of me before I'd done anything, good or bad, in her house?

"Consider it a trial," he said finally. "See how Mary does among the others for the next fortnight. If she cannot be of use to you, then I'll take her back with me to New York, and have some trader put her back on the block. Does that seem agreeable?"

I hugged my knees more tightly. It didn't seem agreeable at all, being bought and sold and traded like one more bag of sugar or flour if I failed to please after two weeks.

"So long as you will abide by my decision, my dear husband," Mrs. Prevost said. "I vow that you are the most tender of gentlemen, for all that you're a brave, blustery soldier in His Majesty's service. And I could not love you more for it."

That was the end to their conversation. I suspect that they retreated to their bed, and took comfort in each other as husband and wife who'd been long parted.

As Chloe and the others came upstairs, I lay on my side against the wall and feigned sleep, not wishing to speak further. Soon they, too, were asleep around me, snuffling and sighing and snoring, and yet still I was too unsettled to join them.

I finally rose and dressed while the moon was still in the sky, and crept downstairs to the kitchen with my shoes in my hand. I was determined to try my best so that Mrs. Prevost would not send me away to be sold. I raked the coals and brought the banked fire back to life with fresh wood. The well wasn't far from the back door, and I drew a bucket so I could fill the heavy kettle over the fire to heat for tea, and whatever else Chloe would require for the family's breakfast.

Next I took the broom from behind the door and swept the back steps clean, and began to do the same with the broad porch across the front of the house. By then the sun had become a warm glow upon the horizon, and I could see all that I'd missed last night when we'd arrived. The house sat on a slight rise, and on the other side of the drive was a green lawn that sloped down to a shining millpond, as smooth as a mirror. Beyond that lay fields nodding with grain that was close to harvest.

Everything was lush and still, with only the first birds chattering in the trees overhead and a soft mist hanging low over the grass. I'd never in my short, crowded, noisy life experienced anything as serene, or as peaceful. As I stood there with the broom in my hand, I tried to imagine what it was to be Mrs. Prevost. Each morning I'd awake to this comfort, this beauty, this peace. I'd be secure in the knowledge that all I saw belonged to my husband, and that our children would never want because of it.

I was so lost in reflection that I failed to realize that I was no longer alone.

"A beautiful morning, Mary, is it not?" said Mrs. Prevost beside me. "This is my favorite time of the day, when the dew is still upon the grass and the children are still abed."

"Good day, mistress," I said, bowing awkwardly with the broom in my hand. To have her find me standing idle and dreaming was not the best beginning.

"It is a good day," she said, looking past me toward the pond and trees. "Indeed, a thoroughly splendid day."

She smiled at the morning, not at me, and stretched her arms before her as if to embrace it. She was wearing a loose dressing gown of flower-patterned silk that floated around her slender form, her feet bare in flat red mules and her dark hair still plaited for the night. Standing beside her, I was surprised by how she wasn't much taller than I was myself; she'd seemed far more imposing last night.

"I'm glad to see that you're an early riser, Mary," she said. "A favorable sign of conscience and industry. Do you know how to make me a dish of tea?"

"Oh, yes, mistress," I said. "Shall I bring it here?"

"Yes," she said, sitting in one of the chairs that I'd just aligned in a neat row on the porch. "I can't begin my day without my tea."

I hurried back to the kitchen, where Chloe was now bustling about the hearth.

"Did you make up this fire, Mary?" she asked, pausing with a spoon in her hand. "Up and awake before the rest of us?"

I nodded.

Chloe smiled with approval, and slowly I smiled in return. I couldn't remember the last time I'd exchanged smiles with another, and it felt both strange and pleasing.

"I was glad to find it done, and I thank you for it," she said. "Mistress likes us to be up with the sun."

"I saw her as I swept the front," I said. "She asked that I bring her tea."

"Ahh, ahh, I believed she was still abed with the Major." In a flurry, she prepared a small handled tea tray with a pot, saucer and cup, sugar bowl, and cream pitcher.

"I can take that," I said, but Chloe frowned.

"Are you sure, Mary?" she asked. "Mistress is most particular about her tea."

I nodded confidently. "My last mistress was a French lady who was most particular, too."

"A French lady." Chloe sighed. "Go, then. But take care. Mrs. Prevost won't be kind if you spill so much as a drop, and I don't want to think what she'll do if you chip one of her precious cups."

While I doubted Mrs. Prevost could ever be as unkind as Madame had been to me, I carried the tray before me with the greatest care. Mrs. Prevost was reading from a small book (an act that I'd never once seen Madame do), and she tucked a slip of paper between the pages to mark her place as I set the tray on the table beside her.

"Very good, Mary," she said, taking up the teapot's curved handle. "I'll pour for myself, since you don't yet know how dreadfully sweet I like my tea. But stay: I'd intended to address you today, and now shall do as well as any other time."

I stood before her and waited as she stirred three snowy spoonfuls of sugar into her tea, the silver spoon clinking softly against the side of the porcelain cup. I waited, and wondered if an English lady like her would ever realize (or wish to) all the misery that had gone into producing that sugar.

"*Mon mari dit que tu parles français,*" she said, delicately sipping the tea.

"*Oui, madame,*" I said, shifting effortlessly into the other language. If Major Prevost had told her that I spoke French, then I'd reply in that language. "*Depuis que j'étais un jeune enfant.*"

"Since you were a young child, Mary?" She glanced up at me over the rim of the cup. "You're scarcely more than a child now. But at least we've established that you do indeed speak the French language, a useful skill. I don't suppose you speak Dutch as well? That would be more convenient than French in this neighborhood."

"No, mistress," I said, more eagerly than I should have been, "but I do speak Tamil and Hindi."

"Then you shall likely be the one person in this entire colony who does," she said wryly. "English will be much more to the purpose here. If you're half so clever as my husband believes, then you shall soon enough be able to understand all others around you. Can you read?"

"No, mistress," I said.

"Then I surmise you also cannot write, nor do sums."

I shook my head, crestfallen, and hating to admit anything that she might use as an excuse to sell me.

"You'll learn," she said, setting her now-empty cup upon the tray. "You should be well seasoned from your time in the Caribbean, and now you must make yourself more valuable to me. You shall be taught to read, so that you may read Scripture. You will attend church, and you will be instructed in the Christian faith, with the hope that one day you will commit your soul to God's grace and mercy."

She smoothed the full sleeves of her dressing gown over her

hands. "So long as you live in this house, I will expect you to be obedient and honest," she said, each word crisp with warning. "Disrespect, thievery, blasphemy, gossip, indolence, and, especially, lewd behavior will not be tolerated."

I couldn't overlook the emphasis she put on lewdness, enough so that I wondered if the Major had in fact told her the circumstances in which he'd found me.

"I will expect you to watch yourself and keep yourself from harm," she said. "I know some masters welcome bastard children among their slaves—their future increase—but I won't. This is a small household, and you will have many responsibilities. I can't afford to have you take time away from your duties to tend to some unnecessary infant. If through carelessness you should conceive and bear a bastard, it will immediately be taken from you and given away. Do I make myself clear?"

"Yes, mistress," I said, trying not to reflect upon the terrible, thoughtless cruelty she was describing.

"I also expect complete loyalty from my people, Mary," she continued. "Whatever you may overhear or witness, whether of my family or of our guests, must never be shared or repeated under any circumstances. I consider myself a fair, even generous, mistress, but I am not reluctant to order the strictest of corrections and punishments to those who deserve them. Do you understand, Mary?"

"Yes, mistress," I murmured, striving to look as meek and obedient as possible.

Mrs. Prevost smiled warmly, confident that everything was exactly as it should be between us. She smoothed her palms across her forehead and over her hair; she'd an old scar above one brow, yet she didn't bother to hide it, the way most women would. Her smile warmed as she listened to the sounds coming from deep within her house. Her family was waking: I heard her husband's low-pitched voice and the laughter of her sons, and she rose quickly, eager to be done with me and join them.

"That is all, Mary," she said, already halfway through the doorway. "Continue as you were."

I bowed, and set to sweeping, the bristles of the broom brushing stiffly over the porch's wide planks. As I were, and as I now was.

* * *

In Pondicherry, and in Saint-Domingue, too, the seasons had been divided into wet and dry, marked by either the presence or lack of steamy torrents of rain, floods, and fevers. Nothing in my experience had prepared me for the changeable seasons of New Jersey.

When the leaves on the trees first began to change their colors from green to golden yellow and brilliant crimson, I marveled at their beauty, even as I worried that some dreadful blight had universally caused these trees to sicken. The others in the kitchen laughed, and told me that it was only the natural course in this part of the world.

Soon these leaves withered and fell to the ground, as the very air grew colder and the sun rose later in the morning and set earlier in the afternoon. Each day seemed to grow colder, too, reminding me of the terrible passage around the Cape of Good Hope. I saw my first snow, an icy wonder, and heard the howling winds of a blizzard rattle the shutters that were latched and barred over the windows. The fireplaces in the house needed constant attention, and at night in the attic Chloe, Hetty, and I huddled together near the brick chimney, finding warmth from one another and from what little heat rose from the kitchen's hearth.

During that first change of seasons, I learned much: how butter should be spread on slices of bread for the family's tea, how to curtsey in the English manner instead of bowing as was done in Pondicherry, how tightly to lace my stays so that they offered me more comfort for tasks like carrying oak buckets of water from the well in the yard.

Gradually Chloe gave me more to do. Although most of my work remained in the kitchen and about the house—washing dishes and floors, sweeping, and emptying chamberpots—I also began to acquire other skills such as sewing, mending, and laundering. My English improved as well, until my very thoughts found their first life in that language.

On Sunday afternoons, an elderly Quaker gentleman in a long gray coat came to our house to teach me to read. He used a babyish primer to teach us letters and words, with rough-drawn pictures of animals. But because I was feverish for learning, I progressed quickly, and soon could proudly read the entire little book of rhymes. To my disappointment, my reward was an equally babyish book of prayers, and the Quaker gentleman ceased to come. I tried to continue on my own, struggling to make sense of the scraps of old newssheets that sometimes appeared in the kitchen, but the leap was too great for a beginner, and my frustration soon exceeded my knowledge.

Still, I must have pleased Mistress with my industry, for she never spoke again of selling me or otherwise sending me away. Indeed, by the end of the year I'd settled so seamlessly into the household's patterns that Chloe said that it appeared as if I'd always been one of them.

In a way, that was exactly what I'd hoped to be. I'd long before learned the value of listening, of remaining quiet while others around me told their secrets. And, oh, the secrets that filled that red stone house, where nothing was as it first appeared.

To begin with, there was the Prevost family itself. On our voyage together from the Caribbean, I'd observed how much deference was paid to Major Prevost, an officer in the Royal American Regiment devoted to his English king. In reality, he was no more English than I, but a French-speaking, Swiss-born mercenary who, with his two brothers, had joined the British army for opportunity in the British-ruled colonies. He had found it, too, having received a sizable land grant not far from the Hermitage, and thus by all rights had become a gentleman officer of rank, power, and property.

And yet, here in his own home, it wasn't so. Mistress's twice-widowed mother, Mrs. DeVisme, and younger half sister, Miss Catherine DeVisme, also resided on his property in the second, smaller house nearby, forming a triumvirate with power of their own. All three were considered handsome women, intelligent yet beguiling in individual ways, and without so much as a hint of the petty silliness that had so characterized Madame. They'd many friends—and many of them male—and the house was often noisy with company and deep voices.

Major Prevost didn't seem to mind, or perhaps his wife gave him no choice. I recalled the first time I'd seen him with her, and how she had waited for him to come to her like a queen with a favored subject. It was always like that between them, and all the more striking considering that he was ten years her senior. They often quarreled when they were alone together at night. The windows were closed now, so the words weren't clear, but the anger was, coming up from their bedchamber beneath me as I tried not to hear them. Yet they were cordial enough before others, even as he deferred to her in most everything.

When Master's leave ended in the autumn and he returned to his regiment in the Caribbean, Mistress had held him close in farewell, and then had stood watching dutifully from the porch until his carriage was gone from sight, their two young sons beside her. But she didn't shed a tear for her husband's departure that any of us saw, and the following day the house was again filled with her acquaintances.

"Mistress married the Major too young," said Hetty after the last guests had departed and the family had retired to their beds and we were left tidying the kitchen for the night. Hetty had a right to her opinion. She was the oldest among us, with tight whorls of white hair beneath her cap and corded veins from years of work along the backs of her hands, and she had belonged to Mrs. DeVisme most of her life.

"Too, too young," she repeated for emphasis. "No girl who's seventeen knows what she wants in a man."

"Young as she was, Mistress knew what she wanted," Caesar said, stacking the wood for the morning fire, "and she got it, too. Those children are proof."

"If *that* was what she wanted," Hetty retorted, "then she wouldn't've married a soldier who's never home to be in her bed. Won't matter if he's left her again with another brat in her belly. Master's wed to old King George, pure and simple. The army's his true wife, and a henpecking old biddy it is."

Uneasily I laughed with the rest of them. This reminded me of the times I'd steal into the kitchen at Pondicherry and listen to Orianne and the others mock Madame's airs and Monsieur's wigs. I could have spoken now, and described how a Tamil bride who was seventeen wouldn't have been considered too young, but instead old and withered. I'm sure I could've made Chloe and Caesar laugh, too.

But talking behind the backs of those who owned us felt dangerous to me. It was a small rebellion, yes, but a shared rebellion nonetheless, and I was not as confident of my place here as the others.

As the Major had promised, I hadn't been whipped once since I'd come to the Hermitage, nor had I seen any others punished with the leather, either. The household was small enough that we answered to Mistress directly instead of to an overseer.

"How long do you think Master'll be away this time?" Chloe asked as she gave a final wipe to the main table. "Will he return again in the spring, or be gone for another year or more?"

"Won't be him doing the deciding," Caesar said, and at once the mood in the kitchen grew more somber.

This was the most fearsome secret of the Hermitage, and the most ill kept, too. The calm and peace that surrounded this house and its sweeping lawns were at heart an illusion. Many of the guests who sat in the parlor here were military men in scarlet coats with swords at their sides, swords that they seemed increasingly desirous to use. As Hetty and I waited on them, unnoticed as we'd carried their food and liquor, we overheard their indignation and their outrage, and how they complained bitterly of the very people whom they'd come to the colonies to protect. Because we were as good as invisible to them, they'd no hesitation of speaking before us of the growing disrespect shown toward them, and toward the king they'd sworn to serve.

"If there's a war," Caesar continued, "why, the Major could be away for years and years, depending on his orders."

"There won't be no war," Chloe said firmly, as if her declaration could make it so. "This country had its fill of heartache and loss in that last war against the French. Not even Englishmen are foolish enough to start another one for the pure sake of being contrary."

"Lucas says otherwise," Caesar said. He made one final straightening to the pile of wood, and then briskly dusted his hands together in a way that wasn't only to brush the wood-dirt from his palms, but to dust away Chloe's reasoning, too. "Lucas says last time he was in New York with Captain Vervelde, the talk in all the taverns was how much Governor Tryon was hated, and how his taxes and laws aren't fair. Lucas says people were planning and plotting to drive him out, no matter what it takes."

"Lucas says, Lucas says, Lucas says," Chloe grumbled, and sniffed. "What makes you believe everything that man tells you?"

"Because he's most always right," Caesar said promptly. "If he says that men in New York are talking about their governor like that, then I believe him. Lucas is as smart as they come, and he tells the truth."

Chloe tucked her chin low and glared at him, her eyes round and bright with warning in the firelight.

"What Lucas is telling is treason," she declared. "You don't work in this house without knowing what that means. Kings and governors are our master's masters, and they don't like being told they're wrong, or can't do something they want to. If Lucas keeps going around repeating nonsense about this and that in New York, he's going to find himself made to answer for talking like a fool. You, too, Caesar."

Caesar shook his head, refusing to give up. "Right and wrong don't mean treason," he said doggedly. "What's right is *right*. Lucas is a free man, and—"

"He's free?" I blurted out with surprise. "He's not Captain Vervelde's man?"

"He was once," Caesar said. "But because he's so clever with horses, and mending leatherwork, bridles and harnesses and such, he was let out to others until he earned enough to buy his freedom from Captain Vervelde. One hundred eighty pounds!"

Caesar paused to give that monumental sum the effect it deserved. I'd no real notion yet of the value of English money; I was never taken to a shop or market, nor did I possess any money of my own to make purchases. But that did seem like a great deal of money, and I marveled at how long and hard Lucas must have had to work on his own time—late at night, or on Sundays—to save so much.

"One hundred eighty pounds," Caesar repeated, clearly impressed himself. "Now he's a free man, and the Captain pays him wages for looking after his horses and stable at Mount Joy, same as he would a white man."

I nodded in silent wonder. I'd always been told that only a master or mistress could grant freedom, and most were loath to do so.

No one had ever explained to me that it was possible to buy one's own freedom.

Chloe sniffed, reading my thoughts. "Don't be getting ideas, Mary," she warned. "Mistress isn't about to set any of us free, even if you worked every hour of the day and the night, too. Especially not then, because you'd be even more valuable to her."

"Don't tell the girl things will never change, Chloe," Caesar insisted. "There's no telling what can happen in this world. Lucas says in New York there's men called Sons of Liberty and they're promising to stand firm and fight back against the governor if he—"

"That's white men, Caesar," Chloe scoffed, her disgust palpable. "That's not you, nor Lucas, neither. White Englishmen talking about *liberty*."

"But if Lucas—"

"Hush, Caesar," Chloe said firmly, lowering her voice. "Just hush. If you keep letting Lucas Emmons fill your head with wrongful notions like that, then you're twice, and twice again, the fool that he is."

I sat to one side in the shadows and listened, fascinated. What Chloe dismissed as dangerous notions of liberty sounded like the sweetest of dreams to me. If the governor was considered a grander form of master, then how bold and daring these Sons of Liberty must be to question his word! I'd never thought that there could be another side to what the British officers said in the Prevosts' parlor, or that it would offer the prize of liberty and freedom.

I longed to hear more, know more, understand more, and the key to all of it seemed to be Lucas Emmons. Who was he, to be able to travel so freely and carry such important news?

I'd my answers within a fortnight. Mistress had invited several friends from the surrounding neighborhood for an evening of music, one of her favorite entertainments. While Mistress herself played the fortepiano, her guests played the fiddle, the flute, or sang. One of these guests was Captain Vervelde, who Mistress gaily declared possessed the finest baritone west of the North River. I was at the front door to take his hat and heavy cloak, both lightly dusted with new snow, when he arrived, and as I carried them down the hall Hetty passed me with a tray of refreshments.

"Go to the kitchen, Mary," she said. "Chloe has need of you there."

I entered the kitchen just as the back door opened, and with a little flurry of snow Lucas Emmons entered as well. He was tall and thin and loose-limbed, with heavy-lidded dark eyes that were filled with wisdom. I saw that at once. Truly wise men are rare, and they stand out from others. He was dressed in a heavy green coat laced with red trim and a black cocked hat with a red rosette, the livery of the Vervelde family, and snowflakes sparkled on his shoulders.

"Good day to you, Lucas," Chloe said, barely glancing up from the pots and skillets on her fire. "Warm yourself if you please, but keep from my way, else you'll find yourself tumbled into the coals."

He laughed, and shook the now-melted snow from his hat. "You always offer a warm welcome to a traveler, Chloe."

Chloe straightened, her hands at her waist. "Cap'n Vervelde is daft to drive out on a night like this. I've dandelion tea if you need something to warm yourself."

"Thank you, Chloe," he said, sitting on the bench to one side of the fire. He'd high, sharp cheekbones, and the warm firelight played and danced across the taut skin. I guessed him to be about thirty years old, a solemn and well-grown man in his prime. "This snow won't amount to much, and the Captain wouldn't miss a night with the ladies. Besides, there's no telling how much longer he'll be welcome in this house."

"The both of you," Chloe retorted. "Mistress will always stand loyal to His Majesty on account of Master serving the army. All your rubbish-talk against the king is just that—rubbish-talk—and won't do anything but put your cap'n and yourself into gaol."

"It's already more than talk," he said, leaning forward with his hands on his knees. "Haven't you been listening to me? Don't you hear when Caesar and I read the newssheets? It's been three years since British regulars murdered innocent men and boys in the street in Boston, and all that came from that is more soldiers in our midst. Things have to change, and there are more and more of us determined to do what we must."

Chloe shook her head as she furiously stirred the chocolate sauce in one of the pots. "That's Boston, Lucas. That's not here. That's not us."

"One of the men killed in Boston was black, Chloe, as black as you or I," he said, his deep voice rumbling with emotion. "You can't pretend otherwise. It *will* happen, and it will happen here in Hopperstown as well as Boston and New York and Philadelphia."

"Rubbish-talk." With both hands wrapped around a thick cloth, Chloe lifted the pan from the crane and marched it to the table. In a single practiced motion, she trickled the chocolate across the little diamond-shaped custard tarts that stood waiting on a wide porcelain plate. She gave an extra swipe of the cloth to clear away a smudge on the rim, then looked up to me.

"What are you gaping at, Mary?" she asked crossly. "You're not hearing anything you need to know. Now go, take these out to the sideboard, and stand there to one side in case Mistress needs you."

I hated to leave the kitchen and this conversation, but I'd no choice. Carefully I took the plate from the table, and glanced one more time at Lucas, who was standing over the fire to ladle Chloe's yellow-green dandelion tea into a tin cup. To a man like him, I was likely only an insignificant little girl, if he'd taken notice of me at all.

Dutifully I carried the cakes to the sideboard in the parlor and waited against the wall while Mistress played and her sister sang. All the while I thought of what Lucas had said, about freedom and a rebellion that, to him, was inevitable.

I studied the ten men gathered in the room before me—half in uniform, half not—and wondered which of them would remain loyal to the king if a rebellion did come, and which would choose the side of those who sought freedom.

Freedom.

"Take away the empty plates, Mary," Mistress said to me. "Tell Chloe the sliced fruit in the punch needs replenishing as well."

I nearly ran back to the kitchen, the plates clattering together in my hands. To my dismay, the bench where Lucas had been sitting was empty.

"Has Lucas gone?" I asked as I set the plates on the table.

Chloe and Hetty both frowned at me, then glanced at each other.

"He's where he should be, out with Captain Vervelde's horses," Chloe said. "Not that that's any concern of yours, Mary, not when—"

But I was already outside without a shawl or cloak against the cold, running across the yard to the open shed where the horses and carriages of the mistress's guests took shelter. It wasn't hard to find the carriage and driver that I sought. Painted green like his servants' livery, Captain Vervelde's chaise was the last in the row, lit by the single lantern that hung from the beam. Lucas stood between the two horses, stroking their noses with his gloved hands.

"Lucas Emmons," I said breathlessly. "What you said before in the kitchen, about liberty and freedom and a war that's coming whether we wished it or not. Was that true?"

"I don't recall speaking of war," he said slowly. "But as for the rest, yes. It's true. I don't speak anything that isn't."

I nodded my head furiously, hopping from one foot to another. It was cold outside in only a short gown and petticoat, and I tucked my hands beneath my arms to keep them warm. Too late I regretted the impulse that had brought me here—what a little ninny he must judge me to be!—but I'd come this far, and I wouldn't shrink away now.

"I know I wasn't born in this colony, and I haven't been here very long," I said in a rush. "But I want to hear more, learn more, *know* more, and I want to—to be ready. The newspapers you've brought here from New York—would you teach me to read them?"

At first he didn't answer, concentrating instead on the horses' noses while I shivered and hopped about and generally felt like more and more of a fool.

"You're the girl Major Prevost brought from Saint-Domingue, the one they called Mary," he finally said. "You're the one Chloe says was so cut up by the French overseer."

I flushed and nodded, wishing he knew of me for some other reason than the scars on my back.

He nodded, too. His shadow was long across the patchy snow, closing the distance between us.

"I'll return on Sunday," he said. "If you want to learn of freedom that badly, Mary, then I'll make certain you will."

CHAPTER 6

The Hermitage
Hopperstown, Province of New Jersey
1773

Heavy snow kept Lucas from returning to the Hermitage that Sunday, and the Sunday after that. I fretted with disappointment, even as I knew he would be a man of his word. He was, too. By the third Sunday, there was enough of a thaw that the roads were passable and he could walk the four miles from Captain Vervelde's place to the Hermitage.

He appeared at the kitchen door in the afternoon, in an old brown coat and a roughly knitted cap instead of elegant livery, though his thick curling hair was still neatly clubbed with a leather strap at the nape of his neck. I'd forgotten how tall he was, and how he had to duck his head to clear the head of the doorway.

It had been an easy day for us in the house, with Mistress and her family having gone to sup with friends after attending church. The rest of us had walked back together, and now sat in the kitchen to relish the warmth of the fire.

Sunday was the only day of the week when we were permitted to take our ease and enjoy light tasks for our own use. I was spinning wool for the purpose of knitting. Hetty had been amazed by how quickly I'd taken to spinning. By comparison to the cobweb-fine cotton I'd once spun in Pondicherry, this thick wool seemed to spin itself between my fingers and onto my spindle.

Chloe was mending an old apron, and Caesar was drowsing, his arms folded over his chest and his head nodding heavily forward. No wonder, then, that we welcomed the diversion Lucas offered. Caesar and Chloe greeted him warmly, while I kept my own excitement to myself. He conversed first with them, sharing news of people from other farms whom I did not know. I listened and waited and tried not to fidget, silently hoping that he hadn't forgotten his promise to me, or dismissed it as inconsequential.

But at last he took a newssheet from his pocket and spread it on the table, carefully smoothing the creases flat with his palm.

"There, Mary," he said, the first time he'd acknowledged me that afternoon. "Choose whatever item you wish, and read it aloud to us."

"What are you about, Lucas?" Caesar asked, curious. "Don't shame our little Mary over nothing."

"I'm not shaming her," Lucas said. "When I was here last, she asked for me to help her learn. There's no shame to that."

Blushing at the attention, I put down my spindle and went to stand at the table, and stared down at the open sheet. In those days, a newspaper truly was a single paper or sheet, printed into four pages, with as many words packed into the columns as was possible on account of the costliness of paper. I wanted to do well to impress Lucas and the others, but the letters were small and dense with ink, row upon row of them, and very different from the humble child's primer that had been my only other experience.

In desperation my gaze landed upon one of the few pictures in the sea of words, a small, crude woodcut much like the ones that had filled the primer. The picture showed a woman hurrying along with a bundle, and I hoped that if I faltered on the words that picture might offer me a clue, the way that the pictures had in the primer.

I put my finger beneath the first word to keep my place.

"'No,'" I began, sounding out the letters the way the Quaker gentleman had instructed. "'No-*tyce*. No-tice. Notice'!"

I grinned, pleased that I'd managed to untangle at least one word.

Lucas nodded. "Go on."

"'Run ah-wah-yy,'" I continued slowly, sounding out most words, but recognizing others. "'Run away. From. Her. Maa-stt-er. Run away from her master.'"

I frowned, the meaning of the little picture suddenly becoming clear.

"That's plenty of reading for now, Mary," Chloe said quickly. "Fine reading, too, but no more."

"Let her finish," Lucas said, his voice firm. "She won't learn anything by quitting now. Read to the thick line at the bottom, Mary."

"I'll finish," I promised. "I won't stop."

Part of me wanted to. I could guess what more I'd read before I was done, but now that I'd begun I didn't want to disappoint Lucas. I went on, slowly, carefully, taking my time to find the sense in each painful word by speaking it aloud, until I could read it all from beginning to end.

NOTICE

Run away from her master, on the fourth instant. A negro wench HANNAH, aged about 15, speaks good English, of slender make and middling height. Her back is much scarred from whipping. Carried with her a coarse blue and white chintz gown, a strip'd petticoat, a red broadcloth cloak, new black cloth shoes, and other good clothes stolen from this house. Whoever returns her to the Subscriber shall have Two Dollars Reward, and all charges paid by JOSEPH LINVILLE.

When I finally finished, the only sounds in the kitchen were the pops and cracks of the fire in the hearth and the constant slow drip of melting snow from the eave outside. I continued to stand by the side of the table, and traced my fingers lightly over the words I'd read.

I'd longed to read and learn more about liberty, freedom, and bravery, the things that Lucas had spoken of before. This notice wasn't what I'd expected. I should've known rewards like this were offered for slaves who ran away.

Seeing the notice printed there in the newspaper, in words that I could read for myself, was a raw and aching reminder of my own history. The satisfaction I'd felt earlier over my accomplishment before the others no longer mattered. Instead, my only thought was for Hannah, who'd run away from her master with scars on her back.

"Thank you, Mary," Lucas said. "That was good reading."

I shook my head, not looking up.

"I hope Hannah ran clear away," I said vehemently. "I hope they never catch her."

"Some do," Lucas said. "Mark and Sary did."

"Mary doesn't know about them," Chloe said quickly. "Didn't see the purpose in telling her."

"Ah." Lucas frowned. "Then I will. Mark and Sary belonged to your Mistress and Master, and they ran away before you came. Major Prevost offered a reward for them like this, too, but they were never found, nor taken."

I nodded, though for once I wished he hadn't told me what I hadn't known.

"I am not surprised," Lucas continued, "for Mark is a brave, resourceful man. God willing, he and Sary are free and happy."

"God willing," Chloe echoed. She turned back toward me and tapped her fingers on the advertisement I'd just read. "If this little girl Hannah was quick and clever like Mark and Sary, and had friends that was already free to help her, then she could've gotten herself away and safe."

"I didn't." I'd never before spoken of my own past to them. Now I couldn't help myself, the words coming fast in a rush of bitterness and regret. "I tried to run away. I tried over and over. I never went far. They always caught me, and beat me for it. When I wouldn't stop trying, they put a collar around my neck, and then they chained me at night to my mistress's bed. And I . . . I stopped running, because I couldn't."

Chloe came to stand beside me, her arm around my shoulder.

"Poor little duck," she murmured, holding me close. "What a share of misery you've had."

I know she thought I'd cry. But at that time in my life, I'd already wept so much that I felt as if my sorrows were too much a part of me, like the scars on my back and around my throat. They couldn't be soothed over with the pat of a hand. My sorrows were buried so deep that they'd be impossible to separate and mourn with tears.

Yet Lucas understood. I could tell by how he didn't try to comfort me, but only nodded once.

"We all do what we can, Mary, and what we must, no matter what others do to us," he said. "We must try, always try. Continue that path and you will find your own reward, whether in this life, or the next."

Chloe's arm tightened protectively around me. An ungrateful part of me didn't want her protection or, worse, believed I'd no need of it.

"Don't tell her things like that, Lucas," Chloe said. "If she tries to run like Mark and Sary—"

"I didn't say she should," he said.

"Then I don't know what you said," Chloe said angrily, and I sensed her anger included much more than Lucas alone. "Anyone else who tries to run from Mistress now wouldn't even get free of this county. This time Mistress'd have soldiers on horses and dogs after them so fast to make sure they was brought back."

Lucas frowned, rubbing his forefinger over his cheekbone. "That's not what I meant. There's other ways to freedom besides running away."

"Maybe there was for you," Chloe retorted. "Not for the rest of us, specially not for us women. The world is unfriendly enough without your nonsense."

"Forgive me, Chloe, but what Lucas says is true," I said slowly. "Besides, he didn't make me read that notice. I chose it. I read it. He didn't."

"You did at that." Lucas rose, and reached out to slide the newssheet away from me. Before I could protest, he'd refolded the paper and tucked it back inside his waistcoat. "I should leave now. The Captain is traveling in the morning, and he'll want everything ready and done tonight."

"Please don't leave yet," I said quickly. "I wanted to read about change and freedom and all those other things that you said before were in the newssheets from New York."

He pulled his cap over his ears and smiled as he unlatched the door. "That's what you did read, Mary. You might not have realized it, but you did."

And I had. The more I thought of what Lucas had said, the more I realized how right and wise he'd been. He couldn't have guessed that I'd choose to read the runaway notice, but once I had he'd made me see that the lesson to be learned was much more than simply sounding out letters and words.

I came to understand this more clearly every time that Lucas returned to the Hermitage. From him, I learned the geography of the American colonies, of Boston to the north and Philadelphia, Williamsburg, and Charleston to the south. I learned that fiery speeches and protests were being made in all these places, but only in Boston had blood already been shed. And I also heard for the first time the notion of free white men who believed themselves in bondage because of taxes, not actual chains or whips, something that even Lucas could not fully explain.

In my short life, I had never been blessed with a father, a brother, or an uncle who had cared to view me as a worthy person. Before long Lucas became all these to me. Whenever he spoke, I listened. This was, of course, to be expected from any young woman. But what was so much more rare was that whenever I spoke, Lucas in return listened to me, my words and my thoughts.

As the weather warmed, we often sat outside. Sometimes the others joined us; sometimes we were alone. It was then that I shared my history and he shared his: how as a boy in Gambia he'd been captured by warriors from another tribe, sold to slave traders, and brought to New York. There he'd been bought first by a stable owner, where he'd learned to work with horses, and then by Captain Vervelde. He'd known pain and loss, as had I, but the greater bond between us rose not from the common experience of suffering, but because we'd both survived it.

Once winter became spring and then summer, Hetty spent most days and nights at the other house with Mrs. DeVisme, leaving

Chloe and me together to keep Mistress's house, launder and press the clothes, tend the kitchen gardens and fowl, and prepare and serve the meals for the family and refreshments for evening entertainments.

My day was ordered by the desires of others. I had no choice in what I did, who I saw, what I wore or ate, or where I went. I cooked and served food that I was permitted to taste, but forbidden to eat. I had neither friends of my own age, nor any family. I was paid no wages, and owned nothing, but was instead the property of another.

Mistress did not understand this. Like every other white person in my life, she truly believed that I had been improved by her ownership. Because my skin was a different color than hers and I'd been born in another country, in her eyes I would forever be childish and incapable of acting upon my own.

It was always the same among the English and the French, even for a woman as learned as Mistress. She wasn't silly or selfish, as Madame had been. Instead, she read many books and wrote many letters, as if she were a gentleman instead of a lady. In company, she didn't simper or demur like other ladies, but spoke her thoughts aloud, which made the gentlemen admire her all the more.

She hadn't before kept a lady's maid, but once she learned I'd helped attend Madame she'd begun to summon me to dress and powder her hair for special evenings. With little personal vanity, she was considered handsome rather than a beauty, and as I brushed and pinned her hair, she sat as docile as could be, without any suggestions or judgments. Most often she read from a book in her hand rather than gazing at her own reflection in the dressing-table looking glass, the way Madame had done.

"You are quite skilled at hairdressing, Mary," she said as she sat before me one evening. "I marvel that your last lady would have parted with you."

"She died, Mistress," I said, carefully rolling a thick curl with my fingers to pin against her temple. She'd never spoken to me like this, as a friend might. It made me uneasy, and from instinct I fell back on the simplest of answers.

"I am sorry," Mistress said gently, consoling me as if I'd felt any genuine loss or sorrow for Madame. "That must have been terrible for you."

"Yes, Mistress." What had been terrible had been my life at Belle Vallée. Given how Madame's dislike of me had grown on the voyage from Pondicherry, I doubted she would have done much to protect me had she lived.

"I am so grateful that the Major was able to rescue you, and bring you here to us where you're safe," she said. "Especially after being sold from your parents as an infant."

"I was eight years old when my uncle sold me, Mistress." I don't know why I told her that. I still don't. Perhaps, in that moment, I spoke that truth for my mother, who could not. "My mother died when I was born."

"Oh, poor little Mary!" she exclaimed, twisting around on the bench to face me. "What of your father? Did he not look after you?"

"My father was an English soldier, Mistress." My voice hardened and grew flat, the way it always did when I spoke of the faceless man who'd sired me. "He did not know of my birth."

"Ahh." Mistress's dark eyes softened with sympathy I did not want. "That explains so much."

I flushed, and turned away to take more hairpins from the dish. I could guess that what was explained to her was the color of my skin and eyes.

"There are few things in this world more irresistible than a handsome man in a red coat," she continued softly. "It's only later, when the heart is less blind, that the true measure of the man appears behind the gold lace."

I listened, mute, as she'd twisted the nightmare of my mother's rape into a romantic tale of broken hearts and handsome officers.

Later, on Sunday, I told Lucas what she'd said.

"I was wrong to speak of my mother to her," I lamented as we walked together in the shade beside one of the ponds. "I should never have told her. I don't know why I did."

"You weren't wrong, Mary," he said. "There's no harm done."

I shook my head, unconvinced. "But for Mistress to think my mother would have loved the man who—"

"She didn't know," he said. "I doubt she would have said that if she had. She is not a bad woman, like your first mistress. She showed you kindness, and you warmed in it. There is no harm, no sin, to that."

I sighed, kicking restlessly at the tall grass beside the path. Even though I had no memory of my mother, I'd always defended her. It was all I had, and all I could do.

"Think instead of what she told you," Lucas continued. "She as much as confessed that she's unhappily wed."

I glanced up at him quickly. "Why would she tell me that?"

"Who else can she tell?" he reasoned. "She told you, because you cannot judge her."

I frowned, thinking. I accepted most of what Lucas said, but I wasn't certain of this.

"But how do you know that Mistress is unhappy?"

"Women and love are not difficult to understand," he continued. "When you are older, you will understand these matters for yourself."

I didn't like it when he reminded me of how young I was, and stopped walking. "You're not married, Lucas."

He stopped, too, looking away from me and up at the trees. Sunlight through the leaves dappled his face, and masked his true emotions.

"No, I am not," he said evenly. "I won't marry until I can support my wife and children by my own labors. That is what a man does."

"Major Prevost has done that for Mistress and their boys," I said. "Besides, she still writes letters to him. Long letters, too."

He began to walk again. "Do you ever see those letters?"

"I?" I hurried to rejoin him. "No. I know when she writes to him because she takes care to guard her words against anyone else reading them."

"As she should," he said. "But the time is coming when being a British officer's wife will not be a good thing for her."

It wouldn't be good for me, either. If the Major's enemies came to attack his wife here, they likely wouldn't pause to ask my name or beliefs. I'd only be considered another of her belongings, more plunder of war. I didn't want to think of what would become of me then, and my trepidation must have shown on my face.

"If you ever see or overhear anything that hints that she—or you—might be in danger," Lucas said slowly, carefully, "send word to me at Mount Joy, and I will tell Captain Vervelde. He has always considered Mrs. Prevost a friend, and will do what he can."

I nodded, every bit as solemn as he. So long as I kept to the fields instead of the roads where I might be seen, I could find my way to Captain Vervelde's house if I had to.

I hoped I never did. It was no secret that the Captain's loyalties lay with those opposed to the king, and while he was still invited to the Hermitage, I'd noted that those invitations only came on nights when there were no British officers in attendance. Mistress was already keeping the two sides separate from each other, and though there was still plenty of laughter and music in the parlor, there was often a tension to the conversations that had not been there before.

Lucas had never revealed how deeply the Captain was involved with groups like the Sons of Liberty, or exactly what manner of business took him again and again to New York. This promise of protection, however, hinted at more connections and power than I'd ever have guessed, and also of more danger, too.

On a cold, clear day in January, Chloe and I were together piping white sugared icing over the sides of the Great Cake for Mistress's Twelfth Night supper. The cake truly was aptly named, dark and heavy with rum-soaked fruit beneath the icing, and larger than any other I'd ever baked. Chloe had already made the twelve little sugar swans that had been set aside to harden before they were placed in a circle around the top of the cake.

Although it was afternoon, Mistress herself was lying abed with one of the fierce headaches that had begun to plague her, and trusting that an hour's time with the shutters drawn and a cool cloth across her eyes would make it depart before it was time for her to dress. The boys had been sent to their grandmother across the field, and the house was quiet and still, as if it, too, were resting before the night.

Working in the back kitchen as we were, neither Chloe nor I heard the rider pull up outside the front porch, his horse's hooves muffled by the packed snow, but we both jumped when the man thumped his fist loudly on the door.

"Bah, what a racket!" exclaimed Chloe. "Go to the door, Mary, and tell him that Mistress won't receive company for another two hours."

I wiped my hands on my apron and hurried through the house, glancing quickly into the parlor to make sure the fire there was still respectable. Chloe could bluster all she wanted about turning away whichever gentleman had arrived early, but I knew Mistress would want him welcomed regardless, and settled into the parlor with either tea or punch.

I unlatched the heavy door, leaning my weight into the lock to open it against the ice that often made it stick. But instead of the gentleman I expected, there was a young British soldier on the porch, his cheeks red from the cold and his cocked hat tied in place with a checkered scarf, with a letter for Mistress. As I closed the door, I turned the letter over in my hand. I recognized the signet pressed into the red wax seal, the insignia of Colonel Faulkner, the commander of the British troops in the area.

"Mary, who was that?" Mistress asked, her voice faint from the top of the stairs. She wore her silk dressing gown over her shift, the color as bright as a flame in the winter shadows.

"A British soldier, Mistress," I said, climbing the stairs to her with the letter outstretched. But instead of accepting the letter, she returned to her bedchamber, clearly expecting me to follow. She climbed back into the bed without taking off her dressing gown, and with a deep sigh drew the coverlet high over her chest and squeezed her eyes shut. By the light of the fire, her face was pale and pinched, with the pain of her headache twisting her brows together.

"Faulkner and his infernal letters," she muttered. "Few things are as tedious as a self-important colonel with more ink and paper than sense."

I dipped the cloth in the bowl of lavender water on the table beside her bed, and wrung it out. Gently I placed it across her eyes, and then began to make tiny circles over her forehead with my fingertips, the way I'd learned to do long ago for Madame.

"You are a godsend, Mary," Mistress said, sighing with relief. "That is better, much better. Perhaps I shall return to dwell among the living after all."

Her breathing grew more measured, and I thought she'd fallen back asleep when abruptly she spoke again.

"Mary, that letter," she said, still masked by the damp cloth. "I'm certain it will be of no importance whatsoever, but I suppose I should know its contents before tonight. Are you able to read it aloud to me?"

"Yes, mistress." I carefully slipped my finger beneath the seal, unfolded the sheet, and went to crouch beside the fire to read aloud by its light.

> *Madame Prevost,*
> *I trust you are well and in good health despite the cold weather. I have had fresh reports this day from Boston that will interest you and other citizens loyal to His Majesty. The city remains in a state of war-like confusion, with the lawless mob having destroyed significant property. Governor Hutchinson has requested Parliament to send a military force to the city at once to restore peace. Sorrowful tidings indeed, but it is hoped that this act will soon quell the unrest for the good of us all.*
> *I remain, madame, your—*

"My obedient servant, on and on and on," Mistress finished for me, and sighed again. "The fellow can scarcely contain his glee, can he? All these foolish men long for a war, as if death and mayhem have ever solved anything. No matter. I shall write and praise him tomorrow as if he were Mars himself, clad in the shining armor of victory that still won't hide his belly."

"Yes, Mistress," I said, refolding the letter, and resolving to share this news with Lucas as soon as I could.

"You read that letter very well, Mary," Mistress said absently. "I didn't realize old Mr. Satterthwaite was such an uncommon tutor."

"Yes, Mistress, he was." There was no purpose—and perhaps some harm—in revealing that old Mr. Satterthwaite had taught me only the barest of letters, and that it was instead Lucas Emmons who had made a reader of me. "Will that be all, Mistress, or shall you dress now?"

"Return to me in another quarter-hour and I shall dress then," she said, drowsy.

I was already closing the door after her when she called back to me.

"And Mary," she said in the same drowsy voice. "Pray recall that what you read in Colonel Faulkner's letter is not to be repeated or discussed with anyone. Do you understand?"

"Yes, Mistress," I said, already understanding far more than she'd ever know. "I do."

Mistress needn't have pledged me to secrecy. By the time Lucas came the following week, Colonel Faulkner's "fresh reports" were so widely known as to have been printed in the broadside that Lucas brought in his pocket.

"You see how in Boston the people are taking matters into their own hands," he said, scarcely able to contain his excitement as he pointed to the broadside from the *Boston Gazette.* "Instead of being forced to pay the king's tax on tea, our men disguised themselves as savages, intercepted the ship carrying the tea, and tossed it all into the harbor. Not a single man, patriot or Tory, was injured, and all was done as civilly as could be. Read it for yourself, and may His Majesty do the same."

Caesar and I crowded together to read the broadsheet, while Chloe sniffed and ignored it, and Lucas, too.

"Three hundred and forty-two chests of tea tossed into the sea!" marveled Caesar. "That's a poke in the eye to the old East India Company, isn't it?"

"'The people are almost universally congratulating each other on this happy event,'" I read aloud. "Do you believe that, Lucas? That this—this destruction was celebrated? So many crates of tea must have made for a considerable loss."

"A loss that the East India Company is bound to miss from its pocket," Lucas said blithely. "It's all the fine work of the Sons of Liberty, true patriots all, and I only wish we'd acted first in New York. But we will. We *will.*"

"Colonel Faulkner wrote to Mistress that British troops were already on their way to Boston," I said uneasily. "What if they come next to New York, or New Jersey?"

"If they do, then they'll find they'll have more than they reckoned for," Lucas said. "If they want a fight, then we shall give them one. It's for the sake of freedom, Mary, freedom for us all."

His eyes were bright with fervor for his cause, his jaw set and determined. I desired my freedom as much as anyone, but not this way. Not like this.

I had been only a small child when the British army had fought the French over Pondicherry. None of us who'd been born there had cared which army of foreign soldiers claimed victory. But I remembered all too well the desolation that their fighting had caused, with once-fine buildings destroyed and torn and bloated corpses rotting in the sun and devoured by the hyenas that had come out of the brush. I remembered the famine that had followed after fields of crops had been burned, and new widows wailing in the smoldering ruins of their homes.

And I remembered, too, what Mistress had said after I'd read her the Colonel's letter: that all these foolish men longed for a war, as if death and mayhem have ever solved anything.

War had solved nothing in Pondicherry, and it wouldn't here in the colonies, either, and as I listened to the excitement in the voices of Lucas and Caesar I could only fear where this all would lead.

I could always tell when Lucas had come from New York. In place of his livery, he'd be dressed like a common sailor or dock-worker, in patched loose trousers, a shapeless jacket, and an old kerchief. To my eyes, it was not a good disguise: Lucas was too tall, his gait too distinctive, for clothing alone to change his appearance. He claimed it didn't matter, that to the watch he was only one more Negro. Nor did they know or care that he was a free man. If stopped, he need only say that he was on his master's business and he was permitted to pass.

When we walked together outside the house, out of the hearing of anyone else, he told me more, of how he and others like him took delight in intimidating New York Tories, shouting foul names, throwing stones at their carriages, and breaking the windows of their shops. To him, they were the enemy; they deserved no better. He explained to me how the Sons of Liberty were creating secret stockpiles of gunpowder and arms around the city in readiness.

"In readiness for what?" I asked uneasily.

"For the time when we must take action to set ourselves free," he said, the words sounding glib and practiced.

"For war," I said softly.

"If necessary," he said. "Mary, consider what we can achieve. Imagine a country where we rule ourselves, without the interference of a king or parliament. Imagine a land where everyone is free, a land without slavery of any kind."

I nodded, wishing I could believe these sweet and heady dreams as completely as he did.

"But at what cost, Lucas?" I said. "You've seen how Parliament has treated Boston. You've told me yourself of all the acts and laws they've passed to try to stop us. What will you do if they send warships to New York?"

"We will do what we must," he said resolutely. "Mary, we know what kind of world we'll have if we do nothing. Isn't it worth fighting for the chance to create one that's better?"

There was no quarreling with him, and I sadly knew that nothing I could say would change his purpose. He was determined, and he'd company enough with the same beliefs.

In December, Lucas had told me of how the grand mansion of New York's royal governor was burned to the ground, with all the governor's belongings inside. He said the flames were the brightest he'd ever seen: the flames of the righteous destroying the corruption of the Crown. What I saw in the newspaper was the price of this righteousness: the cost of the damage was placed at over five thousand pounds. I feared for Lucas, knowing how he and his Sons of Liberty took credit, though not a one was charged with the crime.

In April, they grew bolder still, and copied the actions of their brothers in Boston. As soon as the tea ship *London* arrived in the harbor, they painted their faces like savages and set upon the customshouse and ship itself. They dragged every crate of the tea from the hold to the deck, and took care to break the crates open with hatchets before heaving them over the side, so the tea could not be salvaged.

"The harbor was afloat with these tea leaves, Mary," Lucas told me afterward. With a carelessness that terrified me, he hadn't bothered to wipe away the last daubs of paint along the edge of his jaw and around his collar. "They say the governor wept with fury when he heard the news—not that his tears could undo what's already been done."

On the kitchen table before me, he placed a long leaf of tea that he'd fished from the water, still wet with salt water. He'd thought I'd want it as a memento of liberty's cause. I refused to touch it, and I was glad that the next morning Chloe tossed it into the fire.

By June, the rebellion—for so it was—came closer to us in New Jersey, with most of Mistress's neighbors declaring themselves as Whigs and openly supporting the new Continental Congress in Philadelphia. Those who did not were branded as Tories.

In public, Mistress took no sides, and continued to welcome old friends to her home, regardless of their beliefs. She gaily, and bravely, made it a rule that no politics would be discussed in her parlor, and because of the goodwill and hospitality she'd so carefully created over the years, her friends obliged.

But Lucas told me her loyalties were openly discussed and questioned and Major Prevost's continued absence only fueled the talk for both sides. Some of her oldest acquaintances began to speak against her in public, and I heard guests in her own house question her allegiances the instant she stepped from the room.

I now could see for myself how on edge New Jersey had become, not only in Mistress's parlor, but on market days and at Sunday worship. The more I witnessed and overheard, the more I began to fear for my own safety, too.

One rainy morning late in April, Lucas came to me full of excitement, and waving the newssheet that told the world of what had occurred in a small village outside of Boston, a village that could just as easily have been Hopperstown. The heading was "BLOODY NEWS," and indeed it was: an unprovoked attack by the king's soldiers on a group of humble farmers and townspeople before their own homes, as their wives and children watched in terror.

> Last Wednesday the troops of his Britannic Majesty commenced hostilities upon the people of this province. . . . We are involved in all the horrors of a civil war.

Nothing in my life would ever be the same.

CHAPTER 7

The Hackensack Valley
Province of New Jersey
May 1776

"That is not an inspiring sight, is it?" Mistress said to her sister and mother. "I wouldn't wish to trust my welfare to the defense of soldiers such as those."

"Not at all," Mrs. DeVisme said wryly. "But then Dutchmen aren't by nature fighting men."

They were standing on a small bluff overlooking the field set aside for the local militia's training and drills. The three women in tailored habits and feathered hats were so well known in the county that they'd already been recognized and greeted by most everyone they'd passed.

I stood a short, respectful distance behind Mistress and her mother, but still within hearing in case they required me. We had come here to Hackensack, the largest town in the County of Bergen, so that Mistress, her mother, and her sister could visit the shops. I'd been brought as well to carry their purchases, and while I'd waited for them I'd picked a few bright yellow dandelions and tucked the nosegay into the front of my bodice. Their cheeriness matched my humor. How could it not when the sky overhead was a cloudless blue and the sun was warm on my back and shoulders?

Our final stop had been to come here to the militia drill, where we stood among several other little groups of spectators. But Mistress and her mother were right: there was little enjoyment to be found watching this ragtag drill.

The first war fever that had infected the country with patriotism in the spring of 1775 had long since faded.

It became clear that the British army wasn't at all intimidated by the patriot resistance and militias made up of farmers, and instead of retreating, as most believed would happen, Parliament sent more troops to Boston. But as long as they remained in Boston and posed no immediate danger to New Jersey, then New Jersey had become less and less interested, and instead went about their own affairs as usual.

The company of militiamen drilling here before us in Hackensack was the sorry proof of that. There were fewer than a score of men, when last autumn the number had been a hundred or more.

Mrs. DeVisme left no doubt of which side she supported.

"Mrs. Lynch told me just last week that General Washington's army was melting away because their enlistments were ending," she said. "Meanwhile good King George has so many men clamoring to join his side that I've heard they're being turned away."

Mistress glanced at her sideways from beneath her hat. "What you heard, Mama," she said evenly, "is that British agents are offering a five-guinea bounty and two hundred acres of land to any Jersey man who'll fight for the king. That's hardly the same as the Jersey men accepting."

Mrs. DeVisme sniffed. "What will it matter, when this sorry excuse for a war will be over before it's begun?" She waved her hand absently toward the drilling militia. "Consider your brave husband and his men, Theodosia. Then consider these sorry fellows."

Mistress ignored her. Her younger sister, Miss DeVisme, did not, pointedly turning and flicking her petticoats away from the militia's field.

"This isn't why I came here today," she declared peevishly. "I expected to see fine military gentlemen of honor, not stripling lads with tufts of hay poking from their ears."

"We are here to show our appreciation to these men for following their duty, Caty," Mistress said, raising her voice so that the other spectators around us might hear her, too. "We are not here for you to find a new beau."

That startled me: not that Mistress would scold her sister, but that she wished to make a public demonstration of her own support for the local Whig militiamen. What of her husband the British major?

"You can say what you will, Theo," her sister said, "but if you can marry an officer of the king, then so can I—not that I'll ever so much as glimpse a gentleman like that here."

She turned briskly, petticoats in her hands, and came up the rise of the hill toward me.

"Mary, have you my new gloves?" she demanded. "I trust you haven't mislaid them."

"No, miss," I said, reaching into the basket. "They are here, miss."

"I should hope so," she said. "You can be so slow with even the most simple of tasks, Mary."

Silently I handed her the new kid gloves she'd bought earlier, still wrapped in paper. She pulled off her old gloves, dropped them in a crumpled ball into the basket on my arm, and pulled on the new gloves instead, letting the shopkeeper's paper drift across the grass.

"Don't be wasteful, Catherine." Behind her, Mistress picked up the paper herself, folded it, and tucked it into her pocket for some later purpose. "Now pray that you take care of those gloves. If New York and Philadelphia are blockaded like Boston, then it will be a long time before you'll have another pair from London."

Miss DeVisme didn't answer. Still standing before me, she snatched the little dandelion nosegay from my jacket, crushed it, and tossed it away.

"Slaves don't wear flowers, Mary," she said tartly. "It's vain of you to do so."

I flushed, and looked down at the yellow petals scattered on the grass. I told myself that they didn't matter. Dandelions were only weeds. I slipped the basket's handle over my shoulder and trudged after the others.

And yet as Caesar drove the carriage back to the Hermitage, with me squeezed onto the bench beside him, I still wasn't nearly as resigned as I wished to be. Miss DeVisme's harshness was likely more difficult to swallow because we were close in age. I believed this to be my sixteenth summer, though I wasn't certain. Regardless, I was by now a woman grown, with a woman's form and manner, and a woman's passion as well, though I was loath to admit it to myself.

Chloe, however, had no such qualms.

"Was Hackensack as fine as you'd hoped, Mary?" she asked as soon as I'd returned to the kitchen with spices and other sundries that Mistress had bought for cookery.

"It was well enough," I said, terse with ill humor.

Chloe glanced over her shoulder. "Was it now?"

"Miss DeVisme was unhappy that there weren't any gentlemen to admire her at the drill," I said as I unloaded the basket, slamming each item down on the table as I did. "She turned sharp as any bitch toward me."

"I'd guess she wasn't the only one disappointed at that drill," Chloe said. "I'm guessing Captain Vervelde wasn't there, either?"

"No, he wasn't," I said. "It was only the militia that was drilling, and besides—"

I broke off before I said more.

Chloe raised a single brow. "You were hoping that much to see Captain Vervelde, Mary? Or maybe it was someone who's with Captain Vervelde, someone who—"

"Lucas Emmons wasn't there, either, if that's what you're asking," I said tartly, even as I knew I sounded every bit as sharp as Miss DeVisme had been earlier.

"I wasn't asking," Chloe said. "But there's no harm in wanting to know how Lucas is faring with the army. It's been a long while since we saw him here."

"Weeks and weeks," I said, then frowned when I realized again how she'd led me to speak more than I'd intended. "A long while."

"There's no harm in caring, either," Chloe said softly. "Even a fool could see that you and Lucas are fond of each other."

I sighed, the irritation fleeing from me before the truth. "Lucas is my friend," I said carefully. "But to him, I'm sure I'm no more than a child."

"Maybe when you first came here, but not now," Chloe said. She spoke not to tease me, but as fact. "He's not so old, and you're not so young. You're clever, like he is. Why wouldn't Lucas admire the woman you've become? I saw how you looked at each other before he went away."

I dropped heavily onto a stool, trying to make sense of what I didn't want to acknowledge. I'd last seen Lucas at the end of February, when there'd been a long thaw in the weather. Soon after that, he'd gone off with Captain Vervelde to Long Island or Staten Island (I wasn't sure which) to help with fortifications there.

Although Lucas was a free man, his affairs were still closely tied to the Captain, who paid his wages and provided his lodging on the Vervelde property and expected loyalty and gratitude for that, the way white people did. I'd long suspected that it had been Captain Vervelde, now an officer in the militia, who had entangled Lucas further into the politics of the war. It would have been easy enough. Lucas was a fervent patriot, and eager to help the cause of freedom any way he could. It was part of the reason I found his conversation so exciting, and also why I'd picked the dandelions for my bodice today, because I'd hoped Lucas would be there. I'd wanted to look pretty for him.

That seemed so foolish now, as foolish as anything that Miss DeVisme might say: *I'd wanted to look pretty for Lucas.* No wonder her spite had stung me. I usually could ignore her, but this time her meanness had been able to creep right into me through the weakness of my own disappointment. I couldn't let that happen again.

Still I worried for Lucas, wherever he was, and the longer he was away, the more I feared for him. He wasn't a young man to be out digging fortifications and sleeping in a cold field. For small comfort, I knew he wouldn't see any true fighting. As a Negro (even a free man), he wasn't permitted to enlist in the army.

Was that worry what Chloe meant? Did that translate into the fondness and caring that she'd seen?

Chloe sat on the stool beside mine, bringing with her the basket of apples from the cellar that she'd been peeling.

"Mind me, Mary, and what I say," she said gently as her knife slid deftly beneath the next apple's skin. "People like us don't know what each day will bring us, or what it won't. This war's only making it worse. We must find our happiness wherever we can. If that means you love Lucas, why, then, you make sure you tell him so the instant he returns. Don't you wait. It's better to tell him than to be left with only a heart filled with regrets and wonderings."

I nodded, hugging my arms at my sides and trying to understand. I'd no experience with love of any kind, and the very thought of it made me skittish and uncertain.

I'd no such trouble recalling Lucas: his heavy-lidded eyes as he watched and listened to me, his slow, wide smile that could warm me like a fire, the burnished gleam of his skin, the way he'd finish a thought by spreading his hands and fingers wide, like the rays of sunshine.

"You're smiling," Chloe said as a perfect, unbroken curl of apple peel slipped from her knife into her apron. "That's answer enough."

"Lucas is a free man," I said softly. "I'm Mistress's property."

"Mistress doesn't own your heart," she said, bending to reach for another apple. "It's yours to give or keep. You've found plenty of ways to see each other before this, haven't you?"

I didn't answer, unable to let myself dream that far.

"There's plenty of people who make do between houses," Chloe continued. "If the love's strong enough, then that won't matter. And if Lucas loves you so much he can't live without you beside him, then he could buy you from Mistress, and make you a freewoman."

"Free?" I repeated, stunned by such a possibility. "But I can't—"

"Don't go thinking of what *can't* happen, Mary, and think instead of what *could*," Chloe said firmly. "He wouldn't be the first freeman to buy his wife from bondage, and there's been some who've bought whole families of children, too."

The Major had paid over three hundred *livres,* or about twenty-five pounds, to Monsieur for me. Now, four years later, my value would only have increased. I spoke both French and English, and from being so often in Mistress's company, I spoke her English, with her words, and with only the faintest accent remaining from Pondicherry. I'd learned the arts of housekeeping, mending, and laundering, and I'd become a passable lady's maid. I could cook in both the French manner that I'd learned from Perroquet and the English manner from Chloe, and I still recalled how to make a fine curry, if anyone in New Jersey would desire it. I'd also survived Saint-Domingue; the English called this seasoning, a prized quality.

I did not want to consider exactly how much I now was worth. But Mistress surely would, if Lucas were to ask to buy my freedom.

Love and freedom, freedom and love, and now entwined together. It had taken Lucas years to buy his own freedom, and it could take him more years to buy mine.

Could he love me that much? Did I love him enough to ask that of him?

I turned on my stool to face Chloe. "Did you—have you loved, Chloe?"

"I have." Her knife paused, a curl of red peel hanging from the blade. "His name was Jem. He was bought by my old master in the same sale I was, so we came to the house together. From the start, we just belonged together. After a time, he asked Master if we could marry. It was a fine wedding, Mary, in the garden behind Master's house, when there were pink flowers in the trees. Master watched from the steps. We even had the minister from meeting wed us, so we'd be sure to stay married. We was happy then. Oh, my, yes, we was happy."

She paused, lost in memories, before she roused herself with a shake of her shoulders. She finished peeling the apple, tossed it into the bowl, and reached for another.

"We had scarcely a year," she said, her voice heavy. "One morning Jem was helping the blacksmith with one of Master's horses and the beast reared up and kicked him in the head. Just like that, he was gone. Then Master died, and his son sold me to Mistress here."

I reached out to rest my hand on her forearm, the way she'd often done to me. "I'm sorry."

"I am, too," she said wistfully. "But I had that time, and Jem's with me still."

She placed her palm over her chest, over her heart like a pledge. "I keep him right here, where no one can ever take him from me."

I nodded. Finally I could understand. So much had been taken from me that having Lucas forever as my own—that would feel right.

"You mind what I say, Mary," Chloe said. "You tell Lucas your heart when he comes back. You *tell* him, and the rest will follow as it will."

* * *

Toward the end of June, not long after we'd gone to Hackensack, Mistress decided that the weather was warm enough for a good cleaning of the house. She ordered all the windows thrown open as far as they could be so the fresh air could come inside and clear away all the winter, and set Chloe and me to scrubbing everything that could be scrubbed. Floors and windows and steps and sills, all were to be scrubbed to her satisfaction, until I thought I was back on my hands and knees scrubbing the decks of the *Céleste*.

In every bedchamber, the hangings were taken down from the rods of the bedsteads to be shaken out of doors, all the linens washed, and the mattress and pillows plumped and turned. The clothes in every cupboard and chest were likewise taken out, aired, and refolded.

The last room in the house to be cleaned was the tiny room that belonged entirely to Mistress: her closet, she called it. This was where she spent more time than anywhere else in the house, and we all knew better than to disturb her when she was within.

Here was her mahogany desk, placed before the single narrow window for the best light, and scattered with stacks of papers and letters kept in place by stones her sons had found for her in the fields. Here, too, was a porcelain vase filled not with flowers, but with the tall, pointed feathers of pheasants. This desk was where she wrote, her pen furiously racing across the page as she composed letter after letter after letter. For every acquaintance who called at the house, there must have been another half dozen in other places with whom she'd correspond.

This was where she read, too, with a large standing shelf, or case, for her books. Some were bound in leather and stamped with gold, some in humble, worn cloth, some many pages long and others as slender as a pamphlet. It didn't matter to her. She loved them all. I could tell by how she'd take a book from the shelf, sliding it gently forward until it tipped into her palm, and how she'd open the pages with infinite care, as if to do so was both a pleasure and an honor. Plutarch, Herodotus, and Pliny were among the names on the spines, and sometimes it seemed that these men were her only true friends, or at least the ones she most respected.

In a way, her books were like strong drink could be to others. Ignoring all else in her household, she could sit in her dressing gown and read by the hour and long into the night, absently twisting a strand of her dark hair between her fingers as the candles guttered and burned low.

In my youth, I mistook these retreats of hers for a kind of unhappiness, an unhappiness that I could not comprehend. How could a free English woman with a handsome family, a sizable home and property, and the regard of many friends dare to be unhappy? Only much later did I understand it for what it was: not unhappiness, but restless dreaming, and yearning for more than what her life already held. I understood, for I came to share her restlessness.

It was my task to dust Mistress's books. As she instructed, I knelt and spread a clean cloth on the floor, and placed the books from the bookcase upon it, one shelf at a time. Then each book was wiped with another, softer cloth along the spine, followed by the end pages. Finally the shelf itself was cleaned and the books replaced in the exact order in which they'd been before. Mistress watched me do several books before she returned to her desk, and whatever letter she was writing that morning.

As I took each volume down from the shelf, I longed to open the covers and read them for myself, and if Mistress hadn't been nearby at her desk I would have. Since Lucas had been away, there'd been no fresh newspapers for me to read, no broadsides or pamphlets, and I was fair starved for words and knowledge. I wanted to know what was written in these books that so held Mistress's attention. Lucas had told me that the books English people read could be filled with stories or histories or politics, or explanations of the world's ideas and mysteries. I ran my fingertips lightly across the volume in my hand, the brown leather burnished from wear and the binding loose.

"Take extra care with that one, Mary," Mistress said from her desk. Of course she'd seen me; sometimes it felt as if she saw everything. "It's one of my father's old lawbooks. *Modern Reports, Being a Collection of Several Special Cases in the Court of the King's Bench.* Isn't that the title?"

There were no words on the spine or cover, and I paused, unsure of what to do or say.

"Open to the title page, Mary," Mistress said. "You can read that much. I'm curious to know if I'm right."

Gently I opened the book, the paper soft and velvety to touch. The first pages were blank, but then came a page with the title she'd just spoken, and every line a different size of letters.

"Yes, Mistress, that is right," I said. "Though there are more words written below it. 'In the last years of the reign of King Charles II, in the reign of King James II. And in the two first years of his present Majesty, together—'"

"That's sufficient, Mary, thank you," she said, chuckling. "What dry, dull stuff the law is! How fortunate I wasn't born a boy, or I'd have been doomed to follow in my father's vocation, instead of merely inheriting his name."

"Yes, Mistress." On the page opposite the title was a small pasted label with her father's name: *Theodosius Bartow.*

"I'd no notion that book was so old," she mused, idly tapping the barb of her pen against her wrist. "The two first years of his present majesty must have been from the time of George the First, and now we're sixteen years into the reign of George the Third, though I wouldn't dare venture to say how much longer we'll have him."

"Yes, Mistress," I murmured as I set the book aside and moved on to dusting the next.

But Mistress wasn't done.

"So which party do you favor, Mary?" she asked playfully. "Do you consider yourself a patriot, or a Tory? Would you drink a bumper to General Washington, or His Majesty?"

I sat back on my heels. This would be a game for her, but a game I couldn't play in return. My world was filled with people like me who'd let themselves become too easy with their mistresses and masters, and had the scars on their back to show for it.

"I've no right to speak on such matters, Mistress," I said carefully. "But if I must choose, I should follow the beliefs of this house and my master, and be a Tory."

"Hah!" she exclaimed, pleased, and sat back in her chair with her arms folded over her chest. "Cleverly said, Mary, and wisely said, too. They should send you to their Congress instead of—Now who can that be?"

She slid from her chair and peered from the window, keeping to one side so that whoever was riding toward the house wouldn't see her.

"By all that's holy, it's Mr. Hendrick, riding like the devil himself is on his tail," she said. Swiftly she gathered up the letter she'd been writing and tucked it deep inside one of the books on the desk. From the bottom of another pile of books she pulled out a ledger and placed it in the middle of the desk, spreading the pages wide so that anyone might read the columns.

She ran her hands over her hair to smooth it and took a deep breath, folding her hands neatly at her waist.

"Go, Mary, and greet Mr. Hendrick," she said. "Bring him here to me."

"Here, Mistress?" I asked, unable to keep back my surprise. I'd never once shown any gentleman to her closet. I glanced down at the cloth on the floor with the books and my half-finished dusting. "Should I gather this up first?"

"Leave it as it is," she said, "and when you bring Mr. Hendrick here, I want you to resume the dusting. Your presence will keep him from lingering overlong."

She closed her eyes for a moment, visibly composing herself, and then smiled quickly.

"Don't fear, Mary," she said. "I know what I'm about."

I hoped she did, for Mr. Hendrick was already knocking at the front door, loud and purposeful. I curtseyed, and hurried through the front hall, smoothing my own apron as I went.

Mr. Hendrick was no stranger to the house. Once a merchant in New York, he'd become sufficiently prosperous in trade that he'd bought himself a gentleman's estate not far from the Hermitage. Because Mr. Hendrick was considered a staunch Whig and patriot in the valley, he visited Mistress less frequently than he once had, and it was unusual for him to call now, so early in the day.

"Is Mrs. Prevost at home, Mary?" he asked as he came striding into the house. He was a heavyset gentleman, and he was breathing hard from his ride with the bottom of his wig damp and drooping with sweat. "I've news for her that cannot wait."

"She is at home, sir, yes," I said. "This way, if you please."

I led him back to Mistress's closet. She hadn't been idle in the short time I'd been away. From another room she'd brought a spindle-back chair that would be uncomfortably small for a man of Mr. Hendrick's size and set it beside her desk: welcoming, but not.

She herself was sitting bent over the open ledger, scratching away with her pen, and only looked up with a great show of surprise.

"Mr. Hendrick, good day," she said, managing to look both sheepish and vulnerable. "You catch me at my household reckonings, I fear. With Major Prevost away, you know it all must fall to me."

"I know your husband must follow his duty, but he has left you with a considerable responsibility for a lady," Mr. Hendrick said solemnly, his hat in his hand and ignoring the offered chair. "Yet if any lady can manage, I'm sure it's you, Theodosia."

"Oh, it isn't the vagaries of accounting that fuddle me." She sighed as if all the worries of the world rested upon her slender shoulders. "It's how very dear everything has become since the patriots took over New York. There are many Whig merchants who will raise the prices of their goods for me, or refuse to sell to me outright. Mary, come continue your work."

I slipped past Mr. Hendrick and did as I was bidden. I was glad not to be dismissed, for I was curious to see what exactly Mistress was planning.

Mr. Hendrick's expression shifted from solemn to grave.

"I regret to hear that," he said. "No matter what your husband's allegiances are, you have always been a good neighbor. I'll speak to others in the valley to make certain you'll be spared."

"I appreciate your kindness, Abraham." Mistress smiled. "Do not put yourself at risk on my behalf, I beg you."

"Not at all," he said gallantly. "I've just received several pipes of excellent Madeira from my warehouse in the city. I hope you'll permit me to have some sent here to you."

She gave a genteel little gasp. "I can't possibly—"

"I insist," he said. "Consider it a small gift between friends. But I fear I've come here on much less agreeable business, Theodosia. This morning I've word—reliable word—that there are over a hundred British sail moored inside Sandy Hook. Most are troopships, alive with thousands of redcoats, and they're putting those men ashore on Staten Island."

I bowed my head over the book in my hand so they wouldn't see the shock that must surely be on my face. The last word I'd had of Lucas's whereabouts had placed him with Captain Vervelde's militiamen on Staten Island—the same Staten Island that was seemingly now the destination of thousands of British soldiers.

"So Admiral Howe does indeed intend to invade New York," Mistress said. She'd abandoned the role of a fluttering, genteel lady, her shoulders now set and her voice all seriousness. "Are there any rumors as to when he might act?"

Mr. Hendrick shook his head. "Not yet, no," he said. "But some of the ships are sailing to the north as well, and have put down near Haverstraw Bay."

Mistress nodded, once again absently tapping her pen. "Haverstraw isn't so far from here," she said. "Thirty miles at most."

Until now, the war had been something that happened far away in Massachusetts. The Hermitage had been an island for us who lived here, green and peaceful and safe. Now that could change, and change quickly. I swept the cloth over the book, trying to continue as if my hands weren't shaking.

"Be honest with me, Abraham," Mistress was saying. "Do you think Howe's troops mean to concentrate their forces on New York, or will they come ashore on this side of the river as well?"

"A few already have," he admitted. "Across the line in New York, in Orange County. They seem more intent on foraging than attack, with parties from the ships looting as they please the farms that decide, rightly or wrongly, to harbor patriots, and then setting fire to the houses and barns as they leave. It's a dirty, dangerous business all around."

"That is the nature of war, isn't it?" she said. Mistress had been an officer's wife for many years, and the hazards and losses of battle were not new to her. "What do you suggest I do to preserve my family and my property?"

Mr. Hendrick rubbed his hand along the back of his neck, uncertain of what to say.

"You are most likely safe here," he said at last. "I expect Howe is more determined upon New York than to scatter his forces by sending them here into our valley. But I'll be blunt, Theodosia. The British will know of your husband, and that this is his home. The knowledge should be sufficient to keep you safe for now."

"Perhaps." Her smile was quick, with no humor to it. "We both know how often soldiers from any army will act without pausing to ask whether friend or foe."

He nodded, his expression grim. "Take care, Theodosia. For now you're safe enough, but guard yourself well. Trust no one. These are perilous times for us all, and I fear they shall only grow worse before we dare hope for freedom, and victory."

Soon afterward, I showed him from the house, and returned to find Mistress sitting at the desk, her face buried in her hands.

"Should I leave the books until another day, Mistress?" I asked softly.

She raised her head slowly, her face taut with strain.

"Most likely we should now prepare for a visit from one of Colonel Faulkner's men," she said, closing the ledger that had gained so much sympathy from Mr. Hendrick, as well as a gift of Madeira. "If the Continental Army is in disarray over a coming invasion of New York, then I expect the Colonel will send one of his men to warn me, too. Fetch my husband's old coat from his dress uniform, Mary, the one folded in the chest by the bed."

I did, while she found her hussif, the small kit in which she kept her sewing needles, pins, and thread. Exactly as she'd predicted, a young lieutenant from Colonel Faulkner's staff did arrive later in the day, bearing the Colonel's compliments and a letter for Mistress that assured her continued protection. The lieutenant was given a small glass of wine for his trouble, and returned to his camp to tell his superiors of how Mrs. Prevost was the ideal of a dutiful Loyalist lady, sitting in her parlor and mending the uniform of her officer-husband.

I hadn't realized until now exactly how elaborate her lies had become as she played one side against another. The prize, of course, would be her own survival in the middle of a war, but I wondered how long she could keep the game going, and what would become of all of us if she couldn't.

In the coming weeks, the news that came to us in our little island of peace grew only complicated. In early July, Mistress told us in her household that the Continental Congress, to the south in Philadelphia, had voted for independence and officially declared the colonies free of British rule. Afterward she retreated to her bed with one of her headaches, one that was so grievous that it left her retching over a chamber pot.

I shared her fears. I lay awake long into the night, staring up at the sliver of a new moon through the narrow gable window. When I finally slept, I dreamed of Lucas, proudly reading this declaration aloud from a newspaper in the kitchen as he doubtless would have done had he not been with the army. In the voice I missed so much I heard the magic words of freedom and liberty and how all men were made equal, and with all my heart I wanted to believe they were meant for me, too.

But before my dream-Lucas could finish his reading, I was jerked away by the screams of a dying rabbit as it fell prey to some fox or owl in the fields beyond the house. My heart pounded painfully, willing for an end to the poor creature's agony. The rabbit took a long time to die, the screams growing more shrill and weaker until, abruptly, they ceased. I couldn't return to sleep, but lay curled in a tight knot on my pallet, trying not to think of this as a fearful omen of what might come.

In late August, the British first attacked Long Island, on the far side of New York, forcing the overmatched Americans to flee and retreat, flee and retreat. Other battles swiftly followed that fall, one after another, and with each costly American defeat my hope for Lucas's return shrank a fraction more. By Christmas, the Continental Army had been pushed so far back that the Hermitage now lay on the edge of the British lines, with only a few American troops left to guard the west in the low mountains called the Highlands.

Mistress's Jersey Dutch neighbors were helpless to stop the soldiers who stole away the grain, hay, and other crops they'd put by after harvest, cut down trees and fences for firewood, slaughtered their hogs, drove away their horses and cattle in the name of forage, and then, with local Tories, looted and burned the barns and houses of known Whigs. Many from both sides left with their families, heading to the safer north. Still Mistress remained, determined to trust in the goodwill she'd so carefully cultivated.

Most terrifying to me were tales that slaves owned by Whigs were claimed like more cattle, and carried off as well to be sold or kept as officers' prizes. None of Mistress's guests explained further, because the fate of these poor people mattered much less than the fact that their owners suffered their loss. Yet for me it was one more worry, one more fear, in a time where every day seemed to bring tenfold.

In December, the British raids came to Hackensack and Hopperstown, so close that we smelled the smoke of the fires. The only guests who called on Mistress now were those who proudly called themselves Tories, or British officers themselves. They also brought Mistress food and other supplies as gifts; she accepted them graciously, and ignored how everything had likely been plundered from another neighbor. As hers was a household of three women and two children, she could not afford to do otherwise.

Yet as winter deepened, even those visitors dwindled. No letters, no newspapers, and no news of the war came to the house. Mistress listened to her sons' lessons, read, wrote, and sewed, and now her only guests were her mother and sister from the other house.

One January night, I alone was left below, and charged with putting the kitchen to rest for the night after the others had gone upstairs to bed. The pots and dishes had been washed and dried, the remaining food put aside for keeping, and the table scrubbed down. As I raked the coals and banked the fire, I noticed we needed more wood for the morning. It was Caesar's job to carry wood inside from the shed, but it seemed easier to bring in enough for the first fires myself than to go up the stairs to rouse him. I wrapped myself in one of the rough wool cloaks that hung by the door, and slipped outside.

I didn't need a lantern to cross the yard. The moon was nearly full, and its pale light washed over the banks of sparkling snow. Yet I didn't linger, not liking to be alone out of doors at night, and my gaze swept uneasily over the yard and fields as I hurried to the woodshed. There I filled my arms with small split timbers, and rushed back, my petticoat catching on the ice on either side of the path. At the door, I awkwardly shifted the wood in my arms to unfasten the latch. The bark snagged on my cloak, and I muttered wordlessly. There was no reason for the latch to be jammed, no reason for—

The man's large hand in a thick leather glove came from behind, reaching around me toward the door. I hadn't seen him when I'd been in the yard, and I hadn't heard his footsteps in the soft snow. I gasped, and dropped all but one piece of the wood, holding it tightly with both hands as a makeshift weapon as I swung around to confront him.

"Mary, oh, Mary," Lucas said softly. "What kind of welcome is that for any old friend like me?"

CHAPTER 8

The Hermitage
Hopperstown, State of New Jersey
January 1777

Many months had passed since I'd last seen Lucas, time enough to make me shy in his presence. All the fancies and dreams that I'd spun about him vanished before the reality of his presence.

I'd forgotten how tall a man he was. He stood near the fire, snow melting from his boots, and taking up much space in a room that I'd always thought spacious. The top of his hat scarcely cleared the beams overhead. In my memory, he'd always appeared in Captain Vervelde's livery, a tidy version of an English gentleman's garments. There was nothing tidy or gentlemanly about him now.

He wore an oversized light-colored hunting shirt with a wide caped collar, the hems and edges purposefully fringed, and made bulkier still by the layers of other garments hidden beneath. A thick leather belt gathered the shirt around his waist, with a sheathed hunting knife and other small pouches slung from it. On his legs were some manner of long breeches or leggings, wrapped close to his calves with leather strips, and he'd a black felt hat with a red-and-white cockade, the brim pulled down low over his brow. Over his shoulder was slung a musket.

Now this might not seem remarkable, considering the countryside was torn left and right by war. But most white people did not believe a black man, free or not, should ever be permitted to carry arms of any kind. The musket Lucas was carrying was the same as every other soldier I'd seen possessed, nearly as long as I was tall, the polished wood of the barrel crowned with the jutting blade of the bayonet.

He caught me staring.

"The musket's mine," he said proudly. "Colonel Vervelde—he's a lieutenant colonel now—and I began in the Jersey Volunteers, but then in September we both joined up with the Fourth New Jersey Regiment. When my enlistment's done, I'll get my hundred acres of land and a pension, same as every other soldier."

Still I stared at the gun, unable to look away from it, or stop thinking of what it represented. I'd remembered Lucas teaching me to read, gently spelling out words with me in this same kitchen. But that bayonet was proof that this same man had taken the words we'd relished most, words like *liberty* and *freedom,* and carried them with him into battle.

"I thought black men weren't wanted by the army," I said, watching him.

"Freemen were permitted to enlist last spring." He slipped the musket familiarly from his shoulder and sat on the high-backed bench.

It was like old times, and yet it wasn't. There was a restlessness to him now that hadn't been there before, and his gaze was never still, looking from me and around the room to the door and back again. No wonder he'd chosen the bench; it was against the one wall without a window, and faced the door.

So many questions filled my head that I didn't know where to begin.

"If you're with the Continental Army, Lucas, then you shouldn't be here," I said urgently. "This house lies behind the British lines now, and if you're caught here—"

"I'm safe enough," he said. "Surely Mrs. Prevost has heard the news by now. On Christmas Night, our army crossed the Delaware at Trenton, and fought and captured the entire Hessian force stationed there, and sent the British scuttling back to New York, tails between their nether legs like whipped dogs."

"Sweet Providence!" I said, borrowing an exclamation of awe from Chloe. No other that I knew would suffice. "You are certain?"

He chuckled, delighting in my reaction. "Mary, I was there."

Still I shook my head, incredulous. There had been so many defeats that a victory such as this was sweet indeed.

"What excellent news, Lucas!" I exclaimed. "That the army would triumph like that—oh, that's excellent *and* most fine!"

"It is," he said, and smiled. "Our army's made camp for the winter in Morristown, overlooking the British in New York."

I tipped my head to one side. "So we are no longer behind the British lines?"

"We're behind no one's lines at present," he said. He took off his hat and set it on the seat of the bench beside him, and ran his fingers through his hair to smooth it. There was gray in it now over his temples, gray that was new since I'd seen him last. "That's what the Captain told me this morning. This valley belongs to no one."

"But you are here, Lucas, and the army is not," I said, still uncertain as to how and why he'd come to be at Hopperstown. "You—you haven't deserted, have you?"

He smiled again, relishing my bewilderment.

"Could you see that of me?" he said, placing his hand grandly over his heart. "The truth is not so hard. Colonel Vervelde requested a fortnight's leave to come survey the condition of his property. I asked for leave to accompany him, and it was granted."

I glanced again at the musket. "You are on leave, yet you still must be armed?"

"Nothing is certain," he said, the merriment fading from his smile. "There are a thousand dangers wherever one goes. You should not have been alone away from the house at night. What if it hadn't been me?"

"But it was," I said, turning away to tend to the fire. I wasn't going to let Lucas draw me into a quarrel, not tonight.

"No one's done any plundering here," he said. "But then, no one's going to touch Mrs. Prevost's property."

Even with my back turned, I could tell from his voice that he'd something else in his thoughts, just as I did. The rest was all empty words and no more, and my reply was equally empty.

"Mistress can play the crafty fellow as well." I straightened, and came back to stand before him. "One day she is a staunch patriot, and the next she is loyal to the king."

He was leaning forward from watching me, his elbows resting

on his knees and his hands loose. I'd always liked his hands with their broad palms and long fingers, strong and capable yet gentle, too.

"The Major has not returned?"

"He has not," I said, "nor does Mistress speak of him, even to their sons."

He shook his head, silent sympathy for another male, as all men were inclined to do. Yet he was looking at me, looking at me so intently that I felt the heat of it, and not from the coals I'd just prodded back to life in the hearth, either.

"And you, Mary," he said slowly. "She treats you well?"

"Well enough," I said with a nervous little shrug of my shoulders.

"You look . . . well."

A single word, a single word, and yet combined with how he was looking at me it was so much more than all the flowery compliments I'd overheard by the gentlemen in Mistress's parlor.

I gulped, and seized two tin cups from the shelf.

"Wait," I said, "and I'll be back directly."

Swiftly I went to the parlor, to the cabinet where Mistress kept the decanted spirits and wines. With great care, I poured a small measure of Mr. Hendrick's Madeira into each cup, and replaced the bottle exactly as it had been before I returned to the kitchen.

I handed one to Lucas, and he raised a questioning brow as he realized what was in it.

I raised my chin in defiance. We both knew I'd just stolen from Mistress, but I didn't care.

"To liberty, and to victory," I said, boldly raising my cup.

He raised his. "To liberty, and to victory," he echoed. "And to you, Mary."

I nodded, a quick duck of my chin, and tipped my cup, the way I'd seen others do. I'd never before tasted any wine or strong waters. That first sip took me by surprise, too sweet and strong, yet still I drank it.

Lucas drank his all at once, a single long swallow before he set the empty cup on the floor at his feet.

He patted the place on the bench beside him.

"Sit with me, Mary," he said softly. "You know I'll not bite."

"I knew that when you left," I said, making myself drink the rest of the wine as he had done. "I don't know who you are now."

"Yes, you do," he said, patting the bench again. "Join me."

I didn't need to be asked again. With a small sigh, I sat onto the bench beside him, sliding across the smooth wood so that my petticoat brushed against his leg.

"I feared you wouldn't return," I said softly. "The longer you were away, the more afraid I was that you wouldn't come back."

"Some days I feared I wouldn't, either," he said. "The things I've seen, Mary, the things I've done."

His voice drifted off, leaving me to imagine things I couldn't.

"But you fought for liberty, for freedom, for glory." I curled my hand into the crook of his arm. "Exactly as you wanted."

"In the beginning I fought for those things, yes," he said. "But everything changed after that first battle, at Long Island, with men who'd shared my mess that morning cut apart by long shot in the mud all around me. The ones who lived, the ones who died—that's who I fought for after that. Not for words, but for men."

"I'm sorry." I drew closer to him, leaning into his arm with my head against his shoulder. "I'm sorry."

"Don't." He twisted around to face me. "Because I fought for you, too, Mary. No matter how much death I faced, you were life to me."

I kissed him then, and told him everything without the words that I hadn't been able to find. He pulled me across his thighs with rough urgency, and I curled against him, desperate for more. We kissed, with hunger, fire, and most of all life, yet it wasn't enough, not for either of us. The rest followed, with my skirts pulled up around us both as I joined with him, there on the bench. We'd survived where others hadn't. We needed each other. We'd lived, and now we loved as well.

He stayed until nearly dawn, and when he left I crept up the winding stairs to the attic, taking care not to wake the others. I thought I'd succeeded, too, until Chloe rolled over to face me.

"Lucas is back, isn't he?" she whispered in the dark.

I couldn't lie. "He is."

"Joy to you both," she said sleepily, and I knew our secret would be safe with her.

Mistress was another matter. Later that morning, a messenger brought her the news regarding Trenton, the British leaving Hackensack, and General Washington's winter encampment. At once we became again a household that favored the Whigs and the patriot cause, and invitations were sent to similar supporters for a small celebration that evening. Our preparations took most of the day, and I did not see Mistress alone until I went to dress her hair.

"Tell me, Mary," she said. "You were the final one in the kitchen last night, weren't you?"

"Yes, Mistress, I was," I said, hoping I'd keep the uneasiness from my voice.

"Did you see or hear anything in the yard while you were still there?" she asked. "I'd trouble sleeping, and felt sure I heard voices outside."

"No, Mistress, I didn't hear anything," I said, my heart racing. "Likely you heard raccoons or other creatures driven close to the house to forage through the snow."

"It's the creatures that walk on two legs that worry me more," she said. "I've no wish to be hauled from my bed and marched away as a prisoner by some unsavory party of raiders."

"None of us wish that, Mistress," I said. "But there's never been any patrols come trouble you before. Why should they begin now, Mistress?"

"They shouldn't, if there's any justice to this world of ours." She sighed, and frowned at her reflection. "I wish I possessed a measure of your serenity, Mary."

I wished I had it, too. Late each night Lucas came to the kitchen door, after the rest of the house was asleep, and each night I let him in. Knowing we'd only have these few nights and hours before his leave would end and he'd return to the army made them more precious still. He gave me a heart-shaped token that he'd wrought himself from a sixpence, and tied it around my throat for me. In turn I gave him a little drawstring bag of scrap linen that I'd stitched with our initials in red, with a braided lock of my hair and sprigs of rosemary, and bid him wear it for luck in battle. We held tight to the time we had together, and never spoke of that inevitable future.

From lack of sleep, I stumbled through my days, praying that Mistress wouldn't notice. I was breaking so many of her rules: I unbarred the door to him while the rest of the house slept; I gave him wine and food that belonged to her; I risked conceiving his child; I kept the kitchen fire burning longer than was necessary and squandered Prevost firewood.

One afternoon she mentioned she'd seen Colonel Vervelde at another house, and I thought I'd break down from the fear of it.

"He said that tall Negro of his enlisted, too," she said as she stitched a loose button to one of her son's shirts. "I can't recall his name, but I'm sure you know it."

"His name is Lucas, Mistress," I said faintly. "Lucas Emmons."

"The Captain suspects that Lucas has a sweetheart," Mistress continued, turning cruelly playful. "Can you imagine that? He's always struck me as a perfect scarecrow. Perhaps his inamorata is a scarecrow-woman, old clothes stuffed with straw and sticks for arms."

She laughed at her wit, while I did not. But I did tell Lucas himself that night, pouring out my frustration with her thoughtlessness, and my anguish over how we'd only two more nights before he must leave.

"You can't know how much I'll miss you, Lucas!" I cried bitterly. "Miss you, and worry over you, and fear—"

"Hush," he said, stroking his hand gently over my hair. "Don't do any of those sorrowful things. Just love me. That's all I ask. Just love me the way I love you."

He did, too. I never once doubted him. Yet I didn't realize how very much until the last day, when it was too late.

Mistress and her sons were dining with Mrs. DeVisme at the other house, and Chloe had promised to make sure Lucas and I would have the kitchen to ourselves earlier than usual. By now Caesar and Hetty shared our secret. In our little world, it would have been nearly impossible to keep it from them.

I was determined to be cheerful, and to make the night as memorable as possible, without tears and sighs. I'd given the kitchen an extra sweeping and tidying, and scrubbed and polished everything I could reach. I'd set the table with spoons and plates for just two.

Lucas had a great fondness, even a fascination, for my hair. Like every woman from Pondicherry, I'd never cut it, and it now hung nearly to my knees, a thick, shining dark curtain of hair. I didn't dare leave it unbound as long as I was near the fire—I was not so foolish as that—but instead of pinning it into a tight coil beneath an English cap, I plaited it into a braid that was thicker than my wrist, the way I'd done as a girl, and tied it with a scrap of red ribbon that Mistress had discarded. One tug of the ribbon and he could undo the braid himself.

I was ready far too soon, and waited on the tall-backed bench where we always sat together. I took up my spinning to pass the time and occupy my hands and thoughts. The peaceful rhythm of it always calmed me, and it calmed me now as I waited.

Lost in thought, I didn't hear the door at the front of the house, and I jumped when the door to the kitchen from the hall swung open. I thought it must be Chloe, remembering to do one last this or that before she slept.

"I thought you'd be asleep by now, Mary," Mistress said, pausing at the door. "I was startled to see the light from beneath the kitchen door."

I rose abruptly, the spindle still spinning by its thread from my hand. Mistress never came to the kitchen. Chloe and I always went to her. To see her here now, still wearing her red cardinal cloak over her silk dress for evening, felt wrong and misplaced, and dangerous to me.

She stepped through the door, the fire's light catching the faceted red garnets of her earrings and necklace against her pale skin. She paused again, gazing down at the table set with two spoons, two cups, two battered earthenware plates.

"How agreeably intimate," she said, and then looked pointedly at me, doubtless taking note of my braided hair with the red ribbon, and how I'd left off not only my cap, but also the linen kerchief that modestly covered my breasts and throat, and the stays that gave me the false, stiffened shape of an Englishwoman.

"It appears you're planning to entertain a guest, Mary," she said. "A man, isn't it? No, you needn't reply. That was a foolish question. No woman would entertain another of her sex in such charming *dishabille*."

She sat gracefully on one of the ladder-back chairs, spreading her skirts around her. She wasn't outwardly angry, and she kept a pleasant half smile on her face. I wasn't fooled.

"Please, Mistress," I began. "It's not—"

She held up her palm as a sign for me to stop. "My evening was so tedious that I decided to return home and retire early. Now it appears the entertainment has only begun, and I can scarcely wait for the hero of this little piece to appear."

I bowed my head with misery. Stretched too taut by the weight of the spinning spindle, my thread broke. At once the two ends untwisted and coiled like tiny gray snakes, and the wooden spindle dropped and rolled across the floor. I bent to retrieve it.

"Leave it," Mistress ordered. For the first time her voice was sharp, a hint of what was to come.

I straightened, and fell back into the familiar pose of servants: my head meekly bowed, my shoulders back, my hands clasped at my waist.

I do not know how long we stayed like this—a minute, or an hour?—before I heard the familiar steps on the wooden porch, and the double knock on the door.

"Let him in, Mary," Mistress said. "It's ill-mannered to make him wait in the cold."

I opened the door. Unsuspecting, Lucas smiled, and reached for me. Swiftly I stepped aside so that he could see Mistress, and the joy in his face vanished. Instead, his expression hardened, and his mouth grew firm with determination. He didn't wait to be invited in, but carefully stepped past me to approach her.

"Good day, Mrs. Prevost," he said, sweeping his hat from his head. "I trust you are well."

"No niceties, Lucas," she said, pointedly calling him by his first name as if he were still a slave. "It appears you had plans to debauch my girl, here in my own house."

He didn't wilt before her, but instead stood straighter, his shoulder squared with defiance.

"I'm Private Emmons, ma'am, of the Fourth New Jersey Regiment of the Continental Army," he said slowly, deliberately. "And I've no plans to debauch Mary. Rather, I wish to buy her freedom from you, and marry her, and make her my wife."

I gasped aloud, stunned. He had never said such a thing to me, and I was overwhelmed that he would speak it now, with such conviction.

Mistress raised a single skeptical dark brow.

"You wish me to manumit her for the convenience of your lust?" she asked dryly. "Mary is perhaps the most useful and valuable slave I possess. I should be quite mad to part with her."

"However you value her, ma'am, she is worth far more to me," Lucas said. "What is her price?"

"Her *price*," Mistress scoffed. "If I were to sell her—which I am not inclined to do—I would expect her to fetch at least seventy pounds."

I cried out softly at so great a sum, and pressed my hand over my mouth.

But Lucas didn't flinch. "I can pay half that sum now," he said, "and the rest later, as I earn it."

Mistress swept her hand through the air. "How could you possess such a sum?"

"The way any honest man does, ma'am," he said. "Through my own labor and industry. Ask Colonel Vervelde if you doubt me. He'll tell you the same, and vouch for me. When my time in the army is done, I'll have a hundred acres as well, and a pension for my wife and children."

"What if the rebels lose this war?" she demanded. "What if the members of Congress who offer you this pension and acreage are hung for treason against the Crown?"

Lucas smiled. "And what if the patriots do win, and one of the conditions of our country's peace is that all those held in bondage be set free? Freedom for all, ma'am. Then you'll wish you'd accepted my offer."

"No more, sirrah." Mistress stood abruptly, her dark eyes flashing as she wrapped her cloak more closely around her. "I would be the most irresponsible of slave owners if I let this girl wed you. You have no home, and no prospects. You are an enlisted soldier who could be killed at any time. If you die, I'd be left with the responsibility of your wife and your brats."

"Please, mistress, I beg you!" I cried, stepping forward. "If you will not grant your permission for us to marry, then will you at least say you'll not sell me to another?"

She stared at me. I'd likely never made so long a speech to her in all my years with her.

"Are you attempting to *bargain* with me?" she asked in disbelief. "To set conditions for me to obey? You forget yourself, Mary."

"Please, Mistress," I said again, my voice wavering. "If you will keep me until Lucas returns, and can pay you what you ask for my freedom, then—then that would be enough."

She stood in the shadow of the door, her face and her reaction hidden in shadow.

"I've no intention of selling you, Mary," she said finally. "Especially not during this war. There is your answer. Now I shall grant you five minutes to send this man away, and then I will expect you in my bedchamber. And if you so much as consider running away with him now, know that I'll use every force in my power to have you brought back here in chains."

She didn't wait for my reply, but closed the door after herself.

At once I flew to Lucas, and wrapped my arms around him as if I'd never let him go. I wept freely, neither able nor willing to keep back my tears.

"Mary, sweet, look at me," he said, gently turning my face up toward his. "We haven't much time, and I've things to say."

With a shuddering sigh, I nodded, and pulled away only far enough to listen. He took my hand in his, weaving our fingers and pressing our palms together. His hand was so much larger and darker than mine, swallowing up my little fingers.

"Swear to me that you'll be my wife," he said solemnly. "I'll swear to you to be your husband. Those will be all the vows I need to be wedded to you. Say it, Mary. Be my wife."

"Oh, Lucas, you know I will," I said fervently through my tears. I'd been pulled and forced by so many different faiths in my life that I'd none that mattered to me, and none that would solemnize our union as surely as this oath, made between us alone. "I promise by everything that's right and holy to be your wife in any way you desire, and swear to you that I'll love you and be yours always."

He tightened his hand around mine. "I swear by all the Heavens that I will be your husband, Mary, in every way I can. I'll love you, and protect you, and honor you for as long as I live. You have my promise, and my word."

"My promise, and my word," I repeated, and reached up to kiss him.

He kissed me, too, holding me tight.

"Mark what I tell you, Mary," he said. "Once I'm back in camp, I'll see that you're recorded as my lawful wife, and make certain my enlistment papers say the same. I'll tell Colonel Vervelde to make certain that everything that's mine will be yours. It would've been more proper to be married before an English minister, but this must do for now."

I nodded, my heart too full for words.

"My own little wife." He smiled, a smile so tender that my eyes filled with fresh tears. "This war won't last forever. Some say it will be done by the end of summer. Whenever it's over, I'll come for you, and then no one will keep us apart."

"No one *could*," I whispered, my voice breaking. "No one, and nothing. Oh, Lucas, I love you so much!"

"And I love you." He kissed me again, and then broke away. "I must go now, and so should you."

He opened the door to leave, the moonlight on the snow bright behind him. This was how I'd remember him: a dark angular silhouette against the moonlight, a smile full of heartbreak, a gaze that held my very soul. I forced myself to smile, too, so he'd have that memory of me.

"Be sure you come back to me, Husband," I said. "Come back to me, and soon."

In some ways, it felt as if the two weeks when Lucas had returned were only more of my dreams, idle fancies and not true life. Although I felt myself to be forever changed, the world around me had not. The routine of my daily labors continued in the kitchen and throughout the house. I still slept on my pallet with the others in the attic, wore the same clothes, kept the same hours, and worked among the same people.

To my surprise, Mistress did not punish me as I'd expected. Most mistresses would have done so; certainly, my past owners would have rewarded my actions with considerable vengeance. I do not know the reason for Mistress's laxity, either, nor will I ever learn it, not now. I suspect it wasn't kindness or Christian forgiveness or guilt that kept her silent, but simply that she didn't wish the disturbance to her household that would come from punishing me. As long as I was willing to continue to work, with no trouble to her, then she would ignore my transgressions. It was as if her furious ambush of Lucas and me in the kitchen had never happened.

Within two weeks, I also knew there'd be no more lasting consequences of Lucas's visit. My courses came to prove I was not with child. I grieved, even as I knew it was for the best. By the laws of the time, any child I bore would be born into the same bondage as I endured, and would become Mistress's property, to do with whatever she pleased. It wouldn't have mattered that Lucas himself was free, because the laws were based on the condition of a child's mother. Lucas could in time have bought our child into freedom, too, as he'd promised to do for me, but I'd no reason to believe that Mistress wouldn't have kept her threat, and sold or even given away our child to prevent it from becoming a burden to her. Loving Lucas as I did, I'm not sure I could have survived such a loss.

My only small consolation came from Chloe and the others. I'd told them of how Lucas and I had pledged to each other after Mistress had refused to let us be wed more formally through her church. They understood, and congratulated me.

They'd also begun to call me Mary Emmons, the sweetest sound in the world. I'd once glimpsed the record of my sale from Monsieur to Major Prevost, where the clerk had listed me as *Eugénie Bearhani,* giving me a corrupted version of Monsieur's own name. To the Prevosts, I was no more than Mary, the name that the Major had likewise chosen for me. But Mary Emmons was a name I'd taken from love and regard, not bondage, and it gave me rare happiness each time I heard it.

There was little enough happiness to be found at the Hermitage as the winter of 1777 edged into spring, and spring to summer. To be neutral ground meant that the county around us now belonged to neither the British nor the Continental army, but it also meant that it was no longer protected by one or the other. The few inhabitants who remained were now attacked from every side by raiding parties from both armies, as well as by disaffected Americans and Tories, refugees from New York and other places, and those who generally made violent mischief wherever they went.

Yet while serving tea during a call from Mistress's lawyer, I learned that she was facing another danger, too. The state's General Assembly had passed an act to punish those they deemed traitors and other disaffected persons by confiscating their property, and evicting them from it. According to the grim-faced lawyer, the Prevosts owned not only the estate surrounding the three hundred acres that surrounded the Hermitage but also some thirty-five hundred acres more to the west that had been granted to the Major by the British government. All of this could now be legally seized by the state, and the Prevosts left homeless and impoverished.

"Does that mean us, too?" Caesar asked when I reported to the others what I'd heard. "Are we fit to be confiscated?"

"I don't know," I admitted. "The lawyer used many words that made no sense to me. All I heard was that property was being seized, and sold to benefit the Americans."

"I don't want to be sold again," Chloe said sorrowfully, fear and unhappiness combined in her voice. "Not to a Whig or a Tory or no one."

There was nothing we could do to help our situation, except to trust that Mistress would continue to find a way to preserve us all together.

In the summer, she received word from her husband that he had been promoted and was now Lieutenant-Colonel Prevost. Soon after, Mistress's two sons, Bartow and Frederick, were sent to join their father at his post in the Caribbean and begin their military careers as ensigns. It was clear enough that Colonel Prevost had determined the area to be too dangerous for the boys, and that they were being shifted to his care for their own safety as well as for their future careers. From how bitterly Mistress wept the night they left, I suspected that it was not a decision that pleased her.

Nor was the news of the war itself any more encouraging for the American cause. There were more losses, more defeats. Whenever I dared, I took the newspapers that Mistress had left about and read them aloud to the others in the kitchen, just as Lucas had done for us. It was the only way I had to learn where he might be fighting.

Yet with each newspaper I read or rumor I overheard in Mistress's parlor, I worried more over my husband. I guessed that he was among the troops with General Washington, but I'd no way of knowing for certain. How I longed for a letter from him! But letters were for white-skinned officers to write and deliver by way of couriers to ladies like Mistress. Lucas wouldn't have either pen or paper, or a way to send a letter to me even if he could compose one. Nor would I have been able to reply, as much as I might wish it. All I could do was pray and hope that Lucas was unharmed and well, and that he'd soon return to me.

By the middle of September, Mistress learned that the American General Putnam had taken pity on our valley, and ordered a force of regular soldiers to come help the local militia defend against the British. Exactly when and where these men might appear wasn't known, but Mistress told us that they would be warmly welcomed at the Hermitage.

Late one Monday morning in the middle of September, I was sweeping the front porch of the house. The leaves had already begun to change color and fall, and through some trick of the breezes, they always came to land on the porch. I didn't mind the excuse to be out of doors, however. The sun was warm on my face, and slanting just enough before noon to make the deep rosy-pink brownstone of the house's walls glint and sparkle. I'd learned to relish autumn days like this, knowing that the icy tedium of winter was soon to follow.

I paused for a moment, and touched the little silver heart that Lucas had made for me. The cord on which it hung was just long enough that the heart nestled in the hollow of my throat, reminding me of how often Lucas had kissed me there. The heart also rested near the scars that still faintly marked my skin from Madame's hateful collar. Lucas had kissed those, too, with a special reverence for my past suffering that made me love him all the more.

A fresh swirl of leaves gathered at my feet, and with a sigh I returned to my sweeping. I heard the horses and riders on the drive before I could see them, and I straightened, broom in hand. Both armies had been so thorough in seizing horses for military purposes that few remained in private hands, and among these visitors would most certainly be an officer. The only question was whether he'd be wearing a red coat, or blue.

They came past the last of the trees and out from the shadows: three soldiers in the blue uniform with buff facings of the Continental forces. In the front rode the senior officer, a lieutenant colonel, followed by two others as his escort.

It was clear that these men hadn't come to drink tea in the parlor with Mistress. Their uniforms and boots were dusty and grimed, and their jaws had clearly not felt a razor in several days. Most important, they had that same watchfulness about them that I'd seen in Lucas when he'd first returned. They were on their guard, and from the state of their clothing, I'd guess it was with good reason, too.

Quickly I set the broom against the wall, and smoothed my apron to greet them with a curtsey, the way Mistress liked.

The colonel rode directly to the porch, leaving the others a few paces behind. Now I could see that beneath that black cocked hat he'd a handsome face, with a straight nose, curving lips, and large, dark eyes that observed everything. He'd lost the silk ribbon that should have bound his queue, and instead his black hair was untidily tied back with a worn scrap of leather, the roughness at odds with his uniform. He was not a tall man, slight of frame though well proportioned, and he also struck me (from my own great age of seventeen, and a wedded woman at that) as being exceptionally young, and more of an age for a university than a military command. Yet there was no denying the confident, almost aggressive, air of command about him, or how the other two men, older and larger, deferred to him without hesitation.

"Good day," he said briskly. "Is this Mrs. Prevost's home?"

"It is, sir," I said, wary. "May I tell her your name, sir?"

"You may," he said. "I am Lieutenant Colonel Aaron Burr, commander of Malcolm's Additional Continental Regiment. Last night my men successfully conducted a sortie against the enemy in this neighborhood, and having heard that Mrs. Prevost's residence was nearby, I wished to reassure her of her safety. Is the lady at home?"

"Yes, sir, she is," I said quickly, not needing to inquire. I knew she'd be at home to him. I wasn't a fool; I'd been part of this game before. After last night's sortie—how I longed to know more of that!—Colonel Burr had likely come here more to reassure himself than Mistress, and to make certain that she had offered no succor to the same enemy he'd just vanquished. There was a reason that the other two men were slowly moving about the boundaries of the house, making an obvious reconnoiter with their pistols at the ready.

I curtseyed again by way of excusing myself. "I shall fetch Mistress directly, sir."

He nodded, those dark eyes of his watching me so closely that I hesitated, and then flushed because I'd done so. I turned away quickly.

"A moment," he said, calling me back. "How long have you been here with Mrs. Prevost?"

"I disremember, sir." Because I wasn't sure what reply he sought from me, I judged it best to pretend to be uncertain. "Some years, sir. I was brought here as a child, sir, and now I am grown."

Burr smiled, a smile that showed he wasn't fooled at all by my answer.

"You're the wench from India, aren't you?" he asked, but in a way that made it a statement, not a question. "I've heard others speak of you."

There was nothing I could say to that. I was accustomed to being a curiosity, but there was something different about how he regarded me that made me uneasy. Perhaps it was because I stood on the porch and he still sat astride his horse, keeping our faces nearly level. This seldom happened with me, given my small size, and I didn't like having a man—especially this man—able to study me so intimately.

I looked down at my hands clasped over my apron, and away from him, and with the show of modesty that Mistress encouraged. I also did it to avoid his gaze. I wasn't his enemy. He didn't need to watch me like this, as if he could discover secrets I didn't know I possessed.

"I shall tell Mistress you are here, sir," I murmured, and once again I began to turn away.

"I thought I heard voices," Mistress said, appearing at the door behind me. She'd had other visitors earlier in the day, and was still dressed in a dark red gown that was much the same color as the leaves I'd been sweeping. It was a handsome color on her, making her pale skin appear whiter, and with her skirts tossing lightly in the breeze she looked as handsome as the autumn afternoon itself.

Colonel Burr dismounted in a single easy motion and looped the reins around the post at the bottom of the steps. As soon as he'd seen Mistress, he'd forgotten me, and now joined her eagerly on the porch.

"Good day, Mrs. Prevost," he said, bowing over his dusty boots and spurs. "Lieutenant Colonel Aaron Burr, commander of Malcolm's Additional Continental Regiment. Your servant, ma'am."

"Good day, Colonel." She smiled warmly, generously. "How delightful that you could join us today!"

"I fear it's not entirely a pleasurable call, ma'am," he said as he bowed over her hand. "War—and most specifically an engagement with the enemy last night that we must discuss—has stolen that, ah, delight from me."

"Then you must come inside, Colonel," Mistress said, "and tell me all. There is no topic more engaging to me than military affairs."

He drew his brows together and looked solemn and serious as he followed her inside, but I saw how she'd already bewitched him. She had that effect over most gentlemen, particularly the younger ones. Her voice, her manner, her fine-boned elegance, charmed them in a way that more conventionally beautiful women couldn't match. In the midst of war, she offered peace and gentility, and they were drawn to her like giddy moths to a lantern's flame.

I understood. It was the way she'd kept her property and her family untouched, and herself safe.

"You are kindness itself, ma'am," Colonel Burr said, offering his arm to lead her inside.

She took it, but with only the tips of her fingers, her hands as white and delicate as lilies on his dark blue sleeve. I wonder if he realized he'd only learn what she wanted him to know. I doubted most of the gentlemen who came to sit in Mistress's parlor ever did.

She glanced back over her shoulder to me. Her cheeks were flushed, too, for she enjoyed this bantering as much as the gentlemen.

"Mary, light refreshments for Colonel Burr in the parlor," she said. "I can tell that he's quite famished."

He chuckled at that, as he was meant to do, and together they entered the house as if they were already the oldest and dearest of acquaintances. I retrieved my broom, and walked outside the house to the kitchen's back door. I'd no wish to encounter Colonel Burr any more than I must. Besides, he and his men would likely be gone within the hour, and mercifully that would be the last any of us saw of him.

Mary Emmons

CHAPTER 9

The Hermitage
Hopperstown, State of New Jersey
September 1777

I might have been ready to forget Colonel Burr, but when Mistress dined with her sister and mother later that evening the talk at the table was of nothing else.

"Colonel Burr is the commander of Malcolm's Regiment, which is ordinarily stationed to the north of us at the Clove," Mistress explained, rapping her knuckles absently on the tablecloth. "Learning a large party of British soldiers was encamped perhaps two miles west of Hackensack, he himself led a detachment from Ramapo here for a foray against the British last night, when they would best be hidden by darkness."

"Oh, my," Miss DeVisme said, her eyes wide. "That *is* very near."

Mistress nodded. "The British camp is—or, rather, was—indeed close to us. You recall Mr. Timpany's little schoolhouse, near New Bridge? They'd made that one of their guardhouses."

"Poor Mr. Timpany," her mother said, clucking her tongue. "Or Ten-penny, as the boys called him. To think that even a schoolhouse would be used for war!"

I set the final dish on the table and stepped back to stand by the wall. When the three ladies dined together without guests, the meal was generally a simple one, and they often dismissed me from the room.

Tonight I hoped they wouldn't. Unlike most of the ladies who visited the house, these three were as interested and knowledgeable about the military aspects of the war as any civilian gentleman, and spoke frankly about it among themselves. Because of Lucas, I now always longed to know more, too.

"It was Colonel Burr himself who crept among the sentries first to discover their location," Mistress continued, "and then he returned later in the night with a party of his best men. The party waited until the sentries were at their furthest point apart, and then slipped between them to surprise and attack the picket."

"A wise move, that," Mrs. DeVisme said. "It was dark last night, on account of the clouds."

Mistress nodded. "That's what the Colonel said as well. He led the charge, and after fierce combat at close quarters with bayonets, the Americans were victorious without a single shot fired. Several of the British were stabbed to death with the bayonets, and the pickets and a score of others were made prisoners by the Colonel's men, who carried them off in the same silence with which they attacked."

Now I understood the dirt and grime on Colonel Burr's uniform, and how honorably it had been acquired. But I also couldn't help but think that dead men's blood could have been mixed with the other stains. I remembered the sharpness of his gaze, the keen watchfulness to it as he'd studied and appraised me. Soldiers were meant to kill their enemies, but that killing forever changed them. I'd seen it in Lucas, and I'd seen it this day in Colonel Burr's eyes as well.

"But if the British encampment is so large, why didn't they follow, and attack?" Miss DeVisme was asking. "Surely they must have heard something."

"It seems they were such sound sleepers, or deep in their cups, that none of them did," Mistress said. "But here's the best part of the story. When the British officers awoke and realized their pickets had been neatly seized from beneath their noses, they imagined an American source of great strength beyond the hills, and quickly gave the orders to break camp, and depart. They were gone in haste this very morning, a force of perhaps two thousand or more running from fear of a detachment of under a hundred!"

"A daring night's work for Colonel Burr, to be sure," Mrs. De-

Visme said. "But I must be honest, Theo. I'd rather you were telling such a story, with such relish, of your own husband's exploits."

"Don't discredit Colonel Burr, Mama," Mistress said, though even I could see that wasn't what her mother had intended by her criticism. "You can't deny that the sortie was planned and executed with brilliant efficiency, and yet the Colonel described it all to me with the most perfect modesty imaginable."

Mrs. DeVisme raised a single skeptical brow. "I should like to know how any gentleman could describe all that to you modestly."

"I assure you that he did," Mistress insisted. "I'm confident that in time we'll hear a different version of the events from our British friends, because they were made to play the fool, and at a cost, too. But for now I'm willing enough to credit Colonel Burr exclusively."

Miss DeVisme sighed, and sat back in her chair.

"I wish you'd sent for me while Colonel Burr was here," she said. "What manner of gentleman is he?"

"Oh, he is the very model of an officer," Mistress said, dipping a piece of bread into her stew and idly circling the crust around the carrots and onions. "He is brisk and well-spoken and clever. He has served on His Excellency's staff and that of General Putnam, and he fought with both General Arnold and General Montgomery on the campaign to Quebec. His grandfather was a noted philosopher and cleric from New England. He was graduated from the College of New Jersey at only sixteen. He speaks Greek and French, though not as well as I."

"Goodness, Theo," said Mrs. DeVisme. "You insist the gentleman is modest, and yet he told you all that of himself in the course of conversation?"

Mistress smiled without looking up from her plate. "He did not tell it, Mama, so much as I discovered it. For all his talents, he is very young, and couldn't help himself."

"How very young?" asked her sister.

"Very," Mistress said. "He claims to be a mere twenty-one."

"That makes him ten years younger than you, Theo," her sister said, an observation that was as unnecessary as it was pointed. "Has he a wife?"

If her sister's barb struck Mistress, then she hid it well. She pulled away a crust from the sauce-soaked bread she'd been toying with, and slipped it into her mouth, taking her time to chew it.

"No, Caty," she said finally. "The Colonel is unwed. I'm sure you would find him handsome. However, he says that he has not the time for such an indulgence as a wife, at least not so long as the war continues."

"If the gentleman insists on creeping about in the dark alone to spy upon enemy pickets," Mrs. DeVisme said as she reached for her wineglass, "then neither his service to his regiment nor his life will be of any length. Nonetheless, Theo, please write to thank him for his solicitude today."

Mistress smiled. "I have already done so."

"I'm glad." Her mother nodded. "If Colonel Burr should return our way again, we will certainly welcome him. And in the future, pray include Catherine in your conversations, Theo. You yourself have no need of more adoring young pups scattered at your feet."

Mistress slanted her glance at her mother. "You would consider a Continental officer as a suitor for Catherine?"

Now her mother took her time answering as she slowly sipped her wine.

"If the Colonel is half the paragon that you describe," she said, "then I should hope in time that he should see either the error of his allegiances, or the wisdom of them, and adapt accordingly in order to prosper."

With the candlelight playing over her face, Mistress's smile faded.

"You grow more pragmatic by the day, Mama," she said. "Would you say the same regarding James?"

Her mother sighed, looking down at the wine that remained in her glass.

"You already know my answer to that, my dear," she said quietly. "You chose to become James's wife, and have pledged before God to honor him as your husband. He has always been a good man, an honorable man, and he is the father of your children. It is not for him to change."

"You know I've done whatever has been necessary for us to survive," Mistress said sharply, "and for this property, *his* property, to be preserved. You have seen all the letters I've written, the pleas I have made, the—"

"That's another matter entirely, Theo," her mother said. "Do not confuse the two."

Mistress shook her head, quick little jerks of anger and frustration. "I do not know why you refuse to acknowledge that everything is bound together for me, this house and this land and this war, and the side I must choose to—"

"Mary." Mrs. DeVisme turned in her chair to look at me. "Would you fetch another dish of butter for the bread?"

I'd no choice but to nod and leave, and when I returned with it the conversation had purposefully shifted from war to harvest, and whether the corn should be brought in now, or left to stand another week.

But I could not forget what I'd overheard. Because Mistress was married to Colonel Prevost, I had always believed that she would follow his loyalty to the king, and support the British in their efforts to put down the revolution in their American colonies. No matter how often I'd seen her dance back and forth with various callers to the house, I still believed that her husband ruled her beliefs.

After tonight, I wasn't nearly as sure of Mistress's loyalties—not only to the king, but to her husband himself. It seemed that Mistress was fighting another war, another smaller, private rebellion within the greater one that raged around us. Her mother knew it, too. That was clear enough from how she'd tried to quiet her daughter by counseling acceptance. She was wise to do so, for Mistress's actions could imperil not only her own life, but the lives of her husband and her sons as well as her sister and Mrs. DeVisme. What worried me most, however, was how Mistress's rebellions might influence me.

More than ever, I wished I were a free woman. Lucas had once told me that some wives followed their husbands to war, marching behind the army and then being paid to serve as cooks, nurses, and laundresses in camp. I already performed all these tasks at the Hermitage without recompense, and I was certain I could make myself useful to the army. It was true that the dangers and the hardships would be genuine, but I would endure it all to be with Lucas. Each night as I lay beneath the rough beams of the attic, I'd pretend that instead I was curled snugly beside him, his large body warm and familiar, with a roof of canvas over our heads, and the stars and moon beyond that.

Pretending was the closest I'd come to him. While Mistress was recounting the story of Colonel Burr's sortie, much greater, grander events were taking place in other colonies. Two weeks after it had happened, I overheard in Mistress's parlor that General Washington and his army had barely escaped after a horrific, daylong battle along the banks of the Brandywine Creek, and that the British under General Howe now were in full possession of the capital city of Philadelphia, just as they occupied New York.

Later, with a newspaper before me in the kitchen, my voice trembled as I'd read aloud the descriptions of these terrible defeats, and I knew from the silence that followed from Chloe and Caesar that they feared for Lucas, too. The newspapers never listed which regiments had engaged the enemy, or the companies that had suffered the most. More than two thousand American soldiers were killed, wounded, or lost at Brandywine, and I prayed that Lucas wasn't among them.

But soon after, reports came from the north that were more heartening to the American cause. The British General Burgoyne had fought General Arnold and the Continental Army twice at Saratoga, at the top of the North River in New York, finally compelling Burgoyne to surrender his troops and a large contingent of Hessians as well to General Gates.

When all this was done and the season for war with it, I'd hoped that the American troops would once again encamp for the winter at Morristown, so close that Lucas might return on leave to the Hackensack Valley with Colonel Vervelde. This year, however, His Excellency decided he would rather remain close to General Clinton's troops in Philadelphia than in New York. He settled the encampment instead upon a bluff at a place called Valley Forge, overlooking the Schuylkill River, the main waterway from the country to Philadelphia. There his men shivered their way through the coldest months of the winter while the British and Hessian officers made merry in the warm brick mansions of Philadelphia merchants.

We remained in tolerable comfort at the Hermitage, though there was no doubt that the war had taken its toll on the lavishness of Mistress's entertainments. Once exhausted, costly imported spices, raisins, white sugar, and liquor that had been regular features of the kitchen's larder were not replaced unless one of Mistress's acquaintance brought her smuggled goods, and Chloe and I made do with what was grown on our own farm. There were no new gowns for Mistress or her sister. Instead, older dresses were picked apart and the silk remade into new styles, or refurbished with different laces or a freshly embroidered stomacher. Because hair powder was another imported luxury, they now wore their dark hair without it even at the most formal of gatherings, and were praised for their simplicity and patriotism.

"Patriotism" itself became the most favored word in the house. With the British now concentrated in Philadelphia and New York, they were much less in evidence in our corner of New Jersey. To no one's surprise, Mistress more openly embraced the cause of liberty, and the toasts that were offered in the parlor were now raised to the triumph of His Excellency General Washington instead of His Majesty the King. Because of her adeptness, the Hermitage continued to be one of the few estates in the valley undisturbed by looting or vandals.

All this seemed wiser still (or at least fortuitous) when Mistress learned in March that the French King Louis XVI had joined the American battle against the British, and signed an alliance with the American Congress. Mistress celebrated with an entertainment where all guests were required to speak only French, or suffer a forfeit. She included me, and I was ordered to address her guests in French for the evening. I did not enjoy this, being made to perform like a trained dog at a fair, but Mistress's acquaintances were mightily amused by my prowess, and that was all that mattered.

One of the guests was Mr. Hering, the cousin of Lucas's Colonel Vervelde, who was watching out over the Vervelde farms while the Colonel was away fighting. I recognized him at once, and although I couldn't approach him myself, I did dare to address Mistress the following morning.

"If you please, Mistress," I began as she sipped her chocolate over letters at her desk, as was her habit. She no longer resembled the engaging and elegant hostess from last evening, but instead sat with ink-stained woolen mitts on her hands, an oversized shawl that the moths had gotten to about her shoulders, and her hair in the now-tousled braid that she'd worn to bed. She either remained lost in her thoughts or ignored me, and I tried again.

"Please, Mistress," I said. "I saw Mr. Hering among your guests last night. Did he speak of his cousin Colonel Vervelde? Has he had any news of his whereabouts, or his health?"

She still didn't look up from the letter in her hand.

"Mr. Hering," she said absently. "He's a dull, tedious fellow, isn't he?"

"Mistress—"

"Oh, I know what you want, Mary." With an impatient sigh, she sat back in her chair and tossed the letter she'd been reading onto the desk. "You don't have the slightest interest in Colonel Vervelde. It's that beanpole of a Negro of his."

I stood straight and raised my chin. "Private Emmons is not Colonel Vervelde's Negro," I said. "He is a free man, and was employed for wages by the Colonel before the war."

"Don't be impertinent, Mary," Mistress warned. "I know you had an intrigue with the fellow, but that doesn't give you leave to address me in this familiar fashion."

"I do not wish to be defiant, Mistress," I said as evenly as I could. "But Private Emmons is my husband—"

"Your *husband?*" repeated Mistress, more scolding than angry, the way one was with a tired child. "Such foolishness, Mary. All I can tell you is that Colonel Vervelde is stationed with his regiment with the rest of the army at Valley Forge. I'd assume that his man is with him. Now stop troubling me, and go about your work."

It was a small consolation, but it was better than nothing, and I let myself cling to the thought that God and luck still smiled on Lucas, and would preserve him from harm. I also believed that if he did suffer some grievous mishap, then the Colonel himself would find a way to let me know of it.

Just as the winter had been particularly cold, so now summer arrived with an unrepentant vengeance after a spring that seemed to last only a few days. By the middle of June, a rare heat shimmered across the fields. The tender new crops lay wilted on the ground, and the leaves in the trees already had the dry, dusty look of August. The air was still and heavy, and even the slightest task was a trial.

For reasons no one could decipher, the British army had chosen this time, in this heat, to withdraw from Philadelphia, and return to New York. In hasty pursuit, the Continental Army broke camp at Valley Forge, and followed the British back into New Jersey. Farther to the north, we sweated and sweltered, and speculated as to where—or even whether—the Americans would catch the British.

The same heat also brought on Mistress's headaches, forcing her to take to her bed and lie atop the sheets, her eyes masked with a damp cloth and her body covered by only her lightest linen shift. Without the bulk of her clothing, the stays and hoops and petticoats that gave her presence, she looked frail and vulnerable, a side of her she'd rarely reveal. For relief from her pain, she bade me rub her forehead and wrists with lavender water, and then stand beside the bed and sweep a fan slowly back and forth over her until my arm and shoulders ached from the effort and the sweat puddled along my spine beneath my clothes.

But that was not the worst of it. In her suffering, Mistress would hoarsely whisper strange and ominous things like a person possessed by fever, of how her headaches were a special curse cast upon her as punishment for what she'd done. She never said why she deserved to be punished, or what grave sin she'd committed to equal her torment. I didn't wish to be party to her secrets, and I felt only relief when at last she slept and her muttering ended, and I could leave her.

Four days later, when Mistress learned what had occurred at the exact time as she'd been stricken (and not sixty miles to the south of us), she vowed her head must have sensed that pain and suffering, and sympathetically shared it.

On the morning of June 28, the Continental forces under General Charles Lee attacked the British near the courthouse at Monmouth. The two armies then fought for the remainder of the afternoon, in the same torrid heat that plagued us. Clad in woolen uniforms, soldiers later said that the very soil beneath their feet burned like the hearthstone of an oven, with the blast of the air so hot that it became nearly impossible to breathe, let alone fight.

Scores of men and horses were felled by this heat, not gunfire, and many perished from it.

The fighting stopped at nightfall. The British used the darkness to skulk away back to New York rather than resume the battle again the next morning, retreating to Middletown before transport could carry them across the North River at Sandy Hook to Manhattan. The Americans had proved themselves to be excellent soldiers despite the heat, inflicting four times the casualties upon the British than those they suffered themselves. But while the battle at Monmouth was considered a victory, the day ultimately resolved nothing, and won nothing but frustration for the Americans.

It also earned a court-martial for General Lee on the charges of disobedience of orders, misbehavior before the enemy, and disrespect to the commander in chief. The general was found guilty, and relieved from duty, which to many was more shocking than the battle itself.

Soon afterward, Mistress invited several young ladies from New York to the Hermitage as guests, her "flock of fair refugees," as she called them. They were all of a piece to me, sweetly pretty, foolish, and unmarried, and whenever Mistress spoke of them having flown from New York to her sanctuary I pictured them as the brightly feathered little parakeets that had fluttered and chattered through the trees in Pondicherry, and every bit as empty-headed and flighty as these birds, too. Their visit made considerable demands on our household, for of course they brought their own maids and slaves with them, making more mouths to be fed and bedding to be arranged.

While it did seem these idle, vain ladies had little in common with Mistress and her books and letters, she seldom did anything without a purpose. She had heard that General Washington and his army would be marching north through our region. She'd also heard that His Excellency had planned to make his headquarters at the nearby home of her aunt, Mrs. Lydia Watkins.

This, decided Mistress, would not do, not even if Mrs. Watkins was her aunt. She swiftly sent a note of invitation to His Excellency himself, describing the beauty of the Hermitage and the warmth of her hospitality. Whatever she wrote must have been prettily worded indeed, for His Excellency decided to forgo Mrs. Watkins's house, and instead to make the Hermitage the headquarters for his military family while in the neighborhood.

I cannot say which decision was more stunning: that His Excellency would choose the estate of a British officer as his headquarters, or that Mistress, as that British officer's wife, would open her home to his enemy's commander in chief. But while Mistress would never confide her reasons to us in her household, we felt sure that she must have come to some sort of larger decision about her own loyalties and the American cause of freedom. For truly, why else would she have taken such a monumental and very public step as to have His Excellency as her guest?

Before the sun had set on the long summer evening, the fields around the two houses began to bristle like a large town of white canvas. His Excellency's people quickly erected his marquee tent with its red borders and pennants. He would sleep here, apart from all the others on a slight hill to one side and surrounded by the tents of his life guards, as was fitting.

The rest of the army would sleep in smaller tents, more than I could count, and make their meals around their own messes. I heard it said that there were as many as five thousand soldiers here; I knew I'd never seen so many men (and more than a few women, too) gathered in one place since I'd first arrived in Manhattan. Our entire yard was filled with horses and men, and the field beyond that was made home to the artillery, wagons, and other baggage carts.

I was surprised by the variety of the common soldiers' dress. Some wore smartly tailored uniforms in the colors of their regiments, and many more the hunting shirts (such as Lucas wore) that His Excellency had ordered as a more useful uniform in the field. Others looked exactly like civilians, in the clothes they'd worn when they'd enlisted. There were even a few strutting rogues who'd shed their coats and shirts entirely on account of the heat, and walked past with their weapons strapped across their bare chests like savages.

Vainly I searched among all these men for the one face that mattered most to me. I'd no idea if Lucas's regiment was even here, let alone him with it. This wasn't the entire army, of course. Regiments were stationed on various assignments in every state. Even though the soldiers were forbidden to approach the house, it was still my hope that if Lucas was here he'd find his way to the kitchen as he always had in the past. Each time a tall shadow filled our doorway, I swiftly looked up, but the shadows never belonged to my husband.

Not that I'd much time to spare for hopes of my own. The army might be here on Prevost land to refresh themselves, but there'd be no rest for us in the kitchen. Thanks to Mistress's hospitality, there would now be at least thirty to dine at all meals, including His Excellency and his military family (the most trusted officers of his personal staff), the senior officers from the regiments camped outside whom he chose to invite, and the young refugee ladies from New York.

If Chloe was the kitchen's commander in chief for these entertainments, then I was her second in command. Preparing dishes worthy of the honor of serving His Excellency was only part of our challenge. We also were charged with collecting sufficient chairs, linens, and silver for all the guests, and arranging the room to suit Mistress's orders, as well as providing extra candles and chamber pots. Mistress had borrowed other servants to help, but they were often more trial than they were worth, not knowing our ways.

I never saw His Excellency or the splendid company myself (nor overheard their conversations, which I'd been anticipating). Instead His Excellency's own slaves served as footmen and waited at table, resplendent in the scarlet-and-cream-colored livery of his estate at Mount Vernon. Clearly these men believed themselves better than us, and were so full of how things should best be done to please His Excellency that finally Chloe threatened them with a cleaver in her hand if they didn't cease their meddling.

While some of the guests retired early, others still lingered in the parlor at midnight. The ladies had all taken their turns singing and playing the fortepiano, followed by gentlemen singing alone, or with the ladies. The longer the night went on, the more wine was drunk, and the more raucous the laughter became, too.

"General nor private, they're all the same when they've had their share of the bottle," Chloe said with resignation. Most of the washing up was done, but Chloe and I still sat waiting for the guests to leave so that we could finally clean and close the house for the night.

"The ladies are keeping their pace, too," I said. "I wonder if Miss DeVisme has determined which officer to stalk?"

"You know she has," Chloe said, chuckling. "Poor fellow! He'll learn soon enough what it's like to be that lady's prey."

I rose and stretched my arms over my head, and then stepped outside, intending to go to the privy. Even at this hour, the camp had fires lit, bright little flares of light scattered among the rows of tents and drifts of smoke. There were so many unfamiliar noises beneath the moon, a constant rustle of movement combined with the murmurs and coughs and distant voices of all those men, women, and horses, even while they were supposed to be at rest. Caesar said he'd ask among the drivers tomorrow for news of Lucas's regiment, the best I could hope for. With a sigh of weariness, I bowed my head and folded my arms over my chest to make myself as inconspicuous as possible as I began across the yard.

"Mary, isn't it?"

I froze, and for one joyful instant I fancied it was Lucas calling my name.

"Mary," he said again, the voice younger, without the rich warmth and love I'd wanted so much to hear. But it was a voice that I recognized, and slowly I turned toward it.

"Yes, Colonel Burr," I said. "It's Mary."

He was sitting on the small, rough bench beside the row of elder trees that lined the fence. Since the bench was part of the kitchen garden, it wasn't used by Mistress, but was instead most often the spot where Chloe and I rested our baskets or tools while weeding the beds. It was a curious place for a colonel to be, here in the shadows beneath the elder trees' canopy of white flowers, and the only reason must be the obvious one: a heavy dose of the strong drink that was being consumed with such gusto inside the house.

Nor did his overall appearance dissuade me of this opinion. True, he wore his dress uniform, as had all the officers tonight, but he was slumped forward on the bench, his legs sprawled before him and his palm pressed to his forehead.

"If you please, sir." I purposefully kept my voice low for the sake of his aching head, the way I did with Mistress. "Might I help you?"

"You may indeed, Mary," he said with a rumbling groan. "I'm in need of some, ah, some assistance."

"I'll fetch one of the men, sir," I said, already half on my way. In my time with Mistress, I'd encountered sufficient numbers of gentlemen in their cups to know that the best thing to be done with them was to send them home to bed, and as swiftly as possible, too. "He'll help you back to your quarters."

"I'm not drunk," he said, his voice crisp and irritated and thoroughly sober. "Though you may choose to disbelieve me, I have for a fact avoided Mrs. Prevost's punch entirely tonight. Surgeon's orders. I fear it's the speeches and the singing that have done me in."

"I'll believe you, sir," I said. Why not, when I'd no reason not to?

He lowered his hand from his forehead, looking up at me.

"It was that infernal heat at Monmouth," he said. "I felt as if I'd ridden headlong into the very mouth of Hell itself. It didn't help that my wretched horse fell atop me, either. I haven't been right since."

"I am sorry, sir." I now regretted judging him to be inebriated. Every man reacted differently to the horrors of war, and even differently to each battle as well. I recalled the confidence, even bravado, that the Colonel had shown when he first called on Mistress last fall. There was none of that now. Instead, he looked drained and wounded from the inside, where the scars wouldn't show. "At least the Continental Army was victorious."

He glanced up at me again from beneath his dark brows.

"We were not victorious, Mary," he said firmly, "and whoever told you that is a damnable liar. We escaped only because Clinton was unwilling to see his troops suffer any further from the sun and withdrew by choice, not because of any attack of ours. Given the blind ineptitude and stubbornness of our generals, it's a wonder we weren't all slaughtered."

"You mean General Lee's cowardice in the field, sir." I was so eager for news that I spoke more freely than I should have.

"I did not mean General Lee," he said, sitting straighter on the bench. "Lee is—or was—the single general our forces possessed with any experience and sense. He had observed the hazards of our so-called commander's strategy, and had wisely called a retreat to protect us against further losses. Yet instead of being honored for his actions, as would have been just, he has been driven from the army by the pride of this same ignorant and uneducated dunder-head of a commander."

I listened, stunned beyond measure. He could only mean His Excellency General Washington. In all the conversations I'd over-heard, both Whig and Tory, rebel and Loyalist, I'd never once heard anyone dare to criticize the commander in chief with such vehement fury.

"I've shocked you, little Mary, haven't I?" he said ruefully, watch-ing me now as closely as he had last September.

"Yes, sir, you have," I said. He had in fact shocked me, shocked me so severely that I could only answer the truth. But I didn't back away, not from him nor what he'd said. I was no longer wary of him the way I'd been last fall. Watchful, perhaps, as I was with all those I didn't know, but not wary.

He smiled, a slow, weary, pain-fed smile. I'd remembered him as looking almost boyishly young. He'd lost that now. Instead, his eyes were filled with things that had no place with youth: disillusion-ment, cynicism, sorrow, and suffering.

Things I understood all too well myself.

"The truth is often shocking," he said, more calmly. "But I'll spare you my further revelations, from fear you'll abandon me. Somewhere in Mrs. Prevost's house she must keep a supply of cream of tartar. If you could find it, and mix a spoonful into a small amount of vinegar for me, I will be eternally grateful. It's the only remedy that brings me ease."

"I'll fetch it directly, sir." I returned to the kitchen, to the shelf in the pantry where the spices, nuts, and various dried powders for cooking were kept. Cream of tartar was one of the imported ingre-dients that would not be replaced until the war's end, but also one included in few of Chloe's recipes. I doubted it would be missed, and besides, it was for one of Mistress's guests.

"What are you about, Mary?" Chloe asked curiously as I found a cup for the mixture and a spoon to measure and stir it.

"Colonel Burr is in the garden and feeling poorly," I explained, "and requested a spoonful of cream of tartar."

"Ah, the poor gentleman," she said. "He must be in a bad way if he asked for that."

"He is." I stirred the powder briskly into the vinegar until it dissolved, then set the cup carefully in the middle of a small tray. I didn't repeat what the Colonel had said about His Excellency or the battle, suspecting that the Colonel himself might not have spoken so if he'd felt better.

Instead, I told Chloe what I knew would make her laugh. "He said he had to leave the parlor. He said the young ladies' singing made him ill."

She laughed, and I laughed with her: not because it was amusing, but because we were both so tired by then that we'd laugh at anything.

I carried the little tray with the cup through the garden to where Colonel Burr was waiting. I'd half-expected him gone and returned to the others, but there he was, waiting for me with the elder flowers like pale stars over his head.

"You are an angel, Mary," he said as he took the cup and began to drink it, grimacing at the taste.

"Curious stuff, this," he said when he was done, "but it does act exactly as the surgeon promises."

He set the cup back on the tray, centering it precisely in the middle.

"Are you here, Burr?"

I turned to see another officer had come around the corner of the house, the moonlight glinting equally off the polished buttons of his coat and his light auburn hair. He stopped there by the kitchen door, and came no farther.

I knew why. He didn't wish to interrupt another gentleman entertaining himself with a female slave, away from the house and in the shadows. It didn't matter that I held the tray with the empty cup, or that I was standing while Colonel Burr still sat. The other officer would see what he expected to see.

Nor was the Colonel himself averse to letting the other man see it, either.

"I'm here, Hamilton," he said, rising to his feet and taking a single step so he stood close beside me. "Am I being summoned?"

"We're returning to quarters," said the other man. "You may join us or not, as it suits you."

"I'm finished here," the Colonel said.

As he stepped around me, he paused long enough to run his hand down my spine beyond the edge of my stays, and over the curve of my bottom through the two thin layers of worn linen. He let his palm settle there, his fingers spreading wide to cup my flesh and fondle it. I gasped and stiffened at the unexpected caress, the cup rattling on the tray in my hands, but I could do nothing more. I hadn't forgotten the lesson I'd learned long ago at Belle Vallée, when I'd dared to fight back. My body was not my own. Colonel Burr was a gentleman, an officer, a guest, and while in this house he was as entitled to my person as he was to the pantry's cream of tartar.

In truth, the Colonel's hand was on me for only a moment before he'd moved on to join the other officers. He said nothing more to me, nor looked back. It was as if in that same instant I'd ceased to exist for him, if I had even existed at all.

I took my time returning to the kitchen alone, composing myself before I saw Chloe and the others again. I didn't want to tell them what had happened. Such things occurred more often than they didn't. My body was young and strong and ripe, and no matter how modest I tried to be, I'd be blamed for the temptation I unwillingly offered. It was that way for every woman in bondage. Likely the only reason I hadn't been used by an Englishman since I'd come to the Hermitage was because I lived in a household of women.

Still, I was more angry at myself than at the Colonel. It was my own fault for lingering with him alone in the dark, for answering him with more words than I'd any right to, for letting myself pity him in his illness. I was fortunate he hadn't attempted more, for he would have overpowered me easily enough.

Mistress had said the army would remain here for four days. It wasn't just Colonel Burr I'd have to avoid over that time. I'd seen how other officers had looked at me, too. Lucas had once warned me that soldiers after a battle were like beasts in rut: having survived death, they wanted nothing more than to prove they still lived by planting their seed in the first womb they happened upon. The young officers in this encampment might stand about in Mistress's parlor and listen to white-skinned young ladies in pink silk sing warbling songs of doves and roses, but afterward in the dark they'd hunt for women like me. All I could do was avoid them, Colonel Burr in particular, and count the hours until the army departed.

CHAPTER 10

The Hermitage
Hopperstown, State of New Jersey
July 1778

Early the next morning, Mistress had us move all her belongings from the back parlor that was ordinarily reserved for dining, so that His Excellency's staff could make use of the room as a field office. His Excellency himself took possession of the smaller parlor for his own work and private discussions.

Sure enough, within the hour his men had brought in extra furnishings, set the chairs before the long tables that served as desks, and covered the tops with green baize cloths. Soon His Excellency's aides-de-camp were settled in their chairs and scribbling furiously away at letters and orders and fair copies, conducting the tedious ink-and-paper side of warfare while most of their officer-brethren were gallanting about with the young ladies from the neighborhood. Mistress's orders to me were to make certain the dutiful gentlemen indoors were kept well supplied with hot coffee to fuel their labors, which I did, offering a cloth-wrapped pot whenever a cup ran dry.

I recognized one of these officers as Colonel Burr's acquaintance from last night; his red-gold hair set him apart from the others, as did his bustling manner. He was Lieutenant Colonel Alexander Hamilton, and he appeared to be trusted with more responsibility than the others at the desks, and so occupied by it that he didn't recognize me from the garden, or perhaps chose not to.

To my relief, there was no sign of Colonel Burr in this room. I recalled Mistress having said he'd once been an aide-de-camp, too, but had resigned the post after a short time, preferring a field command. If he'd ever shared the same ill-worded opinions with His Excellency as he had with me last night, I could well understand why the appointment had been brief.

For the remainder of the day I retreated to the kitchen to help Chloe first prepare dinner for His Excellency, his staff, and chosen guests, and then the lighter supper for later in the evening. There was more than enough work to be done for all of us, and far into the night, too.

On the final afternoon, soon after dinner was done and the officers had returned to their makeshift desks, Mistress sent for me to bring a large service of tea to the front parlor where His Excellency now reigned.

As soon as I'd entered with the tea equipment, I realized that this was no ordinary gathering. For one, the windows were shut for privacy's sake, no matter that it was a warm afternoon. Then there was the company itself: Mistress, of course, and several other officers who left soon after I'd entered, and another tall and imposing gentleman who I realized was His Excellency himself. In a well-tailored uniform with gold epaulets, his hair neat with pomade and powder, he had the grave, dignified manner of a natural leader. I'd heard his slaves speak of him, some believing he was a reasonable master, but more declaring him to be vengeful, harsh, and demanding. I was more inclined to believing the latter. Still, there was no denying that His Excellency was the most important gentleman in America, and I was awed simply to be in his presence.

He was sitting in one of the tall-backed armchairs and listening intently to Mistress, his thumb and forefinger resting against his chin. She wore a white silk gown sprigged with pink and blue flowers, kept from being cloyingly sweet by a kerchief of black lace twined around her neck and bosom. Even His Excellency was not immune to her considerable charm and intelligence, and listened with respect to every word she spoke.

"I'm sure in her wisdom Mrs. Washington has told you the same thing, Your Excellency," she was saying. "We ladies may not wield guns or swords, but we can make contributions in our own gentle ways to the great cause of liberty."

"My dear wife doesn't need to tell me, Mrs. Prevost," the General said. "I have observed it countless times myself, most recently here in the case of your own most generous hospitality."

"You are so very kind, Your Excellency," she said. In this room she always sat in her favorite chair placed beside the same window, so that the daylight would fall on the more pleasing side of her face, the one without the scar. "You know my only wish is to do what I can, and remain true to my own loyalties."

I listened as I bent over the tea tray, filling the cups with boiling water from the kettle to warm them, and marveled once again at how easily Mistress could profess the deepest loyalty to one side or the other. Surely General Washington knew she was married to a British officer. But how had Mistress persuaded him so thoroughly of her loyalty? Had she finally decided the American cause would overrule her husband's and she was at last speaking the truth of her heart?

His Excellency nodded. "I do know it, ma'am," he said. "I've been considering how best to make use of your rare talents, and yet preserve your delicacy as a lady."

She smiled. "I'm not so fragile as that," she said wryly. "I believe you'll find me perfectly capable for the assignment we discussed earlier. Mary, His Excellency will take his tea now."

"Yes, Mistress," I murmured. Somehow she always knew the exact moment I'd emptied the boiling water from the now-heated cups, wiped them dry, and was poised to fill them with hot tea. She didn't even have to look. Most ladies liked to prepare their guests' tea themselves, but Mistress preferred to have me do the small rituals, so that her attention remained entirely upon her guests. I poured the tea into the porcelain cups, set them on the smaller tray, and carried it across the room to the General.

I was proud of my skill at this. I held my head up, walked with gliding steps, and never spilled a drop, not even as I curtseyed. I understood that I was one more elegant and valuable part of the tea equipage, my grace as important to the effect as the Chinese porcelain and polished silver, but even so, I found pleasure in it, too, especially as I held the tray for His Excellency. He was my husband's general, and I only wished I could have told him of Lucas, and how honored I was to serve him because of that.

"Well done, Mary," Mistress said softly as I came to her next. It was a rare compliment, likely more for the sake of the General than for me.

"I've always found mulattoes served best for labor within the house," His Excellency said with approval. "They're more easily trained to perform genteel tasks."

My pleasure faded. I'd been honored to serve the General for my husband's sake, yet in his eyes I was the same as the cattle on his estate, bred to perform his wishes.

"Mary was a gift to me from my husband," Mistress said watching me with pride, as if my accomplishments were her own. "He purchased her from a French family in Saint-Domingue. She has learned my ways quickly, especially given her youth. I'm considering bringing her with me on our little junket to Fishkill for just that reason."

I worked to keep the excitement from my face. Since the war had intensified for our valley, it had become hazardous for Mistress to leave her land, and the few times she'd ventured to the house of a friend, she'd left me behind. This junket, as she called it, would by necessity take us away from the Hermitage for at least one night and likely more.

"An excellent suggestion, Mrs. Prevost." The General sipped the hot tea with care, the cup looking foolishly small balanced in his oversized fingers. "Mr. Eltinger and the others are sure to have their people with them, and often their gossip is more revealing than that of their betters, as they are by nature more impulsive and less given to reticence."

I could think of few people more reticent than those of us forbidden to speak our own thoughts, or who were expected to stand mute and invisible.

"Then I shall bring Mary with me," Mistress continued. "I'll also bring my man Caesar, to help with the horses and luggage."

The General nodded. "What of Miss DeVisme? Will she require a servant?"

"No, Mary shall do for us both." Mistress brought her teacup to her lips, musing while she sipped. "Have you considered which officer will be accompanying us as our escort?"

"I haven't," the General admitted. "There are several who would do, but I've yet to decide."

Mistress set the cup down on the saucer on the table beside her, gently, with just the slightest of *clinks*.

"I know to make such a suggestion is vastly presumptuous of me," she said, "but there is Colonel Burr."

To my surprise, the General's expression darkened. "I would not have thought Burr would be your suggestion, Mrs. Prevost."

"Ahh!" she said, a soft, vaguely distressed exclamation that made gentlemen want to rush to her rescue.

"Pray forgive my boldness, Your Excellency," she said. "I'd have thought Colonel Burr would be your first choice. Hasn't he performed your recent requests for intelligence of the enemy's shipping upon the North River with both efficiency and reticence?"

The General frowned. "Has Burr spoken to you on his own behalf, ma'am? Because if he has—"

"Not at all, not at all," Mistress said quickly. "If one of us is at fault, it is I, to repeat what was told me in confidence. Yet I have no shame in my words, nor do I regret speaking on a capable officer's behalf."

"The intelligence Burr is compiling has indeed been useful," the General admitted grudgingly. "His diligence in this matter was, and continues, to be exceptionally thorough. Malcolm cannot praise him enough."

"But you have doubts." Mistress cocked a single brow. "Unspoken, but there."

"I do, ma'am, I do," he said, and sighed. Motioning for me to come take his now-empty cup, he then rose, and crossed the room to gaze from the window beside her chair. "I must ask for your confidence in this, Mrs. Prevost, so that I may speak plainly."

"You know you have it," she said quietly. "Always. My word, honorably given."

He sighed again, his hands clasped tightly behind his back.

"I am certain that you have by now heard of the actions of General Lee at Monmouth last month," he said. "His disobedience, his disrespect, were insupportable, and clearly proved by the court-martial. Yet he has his misguided followers. Burr has been vocal among them."

"Then what better way to test Colonel Burr's loyalty than to send him to escort the Tories to New York?" Mistress asked. "If he returns with fresh intelligence that he's gleaned from these men, then you have your answer. If he is sufficiently disillusioned and chooses to remain on the far side of the British lines in New York, then you'll have another answer, too."

His Excellency didn't reply, but continued to stare out the window. I wondered how much of the scenery he was actually seeing, and how much he was occupied instead by this tangle of loyalty and betrayal.

"This assignment could be a test of his loyalty," Mistress continued, idly wrapping one scalloped end of her lace kerchief around her finger. "It could, I suppose, also be perceived as a test of mine."

He glanced over his broad shoulder at her, his expression revealing nothing.

"I have already considered that, ma'am," he said evenly. "Nor for the first time, either."

"As have I, Your Excellency." She smiled slowly, raising her chin a fraction toward him as she did. "As have I. Would you care for more tea?"

"Back and forth, back and forth," grumbled Caesar as we stood on the dock beside the pile of trunks. "You'd think crossing that river once was enough for any Christian."

"Hush, Caesar," I said, pulling my shawl more tightly around my shoulders. We stood on a small dock on the bank of the North River, not far from the town of Fishkill. The breeze off the water was chilly so early in this gray day, and Caesar and I had been waiting here for over an hour. The sloop was moored at the dock, but her master hadn't wanted to take on Mistress's belongings until the others were here as well with theirs. Caesar and I had been left to stand guard over the trunks while Mistress, Miss DeVisme, and Colonel Burr had gone inside the little coffeehouse nearby to wait in comfort.

"We crossed the river once in next to no time," I continued.

"Today we'll be bound to Manhattan, and that will only take a few days with the current to do all the work."

"Where in blazes are those Tories keeping themselves, anyway?" Caesar pulled a worn red-dotted handkerchief from his pocket and blew his nose loudly. "D'you think they've changed their mind, and turned Whig?"

"It's too late for them to do that," I said, stamping my feet up and down to warm my legs. "I heard Colonel Burr tell Mistress last night that these two are the most stubborn old Tories he's ever seen. He said the Commissioners for Conspiracies in Poughkeepsie couldn't get clear of them fast enough."

"'Commissioners for Conspiracies,'" he repeated. "These people've got a commission and a committee for everything, don't they? We'd best be careful, Mary, else they'll start up a Committee for the Righteous Regulation of My Supper."

"Don't let them hear you say that," I warned, "or they likely will."

He wasn't far wrong. Mistress's entire junket (as she continued to call it, as if this little voyage truly were some sort of pleasure cruise) was the work of the Committee of Safety, the Commission for Detecting and Defeating Conspiracies, and likely a half dozen others besides. Two upstanding gentlemen from the state of New York had refused to swear an oath of allegiance to the new country, and because they insisted on remaining loyal to the Crown, the Committee of Safety had declared them to be traitors. They were now being escorted with their families to the British army they so professed to love.

I guessed the gentlemen must be more than ordinary Tories to receive this kind of treatment. Considering two of them were lawyers, one being the former attorney general of the old colony, they were no doubt clever, wealthy, and guilty of troublemaking for the American cause.

I say that I "guessed" all of this because that was all it was: guessing. After the conversation I'd witnessed between Mistress and General Washington, I was more confused than ever regarding her loyalties. His Excellency at first had appeared to trust her, then had doubted her. Yet in the end, he had sent her and her sister here to accompany the three Tories into exile, and with Colonel Burr as our escort as she'd suggested.

In the same way, Mistress continued to receive letters from her husband and two sons serving with the British army in the Caribbean. She and her mother and sister took delight in Colonel Prevost's victories and the military accomplishments of the two as if she were the most loyal of Loyalist wives—enough that I wondered if Mistress and Miss DeVisme were also planning to remain in Manhattan, on the far side of the British lines, and abandon New Jersey entirely.

Yet this very morning as I'd helped Mistress dress, she had made use of the time we were apart from the others to make a special request of me.

"According to the certificate that Colonel Burr was given, the party from New York will be traveling with four Negroes of their own," she said quickly, her voice low so she wouldn't be overheard, always a risk in a public inn. "I want you to make good use of any opportunity you may have in their company to discuss their masters' affairs without, of course, revealing any of mine."

She smiled, as if this in itself were a confidence between us. It wasn't.

"Be sure to repeat whatever you hear to me, Mary," she continued. "You've been in my household long enough to know what I seek. Any information on shipping upon the river, landings, military affairs, the movements of troops. Whatever might be of benefit to the army."

I didn't answer at once, pretending to concentrate on her hair before I did. What if information that I discovered for her was passed along to the British forces, who in turn used it against the Americans? What if I was aiding a cause that wasn't mine, and never would be?

What if, in this small way, I could be responsible for harm to Lucas?

"Which army, Mistress?" I asked finally. "Who shall this information benefit?"

She twisted around to face me, scowling. "Don't be impudent, Mary," she scolded. "Such a question!"

"Forgive my ignorance, Mistress," I said, persisting. "But if I am not told which army seeks the intelligence, then I do not know what manner of news to collect for you."

She sighed dramatically, and turned around again toward her looking glass. It could have been from irritation, but I believed it more likely that she could not in perfect honesty meet my gaze with her own.

"You *are* being an inquisitive jade, Mary," she said. "If you will but recall who has sent us on this junket, then you have your answer."

"His Excellency General Washington, Mistress," I said. "So you wish me to do my best to collect intelligence useful to the Continental cause?"

"At last you understand," she said tartly. "Now tend to my hair so I'll be ready to join the others."

It was an answer, and yet it wasn't, and as I stood here now on the dock with Caesar I thought of how many times Mistress had spoken in this kind of confusing manner. It wasn't just to me. She twisted her words into riddles and clever knots to everyone she addressed. For now I'd have to accept what she'd told me earlier, for I'd nothing better.

"This must be the Tories," Caesar said, looking past me back to the road that led to the dock. "About time they brung their asses along."

Three carriages, a wagon, and a mounted escort of four soldiers were slowly approaching and coming to a halt at the end of the dock. Colonel Burr must have been watching from the window of the coffeehouse, for he immediately came through the door to greet the newcomers. Mistress had only mentioned two gentlemen and their slaves, but there were far more to the party, including two ladies, a young man, and several children, as well as another officer. There were several servants, as well as the Negroes I was supposed to befriend, one of whom was a woman no older than I with a baby cradled in her arms.

It took the rest of the morning for all of these miscellaneous persons and their goods to be stowed aboard and secured. There were no other passengers, and a good thing, too, considering how the sloop had little room to spare, as her master, a bristling Scotsman named Captain Redman, told anyone who'd listen. But at last he cast off, and by late afternoon he'd picked up either the current or the tide (I didn't know which), and with the wind in our favor, we made brisk progress.

I'd been carried halfway around the world and more by sea, across harrowing rough oceans that made the most experienced mariners blanch, so to me this river seemed as placid as the mill-pond at the Hermitage. But members of our party did not feel the same, and we'd scarcely begun our little voyage before several of them were retching either over the side or into the slop buckets that were conveniently placed between the decks.

I was grateful that Mistress and her sister were not among them and therefore did not require my assistance. I'd had enough of those duties on board the old *Céleste* to last the remainder of my life. Fortunately, Mistress and her sister were instead merry with shipboard gaiety, and making themselves the belles of the company. The sloop was so small that all passengers (excluding us low slaves and servants, of course) dined together on a single narrow rough table that was fixed to the deck. Captain Redman sat at the head, the king of his watery kingdom and the indifferent meal that was served.

As was common in most vessels, this table had a small raised bar along the edge to keep the plates from sliding off in rough weather. It seemed, however, that this was a new notion to Mistress, who found it the cleverest invention ever, and she and her sister insisted on trying it by gently sliding their plates against the rail, and then laughing with delight. It seemed to me to be a great foolishness, yet the gentlemen were enchanted by it, and by the ladies. Their enchantment only grew as the bottles were passed about, and I watched Mistress work her usual artfulness until even Captain Redman was making mooncalf eyes at her. If either Mr. Smith or Mr. Colden were carrying any Loyalist secrets into exile, then I was certain that Mistress would have coaxed them away before we reached the City of New York.

Because of the small size of the sloop, there were no separate cabins, but wooden bunks with thin mattresses stuffed with tufts of stale wool. It was left to each passenger to provide any niceties like pillows, sheets, or coverlets, which of course Mistress had brought with her, and I'd made up the bunks as best could be done. Still, with little privacy, no one disrobed, but instead slept in their clothing. Mistress and her sister had planned for this, too, wearing quilted Brunswick jackets and petticoats that were warm and serviceable and wouldn't show wrinkles.

I was to sleep on the deck below their bunks. The day had been long and tiring, and even those who'd been ill earlier were soon asleep.

Yet I remained wide awake. It was not the discomfort of the deck beneath me—not any different from the floor where I usually slept—but the memories of the *Céleste* that returned, unbidden and undesired. Too clearly I recalled the faces of death from that voyage, Madame's staring, red-rimmed eyes and Orianne's mouth frozen in a fearful gasping grimace. I remembered the stench that rose from their corpses, and the singsong prayers in Latin that the old priest had said over Madame, and how Orianne's naked corpse, bloated and stiff, had bobbed along in the water, her long braid trailing after her.

As hard as I tried to think of other things, the very creaking of the sloop's timbers reminded me of all I wished to forget. Wearily I rose, taking care not to wake the others. I'd already unpinned my cap for the night, and rather than try to find it again, I pulled my shawl over my still-coiled hair and around my shoulders. I often did this in the evening, draping the worn wool shawl like the silk *dupatta* I'd worn so long ago as a child. Holding the shawl with one hand now against the wind, I climbed the steps of the companionway to the main deck.

With the single mast and an easy course, the sloop required only a small crew, and besides the man at the wheel and another standing watch, I'd the deck to myself. The breeze from the water was brisk, tugging at my skirts and shawl. The moon hung high in the star-filled night sky, and I guessed it to be an hour or so after midnight. I went to stand by the starboard rail and stared out across the water, struggling to empty my thoughts of the past. The river was dappled with silvery moonlight, the hills on either side looming as dark shadows, and the rush of the water as well as the wind against the canvas all helped me forget.

"Ah, another wandering soul who can find no respite in the arms of Morpheus," Colonel Burr said as he came to join me. "But this moonlit vista is just compensation for those of us who cannot sleep, isn't it, Mary?"

Swiftly I turned about to curtsey. "Good evening, Colonel Burr."

Thus far on this journey he'd taken no special heed of me, reserving all his attention for Mistress and her sister. I don't think he'd ignored me so much as that, in his eyes, I simply wasn't useful to him, which was exactly as I'd wished things to be between us. Sometimes it was good to be invisible.

But now here he was, standing before me on this lonely deck in the moonlight. I'd so little time to myself that I both resented his intrusion, and feared it, too. I'd retreat back below as soon as I could, but it would have to be with his permission, not by my choice.

"Share your misery with me, Mary," he said. "What reason have you to be awake while all the others sleep?"

I shook my head, unwilling to explain.

He sighed. "You realize that if you don't share your reasons for insomnia with me, then you'll be forced to listen to my own dark ramblings instead."

I'd much rather that than confide my own. "I'll listen, sir."

"You were warned," he said, and then fell unexpectedly silent, gazing across the river as I'd done. He wore a dark cloak over his uniform, and with his black cocked hat pulled low across his brow, his pale profile was sharp against the night horizon. I wondered if he remembered how I'd brought him the cream of tartar that evening in the kitchen garden, how he'd called me his angel, and then had caressed me with as little regard as if I'd been some stray cat or dog.

"I cannot sleep because I think too much of death," he said finally. "My mother, my father, my grandfather and grandmother, my general, and more friends than I've any right to have had. All dead, all lost to me, no matter how I'd long for it to be otherwise. There are nights when they haunt me as surely as restless spirits can. The only way I can escape them is to keep from their realm, and remain awake among the living."

I stood very still. Did he somehow know of my own past, so better to mock me like this? He couldn't know, and yet it felt as if he did.

"The eyes of death are a curious thing," he went on, taking my silence as encouragement. "One moment there is life and passion and the spirit of a man, and in the next instant all is cold and flat, a void of emptiness as if he'd never lived. I've seen it in the eyes of those I've killed in battle, and by God, it terrifies me far more than the possibility that I might die myself."

His words struck me so keenly that I couldn't remain silent any longer.

"There are parts of my own life like that, sir," I said softly. "I try to forget them so they can't hurt me. Most times I do, but . . . sometimes in my dreams I remember all the death and unhappiness I have seen, and there's no help for it, and I cannot sleep."

As soon as I'd spoken I regretted it. I'd no right to speak to him so freely, no right to share this part of myself. I glanced at him quickly, anxiously, prepared to apologize if I'd overspoken.

But instead he'd listened, and more: he'd understood.

"Ah, little Mary with the sad and golden eyes," he said. "Somehow I knew you'd share the same sufferings."

"Yes, sir," I said. "Yes."

"I didn't come on deck intending to make a full confession," he said ruefully, again looking out across the water. "I trust you'll grant absolution to me, and in return I'll promise you'll hear no more melancholia. Let us instead consider the vista before us, in all its somber majesty. You'd never guess the war was so close, would you?"

A large island lay to starboard, and the river narrowed to curve around it. He pointed up along the heights of the shore.

"That's our fortress at West Point," he said. "There, behind the walls. If you look carefully, you'll see the cannon trained down upon us."

I looked to where he was pointing, and now saw the stone parapets with the distant shadows of sentries atop them. Below them were the notches in the wall for the heavy artillery, and the ominous dark shapes that were the barrels of the big guns. Suddenly the peace I'd found in the scene vanished, my earlier contentment replaced by this overt reminder of the war.

"You can be sure they're watching us, too," he said. "Fortunately, we're sailing under that flag of truce, there, or we'd be fair game, too."

I glanced up at the white pennant flying high from the mast. I hadn't noticed it before, let alone understood its importance.

"They would fire upon us without the flag, sir?" I asked, startled. He shrugged carelessly.

"Perhaps," he said. "If the sentries are awake."

I nodded and looked again to the fortress. The sloop would be an easy target, all alone in the wide expanse of the river. I thought of everything I'd overheard of forts and guns and ships on the North River and in the bay, and instantly it seemed much more real.

"But sir," I said, daring to speak again, because I longed to know. "This sloop flies an American flag."

"It does indeed," he agreed. "But it wouldn't be the first time a vessel traveled under false colors to hide her true nature."

I nodded, and thought instantly of Mistress. How much like these deceptive vessels she was, living her entire life beneath false colors!

"If that is so, sir, then why do they trust the flag of truce?" I asked. "Couldn't that be false as well?"

"Clever girl." He smiled, but at the river, and not me. "Perhaps the sentries *are* asleep. More likely they've taken note that we're a merchant vessel, with no armament or gun ports, and decided to let us pass. We're safely out of range now, anyway."

"Safe from our own army's guns, sir?" I was speaking too much, asking too much. This kind of curiosity and familiarity had led me into trouble before with him, and there was no saying he wouldn't accept my conversation as encouragement, and touch me again.

But he was telling me things I desperately wished to know, and he was conversing with me as if I weren't a slave at all. Not since Lucas had any man talked with me like this. I knew I should stop our conversation, but I didn't, because I didn't want to.

"Everything could change by dawn, you know," he said. "West Point itself could be seized by the British, or Hessians, or savages from the forests for all I know. That's the way of it in this damnable war."

He paused, thinking, or reflecting, or something else altogether.

Already I'd realized he was not a straightforward man, and in his way he was just as contradictory as Mistress.

"But for now, Mary," he finally said, "and in this moment, we are safe. We're safe."

Repeated, that "we" had a curious, familiar sound to it, as if he meant only the two of us, and not the sloop and all its crew and passengers.

"Thank you, sir," I murmured, the only reply I could muster. I couldn't tell if he'd meant to reassure me. If so, he hadn't. I don't think he heard me, anyway.

"Of course," he continued, "Mr. Colden, Mr. Smith, and the rest of our unhappy guests—those gentlemen 'notoriously disaffected to the American cause,' as my orders call them—they would most likely disagree with our definition of safety. I'm sure they are painfully aware of the irony of this little vessel's name, just as you doubtless are as well."

"I haven't been told the sloop's name, sir." I didn't understand what he meant by irony, either, but it was easier to ask the name of the sloop.

"*Liberty,*" he said, giving it a grand emphasis. "If that isn't ironic, Mary, I do not know what is. Surely you must agree. To convey our traitorous subjects to the City of New York aboard the good sloop *Liberty*!"

"Forgive me, sir, but I do not believe liberty should ever be considered a jest." I spoke more warmly than I realized, but to one such as I, liberty was the sweetest thing imaginable. "That is the entire reason for this war, for freedom and liberty and justice and—and oh, so many things."

That surprised him. He turned to face me, resting his hand on the railing and his eyes hidden in the shadow of his hat. Still I looked down, avoiding the gaze I couldn't see, but felt.

"I recall now that Mrs. Prevost said you've a soldier for a sweetheart," he said. "Is that why freedom is so dear to you?"

"He is not my sweetheart, sir," I said, "but my husband."

"Your husband, Mary?" he said, tipping his head to one side.

"My husband, sir," I said. "Private Lucas Emmons of the Fourth New Jersey."

"A brave and well-ordered regiment," he said, and my pride

swelled a bit more for Lucas's sake. "But I wonder that Mrs. Prevost has made no mention to me of you being married."

"Because Mistress refused permission, sir," I said.

He frowned. "Mrs. Prevost is an intelligent lady of the highest ideals. I'm sure she had her reasons."

I knew her reason well enough. She didn't want to part with me. Her convenience meant more to her than my happiness ever would. I also knew I shouldn't answer him, but I did.

"Lucas—Private Emmons—asked her if he could marry me, sir, and buy my freedom, too," I said, my voice betraying my bitterness. "Mistress refused, sir. But Private Emmons and I pledged to each other, sir, and swore we were man and wife, and we *are*."

Sudden fierce tears of love stung my eyes, and I turned away so the Colonel would not see them. As I did, I turned into the wind as well, and before I realized a gust had billowed into my shawl and plucked it from my head. I cried out and lunged across the deck after it, for I had no other.

But as I scrambled for the shawl, Colonel Burr caught it first, easily gathering it into one hand. Silently he handed it back to me, but as he did he was staring, as was the sailor behind him.

When the wind had pulled away the kerchief, it had also pulled away the handful of pins that had held the heavy coil of my hair to the back of my head. Now my hair was free and unbound and tossing in the wind. These American men had likely never seen an Indian woman's hair like mine, and I could only imagine how it must look to them: an exotic curiosity, a seductive excess. I felt ashamed for them to see it, as ashamed as if they'd caught me in my shift alone. I had so few things that were my own. My unbound hair was my own private glory, and for my husband's delight, not theirs.

But Colonel Burr continued to stare even as he offered my shawl back to me.

I stepped away from him, struggling to gather my hair. Still he stood waiting with the shawl in his hand until I'd twisted my hair into an untidy knot at the back of my head.

"Mrs. Emmons," he said gallantly, holding the shawl out to me.

I flushed. No gentleman had ever addressed me like that, a small, complicated kindness. My gaze downcast, I swiftly took the shawl from his hand and wrapped it over my head and shoulders.

I should have thanked him then. I should have waited for his permission to leave his presence, and I should have stood meekly before him until he'd given it.

I did none of these things. Instead, I fled back down the companionway to where the other women were sleeping, and I did not look back. Once again I lay down on my pallet, my knees curled to my chest. I closed my eyes and wrapped my fingers tightly around the little necklace that Lucas had made for me. But my heart beat too fast and my jumbled thoughts still raced, and no matter how I tried, I could not sleep.

CHAPTER 11

The North River
September 1778

Our voyage to the City of New York was a brief one, only five days of fair, easy weather. Beyond helping Mistress and Miss DeVisme tidy their hair and clothes, I'd little to do except sit on the deck to the aft with the other slaves, and keep from the way of the sailors and our masters.

I might have been idle, but I'd never seen Mistress toil as hard at beguiling the Tory gentlemen in the party. She ignored Colonel Burr and Major Edwards, who purposefully kept apart from her, most likely by agreed design. Instead, she devoted herself to Mr. Smith and Mr. Colden. She coaxed; she teased; she fluttered; she laughed at jests that were not amusing and never would be. She scattered witticisms in both English and French, and she always made sure to keep a hand lightly touching the nearest male: not seductively, but to reinforce her own dainty helplessness, and how much she required his manly strength.

It was all a farce, of course. Although she was slight in stature, I knew Mistress to be stronger, more cunning, and more resolute than all these men combined. I also wondered how much longer she could sustain this game before the stress grew too great and she'd be wracked with one of her fearful headaches. At the Hermitage her guests departed, but here she could not avoid their company from the earliest hour of the day to far into the night, and the next morning after that. As I watched her parading up and down the narrow deck, or commanding Captain Redman's dining table as if it were her own, I could see her becoming more brittle, more fragile, and I knew only sheer will kept her acting her role.

How long would it be before I'd be the one who'd have to put her to bed, to mix her remedies and clean up her vomit as she wept from the pain?

"How your mistress goes on!" whispered Mag, the youngest of Mr. Smith's slaves and the closest to me in age, too. We were sitting cross-legged together on the deck, which was a fine place to be. We felt the warmth of the late-summer sun, but were shielded from the breeze and the spray from the water by the sloop's tall sides. Beside us her mother, Martha, sat dozing, her head wrapped tightly in a bright red cloth and nodding and swaying like an oversized blossom.

We'd an excellent view of Mistress walking with Mr. Colden, her hand tucked into the crook of his arm. He was an older gentleman in a snuff-colored wig, so much older that he doubtless judged Mistress to be young and fresh, and was therefore flattered by her attention. She wore a black chip hat with a flat, wide brim tipped cunningly over one eye and whose daggered red-striped ribbons danced like pennants in the breeze. Her petticoats swung gently with every step, lifting just enough with the breeze that her pink slippers and green stockings were visible beneath them.

As Mag and I watched, Mr. Colden said something that made Mistress lift her chin and smile winningly, and give his arm an extra small pat as a reward.

"What would your master say to that?" Mag asked. "He's riskin' his life in the war, an' she's playin' a whore with old Master Colden."

"Hush, hush," I said, bending my head over the stocking I was knitting. "Don't let her overhear you saying such things."

"It's truth, an' you know it," Mag said. In her arms she was holding her baby, a handsome small fellow named Little Simon, and rocking him gently with the rhythm of the waves. "No man, white nor black, wants his woman doin' that with 'nother man."

I sighed, squinting into the sun. "It's been years now since she saw Colonel Prevost."

"No excuse," Mag said promptly. "He's her man, an' she's his woman. She can't go givin' herself to any other."

"It's on her conscience, not mine," I said, but I doubted Mag even heard me.

"You know my Simon's 'bout the strongest man ever seen in Dutchess County," she said, wiggling her knuckle against Little Simon's gums for him to suck. "No one else comes close. Why, there was a wagon run up on 'nother man's leg by accident, an' he's lying there screaming like death. Driver's afraid t'make that horse go up or down, an' hurt that man more. My Simon came running over, an' he lifts that old wagon up right off that man, like it weighs same as a feather. Saved that man's leg, an' I 'spect his life, too."

I was only half-listening by now, having heard this story of Big Simon and the wagon at least three times before on our voyage. I was glad I had my knitting, to keep my impatience from showing. Thus far Martha, who seemed to know only a few words of English, had said almost nothing, while Mag had prattled on about Big and Little Simon, and how sorry she was to be forced to leave friends behind at her master's house and farm in New Paltz. When—or if—Mistress asked me if I'd any intelligence to offer, I'd disappoint her.

I looked down at Little Simon, wrapped loosely with a patched blanket and cradled in Mag's arms and against her aproned lap. She'd seated herself on the deck so he'd be shadowed from the sun by her body, and he was as peacefully asleep as a babe could be, one tiny fist curled against his cheek.

Because of the turns my life had taken, I'd no experience with infants or mothering. I never tired of watching Little Simon, his plump limbs twitching in his sleep, his full pouting lips, his velvety brown cheeks, and the luxurious sweep of his black lashes. I watched him, and felt the dull ache of longing for what I didn't have. I longed to bear Lucas's child and hold him like this, to feel and give this kind of mother's love, and make my own child feel snug and safe against whatever the world might try to do.

That was why Lucas was fighting, and why this war was so important: so our children would be born free, and belong only to us.

"I needs tell someone," Mag was saying, her voice low and excited. "You're quiet, Mary. I can tell you."

"Tell me what?" I said absently.

Quickly Mag glanced toward her mother to make sure she still slept. "Soon as we get to the City o' New York, I'm to look for Big

Simon. He sent word that he'll come for me, me an' Little Simon and Mama, too, soon as his regiment's finished in Jersey."

That caught my attention. "He's a soldier?"

"His Majesty's soldier," she said, smiling with pride. "He's no rebel, not my Simon."

I thought of how glad I was now that I'd never mentioned Lucas to her.

"What regiment is he with?" I asked.

"The Seventh Royal Foot," she said. "Cap'n MacLaren. Big Simon sent word to me that they's been ordered to board a ship for cruising up an' down the coast o' Jersey to hunt privateers an' burn their vessels an' towns."

I made myself pause as I knitted three more stitches, slipping them from one needle to the next. "How long do you think they'd be there?"

"I 'spect 'til they have the task done, and them rebels is done, too," she said. "Then Big Simon's coming for me, me and Little Simon and Mama, an' His Majesty will make me free."

I frowned. "His Majesty can't do that. You don't belong to the king. You belong to your master."

"So did Big Simon," she said, her voice dropping to a whisper. "But when he heard His Majesty'd free any man-slave who'd join his army, why, Big Simon ran from Master, him an' two others. Now he's a free man, an' soon as he finds me in New York, he'll help me run, too, an' His Majesty'll make me free like him."

Lucas had told me that the British had promised freedom to any man who ran away from his master to enlist, but he didn't trust them to keep their word. I'd never heard of a black woman earning her way in such a fashion, either, not once. We weren't of any use to His Majesty in fighting his war.

"Don't you worry that your master would post a reward and hunt you down?" I asked, remembering how Mistress had threatened me, as she'd done with Mark and Sary. "They've so many ways to find—"

"No, no," Mag interrupted, raising her chin with defiance. "Master couldn't find Big Simon when he ran. He won't find us, either, not in all o' New York. That's why he brung only us women with him. He didn't think we run away like men would."

She leaned closer, over her sleeping baby. "Come wit' us, Mary," she whispered with fresh urgency. "You don't owe anything to that whore-mistress of yours. We could all run together, an' then His Majesty will free you, too."

"What happens if the Americans win the war?" I asked. "Then you'll be a traitor, and a runaway."

"They won't win," she said firmly. "Rebel scum! God save the king!"

I sighed, and looked back to my knitting. I refused to quarrel with her over something as vague and foolish as this. I knew we were close in age, and she already a mother, too. Yet in that moment I felt infinitely older, and with a wider view of the world and all its flaws and sorrows than she could ever know.

"It's kind of you to offer to share your lot with me," I said carefully. "But I believe I'll trust to whichever side wins this war to treat me fairly."

Mag made a scornful small puff of contempt, holding Little Simon more tightly to her breast.

"Then you're a fool *an'* a coward, Mary," she declared soundly. "Don't you know you can't get nothing in this world by sittin' where you are, without liftin' a finger to help your own self?"

With more muttering to herself, she clambered to her feet so fast that Little Simon began to cry. That woke her mother as well, and the three of them bustled off across the deck and down the companionway, with enough outrage to them that everyone else on the deck turned to look with curiosity, too.

I returned to my handwork, trying to pretend that none of this had affected me. Being the center of an outburst like Mag's made me uncomfortable, and I hated having Mistress and the others watch as if our every word and action were some low, coarse drollery for their entertainment.

As if to prove it, Mistress came over to me.

"A squabble among the biddy hens, Mary?" she asked archly.

I rose, and curtseyed. "No, Mistress," I said evenly. "No squabble."

Beside her, Mr. Colden laughed. "Well, now, to my eye, that was a great deal of cackle and cluck-cluck over nothing."

Mistress laughed, too, while my face grew hot. But since I remained silent, there was no further sport to be made at my expense, and they moved along and left me. With a sigh, I sat again, when one more shadow fell across me.

"Is all well with you, Mary Emmons?"

I looked up to see Colonel Burr gazing down upon me. His hat was pulled low over his forehead against the wind, as it had been the entire voyage, but now through some trick of the afternoon sun on the water, his face was clearly lit from beneath. He wasn't smiling, but there was a sympathy in his eyes that I hadn't expected, as if he understood how difficult the last quarter hour had been for me.

Again I began to rise to my feet to curtsey, but he put his palm up to signal me to stay as I was.

"Continue with your work, Mary," he said, his voice low so that no one else heard him. "I've no wish to disturb you. But it will doubtless please you to know that according to Captain Redman, we'll reach the landing specified by our truce by sunset, and there bid our guests farewell."

"Thank you, sir," I said, and smiled. Most days, I learned what would come next when it occurred; Mistress seldom thought it necessary to tell us anything. But it was not only the fact that Colonel Burr had told me, but that he'd done it immediately after he'd witnessed Mag's outburst. He'd intended to ease my distress, a small thing, but one that meant much to me.

He'd been right, too. We did dock soon after the sun had set. A small contingent of disinterested British soldiers and their lieutenant greeted us, and curt pleasantries were exchanged between him and Colonel Burr as our passengers disembarked and their belongings were unloaded from the sloop into waiting wagons. Mag did not bid me farewell, nor did I her. I wished her only the best, however. Her main sin was innocence, muddled with an overabundance of optimism and inexperience. I prayed that Big Simon found her and their sweet babe, and that they'd make a long life together after the war was done, but the odds of that happiness would not be in their favor. For that matter, the odds weren't agreeable for Lucas and me, either.

I also saw Colonel Burr, Major Edwards, and the British lieutenant purposefully ignore the sizable amount of new cargo that was loaded onto the sloop. By the conventions of the flag of truce, Captain Redman was permitted to take on nothing beyond provisions for his return voyage. Anything else carried across the enemies' lines was considered smuggling and forbidden, yet clearly neither party cared overmuch about enforcing the law.

I thought of the luxurious goods—the sugar, spices, coffee, and wine—from England and France that had continued to appear at the Hermitage throughout the war. Officers and rich folk would always have their necessities, while poor soldiers like Lucas and his fellows in the field did without.

In a more just world, using a flag of truce while smuggling would be immediately reported and punished. But not in this war, and not among white people, either. And so, with Caesar beside me, I watched from the rail as this cargo was loaded into the hold beneath us, and together we idly guessed what each crate or cask might hold. By the time Mistress and the others had returned aboard after dining at a tavern, I'd put aside my conscience and conveniently forgotten everything I'd witnessed, exactly as she would have wished.

On the following day, I found time while I helped her dress to tell her what I'd learned from Mag about the British ship, stationed in the city of New York, hunting for American privateers along the Jersey coast.

"Most excellent, Mary, most excellent indeed!" she exclaimed. "You are certain of this?"

"Yes, Mistress," I said. "Mag had no reason to lie."

"Would that the rest of the world was the same," she said. "Did she say when the troops were expected to depart?"

I shook my head. "Not by exact date, Mistress, but she spoke as if it would be soon. Before winter."

"That would make perfect sense," she said, musing. "One cannot send troops ashore in a snowstorm. I shall share the information with Colonel Burr directly, and write to General Washington himself the moment we are returned to land."

"Yes, Mistress." I smiled, for her satisfaction and my own. "I hope it will help His Excellency and his soldiers."

"Oh, I'm sure it will do that," she said. "It could also save ships, and property."

I nodded, pleased with what I'd done. But Mistress was already thinking of other matters.

"Do you wish to know the most interesting item that I learned?" she said. "That a gift from Queen Marie Antoinette intended for Mrs. Washington was seized from a French ship! Mr. Colden could not speak of it enough, as if intercepting gifts between ladies were the height of wartime accomplishment."

"Truly, Mistress?" I said.

"Oh, there were a few other more useful morsels," she said, waving her hand airily. "But I'm most pleased with you, Mary. You listened; you observed; you remembered—all the perfect attributes for gathering delicate information."

With her palms, she smoothed the front of her bodice, fiddling with one of the pins as she spoke.

"I was also pleased by how well you comported yourself on this sloop," she said, "even when provoked by that other young jade. I saw it. We all did. Yet your response was exactly right, an honor to my household."

She smiled so warmly at me I could almost pretend she meant it.

"In fact, I believe you deserve a reward," she continued. "What would please you? An ell or two of linsey-woolsey for a new petticoat? A length of pretty ribbon to freshen your cap, or a string of glass beads?"

What I'd done was for the American cause, not for a cheap magpie gift. But if she was offering gifts, then I instantly knew what I wanted.

"If you please, Mistress," I said. "I should prefer paper for writing."

"For writing?" she repeated, incredulous. "That is what you wish? Paper for writing?"

"Yes, Mistress," I said. "That's what I wish."

It was. In my eagerness to write as well as read, I'd cut turkey feathers into makeshift pens, and mixed my own ink from ground berries and candle soot. The only paper I had for practicing my penmanship, however, was the scraps Mistress had discarded and I'd retrieved. Not only did I cover every empty space with my writing, but I also used her letters as a kind of primer for penmanship, carefully copying her elegant letters and looped swirls until they became my own. No one would mistake my efforts for a lady's hand, but I was proud of how I'd taught myself through practice alone.

What I wished now was to write a letter to present to Lucas, a true letter, filled with all the thoughts and promises that I'd been unable to tell him these months we'd been apart. I wanted to give him something that he could keep, and reread, and know all the love I had for him wherever he was.

For a woman like Mistress who wrote a dozen letters a day, this would seem as nothing. But for me it would mean the world, and I held my breath, hoping she'd agree.

"I'd always wanted Chloe to learn to write," she said, musing, as she rubbed scented cream into her hands. "I'd hoped that she would keep proper records of meals and general housekeeping, and preserve her recipes, but she's always been too lazy to learn. It would be useful to me if you could write down what she says."

"Yes, Mistress," I said, barely containing my excitement. "I can do that, Mistress."

"Very well, then," she said, reaching for her hat. "I'll see that you're provided with paper, pen, and ink as soon as we return to the Hermitage."

Because we were sailing upriver, the trip was longer, a full ten days. The company was much smaller now, reduced to only four passengers besides Caesar and me: Mistress and her sister, Colonel Burr, and Major Edwards. They were much more quiet, too, or perhaps it only seemed that way to me now that Mag was gone from our midst.

At first I thought that Colonel Burr and Miss DeVisme were set to become a match, as Mrs. DeVisme had clearly hoped they would. They were close in age, they looked well together, and they appeared to take pleasure in each other's presence. Most of all, they were both unmarried, and in need of a spouse.

But it soon became clear that the Colonel was far more fascinated by Mistress than her younger sister. I'd witnessed this before, of course. Many officers, young and old, had come to the Hermitage as dutiful guests, only to leave worshiping Mistress as a womanly paragon of virtue, learning, grace, and patriotism. She wrote to them after they left, too, engaging ever more correspondents as the war had progressed.

But Colonel Burr was different. For the first time since I'd known Mistress, she appeared to be as beguiled by this young officer as he was with her. She displayed none of her well-practiced charm with him, nor flattered him into obedience. Instead, they addressed each other with an honesty and directness that was unusual between ladies and gentlemen, at least from what I had observed. They seemed like the oldest of friends reunited after a lengthy separation, rather than new acquaintances, and yet neither could look away when the other was near.

As she always did when traveling, Mistress had brought a small case of books with her on her journey, and these she and the Colonel now read together. Sitting together at the mess table or walking the deck arm in arm, they would take turns reading aloud to each other, or reading together in companionable silence, and then discuss what they'd read. He was dazzled by her learning, for she read subjects more often preferred by gentlemen than ladies: philosophy, history, and the works of the ancients. She in turn was delighted by how scholarly his own tastes were for his age, and how adept he was at defending them.

I suppose this was not surprising, for there was considerable education to be found in both their families. Mistress's grandfather had been a holy minister, while the Colonel could count both his father and grandfather as among the most celebrated preachers of their age. As a likely result, the two of them did relish a loud literary discussion over whatever they'd most recently read, and delighted in the sound of their own voices, much to the regret of the rest of us who'd no choice but to listen.

At this point there was nothing untoward between Mistress and the Colonel; there could not have been, not in the close quarters and limited privacy of the sloop. It was clear to the rest of us, however, that little would be required to fan these nascent sparks of admiration into an illicit passion.

If I'd any remaining doubts, the Colonel himself approached me on the deck on the last afternoon of the voyage, at the time when Mistress had retired to rest, having slept ill the night before. I was once again sitting cross-legged knitting; I'd knitted three pairs of stockings on this voyage, and was nearly done with a fourth.

"A word, Mary, if you please," he said. "Come, walk along the deck with me."

It was an unusual request, but I scrambled to my feet and tucked my needles and wool into my pocket. I didn't take his arm, the way Mistress or Miss DeVisme might, but walked beside him with my hands clasped before me at my waist. He seemed subdued today, and there were circles of weariness beneath his eyes. I wondered if he, too, had slept badly last night, or perhaps been plagued with a headache. This affliction was one more thing that he and Mistress seemed to share, and they'd compared tales of suffering and remedies for its relief.

"I wish you to be honest with me, Mary," he began, frowning a bit. "You have my word that whatever you tell me I'll keep in complete confidence. If, from loyalty, you would prefer not to reply, I'll accept that as well."

"Thank you, sir," I said; not that he'd offered anything worthy of my gratitude, but because some reply was needed and that was easiest. I expected he would ask me about my conversation with Mag, of ships and troops, and I composed myself to answer.

But that wasn't what he'd intended, not at all.

"Tell me, Mary," he said, and cleared his throat with uncharacteristic nervousness. "How long have you been in Mrs. Prevost's house?"

"Nearly five years, sir," I said. "Colonel Prevost brought me to the Hermitage when he last visited himself."

He stopped his walking, incredulous. "He has kept apart from Mrs. Prevost for that long?"

"Yes, sir," I said. "I do not believe it has been from choice, but from Colonel Prevost's duty as an officer."

"But to abandon a woman as fine as Mrs. Prevost, to leave her to the fates and hazards of a perilous war—what husband would do such a thing to his wife?"

I didn't reply, for I had no answer to give, and we walked forward and then aft and forward again in silence before he spoke again.

"Does she receive letters from him?" he asked. "Does he bother to write to her?"

"Yes, sir, he does," I said. "Because their two sons are with him, he writes to her of their doings, and encloses letters from the young gentlemen as well."

He nodded, making sense of this. "Does Mrs. Prevost answer his letters?"

"I do not know, sir," I said. "Mistress writes many letters."

"He does not deserve them if she does," he said, speaking each word as if it were some sort of vow or pledge. "I am limited in my own resources, but I shall do all in my power to offer assistance to her, however she needs or desires."

I listened with growing unease. Mistress already had other champions willing to fight her legal battles, including important judges, lawyers, generals on both sides, and even Governor William Livingston. It was how she'd so deftly managed to keep possession of the Hermitage and her family unharmed throughout the war.

But Colonel Burr's gallantry sounded different, more determined and more personal, and more reckless as well. I doubted a twenty-two-year-old lieutenant colonel could do more for Mistress than the very governor of the state—unless the assistance he promised her was of a different variety altogether.

We landed in the early evening, and because it was so late in the day, Mistress took lodgings in an inn not far from the river, and postponed our departure for the Hermitage until daylight. The next morning was dreary and chill for the season, with rain already beginning to drum against the windowpanes.

Mistress and her sister were to continue south with an escort to the Hermitage, but Colonel Burr would return to his post in Westchester. His farewell to Mistress in the inn's yard was formal and brief. I wasn't reassured, however, since I knew they'd dined alone the previous night, and likely bidden each other a fonder good-bye at that time.

The rain grew heavier, and followed us all the way back to Hopperstown. The resulting mud made travel slow, wet, and difficult, and it took us four miserable days to cover thirty miles. While Mistress and her sister traveled in the carriage, Caesar and I rode in the open wagon with the baggage. All our clothing was soaked by the rain, and remained that way. The escort left us not far from where

Mistress's property began, and with no further need to remain together, the carriage hurried ahead, and left us to follow more slowly. I'd never been so eager to see the chimney of the Hermitage, knowing there'd be a warm fire, drink, and food waiting.

"Whose gelding is that?" Caesar asked as we drew the wagon into the yard. A visitor's horse was tied just inside the barn, leaning close to one wall to keep dry from the rain.

"I don't know, nor do I care unless he can help me bring Mistress's belongings into the house," I said as I climbed down. With a hatbox in one hand and a satchel in the other, I trudged from the wagon across the muddy yard to the kitchen.

"You're back," Chloe said as I stepped through the door. She didn't smile, or demand to hear of our trip, as I'd expected. Instead, she stood before the fire, her hands twisting anxiously in her apron. "Mistress said for you to come to her in the parlor the instant you returned."

Grumbling, I removed my cloak, my shoes, and my stockings, not wanting to track fresh mud into the parlor. My petticoat was sodden and splattered with mud and my cap and hair bedraggled, but if Mistress wished to see me directly then she'd have to take me as I came. Most likely she wished tea brought to her and her visitor, and with some sort of special, specific nicety that she hadn't wanted to entrust to Chloe, and I hurried barefoot down the hallway.

"Here you are, Mary." Mistress had removed her cloak, but still wore her traveling clothes. She was sitting on the edge of her chair, her back very straight, and her visitor stood before her, his back to me. She was pale, her lips pinched together and her eyes large.

Bad news, I thought at once, bad news. Her husband, her sons, her property . . .

Then the gentleman turned, and I saw it was Mr. Hering, the cousin of Mr. Vervelde, and my heart froze in my breast.

The bad news wasn't for Mistress. It was for me.

"Sit here beside me, Mary," Mistress said, pointing to the plain chair beside hers. She'd never once bid me sit before.

I didn't sit. I'd hear it all standing.

I knew. Oh, I knew.

Mistress sighed, her gaze avoiding mine as her hand fell back

into her lap. "You recall Mr. Hering, who has kindly been looking after Colonel Vervelde's farms at Mount Joy while he has been
away."

I recalled him, a sly man from the city whom Lucas hadn't
trusted and thus I hadn't, either.

He was frowning hard, his brows knotted tightly together, and
turning the brim of the hat in his hands round and round like a
wheel.

"I regret that I've received some, ah, terrible news today. I fear
my cousin and several of his men have been killed to the south, near
Somerset Falls. They had stopped to rest at the farm of a friend to
the cause, but they were betrayed by a Tory sympathizer to British
troops in the area."

"Mary," said Mistress gently. "I fear your friend Lucas was
among those lost."

"When?" A single harsh word, all I could manage.

"I believe it was ten days past," Mr. Hering said. "It has taken
that time for the dead to be identified, and notification sent."

Ten days past, the night on the sloop when I'd dreamed of death
and dying, and so had Colonel Burr. Somehow, I'd known.

*Oh, Lucas, my love, how could I have lost you before you were
truly mine? What of our life together after the war, and the children
we'd now never have?*

My fingers trembling, I fumbled for the heart he'd made for me,
resting there against the hollow of my throat. The silver was warm
from my skin with my own heartbeat beneath it. How could he be
gone and I still lived?

"It is a tragic loss to the cause of freedom," Mr. Hering said.
"My cousin always had nothing but the most generous praise for his
Negro's courage and loyalty."

"Private Emmons was a free man, sir, and didn't belong to Colonel Vervelde or anyone else," I said sharply. "He'd bought his freedom."

He and Mistress glanced at each other, a glance I understood
all too well.

"Mary, please," Mistress said, her voice at once soothing and
condescending. "There's no question that your friend was a brave

and courageous man, and that he died in the defense of his country."

"He wasn't my *friend*," I said. "He was my *husband*."

Swiftly, before she'd say more, I turned from her to Mr. Hering.

"Where is my husband's body?" I demanded. "Where are his belongings?"

"Mary," Mistress said, turning my name into a warning. "I won't have you addressing Mr. Hering with such disrespect."

Mr. Hering held up his hand, his index finger raised, to reassure her, not me.

"I believe he and the other men including my lamented cousin were buried close to where they fell," he said. "I understand that is the custom for the army."

I prayed that was so: that he now lay with his friends, his fellow soldiers, and not apart and alone and forgotten because his skin had been black.

"As for his belongings," Mr. Hering continued, "his musket and other military equipage were divided among his fellows. He must not have left any personal belongings of value, for none were sent with those of my cousin."

"They would have had value to me!" Hot tears finally filled my eyes: not tears of sorrow, but of anger. Lucas had been such a good man, a wise man, and he hadn't deserved this from them. "What of the belongings he left in his quarters at Mount Joy, sir? His tools, his clothes, his furnishings from his employment with Colonel Vervelde?"

To have anything of his would be a great comfort to me now. I remembered an old threadbare shirt he'd had that was more darns and patches than new. As worn as it had been, I'd still embroidered his initials—*LE*—in tiny red crossed stitches beneath the opening at the neck on that shirt, exactly as I'd done for the other two shirts he'd taken with him. He would have been wearing one of them when the British had killed him, and was wearing it now in his grave, and I felt my eyes fill again with more tears.

"I know it won't be much, sir," I said, finally letting the tears flow down my cheeks, "but his things should come to me as his wife."

Mr. Hering ducked his chin and frowned again.

"I am sorry that you have been misled, Mary," he said. "But when Lucas enlisted, he named my cousin as his survivor, having no family of his own. By law his belongings, as well as any back pay owed him by the army, are now considered part of my cousin's estate."

"No!" I cried with anguish. "That cannot be, sir! That cannot be!"

"The law of this state is quite clear," Mr. Hering said. "Unless you can produce a certificate of marriage that proves—"

"No!" I cried again, my heart breaking with the weight of the truth. This was not what Lucas had wanted for me, for us, and I'd never believe otherwise. "Lucas told me I was his wife, and that he would register our marriage with his regiment's clerk, and that it—it would be so! He loved me, and he promised he'd buy my freedom, and then after the war when he'd received his acres—"

"Mary, that's enough," Mistress said, rising from her chair to take me by the arm. "Come, I'll call for Chloe to look after you."

I jerked free of her, my bare feet stumbling beneath me.

"He loved me, Mistress," I sobbed. "Lucas loved me as my husband, and I loved him as his wife, and you . . . you wouldn't—"

But before I could finish, Mr. Hering struck his fist across the side of my face, so hard that I toppled backward to the floor.

"Kindness does not serve with Negroes, Mrs. Prevost," he said sternly, and smugly, too. "They are like wicked children, and will only find their advantage if you show them a gentle hand. You must be firm, ma'am, and you must be strict. This little wench may be sullen now, but I'll wager she won't challenge you again."

I wasn't the first woman he'd hit. He'd known exactly where to strike me, to make sure the hard knot of his knuckles caught the bone of my cheek where there wasn't much flesh to cushion the blow. The pain splintered through me, bright shards of it that I couldn't escape. Years had passed since I'd last been punished. Time enough for me to grow careless and forget how to be on my guard to dodge and duck and escape the worst. Yet I wouldn't give Mr. Hering the satisfaction of clutching at my face, or weeping, or begging for mercy. That much I remembered. That much I'd do.

Slowly I rolled to my knees in my mud-splattered petticoat, steadying myself. I'd had Lucas torn from me, along with the sweet promise of his love and a life we'd one day meant to share. But with him I'd also lost my best hope for freedom, the freedom he'd died trying to gain for me and the children we'd never have.

I willed myself to stand, to keep my balance, to lower my eyes, to curtsey.

"Leave us, Mary," Mistress said, returned to her usual chair by the window. "That will be all."

CHAPTER 12

The Hermitage
Hopperstown, State of New Jersey
October 1778

I sat alone in the kitchen, with only the fading coals in the hearth and a single candle near the window for light. It was the middle of the night, and outside the darkness was velvety and the sounds of wild creatures rustled in the fallen leaves near the house. I welcomed their company. They'd ask no questions about my husband, nor offer me empty pity for his death.

I'd reason to be sitting here, of course. I wouldn't be permitted to squander the light of a candle without one. Mistress trusted me to be the one in her household who wouldn't talk or carry tales about the visitor who came and went by the kitchen door in this darkness. She could have waited here for him near the kitchen door herself, but even at this hour a lady wanted a servant to open the door to her guests.

She had not spoken again of Lucas to me, nor had Mr. Hering returned. On the day I'd been brought to this house, Master had promised me I'd never be punished by force while I was his property. That promise had held until Mr. Hering had struck me. I was sure that if Master had been at home, Mr. Hering wouldn't have dared touch me. But I also knew that Mistress couldn't afford to make an enemy of any gentleman in the Hackensack Valley, especially one whose property adjoined hers. That was the price of my grief and my battered cheek.

In this kitchen and the attic, Chloe and Caesar and I spoke often of Lucas, and they mourned him with me. To Mistress, however, that day and the awful news that had come with it had been forcibly forgotten. She didn't care for the sorrow I'd always now carry within me, or the heartache that would never ease. Lucas had been only one more Negro to her, and so, most likely, was I, for all that she claimed to trust me.

From the front of the house I heard the case clock in the parlor chime the hour eleven times. Mistress's visitor was late tonight. The night was clear enough with a new moon, but he'd still have to cross the river with his horse and ride alone across open fields where every shadow could be a deserter, a spy, a thief.

I'm sure upstairs Mistress was trying to distract herself by reading, but I could also picture her having tossed her book aside to pace back and forth across the floor beside her bed, her silk slippers slapping gently against her heels and her dressing gown billowing about her. She was always restless, but tonight she'd be worrying that the visitor had taken one risk too many and been captured by the enemy, and that he could be carrying papers or letters that could incriminate her. She'd be fretting that he'd changed his mind, that he wouldn't return.

Either way, they weren't my worries. I'd enough of my own. Instead, I watched the wool twisting up and away from the twirling spindle, the never-ending miracle of a clump of sheep's fleece transformed. The rhythm of it gave peace to my thoughts, and reminded me of being a child in Pondicherry, learning how to spin damp cotton fine enough to please Ammatti.

I pulled my shawl a little higher over my shoulders, and yawned. I couldn't go to sleep until Mistress's visitor arrived, and then left. Yet my fingers were slowing and my eyes were heavy, and against my best intentions, my head kept nodding forward.

The knock on the door woke me with a start, and I went to the window. He'd already dismounted, and was looping his horse's reins to one of the porch's supports. I unlocked the door and opened it to him.

"Colonel Burr, sir," I said, my voice still thick with sleep. "Good evening, sir."

"Mary Emmons," he said as he entered. He always called me

that, the only white person who did, and I appreciated it beyond measure. "I'm sorry to have wakened you."

He must have seen me through the window, nodding over my spinning. I dipped my head, chagrined at having been caught sleeping.

"Forgive me for keeping you waiting, sir," I said. "I didn't intend to fall asleep."

"Why not, when this is the hour when most of the world is doing exactly that?" He glanced up at the door as if he could see past it and up the stairs as he unhooked his cloak. His movements were brisk and efficient, the way they always were. "How does our Sister P. this evening?"

That was his playful name for Mistress, as if they were both part of the same family.

"Well enough, sir," I said, folding his cloak over my arm. The light from the coals glanced off the row of polished buttons on his coat and on his silver spurs. Although this was a private call, he still wore his buff-and-blue uniform in case he was captured, so he'd be treated as an officer. By the complicated rules of war, if he'd been caught crossing enemy lines while wearing civilian dress he could have been charged as a spy, and hanged.

"Mistress had a wicked bout of the old affliction yesterday, sir," I continued, "but the new physic from the doctor brought her relief."

He frowned with concern. Perhaps more telling of their growing intimacy than any nickname was that she'd shared the litany of her ailments and disorders. Mistress's "old affliction" was a mysterious pain that would on occasion grip her belly and confine her to her bed for the day. Because the doctors had discovered no cause, and since it passed as swiftly as it appeared, she endured it as best she could.

"She did not write of that to me," he said, again glancing toward the stairs. "Perhaps I shouldn't disturb her, but let her rest."

"She desires to see you, sir," I said quickly. "She would be very unhappy if she didn't."

He relaxed, and smiled again. Although he looked younger— or rather, his true age of twenty-two—when he smiled, there were circles of weariness beneath his eyes that weren't entirely from riding late at night. I'd heard Mistress say that the fevers and weakness that had resulted from old battles plagued him still, and I could see the suffering in his face, despite the smile.

"It's always an agreeable thing to have one's company desired," he said, turning my words into a kind of teasing jest. "What man—or woman—does not wish to be desired?"

The playfulness of it combined with his smile was close to flirtation, close enough to make me uneasy. With purpose I crossed the room to hang his cloak and hat on one of the pegs near the door, and to put some distance between us. He hadn't touched me since that night last summer, but that might have been because I gave him as little opportunity as I could.

It didn't matter that he was here to see Mistress. I knew how gentlemen could be. They could pledge the most fervent and eternal devotion to the white ladies who'd captured their hearts, yet still think nothing of hunting after any bondwoman who caught their notice. Because of the color of our skin and our circumstance, we didn't count as an infidelity to them. We were simply theirs to take as they pleased.

When I turned back toward him, he was looking not at my face but lower, at my body: at my breasts beneath my rough wool bodice, at my waist with the apron strings tied around it, at the swell of my hips made fuller by my patched linen petticoat. Only with effort did he raise his gaze, though his smile—now more hungry than playful—remained.

"Shall I show you to Mistress, sir?" I asked. That was more than I'd usually dare to volunteer, but I didn't wish to remain alone with him any longer here in the kitchen.

"In a moment, Mary," he said easily. "I've something for you first."

I kept my guard, and moved no closer. But all he did was reach inside his coat to draw something small and flat and wrapped in brown paper from the front of his waistcoat, and hold it out to me.

"Here," he said, his hand outstretched. "Consider it a little beneficence in recognition of your loyalty."

Still I hung back. I'd no notion of what a beneficence might be, but I wanted none of it from him.

"What I did on the sloop, sir, I didn't do for a reward. I'll tell you what I told Mistress. I'll always do whatever I can for the American cause, sir, as a patriot should."

"That is admirable," he said. "God knows our country needs all the assistance that can be offered. But I meant your loyalty to Mrs. Prevost. You have given her every reason to place her trust in you."

I would not have called it loyalty. I'd obeyed Mistress's wishes to keep the secret of Colonel Burr's visit as I did everything else, because obedience was demanded of me.

He took a step closer, his hand still extended toward me with his gift.

"Come, Mary," he said, coaxing. "You've no reason to be frightened of me."

I'd every reason in the world. Gifts from gentlemen spoke of obligations, not generosity.

"No, thank you, sir," I said, shaking my head. "I've no need of anything."

"I think it's something you will enjoy," he said with a hint of impatience. "I'll be most grievously disappointed if you don't accept it."

There it was: I'd no choice, even with a gift. Reluctantly I took the package from him, and he smiled with encouragement. A length of ribbon on a card, I guessed, something gaudy and bright.

As he watched, I untied the string and unwrapped the paper. To my surprise, it was a small book with a red patterned cover, perhaps a hundred pages stitched together with heavy thread. Carefully I opened it: the pages were all blank, and I looked up at him, questioning.

"It's a commonplace book," he said. "For you to fill with whatever you wish to remember and note for your personal interest. No one else need ever see what you write. Consider it a way to write letters to yourself, if you will. Not quite so formal as a diary, though you're perfectly free to use it as such."

Stunned into silence, I looked down and slowly flipped through the blank pages. Lucas had believed that I was clever enough to read and write, and had taught me to do so. But this was the first time any white person had judged my thoughts worth preserving, let alone given me a book of my own in which to do so.

He misread my silence as disappointment.

"Mrs. Prevost mentioned that you were attempting to improve yourself by writing," he said gruffly, an awkward half apology and half explanation. "I thought this, ah, I thought you'd like this for practice."

"Oh, sir, I do!" I exclaimed softly, barely keeping back my tears as I ran my fingertips lightly over the little book's stitching. If he'd given me the more ordinary ribbon or buttons, I would have remained guarded, but there was something about the very thoughtfulness of his choice—a choice that most other women would have scorned—that made me forget my defensiveness. Truly, what gentleman would use a commonplace book as a step to seduction?

"I've never been given anything so fine, ever," I said, "and I—I thank you for it, sir."

His smile warmed, and he nodded with satisfaction, and perhaps relief.

"I am glad," he said, and glanced toward the door. "Mrs. Prevost must be wondering where I am."

"Yes, sir." I tucked the commonplace book into my pocket, took the candlestick from the windowsill to light our way, and hurried forward to lead him upstairs.

Although Mistress often had guests at the Hermitage, she was at present the only one in the house (besides us house servants), yet she still insisted on the formality of having me knock on her bedchamber door to announce Colonel Burr's arrival. When she replied and I opened the door for him, she was posed sitting beside the fire in her yellow silk dressing gown, the thick plait of her dark hair trailing over her shoulder and her ankles crossed. Feigning surprise with an open book held elegantly in one hand, she looked up and smiled, as if she hadn't been waiting for hours for him to arrive.

He quickly stepped around me to join her, and all pretense fell away. Their eager expression when his gaze met hers, the wondering smiles that each had for the other, bespoke of affection and admiration, but more of passion.

"That is all, Mary," she said breathlessly as she held her hand out to him. He grasped his fingers around hers, and kissed her hand with great fervor, as if he longed to devour it and the rest of her as well. "I'll see the Colonel out myself. You may retire for the night."

I curtseyed and left them together, but instead of going to the attic, I returned to the kitchen. From the top shelf of the cupboard, I took down the basket where I stored some of my own few belongings. Among these was the paper and ink that Mistress had given to me the day after we'd returned from the City of New York, and the day after Mr. Hering had struck me.

I'll grant that Mistress had kept her word, but to the letter, not the spirit. Perhaps it was guilt that made her present these items to me at that time, or perhaps she'd intended to all along. Even as I'd thanked her, she'd been unable to look at me directly, refusing to see the angry, swollen bruise that Mr. Hering's fist had left upon my temple.

More guilt, I'd thought grimly, more guilt for a woman who surely carried a bushel of it.

The dozen sheets of paper she'd given me were clearly castoffs of her own, with smudges of dirt, folds, and crumpled edges, as much to say that though this paper was unacceptable for her, it would do well enough for me. The bottle of ink, too, had been opened and was only half-full.

When I'd first asked for paper on board the sloop, I'd intended to write a letter to Lucas filled with my love. Now that he was gone, I'd wanted to turn that love letter into a tribute to all his qualities and virtues that I could share with others, like the tributes the white people made to their dead. Even if I was the only one who ever read it, the list would be a way that my Lucas would be remembered, and not forgotten.

But the power of what I now could do intimidated me into silence. That first night, I'd waited until the others had gone to bed before I'd sat at the kitchen table with the freshest of the sheets of paper before me. Carefully I'd dipped my pen into the ink, and held it ready over the page, yet I couldn't think of a single word worthy of my husband's memory. I'd wept with frustration and grief, until I'd finally put the paper aside for another day.

The weeks had passed, and that day had never come. I'd remained too much in awe, too overwhelmed, by that creamy paper with the faint lines running through it, and too aware of my own limitations, to do Lucas the justice he deserved.

But on this night, with Colonel Burr's commonplace book, I had no such trouble. As soon as I began to write, the words flowed like a river from my pen. I'd no hesitation, because no one else would ever read what I wrote, exactly as the Colonel had told me. The blots and cross-outs and uncertain spelling didn't matter.

Instead, I drew the words from deep inside me, and wrote of how the constant ache of my grief had yet to lessen. I wrote of the anger I felt that the war had claimed a fine man like Lucas while others far less worthy remained untouched.

I wrote of how the loneliness that had been my companion through so much of my life was cruelly once again beside me and within me, a constant, harrowing presence without respite or ease.

And I wrote of how much I hated being chattel to Mistress, obeying and obliging her even when I knew what she asked to be wrong. I wrote of her husband, the gentleman who'd rescued me from Belle Vallée, and how she was even now betraying him with another man that she'd invited to their bedchamber.

I wrote, and I wrote, until the candle threatened to gutter out on the table beside me. Only then did I carefully close the little book, and put it into my pocket before I slowly climbed the stairs to the attic.

Yet I felt strangely more at peace than I had since I'd learned of Lucas's death. After I'd hidden my new book in a space between the rafters (for my words, now written and preserved, would be a considerable hazard to me if read by the wrong eyes), I lay down to sleep with a rare and welcome easiness.

Colonel Burr's gift had been much greater than either he or I had realized. And if I was wise, I'd never let him know it.

Several weeks passed before Colonel Burr returned, being much occupied with his military responsibilities. On account of his familiarity with New Jersey and the City of New York, General Washington had sent him on several more missions for reconnaissance of the area and the movements of the British troops.

When at last he sent word to Mistress that he could be spared, the night was arranged, and I was set to watch for him alone in the kitchen, as I'd done before. Autumn was shifting into winter, and white frost glittered on the grass and ground around the house and iced the windows with star-patterned crystals. This would likely be the final time he'd be able to visit before the snows came and made his overnight rides impossible.

When I opened the door to him, I was startled by his appearance. Clearly his own recurring illness coupled with his pressing duties had taken further toll upon him. He'd tried to look spruce, as any gallant would, with his dark beard shaved close and his hair neatly powdered and clubbed into a queue with a black silk bow. But although his face had been whipped to ruddiness by the wind, the circles beneath his eyes that I'd noticed before were deeper, and his face was thinner. He'd overall lost flesh, and when I took his cloak I could see how his uniform hung loose about his form.

Most of all, his demeanor was much changed. There was none of his old bravado, none of the briskness that I'd come to associate with him. Instead, he dropped heavily into the old wooden chair before the fire as if exhaustion had claimed him, his boots stretched toward the coals and his hands resting on the arms of the chair.

"Mary Emmons, Mary Emmons," he said wearily, unwrapping the long woolen scarf he'd worn around his neck and chin against the cold. "Might I trouble you for something to warm me from within before I go upstairs. Coffee would be best, and I care more that it's hot than that it's fresh."

"I've coffee that's both, sir," I said, stepping around him. I wrapped a corner of my apron around the handle of the pot to keep from burning myself, and lifted it from the crane where it hung over the coals. Mistress had requested that coffee and tea both be ready so that she could play the graceful hostess and pour for the Colonel. She would be sorry that he hadn't waited so they might take their refreshment together, but that was not my affair. "I'll fetch one of Mistress's good cups, sir."

"No, no, whatever you have here for your own use will be satisfactory for me," he said. "You forget that I'm accustomed to the crudeness of a military camp. I'd rather have something I can wrap my hands about than a dainty bit of porcelain."

"No porcelain, then, sir," I said, thinking to my amusement of how Mistress would hate the thought of him or any of her guests drinking from a common kitchen cup. I stood on the stool to bring down one of the blue-and-white earthenware mugs from the cupboard as he'd requested, though I did take care to choose one without a chip or crack. "Would a splash of brandy in the bottom warm you further, sir?"

For the first time this evening he smiled, albeit wearily. "It would indeed, Mary, if it's no trouble to you."

I hurried to the cabinet in the parlor where the spirits were kept, poured some smuggled French brandy into the mug, and then returned to fill the rest with coffee. The scent of the brandy blossomed as it mingled with the hot coffee, filling the kitchen in a most pleasing way.

It must have filled him in a pleasing way as well, for the expression on his face as he sipped from the cup was such blissful contentment that I couldn't help but smile.

"Now that is surpassing fine, Mary, and beyond what a poor, ragged soldier deserves," he said, his palms and fingers cradling the cup. "Will you sit and take a cup with me?"

I hesitated, for there was always the chance that if Mistress had heard his horse she might come downstairs to look for him.

"Mrs. Prevost won't mind," he said as if reading my thoughts. "I'll tell her it was my doing, not yours."

"Thank you, sir," I said, sitting on the end of the bench, but not pouring any of the coffee for myself. That would have been too much for even him to explain if Mistress caught me. Coffee was imported and costly and likely smuggled like the brandy, and meant only for Mistress's family and guests. It was forbidden to us in the kitchen, who must be content with the teas that Chloe brewed for us from wild dandelion and chicory.

"I'll sit only for a moment, sir, while you drink your coffee," I said, picking up my spinning again, drawing the thread out between my fingers.

"Be idle for once." His eyes were heavy lidded as he watched me through the hazy steam rising from the cup. "It must be midnight by now. You needn't always be such a paragon of industry."

I smiled, and kept to my spinning, an excuse for keeping my gaze downcast and away from his. But the silence that now grew between us was surprisingly companionable. I wouldn't have expected that, nor did I expect what he asked next, either.

"Tell me, Mary Emmons," he said. "How are you faring these days?"

I glanced up at him with surprise, unsure of what he was truly asking. "Well enough, sir."

"You're still a new widow," he said, his voice low and compassionate. "You lost your husband to this cruel and endless war. No woman can make a greater sacrifice than that."

I didn't want to speak of Lucas, not to him. Lucas was *my* memory, and besides, if I began to speak, I knew I'd weep, and not stop.

"I am well enough, sir," I said, repeating each word in turn. "I am well enough.

"What you are, Mary Emmons, is a golden-eyed sphinx," he said, "full of mysteries and secrets."

I'd no notion of what a sphinx might be, but mysteries and secrets I did possess, and in abundance, too.

He leaned toward me, making our conversation more confidential, almost as if between true friends.

"I didn't intend to press you," he said. "I regret it if I did. Secrets should be kept, whatever yours may be. All that I'm saying is that you've a widow's right to grieve for your husband, and to mourn him how you please. War always brings suffering and loss in its wake, and each of us must find our own way through it."

He tapped a single finger against the side of his cup, and fell back into silence—a silence that had now turned as uneasy as that tapping finger.

"Forgive me, sir," I said softly. "But how do you fare yourself?"

At first he did not answer, and I feared I'd erred by asking at all. Then he sighed again and shook his head, as if to shake away his reply as well.

"Ever since Monmouth, I haven't been right," he said, regret and bitterness welling up in his voice. "The wound from a saber or a musket ball is seen and revered, visible proof of honorable combat. But the indisposition and headaches that reduce me to a worthless invalid are not so apparent to others."

His confession startled me, and concerned me, too. "What have the physicians told you, sir?"

"They say I require rest to recover myself," he said, frowning down into his cup. "They say that time alone and away from my regiment will cure me."

"Physicians are wise gentlemen, sir," I said. "They know the best remedy."

"But I am an officer, Mary," he said. "I've sworn to lead my men. I do not have time to squander on self-indulgence that makes me unable to fulfill my duty. I try, and yet . . ."

His words drifted off.

"You must heed their advice, sir," I said softly, freely. "You don't wish to injure yourself further."

He didn't look up. "I have written His Excellency to request a medical furlough," he said. "To take effect as soon as he'll grant it. I'll refuse my pay for the duration of the furlough, of course, but there is no choice left to me. I cannot continue as I am, and serve my country as I wish. I need to be removed from the noise of war."

I knew enough about gentlemen and soldiers to realize how difficult this decision must have been for him. General Washington was not only the commander in chief of the Continental Army; he was also an exceptionally tall and powerfully built gentleman. His very presence made him a natural leader, but it also created a standard of masculine fortitude that few of his troops could ever match. No one could question Colonel Burr's bravery or accomplishments in battle, but he would always be of a slighter size and less robust constitution, especially compared to his gigantic leader. Men being what they were, I'd wondered if his occasional criticisms of His Excellency were at least partially born from jealousy at the different lots that Nature had given each of them, just as I'd suspected that the Colonel had driven himself all the harder to succeed because of it.

"Have you told Mistress of your decision, sir?" I asked.

"She knows I've considered it, yes," he said. He smiled at the mention of Mistress, an odd little smile that he clearly wished to contain, but couldn't. "I have vowed to be in complete honesty to Mrs. Prevost in all matters, as she has done to me. It cannot be otherwise between us. Her virtue and chastity are supreme among ladies, equally combining the reputations of both the noblest Roman matron and a Christian lady. I would not be worthy of her inestimable regard if I were to offer anything but the most complete truth to her."

There was an uncharacteristic earnestness to this wordy speech that, combined with that smile, made me realize with surprise that their attachment must still be physically unfulfilled. I thought of how she'd received him in her dressing gown, in her bedchamber, and the measures they'd taken to keep their meetings secret. I myself had discovered passion driven by the uncertainty of war, and knew how powerful it could be. The very way they gazed at each other had made me look away.

How could they have remained so chaste? Was withholding the final prize the way that Mistress convinced herself she was still faithful to her marital vows, or did she do so to keep her younger lover's interest from flagging?

There was one more possibility that I refused to accept: that the two of them did in fact respect and love each other, as the Colonel had described to me. I could not believe that he (or any gentleman, if I was honest) could care so deeply for a woman as heartless as my mistress.

But there was no doubt that Mistress had become more preoccupied, and that when I entered a room I'd often come across her gazing from a window with the familiar mooncalf smile that I'd seen on the Colonel's face. It was so obvious to me that I marveled that no one else seemed to take notice of it: not her sister, nor her mother, nor any of her acquaintance.

Regardless, those chaste memories were all that Mistress had to sustain her for the weeks and months that followed. The Colonel was granted his furlough (though His Excellency insisted that he take his pay), and he stepped away from his command to recuperate. He retreated to Elizabeth, a New Jersey town familiar to him from his schooling as a boy and a place he'd still many friends, as well as several physicians he trusted. But while his physicians had urged him to take a lengthy furlough, he placed his health second to his duty, and, I suspected, his fear of what other men were saying about him. After only a short fortnight he was back at his post.

His new assignment was much more taxing as well. Although he was only a lieutenant colonel, his old friend and superior General McDougall put him in command of the brigade at White Plains, in Westchester, a place known for its lawlessness. According to Mistress, the Colonel replaced an officer accused of corruption and plundering, and he was immediately faced with undisciplined troops, horse thieves, and even low women among his ranks.

Despite the Colonel's continuing ill health, he had punished the miscreants, ended plundering, restored order, and secured the law within a matter of weeks. He received the praise of his superiors as well as the civilians who had suffered, as Mistress would proudly recount to whoever would listen. It struck me to be a great deal of accomplishment for a gentleman who had just completed his twenty-third year, and in poor health as well, and I suspected that perhaps Mistress (or the Colonel himself) had exaggerated that accomplishment for effect.

Yet as heroic as all this was, even the Colonel had his limit, and by March of the new year he reached his. He and Mistress spoke endlessly of it; sometimes it seemed as if they spoke of little else, at least while they were in my hearing. No matter how much his soldier's spirit wished to continue, his body would not. This time, the letter he submitted to His Excellency wasn't a request for a furlough. It was to resign his rank and his command in the army.

For the next weeks, he took to his bed under the care of a physician in Connecticut, exactly as Mistress had wished for him to do. His plan was to recover sufficiently to return to his study of the law, which had been interrupted by the war several years before. He'd even discussed returning to the town of Princeton to study side by side with an old friend of his, Colonel Robert Troup, who'd likewise resigned his commission for private life. Princeton was what Mistress wanted, for it was not so far from Hopperstown. In the end, he decided that he would first study with Judge Titus Hosmer in Middletown, in Connecticut, and therefore be close to his sister and brother-in-law in Litchfield.

First, however, he decided to return to the Hermitage as Mistress's guest. Mistress announced his reason to be purely a medical one: he meant to take the healing waters of a hot spring on the edge of Mistress's land as an aid to his recovery. Nor was it unusual for gentlemen to make a lengthy stay at Mistress's house, or her mother's. Recently the British army had sent two physicians, Dr. Joseph Browne and Dr. Samuel Bradhurst, who had been captured on the battlefield while treating American soldiers and placed them under house arrest at the Hermitage. They'd been treated more like honored guests than prisoners, which was likely due more to Mistress's complicated loyalties (and to the fact that Miss DeVisme had taken a fancy to Dr. Browne) than it was to her hospitality.

But Colonel Burr was different. From the instant that Mistress welcomed him at the door, taking both his hands in her own and kissing his cheeks in the French manner, it seemed as if he'd already earned his place in the house. Their mutual fondness was constantly on display in a hundred little gestures and glances, and they were seldom distant from each other's company. Before now, I'd been the only one who'd witnessed this during his nighttime visits last autumn, but it soon became clear to everyone else that more affection lay between them than mere friendship.

Yet he was still unwell, and the improvement of his health was not only the professed goal of his visit, but also a necessity. With Caesar to accompany him, he dutifully rode out early each morning to bathe in the curative hot springs not far from the Hermitage. He swore off tobacco and strong spirits. Mistress had given him the bedchamber with windows on two walls for the freshest air, and had the best mattress laid upon his bedstead, with extra coverlets to keep away any chill.

She was also particular in the food that Chloe prepared for him, requiring only plain fare combined with fortifying possets and gruels. Chloe and I agreed that Mistress was keeping him to food more fit for a puling infant than a gentleman in his prime who needed to rebuild his strength and blood.

How I longed to make a fine, rich curry for Colonel Burr, and see how quickly coriander, cumin, and turmeric would restore him. The fancy became so vivid to me that I could almost smell the spices once again, and I even pictured myself serving it to him upon one of Mistress's best porcelain plates. Yet this imagining made me sad as well, for I realized how distant the recollections of the scents and tastes and colors of my long-past childhood had become.

Within the week, I'd had more such memories dragged from within me, and not by my own wish, either. Much like Mistress, the Colonel had some days where the two of them would walk beneath the trees and take turns reading aloud to each other, and others when a headache would force him to keep to his bed with the curtains drawn against the light.

On one such day, Mistress was similarly stricken, and I scurried back and forth between their bedchambers to wait upon them both. Mistress took the tincture prescribed by her physician to ease her pain, and was soon deep in sleep. The Colonel, however, had no such remedy. Instead, he was restless and bored because his eyes plagued him too much to read, and therefore he expected me to run up and down the stairs to answer his every whim.

He grimaced as I brought him the tea with milk that he'd last requested. He was lying in bed, propped against a mound of pillows with only a sheet across him. Because he'd decided the fresh air was too chill, he'd had me shut the windows earlier, and now to me the room seemed close and still.

Gone was the pomp and tidiness of a Continental officer, and he wore only a plain linen nightshirt. He'd shoved the cuffs and sleeves high over his forearms, and the collar was unfastened and widespread to reveal the curling hair upon his chest. His dark hair was unbound and loose around his shoulders and against the white pillow bier, his jaw shadowed with several days' worth of beard, and he looked more like a deserter or other brigand scuffling over the enemy lines than a lieutenant colonel.

"You're kindness personified, Mary," he said as he sipped the tea. "No wonder your mistress values you so highly."

"Thank you, sir," I said. "Is there anything else, sir?"

"There is another thing, yes," he said, his lips brushing over the gold-edged rim of the cup. "Mrs. Prevost has told me that when she is in the grips of her worst headaches, you alone can bring her comfort by rubbing lavender water upon her temples."

"That is true, sir," I said. "If Mistress orders me to do so, yes."

"If it is such a salubrious remedy, then I should like to try it for myself," he said. "My head aches like the very devil today, and nothing else has helped."

I hesitated. I didn't care how much his head ached. It was one thing to hand him a cup of tea, but another entirely to lean close to him as he lay in bed and stroke my fingers across his brow.

"I am not sure Mistress would wish me to do that, sir," I said uneasily.

"I've no doubt you can creep into her room for the lavender water without waking her," he said, setting the teacup on the table beside the bed. "She would not have described the remedy to me if she didn't wish me to try it."

I couldn't refuse him, but still I lingered by the bed hoping he'd change his mind.

"Come now, Mary," he said, settling back more deeply into the pillows. "Don't make this infirm old soldier suffer any longer than I must."

If he were truly infirm, I'd have had no worries. But headache or not, he was still sufficiently strong to cause me mischief, and as for being old—why, he couldn't have been more than four years older than I was myself.

"Mary," he said again, turning my name into both a warning and a command that I'd no choice but to obey.

Taking care not to waken Mistress, I went to her room and took the bowl of lavender water and a fresh handkerchief from her dressing table, and returned to the Colonel's bedchamber across the hall. His eyes were closed, and I dared to think he was asleep, but he spoke as soon as I entered.

"How does Mrs. Prevost?" he asked, not opening his eyes. "I worry for her when she's ill. It pains me doubly to be lying here like this when she needs me to be strong."

"Mistress will likely sleep the afternoon through, sir." I dipped the handkerchief into the water and wrung it out. "She's said herself that she'd rather you improve your own health, sir, than worry over hers."

He drew in his breath sharply and frowned as I laid the cool, damp cloth across his closed eyes. I began to trace small circles with my fingertips along his temples to the center of his brows and back again, gently increasing the pressure as the warmth of the closed room made the lavender scent blossom and grow.

I tried not to think of how I was doing this for a gentleman, not a lady, or how my touch was making his face relax and the pain subside. I was standing close beside the bed, leaning over him, and uncomfortably aware of how close my body was to his face. Even blindfolded like this, I wished he wouldn't smile. I'd ease his pain because he had bidden me to do so, but I didn't want to go further, and give him pleasure.

"Is that better, sir?" I asked, hoping he'd say yes so I could stop.

"It is indeed," he said, his voice low and deep with contentment. "Where did you learn such an art, Mary? Is it some bewitching magic passed along from an Indian mother to her daughters?"

"No, sir," I said. "I was taught by another servant so that I might ease my French-born mistress in Pondicherry."

"Pondicherry," he repeated, letting the word play on his tongue. "I take it that is a city in India?"

"It is, sir," I said, a brief wave of longing for the place sweeping over me. "I was born there. It's an ancient city, sir, full of beauty, that lies on the shore beside the sea."

"You surprise me, Mary," he said. "Mrs. Prevost told me you were from Calcutta."

"Mistress must have forgotten, sir." In truth, Mistress had never asked where I'd been born, because I doubted she cared. "Calcutta is not the only city in India, though it is the one most commonly known by Englishmen. There are many others besides it."

"I'm sure there are," he said, intrigued. "Speak to me in the language of the place, Mary. Say something in Indian."

I couldn't keep back a little sigh. "There is no single Indian language, sir. It would be the same as if I asked you to address me in European."

"Then say something in the common tongue of Pondicherry."

I wanted to tell him how there was no single language spoken in Pondicherry, either, exactly as there were several—English, Dutch, French—common here in New Jersey. But I'd already corrected him once, and it seemed unwise to do it again.

"Nīṅkal aiyā virumpukiṟīkaḷ," I said softly, thinking of how long it had been since I'd spoken in Tamil.

"What an extraordinary sound." He smiled with delight. "Did you cast an exotic spell upon me, Mary?"

"No, sir," I said. "All I said was 'as you wish, sir.'"

The corners of his mouth twitched. "For all I know, you could have just placed a curse on my house for all eternity."

"I didn't, sir," I said evenly. "Having been born in Pondicherry does not make me a witch."

"Not a witch, no," he said. "Although I doubt you were born a Christian."

"No, sir," I said. "But there are many ways to worship, just as there are many languages in which to do so."

"Ahh," he said. "Much as there is a difference between worshipers in Boston and Philadelphia and Charleston."

"Forgive me, sir," I said, "but there is a much greater difference between Hinduism and Islam."

I hadn't expected to have a conversation with him regarding religion. For that matter, I hadn't expected to have a conversation with him at all. But now I understood why Mistress found discussions with him to be so intriguing.

"The people of Boston and Philadelphia and Charleston are more alike than not, sir," I continued. "They are all considered Christians."

"Oh, Mary, Mary," he said grandly. "Do not dare tell a Boston Puritan that he is the same as a Philadelphia Quaker or a Baltimore Roman, and as for that Charleston planter—he shall always believe, war or no war, that his soul is ruled by the Archbishop of Canterbury."

"It is still not the same, sir," I insisted. "They all share the common beliefs of Christians."

"I never would have guessed what a proper theologian you are, Mary Emmons," he said. I didn't know whether the lavender water had succeeded in easing his headache or our conversation had simply distracted him from it, but either way he seemed more his usual self. "A veritable marvel of argument! I wish my grandfather were here, so that you might address him."

"Your grandfather, sir?" I asked uncertainly, for even from him, this made little sense.

"My grandfather, one of the most feared and fearsome of all New England preachers," he said. "When he thundered from his pulpit, he could describe the burning fires of Hell in such torrid detail that the strongest men in the congregation fell to their knees and wept like babes at the pitiful states of their mortal souls."

While it was difficult to imagine the Colonel as having a holy man as a grandfather, it was easy enough picturing him with one who liked to preach and declaim. "How terrifying for you as his grandson, sir."

"Not at all," he answered, linking his fingers comfortably upon his chest. "I was a mere infant when he died, and whatever sins I'd acquired by that age were of such a humble and insignificant variety that I suspect he'd no interest in them."

"I'm sorry, sir," I said sadly, unable to keep from remembering my own grandmother. "Children should know their ancestors."

"I didn't," he said. "I suppose the very fact that the old gentleman died when he did indicates some manner of divine wrath venting upon me even as a child."

"There is no loneliness like a child forced to suffer the untimely loss of a devoted parent or grandparent, sir," I began softly. "Those who are blessed with a full and happy family can never understand it."

"But you do, Mary." He reached up and lifted the cloth from his eyes to look at me. He blinked, doubtless from the light, but kept his gaze upon me so that I felt my cheeks warm from it. "I should have known that you, of anyone, would."

I was tempted to tell him more of Pondicherry, about my mother's tragedy and my unknown father and how their deaths had been the reason that, in time, I'd been brought here to New Jersey as Mistress's slave.

I wanted to tell him, because I was sure he'd understand, just as I'd understood him.

But instead he continued, not giving me space to interrupt.

"You see everything in this house, Mary, don't you?" he asked, his mouth curling into a half smile. "I am certain you realized it all before I did, how the death of Mrs. Prevost's own father—*vale,* Theodosius Bartow!—in that carriage accident before she was born would bind her even more closely in sympathy to me. It is but one more way that we are alike, she and I, and in as perfect understanding of each other as two souls can be."

I instinctively fell back into my usual silence, head bowed, eyes downcast, hands clasped over my apron, with no opinions or ideas of my own. Of course he meant Mistress. Why should I have been so foolish as to think he'd mean me?

"I believe your ministrations have helped me, Mary." He tossed the cloth aside and sat upright against the pillows as he took up a book he'd borrowed from Mistress's shelves from the table beside the bed. "I feel quite refreshed."

"I am glad, sir," I murmured, gathering up the cloth, the bowl, and the water. They'd served their purpose and were no longer needed, nor was I. I began to turn away with them, and as I did he grabbed on my forearm where it was bare below my sleeve, holding me back.

"A moment, Mary, if you please," he said. As soon as I'd paused, he released my arm, but now he was running his fingers back and forth over my skin, as if he couldn't bring himself to break away completely. As featherlight as this caress was—and I'd no doubt it was a caress, however unintentional he tried to make it appear—it was enough to make me shiver, from surprise and confusion both.

"You must know how much I appreciate you," he said. He paused, his gaze gliding from my face to his hand upon my arm and back again. "You are always an isle of calm and peace and grace in this household, and you have my gratitude for it."

I nodded, mute. His gaze could hold my own by the hour, if he'd wished it. He'd beautiful eyes for a man, large and a rich color that was neither brown nor blue nor green, but a mixture of all three, and framed by thick lashes that any girl would envy. Yet there was nothing soft or feminine about his gaze. It was too sharp, too penetrating, too impossible to evade or ignore.

He was the one who finally broke the spell, and released me. He looked away, pointedly opening the book to read.

"You may go, Mary," he said absently, his thoughts already elsewhere.

I fled, my thoughts tangled and raw.

But later that night, when I turned to the commonplace book he'd given me, I wrote only a handful of words—the last underlined—as a warning to myself.

Keep guard, and do not let yourself become a _fool_.

CHAPTER 13

The Hermitage
Hopperstown, State of New Jersey
August 1780

For the months that followed, Colonel Burr devoted himself both to repairing his health and to Mistress, though perhaps one with more devotion than the other. Although he was occasionally still called upon to perform some small mission or reconnaissance for the army, his military career was effectively done, and he divided his time between Connecticut, where he'd resumed studying law, and New Jersey.

He was so often at the Hermitage that all the Hackensack Valley knew of his interest in Mistress, and gossiped about it, too. On the rare times when Mistress and her mother and sister visited friends elsewhere and took me with them, I was instantly asked by that house's servants for details of the scandal—details that, of course, I never provided.

Indeed, it *was* a scandal. There was no other word for it. For an area that was so besieged and weary of war, the rumors of the wellborn wife of a British officer openly conducting an affair of passion with a much younger gentleman who'd fought for the Continental Army was a titillating diversion. It also became a test of political loyalties. For those who wished to make a public outrage of their Whiggishness, Mistress became an easy target to portray as an adulterous Loyalist harlot. In the way of lopsided English morality, no slanders were cast upon Colonel Burr; but then, what gentleman is ever faulted for loving too freely?

But while Mistress did her best to hold her head high and ignore the tattle from others, she could not ignore her own mother. Mrs. DeVisme was so critical of her daughter's behavior that it became a constant, wearying theme whenever they were together.

The older lady's tirades had only increased in the summer of 1779 when Mistress received most momentous news from Colonel Prevost. With nothing to show for years of fighting the Continental forces in the north, the British had decided to concentrate their attacks on the less fortified southern states, where there were believed to be more Loyalist sympathizers. From his headquarters in the City of New York, General Sir Henry Clinton had sent over three thousand troops to invade Georgia with the goal of restoring the state to British rule—or, as it was said, to remove one of the stars back from the American flag. Mistress's husband was among these forces, and he fought so ably and bravely that, when the British reclaimed the lower half of the state, Colonel Prevost was named acting governor.

All this he wrote in a letter to Mistress, who in turn read the letter aloud one evening to her family and a group of her acquaintances, as she would with any accounting from the war. (It was also, not surprisingly, an evening when Colonel Burr was not in attendance, being at his sister's home in Litchfield.) By attempting to keep her own loyalties in balance as she always did, she tried to direct her pride toward her husband's individual achievements rather than toward the British victories against the Americans. But Mistress erred when she also read aloud her husband's pleas for her to join him and their two sons in Georgia.

Mrs. DeVisme could scarce wait until their guests departed before she began her attack. I was clearing away the cups and plates, and thus overheard it all, though I suspect the older woman's voice could be heard in every corner of the house, she was that distraught.

"You must go to your husband at once, Theo," she said. "He has as much as ordered you to join him. There is absolutely no acceptable reason for a Christian woman to keep apart from the man she has sworn before God to honor and obey."

"Consider the danger of such a journey, Mother," Mistress said, putting her off as she went about the parlor, plumping a cushion here, adjusting the position of a vase there. "The coast bristles with American privateers."

"And not a single one of those impudent little boats would dare interfere with a British transport convoy," her mother countered. "Your passage could be arranged in a matter of days. I'm sure that Sir Henry himself would give the order for it, considering who you are."

"Can Sir Henry order the winter seas to calm, and the storms to abate?" Mistress asked, her back to her mother. "Can a British general control the vagaries of the weather so as to lessen my risk?"

"You are impossible, Daughter," Mrs. DeVisme said grimly. "It is your duty to be with your husband and your sons, no matter the imagined risks. I do not know how you can remain deaf to the talk that—"

"Do you believe I care for such talk?" Mistress demanded, turning to face her mother. "After all I have done, all I have endured, all I have ignored, in order to keep this property and us safe within it! After all of that, how can you believe that I care a fig for the opinions of others?"

Mrs. DeVisme's hands were clasped so tightly about the blades of her ivory fan that I thought she might snap it in two.

"Is it politics, then?" she asked. "Is this—this flirtation with Colonel Burr your misguided attempt to broadcast your sympathies for the Whigs?"

Mistress gave a small toss to her head. "My politics have little to do with my affections, Mother."

"I do not believe that for a moment, Theo," her mother said. "You were always a headstrong, obstinate child, and now that same stubbornness will be your ruin if you let it."

"I am not a child, Mother, and it is my decision to make, not yours," Mistress said, her voice terse and each word clipped. "And though I do not owe you an explanation, I will tell you that I have already replied to Marcus, and I enclosed a lock of my hair so that he would be sure to know it was from me."

As Mistress made this declaration, her mother watched her so closely that she flushed.

"A raggedy lock of hair is poor consolation for a faithless wife,"

Mrs. DeVisme said at last. "You have made a sorry choice, Theo, and I only hope you will come to your senses before it is too late to do so."

Mistress didn't reply, at least not that I heard, for soon after I'd no choice but to return to the kitchen with a tray filled with dishes. There, however, Chloe had opinions of her own once I told her what had happened in the parlor.

"It's pure meanness in that old woman, forcing Mistress t'confess like that," she said. "She knows what her daughter's doing, same as the rest of us. Master is ten years older than Mistress, and the Colonel is nine years younger. What woman wouldn't take the younger man?"

I shook my head as I slipped the dirty cups into the tub of soapy water. My Lucas had been about twenty years older than I, and I hadn't reason to complain.

"She was discontented before she even met Colonel Burr," I said. "I remember when Master brought me here, the last time he was on leave, and she kept apart from him."

"She doesn't keep apart from Burr, that's for sure," Chloe said with a sly laugh. "She's like a young girl with him."

"But it's more than that, Chloe," I insisted. "They speak about books and poetry and politics, and he listens to her as if she were another man. He says their souls are alike."

"Souls and books," scoffed Chloe. "There's one reason that Mistress keeps that puppy around, and it's not souls nor books, neither."

But it was. Chloe might not understand it, but I did. To see Mistress and the Colonel together was to understand how rare their attraction was. There was no arch coquetry, no false gallantry, nothing practiced nor calculated between them as there was with most of the other white gentlemen and ladies who visited the house. Instead, there appeared to be both genuine respect and regard between them, and a willingness to listen and consider what the other said. Their souls truly were alike, as the Colonel had said, and meant to be together.

Which is not to say there was no desire between them. Far from it. Even through the closed door to Mistress's bedchamber, I heard her with him, the creaking of the bedstead and the animal cries of their passion. If once they'd abstained, that time was surely now passed. It was fortunate that Mrs. DeVisme was never in Mistress's house to hear how wantonly her daughter abandoned herself to her young lover, and ignored her vows to Colonel Prevost; I'm not sure the older woman would have survived overhearing such undeniable evidence of their pleasure.

It was difficult enough for me. I'd believed that after all the tragedies and misfortunes of my life, I'd learned to look ever forward, and not let the past hurt me further. But the sounds at night of their lovemaking in the room below the attic made me unbearably sad and lonely, so much so that I often silently wept myself to sleep with grief. When Lucas had been killed, I'd lost not only our future together, but also the solace of love and the joy of another who'd made me whole.

As if to echo the chill in my solitary heart, the winter months of 1780 were the coldest and most bitter that any in the valley could remember, with too many snowstorms to count. General Washington's army had once again made their winter encampment in New Jersey, about thirty miles southwest of the Hermitage. There the army suffered not only from the cold and snow, but also from discontent among the ranks. As the war had continued, the heady patriotic enthusiasm of 1775 seemed long ago, and it felt that far more—in lives, property, and spirit—had been lost than gained. Victories had been few, and because Congress lacked the funds to pay the soldiers, many had quit as soon as their enlistments were done, or simply deserted to return home.

I saw my own dreams of liberty fading, too, and began to think they truly were dreams, and no more. I was most likely twenty years of age then, and all I saw stretched before me was a life of drudgery, bereft of the love that I'd scarcely known, yet always desired. Worst of all, my heart grieved to think that my Lucas might have died for nothing.

It wasn't until spring that we'd learned that His Excellency and his officers had had to put down a mutiny within their own ranks at Morristown that had led to the execution of the instigators. Even after the army broke camp with the warmer weather in the spring, the northern campaign seemed stalled into inactivity.

The only favorable news from this time was that the French King Louis XVI had decided to show more tangible support for the Americans against the British, and was sending ships and troops to join the cause. I thought of the younger son of my first mistress, Madame, who had been an officer in the French army, and wondered if he, too, would be among those sailing to America to fight for freedom of people like me.

Learning that the French were joining the war must finally have decided Mistress's allegiance in favor of the patriot cause, for fewer and fewer British officers and Loyalists now called at her home. We no longer maintained the ruse of placing Loyalist newspapers on tables where they'd be seen, or leaving Colonel Prevost's old red uniform coat over the back of a chair, as if he'd only stepped away from the house for a moment instead of many years.

I guessed that Colonel Burr must have influenced her decision as well. From what I overheard of their conversations, at his urging she had now thrown herself entirely on the mercy and influence of Governor Livingston to keep her home—still technically owned by a British officer—from being confiscated as Loyalist property by the state. She also turned to Judge William Paterson, the state's attorney general. Although she'd known both men for many years, they were also close friends of the Colonel from their days at the College of New Jersey, and I suspected that there were personal favors asked between them on Mistress's behalf. She could not have had any other gentlemen in the state better placed to assist her and vouch for her loyalty as a patriot than these two. But then, she'd always been adept at choosing her allies, and that included Colonel Burr as well.

Her loyalties were soon tested, however, and in a way that no one could have anticipated.

One morning in late September, a young Continental courier brought a letter to the house. I quickly took the letter to Mistress, who was alone at her desk writing letters, as was her custom at this time of day.

She opened it and scanned the contents.

"Is the messenger still here, Mary?"

"Yes, Mistress," I said. "He's watering his horse in the back."

She added several sentences on the bottom of the letter before refolding it and adding a fresh seal of her own.

"Give this to him, Mary," she said, already preoccupied with planning, "and then return to me. We'll have guests tonight, important guests, and we've much to do to make ready."

They were important guests indeed: Mrs. Peggy Arnold, the wife of General Benedict Arnold, traveling with her young son, her servants, and her husband's aide-de-camp, Major David Franks. Mrs. Arnold was traveling from her husband's post on the North River, where he was the commander of the fortress at West Point, to rejoin her family in Philadelphia. The Hermitage was a convenient overnight stop, and no doubt Mistress's reputation for hospitality promised to make it much more pleasant than a common inn or stage stop. Entertaining the wife of a prominent Continental general would benefit Mistress as well, and publicly do much to emphasize her support of the American cause.

But Mistress was certain that there was more to Mrs. Arnold's visit than convenience, as I learned later that afternoon. Mistress had invited several other ladies from the neighborhood as well as her sister and mother to make a proper welcome for Mrs. Arnold, and they'd already gathered in the parlor, dressed in afternoon silk in her honor. I was there, too, standing beside the wall and ready to pour tea for the ladies.

As soon as the carriage appeared before the house, Mistress sent me to open the door while the ladies in the parlor smoothed their skirts one final time in anticipation. But as soon as the footman opened the carriage door and Major Franks handed Mrs. Arnold out, I saw that she was not at all the confident, fashionable wife of a general that they were expecting.

Clutching her baby in her arms, Mrs. Arnold stepped slowly from the carriage. She was small and surprisingly young, likely close to my own age, with full cheeks, a small, red mouth, and a cloud of pale hair beneath the arc of her dark green calash bonnet. She clung to Major Franks's arm as she came up the steps and entered the house. Her child's nursemaid and another servant with a small trunk followed close behind her.

"Good day to you, Mrs. Arnold," Mistress said warmly, greeting

her in the hall with a gracious curtsey. "How honored I am to have
you stop here for the night. If you'd care to join me and the other
ladies in the parlor—"

"Other ladies?" Mrs. Arnold repeated anxiously. "Others? Here?"

Immediately the Major took her by the arm to steady her. "Please
forgive Mrs. Arnold, Mrs. Prevost," he said. "She is much fatigued
from her travels, and it has placed considerable strain upon her fac-
ulties."

Mrs. Arnold shrank against him, holding her child so tightly
that he began to struggle and wail.

"Do not let them steal away my darling!" she cried. "Oh, Major,
hear how he cries from terror! I beg you, please, please preserve us
from these creatures who wish harm to me and my innocent son!"

"You are safe here among friends, Mrs. Arnold," Mistress said,
and reached out to rest her hand in reassurance upon the younger
woman's arm.

But instead Mrs. Arnold whimpered, and shrank away as if
she'd been burned. Immediately the Major took her by the arm and
turned her so she no longer faced Mistress, which seemed to bring
her some comfort.

"Minda, here," he called to the nursemaid, who appeared familiar with whatever ailed Mrs. Arnold. She put her arm around the
younger woman's shoulders and rocked her gently, murmuring the
nonsense most often reserved for infants.

Shaking his head, the Major stepped aside to address Mistress
and the other bewildered ladies who'd followed her into the hall.

"I fear recent events combined with this journey have distressed
Mrs. Arnold," the Major said. "It would be best for her state of
mind if she were to retire to a quiet room, apart from faces that are
unfamiliar to her."

"Of course, of course," Mistress agreed, her expression wreathed
with sympathy even as she organized the next minutes as efficiently
as any field officer. She saw that Mrs. Arnold, her child, and the
nurse were settled in the bedchamber reserved for them. She bid
farewell to the other ladies even as she briskly ushered them from
the house to limit the gossip. Finally she led Major Franks into the
parlor, and had me pour him not tea, but brandy, for surely the poor
gentleman must have needed it.

"You owe me no explanations, Major," Mistress began when she joined him. "But I am saddened to see that poor young lady so grievously afflicted."

"It is indeed a tragedy, Mrs. Prevost." The Major paused, glancing pointedly at me, but Mistress waved her hand.

"Mary has been with me for years," she said, "and I have absolute faith that she will carry no tales from this room."

The Major nodded, though obviously deciding how and where to begin. He was older than most aides-de-camp, and his protective attachment to Mrs. Arnold appeared based on genuine concern, as if that of a conscientious older brother. No wonder he'd been chosen to shepherd her through New Jersey.

"What I shall confide in you now is terrible news, ma'am, though the whole world shall know of it soon enough." He emptied the glass in his hand, and I quickly moved to refill it. "General Arnold has committed the blackest treason imaginable. Apparently he has been in close communication with the British, and had every intention of permitting them to capture his command at West Point, so that he might defect to their side."

Mistress gasped and so did I, the only response that anyone would make to such shocking news.

"I can scarce believe it, Major," she said, her hand pressed to her cheek. "Of all of His Excellency's generals, surely Arnold was the most trusted."

The Major nodded, his expression grim. "I have never seen His Excellency so bereft," he said. "Arnold's plan was only discovered by the accidental capture of one of his confederates, a British officer named John André, who had the damning papers on his person. When word of this reached Arnold, he acted the coward as well as the traitor, and fled to the arms of the British, abandoning his wife and child."

"That poor lady," Mistress said, shaking her head. "I cannot begin to fathom her distress."

"Indeed, ma'am," said the Major. "While I am escorting her to Philadelphia, and into the care of her family, in a rare moment of lucidity she did beg to rest here with you, as a trusted acquaintance."

I listened with surprise, since Mistress had earlier in the day told her sister that she'd never met Mrs. Arnold.

"I am honored," Mistress said, making a graceful turn of her wrist. "She may stay as my guest as long as she—ah, my dear, how kind of you to join us!"

She broke off and smiled, rising to her feet and holding her hand out in welcome. Mrs. Arnold herself was standing in the doorway or, rather, huddled to one side of the door's frame.

"I wish to speak with Mrs. Prevost alone," she said.

"Are you certain, Mrs. Arnold?" Major Franks asked uneasily. "It has been a long and tiring day."

Mistress crossed the room to Mrs. Arnold, taking slow steps so as not to startle her. "We shall be fine together, Major. Isn't that so, Mrs. Arnold?"

Tentatively the younger woman took Mistress's hand.

"I will be safe with this lady," she whispered. "Leave us, Major."

Major Franks sighed, unconvinced, but also unable to refuse. After he left the room, Mrs. Arnold finally took notice of me, studying me warily.

"Mary won't harm you, either, Mrs. Arnold," Mistress said, coaxing. "I trust her, and you should, too. Here, sit, and she'll bring you tea."

Slowly the younger woman sat, holding tightly to the arms of the chair and ready to leap from it if necessary. Mistress closed the door to the room for privacy, and I poured a cup of tea and arranged a plate of small biscuits to offer.

"Is the Major gone from here?" Mrs. Arnold asked.

"I heard him on the stairs," Mistress said, sitting in the chair beside her. "But I can send Mary for him, my dear, if that is what you wish, and she—"

"My God, no." As if she was throwing off a disguise (which in a way it was), Mrs. Arnold's entire appearance changed in an instant. Her expression lost all its previous fear and unease, her gaze became steady, and her posture relaxed into graceful ease. "You cannot know how heartily sick I am of Franks and his endless fawning solicitude."

"You appear much recovered, Mrs. Arnold," said Mistress, her brows raised, and her manner shifting, too, but to cynical observation. "I flatter myself that my tea has worked a miracle."

Mrs. Arnold laughed, her bitterness at odds with her youth and fashionable beauty.

"No miracle, ma'am, but the relief of having put aside the ridiculous sham that my husband—my *husband*—has forced upon me this last week," she said disdainfully. "If he had shown more decision and conviction, then none of this masquerade would have been necessary."

Mistress motioned for me to bring her tea as well, a gesture that, I suspect, gave her more time to consider how best to reply.

"Forgive me for my confusion, Mrs. Arnold," she said delicately. "But I find your meaning difficult to decipher."

"Come now, ma'am," Mrs. Arnold said, tipping her head to one side, the sunlight through the window turning her hair golden. "There needn't be further deception between us. I know Franks has already told you what has occurred. I asked to come here because it's well-known where your own sympathies lie. You are wife to Colonel Prevost. Your two sons serve at his side. Your property has remained untouched while others around you have been ravaged and plundered by Howe's men from New York."

"All that is true, yes," Mistress admitted, but admitted no more. Mrs. Arnold might desire to link their lots together, but Mistress had far more years and experience at this game. I'd witnessed it before: how she listened, and flattered, and coaxed, and learned what she needed without volunteering anything of her own situation.

Mrs. Arnold, however, was too caught up in her own smug declarations to realize this.

"Then you know as well as I that the American cause is doomed to failure," she said, leaning forward. "Their army loses men every day to desertion, they've no funds for supplies or weaponry, and as for their leadership—lah, what a sorry assortment of overweening fools!"

"Indeed," murmured Mistress, all the encouragement Mrs. Arnold needed.

"Oh, yes," she said. "If you'd but seen how easily I was able to deceive not only simpletons like Franks and Varrick, but the ones who believe themselves clever like Hamilton, and even the mighty Washington himself! My breasts bare beneath a fine linen nightgown were all the armament I required to make them forget their duty in favor of ogling the General's wife."

"How extraordinary," Mistress said. "And how very resourceful of you as well. But aren't you concerned for your husband's welfare now that he is marked as a traitor?"

"I needn't worry over Arnold now," she said confidently. "He's safe with General Howe in New York. The British will make him a general as his reward, and see that he prospers, which is far more than Washington and Congress ever deigned to do for him. It could have been so much more, of course, if he'd only heeded me."

Mistress smiled, as if all they were discussing were flowers and babies, not the monstrous confession of treason that Mrs. Arnold had just proudly made to her. How many American lives had she put at risk by displaying her breasts in that fine linen nightgown? How much longer had she forced the war to continue by persuading her husband to turn his back upon his honor, his duty, and his friends and comrades? The more I thought of what she'd just said, the more disgusted I was. Standing beside her, I wished I could pour hot tea upon her golden head, and that would only be the beginning.

"How fortunate for the General," Mistress murmured. "Truly, a wife can be a gentleman's greatest treasure."

Mrs. Arnold sniffed. "I wish Arnold could have listened to you," she said. "I have toiled for *months* for him and his future, writing back and forth to Howe to arrange the terms. If only he had managed to deliver West Point, as he'd promised, why, then the British would in turn have made us wealthy beyond measure. Instead, my husband faltered, and worse, now poor, dear André was captured, and must languish in captivity."

"Major John André?" Idly Mistress reached for one of the short-bread biscuits, tapping it lightly on the plate to shake away the extra sugar. "I've heard he was quite the beau among the ladies of Philadelphia when the British held that town. But then you likely knew him well yourself, yes?"

Mrs. Arnold flushed, her fair skin betraying how accurate Mistress's guess had been. So she'd not only convinced her husband to betray his command and his country, but in turn it seemed she'd also betrayed him with this British major.

"André is a charming gentleman, ma'am," she said, so breathlessly that she left little doubt of her attachment. "There are few women—or men—who cannot help but love him. That is why I am certain an exchange of prisoners will soon be achieved, and he'll once again be among his friends in New York."

"I hope for your sake Major André is soon released, ma'am," Mistress agreed. "Since he is a special friend to you, and your husband."

Mistress broke the shortbread between her fingers, a neat snap into two pieces. Was she guessing, I wondered, or in all those endless letters she exchanged had there been some mention of Major André being more than a mere friend to Mrs. Arnold?

The younger woman's cheeks grew redder still. "I am sure of it," she said quickly—too quickly. "He has been captured before, and his superiors have always made sure he is rapidly exchanged. He is far too valuable to His Majesty's forces for it to be otherwise."

"Oh, I am sure of it." Mistress sighed. "What I wish for above all things is for peace, and an end to the waste and misery of this war."

"That is why I wished to call upon you, Mrs. Prevost," Mrs. Arnold said, nodding. "My husband regretted learning that Colonel Burr had resigned his commission, and how he, too, had been scorned and ignored by those he tried most to please."

Mistress didn't blush or stammer. Instead, she smiled with perfect pleasantness, and dipped one half of the shortbread into her tea.

"I believe Colonel Burr resigned his commission due to his health, ma'am, and not any unhappiness," she said evenly. "But you—or your husband—must ask him directly. I'd never presume to answer for the Colonel."

She popped the dripping shortbread into her mouth as if to say she thought the discussion done.

But Mrs. Arnold shook her head again, refusing to give up. "I've heard that Burr is a, ah, a close and particular friend to you, and that you—"

"I have many close friends on both sides of the war, Mrs. Arnold," Mistress said easily. "I cannot myself bring peace to this country, but I can ask that my friends find peace while beneath my roof, and leave talk of war and politics beyond my porch."

"But Mrs. Prevost, I only wish to—"

"Tell me of your son," Mistress said. "From what I glimpsed, he appears a most handsome babe. I would guess him to be about six months in age?"

That was the end of Mrs. Arnold's remarkable confession, at least in my hearing. She and Major Franks and the rest of their party left the following morning. Mistress never mentioned Mrs. Arnold again to me, proof that her trust in me was indeed genuine.

Yet I thought often of what I'd heard, and of Mrs. Arnold's audacity, likening her attachment to the British Major André to Mistress's with Colonel Burr. There was, of course, a sizable foundation of truth to it: both women were married to older officers, and had taken younger men as lovers. But what Mrs. Arnold had revealed branded her as a traitor as well as an adulteress, and perhaps worse, since she'd been a spy as well.

In a way, I was surprised that Mistress, with her new-decided patriotism, did not share the story with any local official, or even General Washington himself. Perhaps her sympathies were still too tangled for that, perhaps she wished to avoid questions about herself and Colonel Burr, or perhaps she simply felt pity for Mrs. Arnold. Having the younger woman arrested, tried, and punished would achieve little for the sake of the war, and would have taken a mother from her child.

But she must have told Colonel Burr. Even though in September he'd shifted to study with Judge Paterson here in New Jersey, he was concentrating so hard on his readings that we now seldom saw him at the Hermitage. But the next time he visited, on a Sunday in late October, he did speak to me of it. Mistress had crossed briefly to her mother's house while the Colonel had remained to finish a book. I'd come to check that he'd sufficient wood for the fire, for the first serious bite of the coming winter was already in the autumn air.

He sat in the tall-backed chair beside the window, a thick book spread open across his lap. He'd finally begun to look well again, his color fresh and his eyes sharp and keen. Mistress fretted that he toiled too hard at his studies, but clearly the scholar's life agreed with him. Lost in thought, he took no notice of me at first as I slipped into the room and knelt before the fire. It was a necessary skill, to be so quiet at my labors that I became invisible, and caused no interruption or offense.

Yet still I did.

"Mary Emmons, Mary Emmons," he said softly.

"Forgive me for disturbing you, sir," I answered without turning. "I shall be done shortly."

"No, no, you haven't disturbed me at all," he said easily. "I'm the one disturbing you."

I brushed away the last of the stray ashes. Whenever he returned to the Hermitage, I was always startled by how freely he addressed me whenever we were alone together. His familiarity always unsettled me, because it wasn't right.

He said nothing further, and I imagined he'd returned to his book. I swept the hearth clear and slipped the basket with my brushes and cloths over my arm. Only then did I stand, finally turning toward him to curtsey before I left the room.

He hadn't been reading. He'd been watching me as I'd been on my hands and knees, and I flushed when I saw the little half smile on his face, the kind of smile men made when imagining wickedness with the woman before them.

"Is there anything else, sir?" I asked, wanting only to flee.

"Tell me what you made of Mrs. Arnold's revelations," he said, not what I'd expected. "Mrs. Prevost told me you were in the room with her at the time, and I'm grateful that you were. A conversation like that is best held before at least one witness."

I hesitated. It was never wise to fault a white lady, even one who'd boasted of treason.

"Tell me, Mary," he said, his smile now meant to coax away my reluctance. "I've heard Mrs. Prevost's account. I'd like yours as well."

I sighed, realizing I'd no choice. "When Mrs. Arnold was alone with Mistress, she admitted that she'd only pretended to lose her wits. She said she believed the Americans would lose the war, and that she'd persuaded her husband General Arnold to go over to the British, who were going to make him a general and pay him some sort of reward. She also spoke of a British spy named Major André, who she said had helped her, and was a particular friend of hers."

"Oh, yes, a particular *friend*," he said dryly. "But proceed, please. You haven't mentioned how she tried to recruit Mrs. Prevost and me as well."

"She began to do that, sir," I said. "But Mistress would have none of it, and ordered her not to speak of war and politics, but of her baby instead."

"Now that was something Mrs. Prevost didn't tell me." He chuckled, clearly amused. "It doesn't surprise me, however. A pretty little fool like Peggy is no match for Mrs. P., and never will be."

"No, sir." I knew he was laughing over Mistress silencing Mrs. Arnold, but to me there was nothing entertaining about any of that conversation. My words grew warmer, more forthright. "But—but I was glad that her plot was discovered, sir. If she'd forced her husband to act as she'd wished, then who knows how many Americans would have been killed or captured? The loss of West Point could have meant the defeat of the American cause. To hear Mrs. Arnold, that was exactly what she'd desired, sir, and expected, too."

"Spoken like a true patriot." He wasn't smiling now, or laughing, either. "And yet you understand the other side as well, don't you? Even a courageous soldier like Arnold can crumble and turn traitor if pressed too hard. Peggy saw his weaknesses, and as an artful coquette, she was able to beguile him into a marriage he didn't deserve. Fortunately for her, not many will learn her part in her husband's treason."

"I wish they would, sir," I said vehemently. "She deserves to be punished, considering what she has done to both her country and her husband."

He set aside his book and rose from his chair to look away from me and out the window. He stood with his hands clasped behind his back, restlessly clenching and unclenching. His face was all angles in the afternoon light, his jaw set, and he took his time to answer.

"She has destroyed at least two lives by her reckless impulses," he said finally, his gaze unfocused but his voice as flinty as it had been when he'd worn a uniform. "The British will never grant the reward they promised Arnold. His career and his honor are in ruins, and now little Peggy and their son are shackled to him and his disgrace forever. And as for her dear André: within the week, Washington had him tried, convicted, and hung as a spy. So yes, she has been punished, and if she possesses any conscience at all, she'll suffer that punishment the rest of her mortal days."

That was punishment, that was sorrow, and I groaned aloud to think of all the misery the young woman had willfully unleashed.

He swung around to face me, his expression determined.

"You see now why I am urging Mrs. Prevost to take herself from this region," he continued. "If Peggy and her confederates had heard this—this gossip about us, then others will have as well."

"They have, sir," I said. "Servants from other houses often ask me of it."

"I'm not surprised," he said, his dark brows drawing together. "Calumny and lies and innuendo of the lowest sort, exactly the ill fame her enemies hunger for. Mrs. Prevost cannot let herself be linked to any of it, not with the cases regarding her property due to come to court soon. The risk is too great. Peggy did her no favors by stopping here and leaving her taint."

I'd known that Mistress's property had been eyed for confiscation by the state ever since the war had begun, but I hadn't realized that the case was so close to a decision. Yet for that very reason, I couldn't imagine her willingly leaving it, not now.

"Forgive me, sir, but I do not believe she'll go," I said. "This place is too dear to her to abandon it now."

"Oh, I don't expect her to abandon the Hermitage," he reasoned, adding an expansive sweep of his hand for emphasis. "Only that she step away for a time to separate herself from the property. It will sit better with the judges if she is not here to remind them with her presence as Colonel Prevost's wife. Of course, having lived so long apart from him will make it easier for them to explain that she is at heart more a Whig than a Tory. Leaving the state for a short while will only help her cause. Besides, I expect Mrs. DeVisme and her daughter will remain here to oversee the property."

I nodded, thinking how having her further removed from her husband benefited Colonel Burr as well. But I couldn't deny that not only the rest made sense, but also that his careful argument proved how he'd already absorbed many of the lessons necessary to being a good lawyer. At first it had seemed odd to me to see him in a plain but well-cut dark suit instead of the familiar blue-and-buff uniform, but now I was aware of a new air and presence to him that came not from a rank, but from his own intelligence and abilities. He'd always been a handsome man; now he'd become one that would be noticed as well.

"Where will you advise her to go, sir?" I said.

"I've inquired after rooms for her in the home of a respectable widow near Litchfield," he said. "It's not far from the home of my sister and brother-in-law. Removed she may be, but she won't lack for intelligent company. I mean to speak to her about it tonight."

He nodded, as if agreeing with himself, then cocked his head to one side to look at me. "But what of you, Mary? What would you say to a sojourn in Connecticut?"

I didn't say anything, startled that even he would ask my opinion. As a bondwoman, I'd no right to make a decision like that, or any other about my own welfare or agency.

"Well?" he asked when I hadn't replied. "Would you be willing to accompany your mistress on a journey to the north?"

"If Mistress takes me, sir, then I shall go," I said carefully. "But I can no more choose to travel or not than if I were her old horsehair trunk. It is for Mistress to decide, not me."

"You're more clever than that, Mary," he said in the low voice he reserved for persuasion. "The condition of slavery is but a temporary state that can be removed at any time in an individual's life."

"Only Mistress can give me my freedom, sir," I said. It was easy for him to say such things, easy and glib, because it wasn't his life being lived within his "condition of slavery."

But he was listening, and he didn't interrupt, and that gave me the courage (or perhaps the anger) to continue.

"My husband wished to buy my freedom, sir," I said, "but Mistress refused, and said that I was too valuable to her. She won't free me, either, not so long as either of us still lives, or until the war grants me my liberty."

"Ahh, Mary, Mary," he said, taking a step closer to me, then another, before he stopped, and came no farther. "The only thing that is certain in our lives, whoever we may be, is the uncertainty of tomorrow, or even if we live another day. Surely you must know that."

"More than most, sir," I said, at once sorrowful and defiant. I shifted the handle of the basket from the crook of my arm to both hands, holding it before me like a shield of woven splints. I told myself that I didn't want his sympathy, that I didn't need it, yet I held the basket so tightly that the handle cut into my palms.

"You have learned to read and to write," he said solemnly, studying my face as if seeing it for the first time. "You speak languages other than your own. You've seen more of the world than most sailors. You can cook and sew and spin, and likely a thousand other things besides. Your husband wasn't stopped by what others had done to him, and neither, I suspect, will you be."

I swallowed, and looked down and away from the keenness of his gaze, hiding within myself. I couldn't help it. Whenever he spoke of Lucas, I felt the same, as if to hear my husband's name on this man's lips was a kind of betrayal.

"Forgive me, sir," I said, "but I must see to the other fires before Mistress returns."

He ignored me. "The commonplace book I gave you," he said. "Have you filled its pages with your words?"

"Very nearly, sir." They *were* my words, too, and neither he nor anyone else would ever see them. I made sure of that.

"Then next time I come here, I shall bring you another," he said, his voice dropping lower, a rough whisper that seemed to carry his confusion as well as my own. "You are remarkably pretty, Mary Emmons."

I started when his fingertips touched my temple. No, *started* is too brave a word: I trembled, I quaked, I quivered, for his touch was so light and grazing upon my skin that I might have dreamed it.

But I didn't. All he did was brush aside a wisp of hair that had escaped from beneath my cap.

"Go to your fires, Mary Emmons," he said gruffly, and turned away. "Leave me, and go."

And I did.

No matter how Colonel Burr had tried to persuade Mistress to leave New Jersey for Connecticut, she did not go as soon as he wished. Yet not even he could have argued with her reason for remaining at the Hermitage.

In early November, her sons returned. More than two years had passed since they'd gone to join their father and begin their military careers with him. They appeared on the porch without warning, in the care of the elderly merchant who'd accompanied them from Jamaica: Frederick, now nearly sixteen, and Bartow, fourteen.

Both had grown tall and reedy, with hands and feet too large like puppies' paws, while their too-small clothes gapped at wrists and knees. But while they'd all the awkwardness of youths their age, they'd none of the foolishness. They'd been beside their father throughout the battles in Georgia, and had likely seen things no boys their age should see. Now they'd become serious, solemn young men, their boyish mischief gone, and I thought sadly of how they, too, had been marked forever by the tragedy of war.

Mistress had held them close and sobbed with joy. I wondered if she'd wept as much when she'd read the letter they'd brought from their father. Having completed his posting in Georgia, Colonel Prevost had been stationed again in the West Indies, and he had not wanted his sons subjected to the fevers of the Caribbean. He was not well himself, plagued by old wounds and ailments, and he had, it seemed, finally given up hope that she'd ever again join him.

There was no further mention of the boys following the Prevost tradition of military careers with the British army, and I suspected that this, too, had been at the suggestion of Colonel Burr. The Colonel helped Mistress choose the schools her sons would attend, and oversaw their preparations. To his credit, he treated the boys in a most agreeable fashion, and they soon became great friends; not surprisingly, since the Colonel was, at twenty-four, only about ten years their senior, and must have seemed more like a young and benevolent uncle or older brother.

Frederick and Bartow seemed now destined to study the law, like the Colonel himself. The significance could not have been more obvious. Mistress, however, took great pains that he be described as a dear friend only before the boys, and all romantic gestures between them ceased for the sake of the boys.

Early in the new year, Mistress closed up the Hermitage and went to the lodgings the Colonel had found for her in Connecticut. I was the only servant she took with her, Chloe and the others being left behind with her mother and sister. While she told her family that the purpose of this visit was to improve her cause with the state courts, I soon saw that the real reason was for her to strike a friendship with the Colonel's older sister, Mrs. Sally Reeve.

As the only other survivor of the Colonel's family, Mrs. Reeve was extremely close to her brother, and as proof had named her only child Aaron Burr Reeve. I doubt the Colonel would have continued with Mistress if the two women had not pleased each other. Mrs. Reeve was two years older than her brother, with the same pale complexion, dark hair, and large eyes. At seventeen she had wed their childhood tutor, a legal gentleman, teacher, and scholar named Tapping Reeve. Mr. Reeve doted upon his young wife, and it was fortunate that he did, too, for she was weak and so sickly that her bedchamber was on the lower floor of their house, to spare her the exertion of climbing stairs.

But if Mrs. Reeve's mortal body was feeble, her mind was as nimble and quick as could be, and she and Mistress instantly delighted in each other. Together they could discuss books, ideas, and events by the hour, and Mistress became her near-constant companion. With only Mistress to wait upon, I'd little to do, but Mistress had offered my skill with a needle to Mrs. Reeve. Thus I often sat near to them, close enough to be summoned for fresh tea and to hear their conversations, while I sewed new buttons on Mr. Reeve's shirts and mended Mrs. Reeve's household linens.

From the two ladies, I learned that the Colonel had shifted his law studies first to the library of Mr. Thomas Smith in Haverstraw, and then to the capital of Albany, where a wealthy friend in that place, Stephen Van Rensselaer, had fortuitously found him lodgings with a pair of elderly maiden aunts. Yet the Colonel was so determined to be admitted to the bar as soon as was possible that he'd no time to spare from his books to visit Mistress. Instead, he'd send his own newly purchased bondman, Carlos (whom Mistress wryly called her fleet Mercury), with letters. She respected his dedication, and never pined or fussed the way most ladies would. Mrs. Reeve became the Colonel's surrogate, wooing Mistress in his stead with the family's wit and intelligence. I have never seen or heard of a similarly curious courtship, but it seemed to suit Mistress, the Colonel, and Mrs. Reeve.

In this small village, the war seemed so distant as to have ceased. By late summer, Mr. Reeve told us of rumors of a battle to come that many in the region believed would involve the armies of General Washington and General Howe, and would settle which country controlled the City of New York. Mistress and Mrs. Reeve (and I as well) pored over fresh newspapers whenever they arrived, and listened breathlessly to even the smallest whispers of news that Mr. Reeve relayed.

By the end of October, we learned of a siege and battle far greater than any we'd anticipated, which had taken place at a town on the Virginia coast called Yorktown. Overwhelmed by the Continental forces combining with French ships and soldiers, the British General Cornwallis had surrendered outright to General Washington. It was a momentous victory, and one that was hoped would finally lead to the end of the war.

But for Mistress, even more momentous news arrived in a letter from her sister. Writing on the last day of 1781, Miss DeVisme had enclosed a brief announcement carefully cut from a newspaper, an announcement that Mistress immediately shared with the Reeves.

Far to the south on the island of Jamaica in the Caribbean Sea, Lieutenant-Colonel Jacques-Marc Prevost, Major of the 60th Foot, aged forty-five, had died of yellow fever.

CHAPTER 14

The Hermitage
Hopperstown, State of New Jersey
July 1782

"Are you certain the ladies in New York and Philadelphia are still wearing powder?" Mistress leaned closer to her looking glass in dubious scrutiny, turning her face from side to side as I stood next to her with the pot and duster. "It has been so long since I've powdered my hair that I've forgotten how it looks."

"Yes, Mistress, it is still the fashion," I said. "Miss DeVisme asked me specifically to dress your hair with it today, and sent you her own French-milled powder, too. She said the queen of France powders daily, and is considered a great beauty for it."

"Hopperstown is hardly Versailles, any more than I've ever been considered a royal beauty." Mistress sighed, and shook her head. "But Caty would know the fashion. I suppose she'll be wearing an entire cloud of the stuff in her hair."

"Yes, Mistress," I replied absently. I hadn't powdered a lady's hair for a good long time, either, but Madame had always been most particular about how she wished hers to be done, with extra pomade and the powder applied with a light hand. "You'll both make handsome brides today."

Mistress gave a disdainful small sniff. "I've no doubt that Caty will beam and glow as a proper bride should, while poor Burr must take me as I am," she said. "Perhaps a bit more at my temples? It's the curse of black hair, I know. It requires double the powder to look even halfway respectable."

Dutifully I feathered more of the powder over her hair, carefully arranged and combed high from her forehead and over a cushion-like pouf stuffed with feathers, also her more fashionable sister's suggestion.

"There." Mistress raised her chin to smile at her reflection, and gave her hair a final pat. "That looks far better than it's any right to, Mary. Now the gown."

She shrugged free of her old yellow dressing gown, letting it drop from her shoulders into my hands. I slipped the lavender-colored gown for her wedding over her shoulders, the silk skirts floating and settling over the feather-stuffed false rump that made up for Mistress's natural deficiencies in that area. The gown was also a gift from Miss DeVisme and Dr. Browne. In fact, the entire wedding itself had been contrived at their expense, and I doubted if Mistress and the Colonel would even be marrying if her sister hadn't removed every last objection. There had even been a special license issued by their old friend Governor Livingston himself so they could marry today, without having any banns read.

Carefully I tugged the gown into place over her stays and pinned the bodice together. I tied an embroidered white linen kerchief over her shoulders, twisted the ends together, and tucked them into the neckline. A little bouquet of flowers, tied with pink ribbons, was slipped into the neckline as well, and I anchored it all with a gift that the Colonel had had delivered to her earlier: a small oval brooch with a golden topaz, set in silver, that had belonged to his mother. I plucked at her linen cuffs to make them more full; then, satisfied, I turned her gently so she could admire her reflection in the glass.

"Oh, Mary," she marveled, her cheeks flushing with excitement as she touched the little brooch. "Truly you can work miracles, even with this pauper-bride."

"Thank you, Mistress," I murmured. I was so weary of her constant cries of poverty, an empty complaint if ever there was one. Ready cash was in short supply with her, as it was with many people on account of the war, but no one who possessed a fine stone house, hundreds of acres of land, silk gowns, and slaves was truly poor.

"Are you ready, Theo?" her sister called gaily from the bottom of the stairs. "Oh, I cannot wait to see you!"

"Nor I you, Caty." Mistress turned back to me. "Mary, please continue packing the last of my things. Colonel Burr desires for us to leave before dawn tomorrow. You may, of course, watch the ceremony from the windows with the others if you wish, though I don't know how much you'll see. We're expecting a crowd in the parlor."

She hurried eagerly from the room with a shush of lavender silk. While she greeted her guests, I packed away the last of her belongings in the trunks that stood open on the floor. She was taking mostly clothes and books, and none of her furnishings. The Colonel had warned her that their lodgings were so meager that there'd be no room for much else, especially since Frederick and Bartow were coming to Albany, too.

My own few things were already packed in a bundle in the attic. I was the only one of our household whom Mistress was taking with her to her new home in Albany, just as she'd done during her visit to Connecticut. I expected Mistress would eventually return to the Hermitage to visit her mother, but I'd no assurance that I'd accompany her. I'd also overheard Mistress and the Colonel discussing how the entire estate might as well be sold, if a buyer could be found. This could well be the last day I ever spent here. I'd miss the beauty of the place and my memories of Lucas, but I was eager for the change of living in a city.

The day was warm, and every window of the house had been thrown open wide. I stood outside with Chloe and the others—not only the people from the Hermitage, but also the men who'd driven the carriages for the guests. While the fine white guests were within, we servants crowded around the windows to see and hear what we could as we swatted at the bees that drifted toward us from the rosebushes. Still, we were likely more comfortable outside, where we'd catch the breezes, than those who stood inside in all their overwarm finery.

I'd never witnessed an English wedding, and I was surprised by how quickly it was accomplished. The two couples repeated their vows before the minister, who stood in front of the fireplace. It was not so very different from the vows that Lucas and I had said to each other—the vows that Mistress herself had so scorned—and my heart ached as I remembered the promises I'd made to my own husband.

Even though I'd wriggled a place directly before the window, I was so short that I couldn't see over the heads of the guests. I didn't see how Mistress's dress compared to her sister's, or if Mistress and the Colonel had held hands or gazed with love at one another.

I'd one quick glimpse of the Colonel, strikingly handsome in a dark gray coat with one of Mistress's pink roses tucked into his top buttonhole. Although I couldn't see Mistress behind the others, he could not look away from her direction. He was flushed and smiling, as likely from the heat and celebratory brandy taken with the other gentlemen in the yard beforehand as from matrimonial joy, or perhaps that was just how I chose to think of it.

I do not know why his happiness made me melancholy, yet it did. I suppose I was jealous—not of him, but of how he acted as Mistress were the one woman in this world meant for him, the way every bridegroom should. No one looked at me like that now. Maybe no one ever would again.

"That was a fine wedding," Chloe said in the kitchen as we hurried to put the last touches on the wedding cake. Because the day was warm and she wanted the cake to be as splendid as possible, Chloe had waited to beat the egg whites for the sugary icing until the last moment. "Though Mistress would've done better for herself if she'd wed some rich old man. You know she could've had her pick of them."

I nodded. In those days during the war, when death was often sudden and most marriages were made from shared necessities rather than love, no one expected mourning or grief to keep a fresh widow or widower from remarrying swiftly for the sake of security. There'd been plenty of older widowers among Mistress's acquaintance who'd have been very happy to wed her.

"But Mistress, she wanted her young buck," Chloe continued, chuckling to herself. "They say his father left him a tidy fortune before the war, but that's gone now, same as Mistress's. I heard he was jesting about how he'd use the last half joe in his pocket to pay the parson."

"Hush, Chloe, they're not poor," I said irritably as I whipped the egg whites in a large bowl cradled in my arm. "Think of all they have, all they own."

Chloe sniffed, making sure I knew she didn't agree with me. "Mistress's first husband was ten years older than her with property, and now this one's ten years younger without a penny. She'll learn soon enough which was the wiser choice. The Colonel's one of those men who's full of fire. She'll get no peace with that one. He'll be on her day and night now that she's his rightful wife."

"More of the same, then," I said. It was no secret that the Colonel wanted children together; they spoke of it often. "Where's the difference between that and what they've been doing, making that old bed of hers shudder and creak?"

"The difference is that now he'll be after her for a son," Chloe said. "That's what every man wants, and he won't stop pestering her until he gets one."

"He hasn't gotten one yet," I said. "Whatever that parson said to them won't make any difference."

"Mistress knows French ways," Chloe said, lowering her voice. "She wasn't about to have a big belly before she was wed again."

I frowned. "French or no, she wouldn't have much choice."

"French or yes," Chloe said knowingly. "Whether they be ladies or whores, those French women have their tricks. They know ways o' pleasing men that keep the seed away from causing harm in their wombs. But now the Colonel'll be expecting every liberty, and she'll have to give it to him."

In my experience, women had no choice but to bear the children that men got upon them. I wasn't entirely sure what Chloe meant, but I didn't want her to know I was ignorant of a mystery that she so clearly understood.

"Mistress's womb may be too old for more babes," I said instead. "She's thirty-five. Master Bartow's the last child she bore alive, and he's sixteen years old now."

"True enough," Chloe agreed with a show of understanding, if not sympathy. "Birthing's always a trial and a hazard for women like her. Before she's done, she'll wish she'd wed one of those old men who've lost their spunk and mettle."

I thought of this later that night, when the sounds of the newly-weds' lovemaking drifted up from their open window to ours beneath the eaves. Mistress had always been as lusty as her colonel, and they'd never cared who heard their love play, either. I knew exactly why she'd chosen a younger groom instead of some wizened old fellow, nor could I fault her for it.

But still I covered my ears with my arms so I wouldn't hear them on their feather bed, and be reminded again of how hard and lonely my own pallet was beneath me.

We left the Hermitage early the next morning, the way the Colonel had wanted, so early that we needed the moon and lanterns on the hired carriage to light our way. While Mistress and her sons said good-bye to Mrs. DeVisme, I quickly said my farewells to Chloe and Caesar, who'd risen to see us off. We all wished one another well, but took care to make no promises for the futures we didn't control.

While Mistress, the Colonel, and the two boys rode snug inside the coach, I sat on the top between the driver, a plump free man, and Carlos, the Colonel's Negro manservant. The two of them were delighted by the arrangement; I, squeezed tightly between them, was not. I'd found Carlos to be a cocky fellow who clearly believed I should be smitten with him. He was several years younger than I, more boy than man, stocky and strong and handsome enough, but with a sly, darting gaze that never seemed able to settle on any object—including me—for more than an instant. He was also free with his hands under the guise of offering assistance, and I was constantly having to shove him away from me.

"You'll like Albany, yellow girl," he cheerfully told me. "I expect Albany will like you, too."

"Don't call me that, Carlos," I said crossly. "I don't like it."

"Lah, lah, listen to you," he teased, pressing his knee against mine. "*Miss* Yellow Girl!"

I jabbed him in the ribs as hard as I could with my elbow, which made him yowl, but also back away from me, which was all I wanted. I didn't sense he was a dangerous man, only an irksome one. Since we'd be living together in one household, it was better he understood now how things must stand between us.

At least once we'd boarded the sloop I was spared from his attentions. Carlos turned out to be a miserable sailor, even on this mild river on a sunny day, and to the amusement of the true sailors as well as his own master, he spent much of the voyage close to the railing and retching horribly.

Our travels took the better part of a week. Freed of both their schooling and their grandmother, Frederick and Bartow could not have been happier, pestering the crew until they, too, were allowed small sailing tasks that made them believe they'd become true mariners. Mistress and Colonel spent their days deep in their usual conversations with their heads bent close to one other, strolling the deck or sitting in chairs brought up from below for their use. She clearly couldn't bear to be apart from him, while he kept his arm around her waist, though his hand sometimes slid lower, too, as a fond husband was entitled to do.

I sat to one side of the deck and industriously stitched new hems and darned old linens for Mistress, and knitted woolen stockings against the northern winter, which I'd been told was much fiercer than in New Jersey. As was so often the case, the idlers among the sailors tried to make conversation with me, hoping for more, but I was as purposefully aloof, and they soon left me alone.

When the port of Albany finally came into sight, the Colonel made sure to have Mistress on deck beside him so that he could proudly call attention to the finer points of the city that would be their new home.

"That's the seat of General Schuyler," he said, pointing to a large and elegant brick house with outbuildings high on the hill and surrounded by gardens, lawns, and orchards. I put aside my handwork and stood to one side of them, eager to see more, too. Although it seemed the war was nearly done, the British army still occupied the City of New York, and thus all the state's business continued to take place here in Albany. To my country eyes, it seemed a dazzling place, with docks full of ships, warehouses, churches and other public buildings, and more houses beyond counting. General Schuyler's estate appeared the largest, and purposefully placed beyond the city proper to garner the first attention and awe of visitors approaching on the river.

"It would appear that General Schuyler has prospered during the war," Mistress observed. "Or at least he hasn't suffered as many others have."

"Oh, but he has, Theo," the Colonel said. "Don't you recall how

I told you his second house as well as his mills and fields of crops were burned to the ground by Burgoyne? Heavy losses indeed. But you are right that this house remained untouched, and a lovely place it is, too. You must call upon the General's wife as soon as you are settled."

She glanced at him sideways beneath her wide-brimmed hat, the dark blue ribbons fluttering about her face. His mother's brooch sparkled in the sun, pinned there to her bodice; she'd worn it nearly every day since their wedding to please him.

"I *must,* Aaron?" she asked, teasing. "I thought we'd agreed that that word would never be spoken between us."

He chuckled, and raised her gloved hand to kiss it.

"In most matters, yes," he said, continuing to hold her hand. "I meant only that since General Schuyler has shown me considerable kindness by sharing his library with me for study, it would be a welcome consideration if you were to call upon his lady."

"Of course I shall do so, *mon cher,*" she said, her mouth curving in a smile. The cares that had lined her face these last years at the Hermitage had softened now that she'd left that place, and she looked years younger. "It's always seemly to show gratitude."

"Seemly, but also useful to our combined fortunes," the Colonel said. "Schuyler is state senator and one of the most important gentlemen in the region. His favor will help me gain the confidence of all these other old Dutch grandees so that they'll bring their cases my way."

This might have shocked a less practical lady, but not Mistress. Her smile widened, and she tipped her head to one side with perfect understanding. She and the Colonel truly were every bit each other's equals in the politics of being agreeable to the right people.

"And I'd guess you would wish me to win not only him," she said, "but his lady, and whoever else may be in attendance?"

He nodded. "Another lady that surely will be there is Schuyler's second daughter, Elizabeth," he said. "Think back to when the army camped in your fields. Do you recall the aide-de-camp with the sandy red hair who was a special favorite of Washington's?"

I recalled him at once, for he'd been the colonel who'd smirked at discovering the Colonel with me in the kitchen garden.

Mistress remembered him, too, but for other reasons. "An intense fellow, very quick and clever, but short of patience with others," she said. "I also recall he spoke beautiful French."

"That is the man," the Colonel said. "He wed Elizabeth Schuyler, and they are at present living in her parents' house. He's now pursuing the same course of study for the bar that I did. My old friend Bob Troup is assisting him. You may see him as well in passing. Oh, and Mrs. Hamilton has an infant son, if such knowledge is of use to you."

"Among women, a prized infant son would be of the greatest and most delightful importance in conversation," she said. "But you may likewise be sure that I won't leave Madame Schuyler's parlor until I've convinced her and her daughter that I'm wed to the cleverest legal mind in the city. Every word being true, of course."

"Yes, of course, since I am likewise wed to the cleverest lady," he said, and though they both laughed, his smile faded first.

"I promise you, Theo," he said, "one day soon I'll see that you live in a house that's twice as grand as Schuyler's."

"So long as you shall live there with me, counselor," she said, lowering her voice in a way that promised much.

"With you, and our children." He turned her hand in his and kissed her palm, a favorite gesture between them that always seemed so startlingly intimate that I looked away, and returned to where I'd left my basket of mending.

That small motion from me must have been enough to break their lovers' spell, however, because suddenly the Colonel called to me.

"Tell me, Mary," he said. "Wouldn't you like to live in a fine house such as General Schuyler's?"

Reluctantly I looked back at them. He'd released Mistress's hand, and she now smiled at me, bemused, with her hands clasped before her. I wished he hadn't noticed me looking at the grand house as well.

I wished he hadn't noticed me at all.

"Have you no answer, Mary?" Mistress said, her voice still lighthearted. "My dear husband has as much as promised that one day we'll all live in a grand palace of his making. Wouldn't you like that?"

"I shall live wherever I am taken, Mistress," I said evenly.

But what difference would it make to me where they lived? I'd still be sent to sleep in the attic, and the floor of a palace would be just as unforgiving as the floor of the meanest cottage.

But Mistress would not (or could not; I do not know which) see the truth in my words, and instead continued her teasing.

"You are always my petticoat diplomat, Mary, neither agreeing nor disagreeing," she said, a hint of sharpness now to her banter. "You could claim a seat in Congress for all you avoid taking a forthright stand for one side or the other. Now go below, and make sure my trunks and boxes are all locked and ready to be carried ashore."

"Yes, Mistress," I murmured, thinking a score of forthright things about her that I could never say aloud. I curtseyed and slipped my basket over my arm, preparing to do as she'd bidden, and she looked again at the view before her. But as I turned away, the Colonel's eye caught mine. He wasn't laughing, nor even smiling. Once again, he understood, and his eyes were filled with sympathy.

I flushed, and hurried away, and did not look back. Although by law most all of Mistress's property had become his once they had wed, she'd told me that the Colonel had generously let her keep sole ownership of me. I didn't understand entirely how this could be, but so long as I must remain a slave, being Mistress's property was preferable to being his. Still, I didn't want to imagine what would become of me if she ever caught him looking at me like that. At the very least she'd sell me, and make sure I went to a place where I'd be used ill. As comforting as the Colonel's understanding might be (and I am ashamed to admit that it was), I prayed he'd never show me that favor again.

Alas, I prayed in vain.

The first lodgings that the Colonel had found for us were in the upper rooms of an old Dutch-style brick house with a sawtooth roof, not far from where he kept his offices. As soon as I climbed the narrow stairs, I understood why most of Mistress's belongings had been left behind at the Hermitage, and why, too, the Colonel had wanted to promise her that things would be better in the future.

These lodgings were more bachelor quarters than a fit home for a married household. There were only three rooms: a parlor with their bed in one corner, and a dining table before the fireplace, a small chamber for the two boys, and another tiny room that they planned to use for dressing and washing, and where the Colonel sat to be shaved each morning by Carlos.

There was a true kitchen in the cellar that the house's owner said was to be shared, if we wished. I felt only disgust when I first visited it and saw all the mouse leavings about the floor and the water puddled around one wall that stank like the nearby privy. To my relief, Mistress shared my reaction, and instead I made do by cooking light meals in one or two pans and skillets on the hearth in their parlor. This suited Mistress and the Colonel well enough. For those first weeks, it seemed they were content to live on coffee, tea, and love.

Carlos and I slept on the floor of the little dressing room, and I made sure each night to place the two spindle-back chairs between us. But to his credit, Carlos seemed to have lost interest in mischief with me, and we settled into a truce, if not a friendship.

I did soon learn, however, that Carlos was shockingly free with his master's business, and shared with me much about the Colonel that I hadn't known. He told me how through his own brilliance, the Colonel had persuaded the state's Supreme Court to let him take the bar exam without the required three-year clerkship, citing his military experience as a substitute. Because a new law had been passed in New York prohibiting any lawyers with Tory sympathies from practice, there'd become a shortage of lawyers, and as soon as the Colonel had first passed his bar exam, and then a second to become a counselor-at-law, he'd seized the advantage for himself.

According to Carlos, the Colonel's intelligence, handsome appearance, diligence, and confidence combined with his heroic record as an officer during the war and his well-respected family had won him both clients and cases. Even with the two clerks he'd hired, he almost had more work than he could handle.

"You can think you're better than me and know everything worth knowing in this house, Mary Emmons," Carlos said with his usual flippancy, "but you'll see soon enough that I'm right. Master's set his sights on becoming a wealthy gentleman and nothing won't deny him."

It was true that the Colonel appeared to be a gentleman of many accomplishments, and well regarded wherever he went in Albany. Still, I could see for myself how modest our lodgings were, and I recalled how he'd worn an old coat to his own wedding. But Carlos assured me that this was all temporary. As soon as the Colonel began to collect the fees he'd earned, he would move us all to a better house.

To my humbling surprise, Carlos's prediction was soon realized. Before the summer was done, the Colonel had moved us all to another and much more agreeable residence. Although not large, this house belonged entirely to our household, and was more removed from the bustle of the docks and other commerce. Also of brick, it had tall windows that overlooked the North River and the green fields on the western banks, a parlor of sufficient size for entertaining guests, two separate bedchambers, and a respectable kitchen.

Mistress quickly set about making this house into a pleasing home. For her, of course, this meant first unpacking her books, but I soon saw other marks of the Colonel's growing prosperity in the new furnishings and carpets that began to appear. He also ordered a Franklin stove for the parlor to be sure that Mistress would be warm in the winter, a stove that the boys immediately turned into a game of daring each other to touch the cast-iron surface.

Mistress had several new gowns made and older ones refashioned to suit the changing fashions, while the Colonel, too, had two new suits for his appearances in court. A fat-cheeked Dutch girl who spoke next to no English was hired to come several days a week for sweeping and laundry, as was a gardener for bringing order to the small walled garden behind the house so that Mistress and the Colonel could dine there. On nights when they decided to entertain, other servants beyond Carlos and me were hired or borrowed, too.

I was surprised to see how much the Colonel trusted Mistress with his business affairs. She was completely at ease in his office, and when he was away from Albany for a trial or other court business she was the one who oversaw the clerks, and answered questions as if she were herself a lawyer. Given her learning and intelligence, this was perhaps not so extraordinary in itself, but few other gentlemen would trust their wives so thoroughly with their affairs of business.

But Mistress performed more expected obligations on his behalf, too. Upon her first arrival in Albany, she called upon the wives of prosperous and important gentlemen, as she and the Colonel had agreed. Many had been away from their city homes for the warmer months, and now that the weather was once again cooler they'd returned. Just as the Colonel worked long hours to better their situation, Mistress now toiled as well, keeping up a stiff schedule of calls, teas, and dinners. She even began attending the North Dutch Church on Sundays, because it was the church that all the oldest and wealthiest Albany families attended.

As can be expected, among the most important of these new duties was calling upon Mrs. General Schuyler and her daughters at The Pastures, the manor house we'd first seen from the river. Because the Colonel wished Mistress to make the very best impression, he had hired her a chaise (for he could not yet afford to keep one of his own) to carry her the mile between our lodgings and The Pastures, and desired me to attend her.

The last time I'd accompanied a lady like that I'd been a child, traipsing along in a jingling collar and gaudy silk costume as Madame's *poupée*. While I wouldn't be expected to kneel on the floor or be petted like a tame monkey, I knew that my purpose remained much the same, to show to all of Albany that Colonel Burr was sufficiently successful at his profession for his wife to keep a mulatto slave to do little more than follow about after his wife.

This time I'd also carry a basket of shortbread biscuits as an offering. They were the Colonel's favorites, and favorites of everyone who tasted them, too, and we'd always had them at the Hermitage. Now I baked them here in Albany, following Chloe's recipe and thinking of her as I did. I knew Mistress would claim that the recipe was hers, and smile proudly when the biscuits were praised, since I'd seen her do it before. But when I creamed the butter and the sugar and the eggs, I knew the truth: they were Chloe's, and now mine as well. Wrapped in a checked cloth, they'd be a fit offering at any house.

Not that Mistress needed biscuits to win her favor. I'd never seen her intimidated, and she wasn't when the chaise drew before the Schuylers' house. It seemed much more imposing, even daunting, than it had from the river, looming before us with two rows of tall, shuttered windows, double chimneys, and an elaborate white-painted balustrade along the roof. Mistress sent me up the steps first to knock at the door and announce her arrival to the manservant who answered. She then swept briskly up the front steps as if she'd every right to be there, while I followed more meekly with the basket.

I was awed, even if she was not. I'd never been inside so fine a house. The center hall alone was the width of most houses, with large doors open at each end to let the summer breezes through. The walls were ornamented with elaborate and costly printed wallpaper showing scenes of fanciful places and creatures, and through the other doorways I glimpsed rooms filled with fine furniture, porcelains, looking glasses, and carpets. I also noticed numerous Negroes at their tasks, another sign of the General's prosperity, just as I was for Mistress. Like me, their clothing was worn and mended many times, proving that the Schuylers' taste for luxury would go only so far, and was not to be shared with those who'd helped create it.

We were shown into a large, sunny parlor with yellow patterned wallpaper, where several well-dressed women looked up expectantly from their needlework when we appeared. Within minutes Mistress had charmed them all with her usual mixture of flattery and wit. She'd always been skilled at judging what manner of conversation suited which company. Here there was none of her usual droll exclamations in French, or reflections on Lord Chesterfield or Voltaire. Instead, she plunged into tales of her two boys like any other fond mother, and how she'd been forced by the war to make so many little economies in her housekeeping, and how her favorite reading was a good book of sermons. I knew Mistress well enough to understand how calculated all this was on her part, but the other women loved it, and therefore loved her.

She took special effort to be agreeable to Mrs. Hamilton, a lively dark-haired young woman with bright eyes and a ready smile. In turn Mrs. Hamilton was eager to converse with her, and tell her how Colonel Hamilton always spoke so well of Colonel Burr and his brilliance in legal matters. Before we left, Colonel Hamilton himself appeared, kissing his wife before he greeted the rest of the ladies, which made them all sigh over what a gallant, doting husband he was.

In some ways, he reminded me of Mistress's husband: both were young and handsome gentlemen who'd kept their military bearing, even as civilians. Where Colonel Burr had dark hair, a commanding gaze, and a certain dignified reserve, Colonel Hamilton's hair was golden red and his close-set eyes were light blue, and he'd the manner of a man too eager to please. Of the two, I preferred Mistress's colonel as being more gentlemanly, as I assumed she did as well.

But I was not prepared for what she said as we rode home together in the chaise.

"I know Colonel Burr calls you a sphinx, Mary, silent but all-seeing," she said. She'd developed a taste for modish large-brimmed hats, and the wired silk flowers on the brim of the one she'd worn today bobbed and trembled with the jostling of the chaise over the cobbled streets. "What did you make of young Mr. and Mrs. Hamilton?"

"They seemed most content with one another, Mistress." I was more interested in learning that the Colonel had called me a sphinx to Mistress.

"They did indeed," she said, smiling at the memory. She conversed freely like this when we were alone together, perhaps because I was the only woman left from her former life, or perhaps because the joy of her second marriage had made her more at ease. I knew better than to mistake her confidences for true friendship, but recognized it for what it was, more a convenience, a diversion, for her.

"It's a pleasure to observe that kind of wedded bliss," she continued. "Though I'm ashamed to admit I've little memory of Colonel Hamilton from the encampment at my house, especially after he praised my hospitality."

I nodded. "There were other matters making demands upon you, Mistress."

She laughed softly. "Yes, there were a plentitude of those," she said. "All those tents, all those men and horses!"

She turned her head to look out the window, her expression turning thoughtful.

"I hope for Mrs. Hamilton's sake that the Colonel did marry her for love, and not opportunity, though there'd be few who'd fault him for it that he did," she said. "Hamilton has no family, no influence, no prospects to speak of. Simply by marrying that sweet creature, however, he now has everything in abundance, and a dear little son in Philip besides. That child is as beautiful as an angel."

She paused, likely remembering her own two boys at the age of the Hamiltons' son.

"Do you know that once a match was considered between Mrs. Hamilton—Miss Schuyler then—and my Burr?" she said, still looking away from me. "It never went beyond the meddlesome hopes of parents and maiden aunts, but ah! For a great family from Connecticut to wed into a great family from New York!"

Absently she rubbed one of the looped ribbons from her hat between her fingers and smiled, but as she gazed through the window her eyes were filled with an odd wistfulness.

"Elizabeth Schuyler would have made Burr's life so much easier," she said softly. "Her very name would have smoothed over every obstacle, and she'd have given him that son that he longs for so much. He'd never once have to explain why he'd chosen her. Yet instead he married me."

From any other lady, this could have been a declaration plumped with pride, or even gloating triumph. But this was more a confession of love, and one tinged with insecurity as well. How much Mistress must love her husband, to wish unselfishly for his sake and betterment that he'd married another.

I remembered what she'd said again later that month. I'd come up the stairs to bring her tea on a tray, along with the letters that had arrived at the house earlier that morning. Because she and the Colonel often kept late hours, it was her habit to begin her day slowly, and after her husband had left for his office or for court she would return to their bed alone, sometimes to read with a cup of tea, sometimes to sleep further. Although her headaches had lessened since we'd come to Albany, her constitution remained delicate, and I believe the further sleep was her way of keeping pace with her more vigorous husband.

But on this morning, when I entered the room, she wasn't in the bed, but huddled on the floor, retching over the chamber pot.

"Oh, Mistress," I said. Swiftly I set the tray on her dressing table, grabbed a fresh handkerchief, and went to crouch beside her on the floor. I slipped my arm around her waist to steady her, and held her until with a final gasping shudder she raised her head.

"That's all," she rasped, leaning back against the frame of the bed with her bare legs and feet splayed awkwardly before her. "There's nothing left for me to puke up, anyway."

I moved the chamber pot to one side. Gently I smoothed her hair back from her forehead, and wiped sweat from her face and lips with the handkerchief. Her skin was pale and waxy, and her breathing labored.

"Come, Mistress, it's chill here on the floor," I said, trying to persuade her. "You're unwell. Let me put you to bed, where you'll be warm."

"I shall be fine in a bit." She struggled to rise, and I slipped my shoulder beneath her arm to lift her up and onto the bed. Although we were of similar height, she'd always been a wisp of a woman, all bones and skin, while I'd the strength that comes from long hours and work.

She didn't fight me now, sinking gratefully against the pillows with a sigh as I drew the coverlet over her, her eyes fluttering shut from the effort. Most likely it was one of her headaches that had made her sick, as they often did.

"I'll send Carlos to fetch the doctor, Mistress," I said, lightly stroking her forehead. "It's best to be sure."

"No!" she exclaimed, her eyes flying open. "I told you I shall be fine."

"But the Colonel would wish it, Mistress," I reasoned. "He'll fault me if I don't."

"He won't if he doesn't learn I was sick." She pushed herself up on her elbows, rising up more from sheer will than true strength. "You see, I'm already feeling better."

"Forgive me, Mistress, but you're not," I said. "You're whiter than that linen."

"Mary, no," she said, dropping back against the pillow. "I'm not ill. This isn't a sickness or complaint. I've been down this same path before, and I recognize the signs."

I frowned. "The signs, Mistress?"

She sighed again, this time with what seemed to be resignation.

"I'm with child, Mary," she said. "Or at least it was this same way with me the other times, with the other babes. It has been a long while."

"Oh, Mistress," I said, feeling foolish for not understanding. Except for my brief time at Belle Vallée, I'd never been in a household with childbearing women; Chloe would have laughed aloud at my ignorance. "The Colonel will be overjoyed."

She grabbed my arm. "You must not tell him, Mary, not yet," she said, her voice edged with desperation. "Not a word! I don't want him so much as to hope until I am certain. If he began dreaming of his son, and I am mistaken, then he would be devastated, and I—I love him too well to do that to him."

She was right. He spoke so often about the children he wanted to have with her that it couldn't be otherwise. And I thought, too, of the children I'd wanted with Lucas, the children I'd now never bear.

"Be easy, Mistress," I said gently. "I will not tell him."

Her hand fell away from my arm, and again she closed her eyes. Beneath the coverlet, I saw the motion of her hand protectively resting on her belly, over that tiny promise of a child. I pitied her, her and the Colonel both. It wasn't so much that they'd no desire for a daughter, but the boys Mistress had borne during her first marriage had been strong and survived, while the two little daughters had been weak and fragile, and perished before their first birthdays.

Even so, there'd be no certainties where Mistress was concerned, and their fondest hopes might yet be misplaced. Childbirth was a hazard to any woman. If she was this weak and ill now, how could she—or her child—withstand the rigors to come?

And yet as ragged as her voice was, there was no mistaking the determination in it.

"I'll give him his son, no matter what it costs me," she said, "and I promise that no child, ever, will be better loved."

CHAPTER 15

Albany
State of New York
June 1783

No matter how much Mistress wished otherwise, a resolute mind cannot overcome the frail body that contains it. From those early days onward, her pregnancy was a difficult one. She had some days, particularly in the middle months, when she felt better, and was able to rise and dress and go about her day's business and the Colonel's as well, and even make calls and receive others, but for much of the last month she remained in her bed.

It had not taken the Colonel long to discover her secret, though I do not know if he guessed it himself or she finally told him. Whichever was the case, he was as proud and happy as could be expected, but also much worried for the health of both his wife and their unborn child. It was all a mystery to him, as it always is for men, and he brought both midwives and physicians to her bed for consultations. It had taken so long for Mistress to agree to marry him, and they'd now been wed for such a short time, that he could not bear the thought of losing her.

But Mistress's entire concern was for the child growing within her, its health and hardiness. Haunted by the two infants she'd lost long before, she was terrified that her inhospitable womb would somehow produce another who was too weak to survive. She heeded every single suggestion that her midwife and the others made, from sipping French brandy and beef-heart broth to wearing two pairs of woolen stockings and a little bag of fragrant herbs tied around her neck.

On days when she was too weary to sit at her desk to compose letters, she'd have me write down her words for her. I read to her, too, though she became impatient when I could not decipher a word, or pronounced it how it looked, rather than how it was written; still, while her pleasure might have been diminished, my reading and my knowledge improved by her corrections, though that was surely not her intention.

The longer Mistress kept to her bed, the mound of her belly growing larger beneath the sheets, the more I began to assume the household's affairs and responsibilities. This had increased with the arrival in late May of Mrs. DeVisme from New Jersey, who intended to remain with her daughter until after the birth. I was sent on errands about the city, to shops and to the market in Mistress's place. I was trusted with both small amounts of money to spend on purchases and the right to sign for credit in the Colonel's name. When we'd first come to Albany, I'd been a cook who'd also served as a lady's maid to Mistress. Now, in addition, I served as housekeeper to Colonel and Mrs. Burr, a significant accomplishment for someone of twenty-four years.

Neither the Colonel nor Mistress said anything of my increasing responsibilities, being so occupied with their own affairs and concerns, nor did it make any real difference in my own situation. It was not a promotion such as a free white servant would have celebrated. I still slept on a pallet on the floor in the attic. I wore the same clothes I always had. I did not receive an increase in wages, for I received no wages at all.

Of course I longed for it to be otherwise, yet I could contrive of no way to make it so. Late at night in the kitchen, Carlos would often pronounce bold statements about running away and freeing himself that way, but he never could answer the most important question: where would he run to?

For a young woman like me, that question had no answer. I'd no friends or family elsewhere to aid me, nor had I the funds to purchase passage on a boat or ship, or otherwise ease my way. The two servants who had fled the Prevost household years before had had each other for companionship, while I'd no one but myself. My appearance was sufficiently unusual that I could never pass unnoticed, or pretend that I was a white woman. A man could enlist in the army, or go to sea, or disappear into the forests to the west, but a woman could not. Instead, there were a thousand grim ways that I could come to harm or be misused by others.

Perhaps that knowledge made me a coward. Perhaps I thought too much of Lucas, and how he'd promised to buy my freedom for me, instead of contriving a way to free myself. But for now, my one hope was that with the final end of war—which was said to be any day now—Congress would finally make good on the words in the Declaration of Independence that "all men are created equal," and banish slavery entirely. Lucas had believed that they would, believed strongly enough that he'd enlisted in the army and given his life for it. I had trusted him, and now must put all that same trust in Congress.

On days when the Colonel was not in court, it was his habit to come home to dine at midday, and then return to his offices and work until early evening or later, depending on his cases. At his request, I usually sent Carlos to his office with some small refreshment to sustain him until he'd come home for supper. On this particular afternoon in June, I couldn't find Carlos, and thus made the short walk myself.

The Colonel kept his offices in a small clapboard building on South Pearl Street. In the front was a large, open room where the clerks toiled at their desks. Bartow and Frederick were among them, taking this first step toward becoming lawyers. It didn't surprise me to see Bartow industriously copying a letter while Frederick gazed out the window, his chin pillowed in his palm, for that was already the difference between the brothers. I hoped Frederick didn't let the Colonel catch him daydreaming. Neither his stepfather nor his mother would be sympathetic to what they'd perceive as his idleness.

Beyond the clerks' room was the Colonel's office, a smaller room with a door for privacy. The clerks scarcely glanced up from their work when I entered, and I made my way, unannounced, between their desks to knock on his door.

The Colonel rose from his desk as soon as I entered: not from respect, but excitement, and trepidation as well.

"Is there news?" he demanded. "Has Mrs. Burr—"

"All is well, sir," I said quickly to reassure him, "and no sign yet of the child."

His dropped back into his chair.

"Thank God." His face relaxed, and he attempted a half-hearted jest. "I know my poor wife wants only to be safely delivered, but I've a sizable case before the state courts tomorrow, and I'd be much obliged if my son would postpone his arrival until the end of the week."

"He'll come when he comes, sir," I said, setting my basket onto the corner of his desk, the only part that wasn't covered with papers. "Both Mrs. DeVisme and the midwives say the same."

"They would know," he said, "and I would not. Nor would Hamilton, who was here earlier with nightmarish tales of his wife's mother's confinements. It is not agreeable to hear of that poor lady delivering triplets—triplets!—when she was the same age as my wife, and then to tell me that the three pitiful infants perished in the process."

"Oh, sir, that is not what you wish to hear!" I exclaimed, horrified that Colonel Hamilton would thoughtlessly repeat such a sad tale. "At present your child is in no such peril, sir, but quick and lively within the womb."

He nodded, looking so solemn that I saw again how much this former officer, known for his courage and boldness in battle, now feared desperately for the sake of his wife and child.

"I'd much rather take your word than Hamilton's, Mary," he said. "Where's that rascal Carlos?"

"Likely he's on some other errand, sir." I suspected that errand was a girl who lived four houses from ours, but I saw no reason to mention that. "I baked this morning, and brought you a raised pie. Ham, onions, and potatoes."

The Colonel smiled with hungry anticipation as I lifted the little pie from the basket, and a bottle of small beer to go with it. Although he had the room's single window open behind him, the office was very warm on this early summer afternoon. He'd taken off his coat and unbuttoned and folded up his shirtsleeves to his elbows. Those bare forearms made me think not of a distinguished jurist, but of a common laborer eyeing the pie as if he hadn't eaten in weeks.

"I thought I was dreaming that delicious fragrance, even before you appeared," he said, clearing a place on the desk before him. "Before we'd come to Albany, I'd believed that the quality of my wife's table was due to Chloe. How mistaken I was!"

"At the Hermitage it *was* Chloe's doing," I said, coming around the desk to set the pewter plate with the pie before him. "I learned much from her."

"Then the fair apprentice has surpassed her master," he said, and looked up at me over the pie.

"You are generous, sir," I said, and swiftly moved back to the other side of the desk. I felt more at ease with a sizable piece of heavy mahogany between us.

Yet in perfect honesty, he had been so delighted and occupied with his new wife since he had moved us all to Albany that he'd apparently forgotten any unfortunate desires he might once have had toward me. That was as it should be between man and wife. I was grateful for his marital contentment, for it had made me feel less guarded in his company.

Still, I'd always found conversing with him to be easier than with Mistress. He liked to speak freely with me, too, so much so that I was astonished once to hear Mrs. DeVisme describe him as tight-lipped. He was not that way with me. He'd always shown me more kindness than any other white person had. He never berated me, or treated me as if I were half-witted, and he'd never once struck me in anger or as punishment.

Little wonder, then, that I was pleased to have in turn pleased him with my cooking. The way he began to tear into the little pie was proof enough of that. He ate with relish, taking large bites and smiling as he chewed, long and slow to savor the flavors. He broke off pieces of the crust with his fingers and swiped them through the sauce that had gathered on the edges of the plate, not wanting so much as a drop to be lost, and he licked his fingers as well, not gentlemanly, but satisfying to watch. For a cook, there was no happier sight.

"I must return to the house, sir," I said at last. "I must begin supper."

"Supper can wait," he said easily, the way he often swept away objections that didn't suit him. "I was planning to visit the shop down the street before they close for the day, and buy Mrs. Burr some pretty trifle to cheer her spirits. You know her tastes. Come with me, and help me decide."

A short time later, I stood with him in the shop of Mrs. Gysbert, a milliner favored by Mistress. He had, of course, once again buttoned the cuffs on his shirt and resumed his coat, the very picture of a prosperous attorney, and the shopkeeper and her assistant were quick to fawn over him. I stood silently to one side with my gaze lowered and my hands clasped before me, as was usual for me while accompanying Mistress into a shop like this one. It wasn't just to appear meek, but also to keep my hands where Mrs. Gysbert could see them, to make it more difficult for her to accuse me of thievery.

"I do have something exceptional, Colonel Burr, a lovely piece that only came into my possession this very morning," Mrs. Gysbert said, leaning a fraction too far across the counter toward him. She was a stylishly dressed woman, as milliners usually were to advertise their trade, with an extravagantly ruffled cap over her auburn hair. "Agatha, you know which piece I mean, the one Captain Evert brought today.

"Evert, eh?" the Colonel said, smiling as the assistant brought a pasteboard box from the back. "Do not tell me you're encouraging smuggling, ma'am."

Mrs. Gysbert sighed deeply, and touched her fingers to her sizable bosom.

"Oh, Colonel, I beg you, do not be cruel to me," she said. "Widows such as I must do what we must. If Captain Evert were to carry goods to me from the Tory shopkeepers in New York who are all a-panic, shopkeepers who will offer the best prices before they must flee with the British army, then that is simply wise business. Ah, here we are."

She opened the box with a flourish, and drew forth a sizable sheer kerchief, deeply edged with lace.

"There now, Colonel Burr," she said, draping it over her arm to display it. "Imagine how this will please your lady! That's the finest French lace, such as the virgins make in French convents."

"Mrs. Burr does admire lace," he said, lightly touching the kerchief. "Mary Emmons, here. What do you make of this lace? Do you think my wife would like it?"

I stepped forward as he'd asked. Smuggled or not, it *was* beautiful lace, stitched along a square of the finest linen, and it reminded me of long-ago pieces that had been in Madame Beauharnais's wardrobe.

"Yes, sir," I said. "It's Alençon lace, of the best quality. Any lady would like it."

"Come, sir, I cannot believe you'd trust your decision to your mulatto girl," said Mrs. Gysbert, almost scolding. "A gentleman of your discernment can judge the quality of the lace for himself. Goodness knows when we'll see lace this fine in Albany again."

His smile hardened in a way I hadn't expected. "Mary served a French lady before my wife," he said. "I'll wager she knows more about that lace than I ever could learn."

I glanced up at him swiftly. He wasn't just defending my right to speak and hold an opinion of my own. He was saying that my opinion was likely better than Mrs. Gysbert's, or his own.

"Forgive me, sir, but I didn't realize she was French trained," the milliner said meekly, scrambling so as not to lose a customer. "No wonder the girl is valuable to you."

"Wrap the kerchief for Mrs. Burr," he said, ignoring the milliner's comments. "You may put it to my account."

"Of course, sir, of course," she said, handing the kerchief to the assistant. She glanced back at me, then at the Colonel. "In that same lot from Captain Evert were a collection of linen short gowns, sir. If you wish to, ah, reward your wench, I daresay they'd suit."

I expected him to ignore this attempt at a further sale, too, but instead he turned toward me.

"Tell me, Mary," the Colonel said. "How long has it been since you'd a new gown or petticoat from Mrs. Burr?"

"Never, sir," I said, the truth. "Colonel Prevost bought me my clothes when I first came to New York, but they were not new."

"Nothing since Prevost?" he said, his brows rising with incredulity. "Well, then it's past time. Mrs. Gysbert, show us your stock."

This time the milliner didn't drape her goods over her arm, but simply put a stack of folded short gowns and bed jackets on the counter.

"Choose one that you like, Mary," he said. "And a petticoat as well, Mrs. Gysbert. Add them both to the tally."

Boldly I reached out to touch the stack of gowns. The linen was coarse and the prints clumsily done, meant only for servants, and the garments themselves were boxy and unfitted to suit a variety of figures. But never in my life had I been the first person to wear anything, and this rare chance to make a choice of my own was nearly overwhelming, as was the Colonel's unexpected generosity.

"You're wise to dress the wench in new colors, Colonel Burr," the milliner said over my head, as if I weren't standing before her. "It's the best way to catch her if she gets it into her head to try to run from you and your wife. Bright clothes to mark down in the advertisement. That's how General Schuyler caught his runaway Negress last fall. Diana, I think it was."

I forgot the clothes before me, and thought instead of Diana of The Pastures. Had I seen her? Had we stood near each other in that grand front hall? I didn't know her by name, but most likely she'd been somewhere nearby when I'd followed Mistress to call upon Mrs. Schuyler.

"They say she hid with a Scotsman for a time," Mrs. Gysbert continued, "but it was her clothes that betrayed her in the end. At least the General was able to sell her south before she tried again, as a lesson to the rest of his lot."

My thoughts raced back to the first runaway notice I'd ever seen, the first I'd read with Lucas, for the Negro wench Hannah, dressed in a coarse blue-and-white chintz gown and a striped petticoat. To Mrs. Gysbert and so many like her, the gaily printed flowers and twisting vines on the garments before me weren't intended to reflect the taste of the wearer, but to mark her as surely as a brand burned into her flesh or the scars left by a whip on her back, and to make her easy to identify and capture if she dared to flee.

I drew back my hand, all my pleasure gone, and bowed my head. None of it was right. None of it was fair.

"Choose, girl," Mrs. Gysbert said impatiently. "Don't keep your master waiting."

Without turning, I could feel the Colonel's questioning gaze upon me. Yet my thoughts were so mired in anger and confusion and disappointment that I couldn't bring myself to speak, fearing what regretful things I might say.

"The blue flowers, then, and the red petticoat," he said, finally speaking for me. "That will be all for today."

He did not speak to me again, nor I to him, as we walked along

Pearl Street and back to his office. I kept several steps behind him, as was expected, and carried his purchases in a paper-wrapped bundle beneath my arm. Yet I was grateful for his silence, even if it meant he was most likely displeased with me. The milliner's words still twisted and turned in my head and in my heart as well, and it was better I suffered them alone.

I do not know why Mrs. Gysbert's offhanded story of Diana had struck me so hard. I'd heard similar histories many times before, always with the same grim ending of capture and punishment. White people never spoke of the servants who ran away and found their freedom.

Yet I needed that reminder that the small liberties I had with the Burrs—the permission to walk alone on errands, or write down my thoughts at night, or taste the food I cooked for seasoning—were at best hollow, and no substitute for the true liberty, true freedom, that might never be mine. It hurt, that reminder, and as I kept pace behind the Colonel along the dusty street I fought to keep back my tears of frustration.

The skies were leaden and darkening early, with thunder rumbling in the distance to the west. People hurried to be home before the storm arrived, and while the Colonel raised his hat to those he knew, he didn't pause to converse. His clerks had shuttered his office for the night and gone home as well, their desks clear, their inkwells stopped, and the books they'd been consulting returned to the shelves. Both rooms were shadowed, with the only light sliding in through the cracks in the shutters.

I followed him back to his office, intending only to gather up the basket and plate that I'd left earlier.

But as soon as we were together in the back room, he wheeled around to face me, his brow as dark as the clouds outside.

"What the devil do you want from me, Mary Emmons?" he demanded. "I have done my best to be civil—more than civil!—to you, and yet still you torment me."

"I, sir?" I exclaimed, my own anger and hurt overruling my better judgment. "What have I done, sir? What could I have done?"

"Did you know Schuyler's wench?" He pulled off his hat and threw it on the desk with an angry thump. "Was that what made you turn so sullen and ill-humored?"

"Would you do the same to me, sir?" I asked, a demand of my own to match his. "Is that your meaning? If I ran, sir, would you chase me down like a beast in the forest, and sell me away as General Schuyler did?"

He shook his head, incredulous that I'd dare speak so to him. "Do not challenge me, Mary."

"You twist my intentions, sir," I said. "I only ask if you would hunt me if I ran."

"You won't," he said bluntly. "You can't. You are too important to my wife."

"No, sir." My voice was now trembling with the weight of so many years of words held back and unsaid, and words that even now I could not find. "No, sir."

He took a step closer. "You know that if you did dare run away, I would find you, and bring you back."

He'd done this to me before, standing too near to remind me of how much larger and more powerful and more important he was than I. Most times I backed away, but this time I was determined I wouldn't. Hidden in the folds of my skirt I clenched my fingers into tense little fists, willing myself to be strong in my own way.

"You belong to my wife, Mary," he continued, another step closer. His voice dropped lower, too, a rough whisper that forced intimacy. "I'd make sure you were returned to her. I would do the same if anything she valued were stolen from her. A necklace, a horse, even a favorite book. I would make sure her property was returned to her."

Even by the half-light of the shuttered room, I saw every detail of his face above mine: how the band of his hat had pressed his hair flat and damp against his forehead, how his jaw was peppered dark by his beard this late in the day, how the sweat glistened on his upper lip. His eyes seemed fathomless, and so focused on me that my very skin seemed to burn beneath his gaze.

"Is that all the worth I am to you, then, sir?" My voice was a whisper now, too, but because I couldn't find the air in my lungs to make it louder. "No more than the value of a misplaced book?"

He didn't answer, which was answer enough. Each second between us stretched longer, but I refused either to retreat or apologize. Not this time, I thought, not again, and if he whipped me for being sullen, then so it would be.

Instead he shoved my straw hat away from my face and my head until it fell backward over my shoulders and to the floor. He covered my shoulders with his hands, not roughly, but tight enough that I could not escape. Then his mouth was on mine, pressing and working back and forth until my lips parted, not from desire, but in a silent, shocked cry that I couldn't hold back. He tasted of tobacco and the onions he'd eaten earlier, enough to make me choke. He moved one hand to the back of my head, his fingers digging into my hair and pulling it free from its pins while his thumb pressed into my nape.

Yet I did not fight him. I know that does not seem right, but it was so: partly from shock, partly from fear of what more he'd do to me if I did, and partly from knowing that I hadn't the right to refuse him. Instead, I stood still and rigid, my hands not touching him, but clenching impotently at my sides. I let him kiss me because I had to, and he was the one who finally broke away.

Yet still he held the back of my head against his palm, his fingers tangled into my hair as he searched my face. I do not know what he sought, either, or what he hoped (or feared) to discover—pleasure, revulsion, misery? My lips stung from the rough stubble of his beard, and my breath came in quick pants of alarm that I couldn't control, no matter how much I wished to.

"You tempt me, Mary Emmons," he said, more to himself than to me. "My God, you tempt me."

The thunder was closer now, rumbling deep.

Abruptly he released me. He stepped back, still watching me as he rubbed his hand across his mouth.

"Get your things," he said, and turned away to gather a small portfolio of papers from his desk.

With shaking fingers, I smoothed my hair as best I could, picked up my hat, and tied it once again over my cap. I stuffed the plate, the bottle, and the napkin into the basket and slung it into the crook of my elbow, and tucked the milliner's package beneath my arm.

Little things, I told myself, *do these little, ordinary things, and forget what has happened.*

"Come," he said, the order one gave to a dog, and I followed him from the office.

The streets were nearly empty now, and the coming storm was sending little whirlwinds of dust and broken leaves skittering around our feet. By the time we reached the house, the first rain-drops were beginning to fall, random and scattered as if thrown from the clouds.

As soon as we stepped inside the front door, Mrs. DeVisme came bustling down the stairs to greet the Colonel.

"Here you are at last, Aaron," she said briskly. "It seems your child has decided to make its arrival on the wings of this storm. Mrs. De Jong is with Theo now. Go to her, sir. She's been asking for you."

He didn't wait, but raced up the stairs to join his wife.

The baby was born fast and determined, a healthy girl with a lusty cry and a thicket of dark hair that could have come from either parent. Mistress's travail was quick and as easy as possible (which was to be expected considering this was her fifth delivery), and though she was exhausted afterward, all was forgotten in her joy.

But it was the Colonel who was instantly and completely in love with his new daughter. He proclaimed that she, too, be named Theodosia, in honor of her mother, his wife. If he were at all disap-pointed that he'd been given a daughter rather than a son, he kept that sentiment buried deep in his breast. To see her in his arms, I believe he was perhaps more happy in a little girl than if she'd been born a boy. To him she was a paragon among all babies, and already extraordinary when her only accomplishment was to blow milky bubbles and spit up upon his shoulder. Even her half brothers, Bart and Frederick, found her endlessly fascinating, and squabbled over who would be next to rock the mahogany cradle that had once shel-tered them, too.

The distraction of the baby also made it easy for me to avoid being alone with the Colonel. In that first month, the house was filled with well-wishers bringing gifts and drinking toasts until at last Mrs. DeVisme put an end to it, fearing for the health of both her daughter and granddaughter from too much celebration. The Colonel purchased a nursemaid named Ginny, carefully selected by

Mistress and Mrs. De Jong, whose sole purpose was to look after the new baby and launder her clouts and clothes. She was a dark-skinned, quiet woman who seemed to have limitless knowledge about babies, and the ability to calm a fretful child with a gentle touch and a handful of African words. The Colonel returned to his office and court cases and the boys with him, Mistress recovered from her confinement and delighted in her new daughter, Mrs. De-Visme traveled back to New Jersey and her youngest daughter, Mrs. Browne, and the household found its way back to its usual rhythm.

Or at least Mistress believed it to be so. The Colonel and I knew otherwise, with things as restless and uneasy as a stormy sea between us. What had happened in his office the day of his daughter's birth could be neither undone nor forgotten, though I did try to do so.

But one morning as I brought breakfast to Mistress and the Colonel, it was Mistress herself who unwittingly made things impossible to ignore any longer. From his severe attire, he must have been appearing in court that day. He was dressed in a well-tailored black suit and his linen shirt was snowy and immaculately pressed, as he insisted it be. His only ornament came from his favorite shirt brooch, a golden snake knotted back on itself with a tiny pearl in its jaws.

Although Mistress had come to join him at the table, she still wore her dressing gown, and likely her night shift beneath. Around her neck was looped the lace-edged kerchief that he'd bought with me. He'd given it to her in honor of the joyful birth, and because she loved him, she'd found an excuse to wear the kerchief nearly every day.

"Mary, I am disappointed," she said to me as I poured her tea. "My husband told me that some time ago he generously bought you a pretty new short gown and petticoat from Mrs. Gysbert, but I've yet to see you wear either one."

I flushed, and fought the urge to glance at the Colonel. Instead, I lied.

"Forgive me, Mistress," I said. "But the new clothes seemed too fine for everyday. I've put them aside for special."

The truth was that every time I saw the new garments, folded beside my older clothes, I was filled with so many difficult thoughts and memories from that afternoon that I could not make myself put them upon my body.

"I do not know what can be more special than a new baby in the family," Mistress said, tipping a spoon of sugar into her tea. "Besides, it's ungrateful of you not to wear what has been given you. When we dine later this day, I'll expect to see you dressed in the new clothes."

"Yes, Mistress," I murmured. In this as in so many things, I had no choice. Doubtless I'd be made to parade about in a display of gratitude, too.

From upstairs came the wail of the baby, unhappy over some indignity, and at once Mistress set down her tea, her chin raised as she listened.

"It is nothing, my dear," the Colonel said. "You've said yourself that babies cry over everything and nothing."

"But when I left her, Aaron, she was sleeping as peacefully as could be," she said. "Something must have upset her."

"Ginny is with her, Theo," the Colonel said. "She's not alone. Now finish your tea."

"I'll only be a moment." She pushed back her chair and hurried upstairs, her backless slippers slapping on the steps.

And for the first time in weeks, I was alone with the Colonel.

I leaned forward to gather up Mistress's empty plate, hoping to use that as an excuse to retreat to the kitchen. I wasn't fast enough. He caught my arm as I reached across the table, holding me fast so I couldn't escape.

"Mary Emmons," he said softly. "You've avoided me."

"No, sir," I said, another necessary lie. "I've had many tasks that have kept me busy, sir."

"You know I have missed you," he said, his fingers tightening the slightest amount to reinforce his words. "Our conversations, your thoughts. I miss them."

"I am sorry, sir." There'd been a time when I would have said the same of him. No longer. I tried to slip my arm free of his hand, but he held it too firmly. "Sir, if Mistress were to—"

"Shush," he said. "She won't. But here, as proof of how much I trust you."

He released my arm and sat back in his chair, his gaze never leaving my face. This was all a game to him. So why didn't he understand that it was I who didn't trust him, and not the other way around?

Finally I picked up the plate in both hands, but uncertainty made me linger.

He smiled slowly, and too late I realized that by my staying he'd won some small victory.

"Did you not like the clothes I chose for you, Mary Emmons?" he asked. "I thought the color and pattern would please you, but then I should know better than to presume a woman's taste. Is that why you haven't worn them?"

"They pleased me well enough, sir." Another lie, so many for so early in the morning.

This one, however, he recognized for the defense that it was, and looked down at the tablecloth and away from me. His smile had shifted into a wry twist. In many ways we did understand each other, and had from the beginning.

"I'm sorry for what occurred, Mary Emmons," he said, and his voice did indeed sound regretful. "I was wrong to . . . succumb. It shall not happen again. Now go, if you wish to. I won't keep you here against your will."

I did wish it, and fled back to the kitchen. There I considered further what he'd said. He'd offered as much of an apology as I'd likely ever receive from him. But in some fashion he seemed to believe it had been my fault that he'd kissed me, which couldn't have been more cruelly wrong.

Or was it? I reminded myself how, by trade and education, he was a counselor-at-law, and skilled at persuasion and argument. He knew how to parse the finest meaning from every word. Yet had I through my words or actions somehow indicated that I'd welcome his attentions, and encourage his adultery? How could I, through no conscious act, sway such a guileful and intelligent gentleman? Had my loneliness and longing betrayed me, and acted as a beacon to him? I doubted his apology, yes, but I doubted myself more.

He kept his word for another month or so, until one night when he'd returned late from a case in a district court. The rest of the household had retired, and I alone remained awake, putting the last of the kitchen to rights. As I took his coat and hat, he told me he was hungry, but refused the ceremony of the parlor, and instead came downstairs to sit at my rough kitchen table. I fried eggs for him with grilled ham and buttered bread, as simple as could be, and exactly what he wished after a long journey. We conversed most amiably of both politics and his daughter. I liked cooking for him in this manner, with the eggs sizzling hot in the ham's fragrant fat as they slipped directly onto the plate before him, and I liked seeing the contentment I could bring him as he ate. He praised my cooking, and my cleverness.

But afterward he pulled me onto his lap, the muscles of his thighs hard beneath my bottom and his arm like an iron band around my waist. He kissed me longer this time, with more leisure and traitorous care, as if he wished me to find equal pleasure in it. This time, too, he fondled my breasts, his hand deftly finding its way into my bodice to my flesh.

When he finally left and went upstairs, I sat by the dying fire and wept over my shame, clutching the little heart-shaped pendant that Lucas had made for me in my fingers. I'd loved my husband by the light of a kitchen fire, and now, in a place that had always felt most my own, I'd let another man hold me and touch me and kiss me.

A week later, while Mistress was playing her fortepiano in the parlor, the Colonel passed me on the stairs. He crowded against me, drew me to one side, and kissed me quickly, then patted one finger against my lips, as if to say it must be our secret. He continued down the stairs toward the music and his wife, while my heart raced so fast in my chest that I could scarcely climb to the landing.

After that, he left me alone for the better part of the next two years. I know that sounds extraordinary for a gentleman of his appetites, but he'd his reasons, and reasons that had little to do with me.

When the British army had finally evacuated the city of New York at the end of 1783, the Colonel had wasted no time in removing his family from Albany to Manhattan Island. He'd spoken excitedly of the opportunities that were waiting for those who dared seize them, and Mistress had agreed, even to shifting a household with a baby in the middle of December.

I'd only visited New York once before, when I'd been brought there by Colonel Prevost over ten years ago. I'd been so overwhelmed, and my grasp of English still so uncertain, that my memories of the place were jumbled at best. But I did recall a fine city, with many grand homes, gardens, churches, and other public buildings, and docks bristling with the masts of seagoing vessels.

No more. Years of war and occupation plus two calamitous fires had sadly reduced that once-fine New York I remembered. Much of the current city lay in ruins, with empty lots, broken-down walls, and pools of stagnant, standing water in the streets and open cellars. The docks were rotting from disuse, and every last twig of trees, gardens, and fences had long ago been cut or pulled apart for firewood.

The fortunes of war had claimed much of the citizenry, too. The majority of the gentry and merchants, doctors, and lawyers had been Tories, and had fled with their families to Nova Scotia or London when the British army had abandoned the city. Shops and trades with Tory leanings had been looted and burned. Even many of those bound by slavery had vanished, promised freedom in Canada by the British. The gaps all these people had left in the city were every bit as noticeable as the yawning, empty lots where houses had once stood.

This was the city that Mistress saw when we arrived on a late afternoon in the last week of December, in the midst of a storm of sleet and with a tender baby fretful from teething. Although larger and finer than the lodgings we'd left in Albany, this new house that the Colonel had let for us on Wall Street was cold and dark and inhospitable, the front steps glazed with ice and the woodbox empty. When at last we'd managed to light fires, the chimneys had smoked from disuse, making for such an inauspicious beginning that not even Mistress could hide her disappointment and discouragement.

Fortunately it did not take long for her to realize how wise the Colonel had been to seize the opportunity the city presented to a gentleman of his profession. New York was filled with people turning to the courts and law for order and for compensation for property lost or destroyed by the war. Yet because the Tory lawyers (who had formed the largest number of the city's jurists) were now prohibited by state law from practicing their profession, there was a shortage of lawyers to handle the cases, and Whig lawyers were in constant demand. Within months, the three busiest and most prosperous counselors were the same three gentlemen who'd studied together in Albany, and then made the short voyage down the North River: Colonel Alexander Hamilton, Colonel Robert Troup, and, of course, Colonel Burr.

As a result, the Colonel kept long hours, and was often away from home. This meant he was often away from me as well, for which I was most grateful.

But that wasn't all. His daughter, Theo, was not a strong infant and was often ill with mysterious fevers and other ailments, sometimes so perilously that her parents despaired for her life. Mistress had always been an ardent member of her church, and when her little babe was threatened she turned further to the solace of her faith, and often persuaded her husband to join her.

No gentleman who reads his Scripture will find in its pages an excuse for embracing his servant, and I suspected this was the case with the Colonel, especially when Mistress gave birth to a second daughter on the twentieth of June 1785, the day before little Miss Burr's second birthday. This new babe was named Miss Sarah, or Sally, after the Colonel's sister, and was so hearty that her parents rejoiced.

To my considerable relief, during this time there was nothing untoward in the Colonel's manner when he spoke to me, and he made no more attempts to embrace me against my will when I was alone with him. Instead, he gave every appearance of devoting himself entirely to his wife and daughters, and expending all his other energies upon his practice.

But inevitably his contentment did not last, and late in 1786 he began to seek me again.

Mistress's sister, Mrs. Browne, and Mrs. DeVisme were visiting through Twelfth Night, and the three of them had taken the children with Ginny in the carriage to drive along the Battery. I was making up Mrs. Browne's bed, tucking in the sheets and smoothing the pillow biers, when the Colonel appeared in the doorway. Because I'd lost my reason to mistrust him, I thought nothing of it. He watched me briefly at my work, with idle talk of whether or not there'd be snow that night. Then with a suddenness I hadn't expected, he called me a temptress, and pushed me backward onto the bed. Swiftly he lay upon me to kiss me, his weight pressing me down into the feather bed and making the rope springs creak beneath us.

I'd never lain upon a bed before, nor had a man lie atop me, either. The bed was as soft as I imagined clouds to be, while the Colonel's body was hard and heavy and oppressive, even with the layers of our clothes between us. He stroked my cheek with his hand and called me beautiful to calm me, and kissed me again. From fear I whimpered into his mouth and tried to wriggle free, away from him and all that feathery softness beneath me. My resistance seemed to be enough to make him at last leave me, and I thanked God for my deliverance.

Of course my salvation would not last. The following week, he found me alone again when Mistress was out, and again, and again, and again after that. His persistence, his persuasion, his sheer strength, slowly wore away at my defenses, until what I let him do—what we did—became my private shame and sorrow. I'd no one to tell, no mother or sisters or friends to offer counsel. I longed for the companionship of Chloe, long parted from my life. We were now five servants in this house, and I was the most senior among them. I could not confide in any of the others, nor was there any question of going to Mistress. To make it worse, if such a thing were possible, Mistress was once again great with child, her third.

Even on Sundays, when I sat in the upper benches of Trinity Church among the Negro servants from other houses, what I heard in Scripture and in sermons only served to deepen my guilt and wretchedness. Among these Christians, there were but two kinds of women: the ones who were good and faithful wives, daughters, and mothers, and the ones who were not, and who through their wantonness and sin hurt the good women and their families.

If I leaned forward on the bench and looked past the shoulders of the other servants around me, I could see the heads of Mistress and the Colonel in their pew below me, listening to the same words that so tormented me. I wondered if those words ever eat at the Colonel's conscience. Did they ever gnaw into his sleep at night as they did to mine, or did he persuade himself that he was blameless, faultless, without the guilt that so plagued me?

And each day when I saw little Miss Burr at her first lessons or baby Miss Sally in her cradle, both smiling in their innocence and secure in the love of their parents, I thought of how their father sinfully desired me, and the disaster my very presence could bring to the sanctity of their family.

I envied them the sweet luxury of that childish innocence, a luxury that I doubted I'd ever possessed. In its place, I had the harsh knowledge that came from the world and the men who ruled it. I knew it was only a matter of time before the Colonel would cease to be content with kisses and fondles, just as I knew I'd be powerless to deny him when he did.

He'd called me beautiful and beguiling and tempting, a sorceress and a sphinx, but most often he called me clever, the single compliment I believed. It was the one that mattered most to me, too, because only through my cleverness was I going to find a way to save myself.

CHAPTER 16

City of New York
State of New York
December 1786

I dipped the small ladle into the sauce, tasted it, and frowned. My frown wasn't for the sauce, which was exactly as Mrs. Glasse, the cook whose recipe it was, had intended it to be: rich and thick with two pints of cream, onions, the juice of four lemons, and a quantity of butter bathing the fricassee of four chickens, exactly as it should be. If that had been all, then it would have been a fine dish, such as would please any cook to serve, and please the lady who offered it to her guests.

But it was the recipe's seasonings that made me frown with dismay, even disgust. Mrs. Glasse believed that with the simple additions of two ounces of turmeric and a large spoonful of raw chopped gingerroot to the cream, the dish now had a right to be called a "Curry Made in the Indian Way." I could have told her that it most assuredly wasn't. There was none of the subtlety or delicacy of carefully toasted, ground, and blended spices that was to be found in a true Indian curry. This was coarse and common and *English.* I hated to think what Orianne with her treasured *masala dabba* would have said had she seen this dish, an unappealing glowing yellow from a surfeit of turmeric.

But this was the recipe that Mistress, determined to impress her guests, had chosen for this night's dinner. It was a special dinner, too, the first in yet another new house. This one was their fifth home in the course of their short marriage, and though we were scarcely settled here in Cedar Street (formerly Little Queen Street, for even streets had changed their allegiance once the British had left), I'd already overheard Mistress and the Colonel discussing another, even larger house that the Colonel was considering on Broadway. Yet that seemed to be the way here in the City of New York, and of New Yorkers in general. No one was content to remain as they were, and everything was in a constant state of change and improvement.

Mistress had told us servants that this was a dinner for three old friends, now colleagues, and their wives. These gentlemen had all served with distinction in the Continental Army, and all attained the rank of Lieutenant Colonel. Colonel Troup was one of Colonel Burr's oldest and dearest acquaintances, but the same could be said also of Colonel Hamilton, since he and Colonel Troup had shared lodgings together when they'd both studied at King's College. Their wives called upon one another, their children played together, and their houses all stood within a few blocks of one another.

While there was friendship among the three, however, there was a certain rivalry as well. It was not so great with Colonel Troup, stout and pop-eyed, who seemed by nature too mild for such competition. Between Colonel Hamilton and Colonel Burr, however, the rivalry crackled: not only when they were in the courtroom together, as often happened, but outside of it, too. Even we servants knew of it. Carlos was quick to report to us in the kitchen whenever his master bested Colonel Hamilton in a case, or in some drollery at a tavern afterward, often recounting these tales with such unseemly glee that I had to shush him.

There were many triumphs for Carlos to recount, too. It was no secret that while the Colonel was willing to drive himself so that Mistress fretted for his health, he was practical (some would say cynical) in his choice of that labor. He was not an idealist, like Colonel Hamilton. Instead Colonel Burr never accepted a case that he wasn't confident he'd win, for the simple reason that he hated to lose.

Even this dinner would be cause for competition. Originally the Burrs and the Hamiltons had both lived in similar houses near to each other on Wall Street, but this new house of the Burrs was significantly larger and better appointed. There was a separate room for dining, and the Colonel and Mistress, too, were particularly proud of having a library for their ever-growing collection of books.

Nor did the contests between the two men end there. They strove to outdo each other in the importance of their cases and clients, in the length of the hours each worked, and in their horses and equipages. With the encouragement of General Alexander McDougall, his old supporter and commander from the war now turned politician, Colonel Burr had recently completed his second term as a representative in the State Assembly for New York County, while Colonel Hamilton had only just been elected to the same position. Their rivalries extended over the infant brilliance of their children, too: Theodosia Burr, aged three, was already reading and beginning to write, while at five years of age Philip Hamilton was being taught the rudiments of Latin and Greek, or so his father claimed. Even this hideous English curry would be considered part of their competition, a dish both fashionable, exotic, and costly, on account of the imported turmeric and ginger.

I carefully took the chicken from the kettle and arranged it with a frill of parsley upon Mistress's best porcelain platter, painted with orange dragons and rimmed with gold. The other dishes for the meal had previously been carried to the table, and it was now up to me to appear, triumphant, with the curry. Mistress had been most specific about that. It wasn't necessary for her to explain why. By now I'd a perfect understanding of her reasoning. What could be more impressive before guests than having your curry prepared by a cook brought from India?

I smoothed my apron and tucked a few stray wisps of hair back beneath my cap. With additional servants in our household, I seldom served at table now, and remained in the kitchen to oversee the cooking and other preparations instead. I preferred this, though I did miss being able to overhear the conversations during meals. Mistress and the Colonel had always spoken freely before us, and this was often the one sure way to learn what was next for them, and therefore the rest of us as well.

Who knew what I might learn tonight? I carried the platter to the dining room, holding it out before me like the prize that Mistress considered it to be.

"Ah, at last! Here's our true Indian curry," she announced as soon as I appeared in the doorway. Smiling proudly, she patted the corner of the table beside her to show where she wished me to place the dish. The dinner must be going well, for she looked happy and at ease in her emerald-green silk, her left hand resting protectively on the great swell of her belly. She wore the amber earrings that the Colonel had given her for her last birthday, the golden drops gleaming like honey in the candlelight as they swung against her cheeks.

"I don't believe you'll have a more correct curry anywhere in New York," she continued, "thanks to our cook having been born in Calcutta."

There was a polite murmur of admiration from the guests to this long-standing untruth, and one I'd long ago ceased trying to correct, or worrying over, either. Mistress motioned for me to remain standing beside her chair instead of retreating back to the kitchen. Clearly I was going to be displayed among the Burrs' other possessions tonight.

"Mary Emmons is far more than an exemplary cook," the Colonel said, playing the perfect, expansive host as he leaned back in his armchair. It was a role he relished, and played well. He was flushed, as were the other gentlemen, proof that the wine—expensive, imported wine—had been flowing already, and that Tom, another servant standing nearby, had been busy refilling the glasses as the Colonel liked him to do. Yet I knew that he would not drink to excess; unwilling to give any advantage to another, he never did.

"She is a veritable marvel," Colonel Burr continued, smiling warmly at me. "She reads anything you set before her, and writes a far better hand than yours, Troup. She ciphers. And she speaks French worthy of an invitation to Versailles."

Colonel Hamilton leaned forward to study me more closely, close enough that I in turn could see the light freckles that crossed his pronounced nose and jaw. Because his gaze lacked the intensity of Colonel Burr's, it was no trial for me to withstand his scrutiny, even as his gaze slid from my face to my breasts.

"*Est-ce vrai, ma chère jolie créature?*" he asked me. "*Tu parles français?*"

I doubted his wife spoke French, for her expression as she sat beside him didn't change when he called me his dear pretty creature, though Mistress, who did, arched a single, bemused brow.

"*Oui, honoré monsieur,*" I said, proof enough of my fluency.

"She speaks heathen Eastern tongues as well," Mistress said. "Address us in Hindoo, Mary."

I nodded, having suffered this request to perform from her before. Over time I'd contrived a small revenge. Because I knew that I was likely the only person in all New York to speak Tamil, I called them a foolish pack of babbling jackals in that language, adding a little curtsey at the end as an extra flourish. I shouldn't have done it, but I did, and my smile afterward perhaps held more satisfaction than it should have, too.

"The wench is a marvel, Burr, exactly as you say," Colonel Hamilton declared. "What is her price?"

At once Mrs. Hamilton seized his arm and glowered at him in silent, wifely warning. While her family in Albany had possessed many Negroes, I'd noted that when I'd accompanied Mistress to call upon the Hamiltons here in Manhattan their servants had all been white Dutch and English girls, though I cannot say if this was from choice, or economy.

"Her price would be more than you could afford, Hamilton," said Colonel Burr, a measure of indulgence to his words. "Besides, Mary belongs to Theo, not to me. A long-ago gift from her first husband, and one I doubt she'll wish to part with, for sentimental reasons. Isn't that so, my dear?"

"Don't even make such a jest, Aaron," Mistress scolded with mock dismay. "I could never bring myself to sell Mary, no matter what was offered for her."

He tipped his head back and laughed, his white teeth flashing. But I found no humor in either his jest or her response, nor in the way that the rest of the party laughed with him, as if it all were the greatest cleverness and wit.

Only Colonel Troup did not. "It's a damned shame that any accomplished woman, mulatto or not, must wear the shackles of slavery," he said earnestly. "This country will never become the power it could be so long as useful persons are not given rights and freedoms equal to ours."

"I don't see you freeing your slaves, Troup," Colonel Burr said in the same jovial manner as before. "If you expect others to follow, friend, you must be willing to lead the way."

"That should be the role of the federal government," Colonel Troup said, helping himself to a sizable serving of the curry. "Until then, however, there should be a thoughtful discussion among citizens that leads to manumission in place of abolition. That is the entire purpose of the Society, as you know."

"It should better be the entire purpose, when you've called it the New York Manumission Society," Colonel Hamilton said as he took the platter and courteously served his wife first. "But considering how at the present time there is no federal government with any teeth to it, I would venture that your thoughtful discourse will continue for years without much result."

"Congress will never abolish slavery," Colonel Burr declared firmly. "The Virginians and their ilk to the south will not permit it. They'd be ruined."

I listened, hearing them make light of these hard and ugly truths. I'd heard it before, many times, yet the bitterness never faded. Had they forgotten I was standing there beside Mistress's chair, and Tom at the sideboard? Did they think Tom and I were deaf as well as mute by their will, unable to hear what was said without their permission?

And what of the dream I'd held on to for so long, my husband's dream, that the war and this country would bring freedom to everyone in it? I'd come to see that I and all others like me had been told the greatest lie imaginable, a lie I'd treasured and believed, a lie that now crushed both my hopes and my future.

"It would be a loss to you, Burr, as well as many other households and trades here in New York," Colonel Troup said. "How many servants do you keep? Three, four? Why, this wench here must be worth several hundred dollars alone."

This wench. Earlier he'd praised me. He'd heard my name, too. But now I was no more than another piece of valuable property.

"We were discussing a general emancipation, Troup," Colonel Burr said easily, "and not the condition of my private household. But manumission will be the most palatable solution to the most people. A choice is always preferred to legal force."

"Perhaps," Mistress said, for she'd never been afraid to venture into gentlemen's conversations. "But what of that old woman that your brother Tapping helped Sedgewick represent? I recall she herself sued for her freedom based simply upon the state's constitution, and won. Tidy work, that."

"Yes, yes, *Brom and Bett versus Ashley*. A legal exercise, Theo, no more," Colonel Burr said, all mild weariness as he waved for more wine. "You know how Tapping likes a challenge, and Theodore Sedgewick is an out-and-out abolitionist who needed every bit of Tapping's assistance to win his point. Nor was the suit as cut-and-dried as Sedgewick now makes it out to be. After the ruling, the Negress named in the suit was asked by her owner to return to her old place to labor for wages."

"Your sister told me she refused," Mistress said. "Sally said she took to calling herself Elizabeth Freeman, and went her own way, and no one knew what to make of her after that."

"Then there you are," Colonel Burr said, as if Mistress's small-minded comment had proved anything. "But yes, old Bett did sue—or rather, Reeve and Sedgewick did on her behalf—and the court awarded her freedom to her."

From the deepest misery, my spirits now rose to incredible heights. I lived beneath a lawyer's roof. How had I never heard of this decision before? That the Colonel's own brother-in-law had been party to such a momentous decision? I longed to know more of the woman who'd called herself Elizabeth Freeman—*Free*-man!— and learn more of her struggles, more of her daring and courage and how hard she must have fought for her freedom.

Colonel Troup nodded, his full chin quivering with argument.

"'All men are born free and equal' is a powerful constitutional provision, Burr," he said, "and drawn as it was from the national Declaration, it could set an equally powerful precedent."

"It could, but it won't," Colonel Hamilton said, his voice rising as if he, too, were in court. "Decisions made by the Massachusetts Supreme Court will not hold so much as a single drop of water anywhere else. Massachusetts means nothing to Virginia, or Carolina, or Georgia."

"Or New York," said Colonel Burr. "Perhaps most especially New York. You recall how ineffectual my own attempts were in that arena, and how it has soured me forever on the idle game of politics."

"You will never give up politics, Burr," scoffed Colonel Hamilton. "You like the power too well to abandon it."

Colonel Burr smiled again. "I should like it a great deal better if there were more money in it, sufficient for a gentleman to support himself."

Irritated for reasons I'd no knowledge of, Colonel Hamilton leaned forward.

"From what I've heard, Burr, you did indeed manage to derive a certain profit from the office for peddling influence and favors," he said. "At least more than most gentlemen would deem agreeable."

"Tales, Hamilton, idle tales," Colonel Burr said expansively, refusing to acknowledge whatever insult the other man was hinting at. "To be so wonderfully noble, these whispering gentlemen of yours must not live here in New York, and therefore have no sense of the expense of everything from hay and oats onward."

"Because New York is the apex of all that is fine and glorious in not only this country, but the entire world," Mistress declared, raising her chin a fraction higher so she'd be seen over the candlesticks by her husband at the other end of the table. "*Fais moi plaisir,* Aaron, I beg of you, no more politics or law while we dine. All of us ladies here revere Justice as much as, or more so, you gentlemen do, but might we please give her peace this one night, and turn to other topics?"

Colonel Burr smiled to her, a genuine smile, and nodded, conceding with a gracious sweep of his hand.

"My only wish is to please you, *ma chérie,*" he said. "Consider all legal matters banished before the ladies. Here's a topic that will surely be more agreeable to you: I heard this day that there are plans to rebuild the old theater on Beekman, and in time for a proper season in the spring, too."

"I thank you, Your Lordship," Mistress said, teasing him with that title as she often did to make him smile. He did in fact smile, as did the other ladies, and the conversation moved on to actors and plays and other follies, and away from what I wished most desperately to hear.

"What did you make of all that, Mary Emmons?" asked Tom

excitedly when we were both again in the kitchen, and out of the hearing of the Burrs and their guests. "Could we go to court and make ourselves free, too, just like they said that old woman in Massachusetts did?"

"I do not know, Tom," I said with care, not wishing to encourage him falsely. "Lawyers like the Colonel earn their fees by twisting words and meanings into knots."

"But you'll find the truth," he said confidently. "You'll find it, and tell us all."

He nodded, trusting me more than he should. I'd never set out to be a leader or a pathfinder, but because I could read and write and speak as well as many of the white people I served, I'd had that role pushed upon me against my will, like another's cloak draped over my shoulders.

It wasn't only the servants—Carlos, Ginny, Ben, and Celia— who lived in our house, but others in our neighborhood also came to ask me to write letters for them, or read papers, or help them to learn their letters, as Lucas had once helped me. Because of this, and because I was by nature reserved, with a goodly measure of white blood apparent in my color and features, I was credited with more knowledge than I believe I possessed. I'd never yet known a lasting love, or given birth to a child to hold like a treasure in my arms, the things that gave women true wisdom. Yet people will believe what they want, and I did my best to help however I could.

When I told Tom that I would try to learn more about Elizabeth Freeman's case and where it might lead for the rest of us, I'd every intention of doing so. My conscience wouldn't let me do otherwise.

I also knew where that hunt would lead me personally, and how very difficult, even hazardous, it could prove to be. But for a chance to seize my freedom, I would do it. I'd do it.

The following morning, I stood before the closed door of the Colonel's library. I'd no right to be there, since my orders came only from Mistress. This was the Colonel's room, his solitary place that not only held his books and papers, but also served as his office and his retreat, here in the back of the house where it was most quiet. The only time I came into this room was to make certain that Celia had swept and cleaned the grate as she should, and even so, I'd taken care never to send her to do so when there was any chance the Colonel would be there, too, to spare her what had happened to me.

Still I hesitated, unable to bring myself to knock. I knew the Colonel was within. Because he wasn't expected in court today, he hadn't left for his office yet, though Frederick and Bartow had gone ahead. Earlier Carlos had brought the Colonel his coffee, letters, and newspapers, while Mistress was still abed upstairs. She'd only a matter of weeks left until her time, and often slept later because of it.

Once I entered the Colonel's library, we'd be together, the two of us and no one else. It had to be like that if I wished to remind him of the old days in Albany and at the Hermitage, when he'd speak to me almost as a friend would. We hadn't conversed with that ease since he'd moved us to this house.

I took a deep breath, and rapped my knuckles on the frame of the door.

"What in blazes do you want, Carlos?" he called irritably.

Another deep breath. "It's not Carlos, sir. It's Mary."

I heard the squeak of his chair as he rose, and his footsteps as he came striding across the room to open the door himself, and then there he was.

"Why, Mary Emmons," he said, clearly surprised. "Is all well? Is my wife—"

"Mistress is still asleep, sir," I said quickly. "If you please, sir, I wish to speak to you myself."

He opened the door wider for me to enter, and I slipped inside. Then he closed it after me, the latch clicking into place and signifying to me that I was, by my own choice, now alone with him.

"Here, Mary, sit," he said, solicitously offering me a chair. He was already dressed in his breeches, shirt, and waistcoat in preparation for the day, but over them he wore a long banyan of quilted blue silk. This was left open, as was his shirt, still unfastened at the throat. Now I was accustomed to seeing both of the Burrs in various undress. Like all body servants, I knew their most personal secrets, from how often they changed their linen, to when Mistress had her courses, to which nights they lay together as husband and wife, but for some reason this morning the glimpse of his bare chest and the dark curling hair upon it unsettled me.

"Thank you, sir, but I'd prefer to stand," I said as briskly as I could. "What I wish to say shall not take long."

He smiled. "You intrigue me," he said, returning to his own chair behind the broad mahogany table that he used here as his desk. I was grateful to have it between us.

"Before you begin," he continued, "I'd like to tell you again how much I enjoyed your curry dish last night. It was unlike anything else I've ever eaten, yet I cannot stop thinking of it."

"I can do better, sir," I said promptly. "Mistress desired me to follow the English recipe in the cookery book, but it made for a poor sort of curry, and not what is enjoyed in India."

He nodded, considering. "You have a recipe that you prefer?"

"I do, sir," I said, and tapped my chest. "It's not written or printed in a cookery book, but learned and saved here, within me."

"What better place to store what's most dear, yes?" he said. "Would you be willing to prepare it for me?"

For me: not *for my guests,* or even *for my wife and me.*

Just *for me.*

"I do not know if all the spices I'd require might be purchased here in New York, sir," I said, avoiding his request.

"Oh, Mary, everything is for sale in New York," he said. "Seek out a grocer near the docks. You have my leave to buy whatever you require, so that you may make me your best, proper, Indian-style curry."

"Thank you, sir," I murmured. I was frustrated by how I'd wandered so far from my original purpose, and worse, that he could do that to me. "Forgive me, sir, but I—I'd more to say than that."

"More, Mary Emmons?" he asked, his manner teasing in a way that only served to frustrate me further.

"Yes, sir." None of this was easy for me. I was determined to speak as plainly as I could, but if irritation gave an edge to my plain words, then so be it. "Last night you spoke of Elizabeth Freeman, sir. You spoke of how she won her own freedom in a court of law."

Instantly his expression became serious, and his voice with it.

"Then you also learned from me that the case was heard in the state of Massachusetts," he said, "where laws and precedents are entirely different than from here in New York."

I'd expected him to say that, and I was ready with my reply.

"Yes, sir, I did," I said. "I heard as well that you'd little use for Mr. Sedgewick as an attorney. Surely you are much his superior, sir. Surely your learning and experience would make up for those different laws here in New York."

He frowned a bit, his dark brows drawing together as he listened, and in a different way than he usually did. This time, it was not my form or face that drew his eye, but my resolve, and it gave me fresh courage.

"I begin to see your purpose," he said slowly. "You wish me to present a similar suit."

"I do, sir," I said bravely. "I would pay you, too, sir. Ever since we were in Albany, I've sewn for others, and put what I earned aside toward buying my freedom. This would be the same, sir, and every penny spent well if you will but accept my case."

He shook his head. "I wouldn't take your money."

"Forgive me, sir, but I'd want you to," I said, "so everything would be fair between us."

"That's not what I meant," he said bluntly. "You could stitch shirts on Sundays for the rest of your life and not begin to equal my fee."

That stung, but still I wouldn't give up.

"It's what I have, sir," I persisted, my voice rising. "And once I've secured my freedom, I'll earn wages, good wages, on account of all I can do. I can pay you more then, sir, for years and years, if that's what it shall take."

"You must have heard only part of what I said last night," he said in that same direct, almost harsh fashion. "I sat in the state legislature, Mary. The question of abolition is frequently raised, and I can tell you again that this state is not ready to accept it. Two years ago I proposed a provision to a bill under consideration that slavery be entirely abolished within the state. I was soundly denounced for it, and the provision was removed. I can assure you that a suit such as you propose will do nothing to change the collective minds currently in power."

"But that was two years ago, sir," I said, beginning to realize how difficult it was to counter his arguments. Carlos had said that this was how he was in court, piling fact upon fact to confound his challengers. "Things have changed."

"Not sufficiently," he said, and for the first time I could hear the irritation in his voice, too. "New York—especially this city—is still striving to recover from the war."

"But you could try, sir," I said. "If only—"

"Listen to me, Mary," he said. "I will not trouble you with the figures of losses and other expenditures. All you need do is look about you to see the damages that remain on most every street. What man, whether farmer or merchant, is willing to sacrifice the labor to do all that needs to be done?"

"Then that farmer and merchant should pay fair wages, sir," I said, desperation making me be dangerously frank, "and not rely on captives like me to do their bidding."

"Stop," he warned, rising to his feet and coming around the desk to stand before me. "You go too far. Stop now."

I was pressing my fingers so tightly into my palms that they hurt. I couldn't let my voice rise any higher, not and risk others hearing us. Yet my words refused to be held back any longer, else they'd strangle me.

"You've told me yourself, sir, that slavery is only a temporary condition in a person's life," I said in a fierce, tormented whisper. "Why can't that condition be changed now, sir? Why must I wait to taste freedom that my husband earned, and that he died for so that I might have it, too?"

"*Stop,*" he ordered roughly, seizing me by the arm. "Do you believe me mad? That I'd file a baseless suit against my own *wife* on your behalf?"

I tried to pull my arm free, but he held me fast. In the past when he'd trapped me like this, I'd been frightened of him, but now I was too angry to be afraid, or wise, either.

"My *mistress,*" I said, practically spitting the words. "You would rather she kept me her prisoner than do what is right before your God and your country!"

"Guard your words, Mary," he warned. "Consider—"

"No, sir, *you* consider!" I cried furiously. "Consider what you and Mistress have done to me, to my life, to my—"

But before I could finish he shoved me back flat against the wall, there beside the tall case filled with his books. Without pause, he kissed me, his mouth grinding across mine and his tongue thrusting deep. Pinned against the wall, I twisted between his heated body and the cool, smooth plaster behind me.

He still held my arm, and now shoved my hand down between our bodies. He forced my fingers over the front of his breeches, pressing them against his rampant cock.

"That's what you do to me, Mary Emmons," he said, his voice filled with anger that was a match to my own. "I have everything in my life that a Christian man could want, yet still you torment me like some golden, sinful Eve, here in my own house where I cannot keep away from your temptation."

He pushed himself against my hand. I closed my fingers around him through his breeches, just enough to make him groan aloud, vibrating against my temple.

"Then free me, sir," I whispered fiercely, my words as rough and breathless as his. "Set me free, and send me away, and I'll never torment you again."

He groaned again. "You know I can't do that."

"You could, sir." I turned my face up so my mouth was near his and brushed my lower lip against his cheek, just enough to make him shudder. I was smaller, weaker, bound by law to his wife, but in that moment I realized that I had some measure of power over him. I'd never felt this before, not with any man, and especially not one like the Colonel. "Mistress would heed you."

"My wife." He swore, helpless, a sound I discovered gave me great satisfaction.

"Mistress would listen to you if you asked, sir." My breasts crushed against his chest. "She would obey."

"As you do not," he muttered. "I should whip you for your impudence, Mary Emmons."

At once I tensed, remembering the last whipping I'd received, long ago on Saint-Domingue, and the grooved scars I'd carry forever upon my back. But this was different.

He was different.

And so, I supposed, was I.

I'd been expecting what came next for years, and I thought I was prepared for it. But I wasn't, and afterward I realized I never would have been. What woman is?

He grabbed the coarse linen of my petticoat in a bunch and shoved it up around my waist. He was past words now, ripping open the buttons on the fall of his breeches to free himself. He pushed my legs apart, bent his knees, and entered me, roughly, with no care or kindness. I cried out, and he pressed his palm over my mouth.

"No noise, mind?" he ordered in a harsh whisper.

Of course: his first thought would be that no one hear us. I was pinned against the wall, helpless and trapped, yet still I knew what I must say, the only threat I could make. I twisted my face free of his palm, even as his other hand was hooking his arm beneath my thigh to lift me higher.

"If Mistress hears you—"

"Damnation, Mary," he growled. "Not a word."

He worked me hard and fast against that wall. It had been nearly ten years—ten years!—since I'd been with my husband, and he had loved me. There was no love in this. I squeezed my eyes shut and turned my face away, my cheek pressed against the pale blue quilted silk of his banyan and the hard bone of his shoulder beneath it.

I didn't cry.

When he was done, he was breathing as hard as if he'd run a footrace. He stayed pressed against me, covering me, until at last he slipped free of my body, and stepped back. At once I pushed my petticoat down over my bare thighs, and crouched down to retrieve my little linen cap from where he'd knocked it to the floor. My legs trembled and shook beneath me, and I linked my arms around my knees, as if that would be enough to calm myself. His spendings were warm and sticky between my thighs.

"Mary."

I didn't want to look up at him, but I did. His face was flushed, his eyes heavy lidded with satiation.

If Mistress saw him now, she'd know in an instant what he'd done.

"Mary," he said again, his voice gruff. I was thankful he didn't call me by my full name, as he usually did. I do not think I could have borne it to hear him speak Lucas's name just then.

He bent to take one of my hands, and raised me up and into his embrace. He held me close, his arms linked lightly around my waist. I could guess what was coming, and I was right.

"Mary, sweet," he said, in that same low, gruff voice. "You know this must stay our secret."

I didn't answer, letting him wallow in his guilt. I could hear other voices in the distance inside the house, and I'm sure he did, too.

He cleared his throat. "We've always been friends, you and I."

I drew apart from him enough to look him squarely in the eye, where he couldn't hide. I couldn't tell if I was calm or numb. Maybe it amounted to the same.

"We are more than that now, sir," I said quietly. The anger and frustration I'd felt earlier had scattered and vanished. What was done was done. Pitying myself would accomplish nothing. I'd come here with an honorable plan that had failed, and failed disastrously. Now I'd have to scramble to devise another, and quickly, for I might not have another chance.

"Yes," he said. "You're right. We are." He touched his fingertips to my cheek, trailing them down along my jaw. He was already thinking of the next time, and the next after that.

I let him have his dear, wanton dreams for a long moment before I eased free of his arms.

"I must go, sir," I said, smoothing my hair and pinning my cap back over it. "Mistress will be awake by now."

"Of course, of course." He frowned in the face of that reality, and cleared his throat. "We must talk, Mary."

I was glad that he wished to talk. I wished it, too, and raised my chin a fraction.

"Yes, sir," I said. "Any child born to a mother in slavery is likewise a slave, regardless of the father's state."

He drew in his breath sharply. "If there's already a brat in your belly, it's not mine."

"There isn't, sir." My cheeks grew hot at what he implied, but I didn't flinch or look away. "This is—was—the first time since my husband."

I could almost see his thoughts on his face, and how being the first man but one puffed his pride.

"Then I do not believe it requires discussion." His voice softened a fraction, and he smiled, coaxing me to agree. "Surely you will understand that."

"I do, sir," I said. "But I would never want any child of yours to be born into bondage because of me."

His smile disappeared. So he hadn't considered that possibility, and I thought bitterly of how desire could blind even the most brilliant of gentlemen. Yet because I knew how dearly he loved his daughters with Mistress, I was gambling that he'd feel a similar devotion to a child of ours.

And, if I was fortunate, to me as well.

The silence stretched between us, longer and longer still. Why hadn't I been aware before of the little brass clock on his mantel, ticking away every minute of my misery?

My hope faltered, certain that I'd gambled from desperation, and I'd lost. I remembered how on the first day I'd belonged to Mistress, she'd curtly told me that if I ever bore a child she would take it from me and give it away. At that time, I'd thought this uncommonly cruel. Now that I was older and knew more of suffering, I realized that a loss like that would break both my body, and my heart. I, who never cried, now felt my eyes fill. At once I lowered my gaze, unwilling to let him see my defeat.

"Don't cry, Mary," he said softly, gently, speaking at last. "I'll never do that to you." He took my hand and lifted it gallantly to his lips, the way he would have done with a white lady. "You have my word, Mary Emmons. I'll see to it that you'll never want or suffer."

Unchecked, the tears were sliding down my cheeks now, wet and hot. It was more than I'd expected, more perhaps than I'd deserved, and yet the one word I'd wanted most to hear was missing.

"What of freedom, sir?" I whispered, daring.

"In time," he said too easily, his lips grazing the back of my hand. "All in time."

In time, in time. What did that mean? A year, a month, a week, or a lifetime of empty hope?

Perhaps I should have asked him to explain. Perhaps I should have demanded he write and sign his promise, so that I might hold him to it. My life was filled with things like this that had been left undone, some my fault, some not. I told myself I'd pressed him enough. More honestly, I feared what he might say if I demanded more.

Instead, I let him kiss my lips one more time before I left him. He didn't want me to leave, and I believe he would have been on me again if I'd remained. But I insisted, not wanting my absence to be noticed by Mistress.

In the hall, I wiped my eyes with the corner of my apron and tried to set my thoughts only to the duties before me. I felt as if I'd been in the library with him for so long that I blinked with surprise at the morning sunlight streaming through the arched window over the front door. More likely it had been only a half hour's time, scarce enough for the rest of the household to take notice.

I met Celia at the bottom of the stairs, carrying the tray with Mistress's tea and toast.

"Where've you been at, Mary?" she asked crossly. "Mistress's having fits over you not coming to her."

"Then you better let me bring her breakfast," I said, taking the tray without answering her question. "There's no need for her to be unhappy with you, too."

The door to Mistress's bedchamber stood ajar, and she was still in bed, propped against a mound of pillows with open books on the coverlet. With her was her older daughter, Miss Burr, sitting cross-legged on the bed with her small hand pressed to her mother's belly.

"I can feel my brother move," Miss Burr announced importantly, and her dark eyes widened as she felt the unborn baby kick beneath her hand. "There, Mama, there he is!"

"He'll be chasing you about before you know it, Theo," Mistress promised. She raised her daughter's hand and kissed her chubby fingers, one by one with a large smack for each, which made the little girl laugh with delight. "Now go prepare your lessons, and let Mama have her tea."

Obediently Miss Burr slid from the tall bed and trotted from the room as I set the tray on the table beside the bed.

"Where have you been, Mary?" Mistress asked. "You know Celia can't be trusted to carry a tray up the stairs without spilling half the contents, and besides, you're the only one who knows exactly how I like my tea."

"Forgive me, Mistress," I said. "There were matters in the kitchen that required me."

"Well, I require you, too." She sighed, and spread her own fingers across her belly. "What a restless brave fellow this is, even if he keeps me awake at night with his antics."

This had not been as easy a pregnancy for her, and her eyes were ringed with weariness. She was nearly forty-one, old for childbearing, not that any woman with a husband like the Colonel would have a say in that.

"You are certain the child will be a boy, Mistress?" I asked as I spooned sugar into her teacup.

"I am willing it to be so," she said, "because that is what my husband desires. Oh, he loves his two darling girls beyond measure, but every man wants a son in his own likeness. In his heart, my Burr is no different, no matter how content he claims to be."

She smiled, though whether at the thought of her restless son, her darling girls, or her contented husband I cannot say.

On one account, however, I knew she was wrong. I handed her the cup and smiled as she expected me to, and prayed for both our sakes that she'd never learn the truth.

CHAPTER 17

City of New York
State of New York
March 1787

If this were a happier fiction, and not a story based upon truth,
I would write only of days of sunshine and bliss, and how his
friendship—for so the Colonel would now always style our
connection—with me gave us both nothing but pleasure. But this
would be wrong, and the new year was not a joyful one in the Burrs'
house.

For most of January and February as well, the Burrs' house was
filled with guests, visitors from both the Colonel's family and Mistress's, who, having arrived in New York, found them to be far more
hospitable than a public inn, and treated it that way, too. The festivi-
ties of Twelfth Night lingered in the house, with elaborate dinners
and suppers that required considerable toil upon my part to arrange
and oversee. In addition, the Colonel was called upon to travel to
various courts, with his journeys often hampered by winter snows
and days longer than expected.

But then privacy was always a luxury, especially the furtive kind
of privacy required for our friendship. Even without guests, we
were now eleven of us in the house: the Colonel and Mistress, their
two daughters and her sons by Colonel Prevost, as well as the five
of us servants. On an ordinary day, that was only the beginning. As
Mistress came closer to her lying-in, she received friends, tradespeople, and physicians in her bedchamber. Clerks and messengers

and other men of business and law called upon the Colonel in the library. Even little Miss Burr had visitors in the form of the tutors and private teachers that her father deemed necessary for her education.

In such circumstances, the Colonel could contrive few opportunities to be alone with me, and to my considerable relief, too. Despite the benefits I dared to believe might someday come my way in return for having finally obliged his desires, I was not at ease either with what I'd done or said. I took off the heart-shaped pendant that Lucas had made for me; my unhappy conscience no longer permitted me to wear such proof of my husband's love. How could it be otherwise? The shame I felt over what had happened was a constant burden, and one I'd no choice but to bear alone.

During this time, the Colonel and I had but two assignations (another word he used) in his office, early in the day, and another late at night in the kitchen. Although the kitchen offered a greater chance for discovery, I much preferred it, for the kitchen was my room, not his. Either way, he was quick to find his satisfaction. Though he'd often call me sweet names and embrace me when he was done, I knew he said those things to ease his own conscience, in the same way he always maintained that I'd been the one who'd tempted him.

Afterward he'd sit with me upon his lap and talk, about everything and nothing. He'd tell me of cases and clients, of various schemes to buy and sell land to the west that he hoped would make him rich, of unpleasant people he'd encountered on the packet from Albany and the new fortepiano he was considering buying for his daughters. He'd ask me of my days, too, and listen when I replied.

And because I was so trusted by Mistress, he'd ask me about her, most specifically after her health while he'd been away. He worried over her, and did not trust the physicians who attended her. He'd every reason to do so, too. Her constitution was sorely taxed not only by childbearing, but also by the noise and commotion of the city and its society. Of course the Colonel could see this for himself, for it was evident to everyone that she was unwell. But because I was so familiar with her intimate habits, I could also tell him of how her headaches had increased, how she'd other pains that came and went throughout her body, how some days she couldn't keep any food at all in her belly, and how she'd come to rely more and more upon the laudanum to ease her suffering.

I know that this sounds wrong: that the Colonel would show such concern for his wife's welfare even as he was being unfaithful to her with me, and even worse that when he'd asked me of her health I'd answer those questions as directly as I could.

Yet at the time, I understood. Mistress was his wife and the mother of his daughters, and he did love her, even if her illnesses had often kept her from being a true wife to him. I was who—and what—I was. Bound to Mistress, I was expected to obey both her and the Colonel, even if adultery was the consequence. It wasn't my place to question his actions. I wished him to be happy, so that he'd be more inclined to please me in return, and keep his tenuous promise to me that I'd be granted my freedom.

Late in February, the snow and cold that had held the city at last gave way, and in its place came a thaw that no one had expected, but everyone welcomed. To be sure, it was a false hint of spring, for true spring never came in New York before April, but the warmth still brought people from their homes and into the streets to turn their faces up toward the sun. The gray piles of old snows that lined the streets shrank, and the bravest souls opened windows to let winter's stale air out, and fresh air within. From every eave came the sound of melting snow, rhythmic drips as steady as a clock's ticking, and as maddening, too.

On one of these warm nights, Mistress's labor began, and Ben was roused from his sleep and sent running through the slush to fetch the midwife and her assistant. Unlike Mistress's previous travails, however, this one proved long and tedious, and shortly before daybreak the Colonel sent for the surgeon as well, and then Dr. Miles from St. Paul's Chapel, at Mistress's own request. No one spoke aloud what was most feared: that Mistress was too weak to survive an arduous birth.

Her two sons and two daughters were all brought into her bed-chamber. The Colonel asked them to bid their mother good morning with a kiss, but I doubted the older ones were fooled that this was anything but a grim farewell. Mistress's eyes were closed and her face was waxy-pale and shiny with sweat, her breath coming in heaving gasps against her pains. She was so weak she could not lift her head from the pillows behind her. The mood in the entire house was somber, punctuated only by the agonized groans of Mistress.

The Colonel insisted on remaining at Mistress's side, sitting beside the bed to clasp her hand. He'd hastily dressed; his jaw was dark with last night's beard and his hair untied and loose about his shoulders, all more proof of his dread.

At the midwife's insistence, there was a raging fire in the hearth that made the room too warm, and the air was heavy with the fetid smell of fever and sickness. With so many others crowded within, there was no purpose to me staying there as well. Instead, I did what I would have done on every other morning, which was to return to the kitchen to prepare breakfast—even if, on this day, it might prove to be a breakfast that no one wanted.

I sighed as I made my way down the back stairs, thinking of Mistress. No matter what our history had been, I would not wish that kind of suffering upon her. At the bottom of the stairs, a slight movement caught my eye in the shadows, and I turned quickly.

"Miss Burr!" I exclaimed, crouching down to be able to meet her gaze eye to eye. "Why are you here?"

She stepped from the shadows like a little ghost in slippers, still in her nightgown with a pink shawl around her shoulders and her dark hair plaited from the night. She would be four in the summer, a pale, pretty child who already resembled her father, complete with his self-assurance, which made her manner seem that of others twice her age.

"Papa told me that I'd have no lessons today, on account of Mama," she said. "He told me I should do my readings to be ahead for tomorrow, but I was too hungry for it."

"Then come with me to the kitchen, Miss Burr," I said gently, taking her by the hand. "I was already planning to finish making breakfast."

But she hung back, tugging on my hand. "I cannot, Mary," she said. "Papa says I've no place in a kitchen. He says I belong with books, not kettles and pots."

"Did he now," I said. I didn't doubt it. The Colonel was pushing his little mite of a daughter at her studies as hard as if she were a boy. She could already read and write, and was learning ciphering and geography and French and Heaven knew what else, in lessons that often began before dawn and continued until supper. How could mere cooking hold its place against that?

"I think this morning he wouldn't mind, Miss Burr," I said. "You can help me make your mama's tea so it will be ready for when she feels better."

"Once my brother is born," she said importantly. "That's why Mama is ill, Mary."

"Childbirth is hard work," I said. Her fingers had tightened into mine, and now when I began to walk she followed, coming close beside my legs.

She stared about the kitchen, her eyes wide. I realized she never had visited this room, although when I considered it, I realized Mistress herself had been here only a handful of times. I had Miss Burr sit on a chair, close enough to the fire that she'd be warm, but not so close that she'd find mischief.

"What are those things for?" she said, pointing up to where I hung pots and pans and other useful implements from a rack of iron hooks up high, where they'd be both out of the way and within easy reach. Also hanging nearby from the beams were braided ropes of onions and bundles of dried herbs, and on the shelves that lined the walls were plates and platters of every description, plus fluted pans for cakes and pies and shaped molds for sweet jellies. Because I saw it all every day, I thought nothing of it, but to Miss Burr, more accustomed to the tidiness and elegance of her mother's fine parlor, this was probably fascinating.

"Those are all things that I use when I cook for you and your family," I said, taking a well-cured ham from the safe to slice for frying. "Do you think all I must do is snap my fingers and your supper is ready?"

She wrinkled her nose and smiled. While I'd little experience with children, highborn or low, I guessed she'd be like people of any age, and find comfort from familiar food. I placed a thick piece of bread into the toaster on the hearth near the coals, and asked her to watch it carefully and tell me when it was done on the first side and ready to spin. This she did, and took credit for it being perfectly browned. I let her spoon the jam onto the toast herself, large, glistening dollops of blackberries, and I pretended not to see when an extra spoonful disappeared directly into her mouth.

Other servants came for the porridge that was their breakfast before they began their duties. Though they were surprised at first to find the Colonel's daughter in our midst, she made amusing company, and seemed to enjoy us as well. We all were aware that Mistress was laboring upstairs, but everyone took care not to mention it before her daughter. I kept waiting for word that breakfast was wanted in the dining room, and when that word didn't come, I feared for the worst.

I showed Miss Burr how to mix chocolate into steamed milk, and had just set her to work twisting the rod of the chocolate mill between her palms when at the door I heard footsteps in the hall. I turned quickly just as the Colonel opened the door. His expression was carefully composed, yet his fresh grief was too heavy a burden to be shrugged away that easily.

But Miss Burr, in her childish innocence, didn't see it, and clambered down from the chair to run to him, her slippers slapping on the brick floor. He gathered her up in his arms and held her tightly, his eyes closed. She didn't ask any questions, and he offered nothing; even then, they seemed to sense each other's thoughts without words. Finally he sighed, and curled his arm beneath her to make her more secure.

"Come, poppet," he said, his voice heavy. "Let me take you to see Mama."

News traveled fast through our house, and we servants soon learned the reason for his sorrow. Mistress had been delivered of a large and handsome boy, perfectly formed and exactly as they had both wanted, and predicted. But while the child had been lively even as she'd labored, through some tragic mishap he had perished in her channel, and had been delivered stillborn.

Now there are some cruel folk who will say that women grow accustomed to losses like these, and accept them with grace and resignation. This was now the third child Mistress had lost, and I assure you that her grief had no grace, no resignation, nor should it have. She was devastated by so unexpected an outcome after her difficult travail, and it left her broken in spirit as well as body. She faulted herself for her son's death, and refused to be consoled. Finally the Colonel had agreed to the doctor's prescription of a mixture of brandy and laudanum, both to ease her suffering and to help restore her strength through sleep.

I was summoned by the midwives to help wash and prepare the baby for burial. I'd known much of death, but the sight of this poor small body made me add my own tears to those of the others who wept over him. It shook me, that pitiful little man: the limbs still curled from the womb, the dark hair already destined to be like his father's, the cord neatly tied on his rounded belly with the midwife's thread. The other two babes Mistress had lost had remained in this world long enough to be baptized before their tiny mortal souls had fluttered away. This one had not. He'd no name, no blessing, and, so the midwives whispered, he'd no place in the consecrated ground of St. John's burying ground.

As sad as the house had become, there was still a near-constant procession of callers to the front door, come to express their sympathies. Most left a brief note of condolence that was brought from their carriages to the house by servants. Only the closest of acquaintances were shown in to the Colonel, who received them stoically with Mistress's sons in the parlor. It was a long, exhausting day of grief, disappointment, and fear for Mistress.

Yet when I'd finally finished in the kitchen that night, I found I was too weary and on edge to sleep. My thoughts had twisted from Mistress's loss to my own mother, and how she had died while I had lived.

Long after everyone else had retired, I remained in the kitchen, reading one of the household's newspapers by the light of the coals as I did most nights. No matter how arduous my day might have been or how tired I was, there was so much occurring in the city, the state, the country, that I could not imagine keeping myself ignorant, given the chance to be otherwise. On this night in particular, I gave myself over to the printed words as a distraction, sitting at the table with the paper spread before me.

I was so engrossed in my reading that I started when the door to the hall opened.

"I saw the light beneath the door," the Colonel said. "I guessed it would be you."

He paused at the door, waiting to be invited in, which was, of course, unnecessary. He hadn't yet undressed, and wore the same severe black suit as he had since morning. His face was so inexpressibly sad that he seemed to have aged five years in a day.

I rose swiftly, curtseyed, and motioned for him to sit in the best of the chairs, the one with the tall back and arms and a flattened calico cushion. He sank into it with a grunt that was halfway to a groan, and glanced past me to the hearth.

"Is there any coffee remaining?" he asked.

"There is always coffee, sir," I said, reaching for a saucer and cup from the shelf. This was true. Because he often worked at odd hours or roamed the house when he couldn't sleep, I usually kept coffee at the ready for him. "How does Mistress fare?"

"Not well, as is to be expected," he said. "But the doctors and midwife cautiously agree that with rest and time, she shall recover. There is a nurse sitting with her now, even though with the laudanum she'll sleep until tomorrow. She blames herself, no matter what is said to her. To recover from that—that will be the true trial."

"Oh, sir, Mistress shouldn't fault herself," I said softly, handing him the cup. "She took every care."

"So I have told her, and Dr. Walker as well," he said, his eyes unfocused as he drank his coffee. He never sipped at it, no matter how hot, but simply drank it as if it were water. "The child was taken by God, and is at peace now in His embrace."

I sat on the stool beside his chair. "It's not your fault, either, sir. None of it."

"If you had been raised among staunch Presbyterians as was I, then you would understand," he said. "What is more fearsome than a vengeful Lord God?"

He grimaced, his attempt at cynicism failing miserably.

"Nothing you have ever done could merit the death of your child," I said softly. "Nothing, mind?"

I wasn't sure he heard me, until he took my hand and laced his fingers tightly into mine.

"The little fellow never knew how much he was wanted, or loved," he said, his voice low and poignant. "He died without knowing any of that."

"But he did know, sir," I insisted. "Every time he leaped and turned within Mistress's womb at the touch of her hand, or the sound of your voice, or even his sister's laughter, he knew it."

He shook his head. "I'm not certain of that, Mary. It's well-argued that life—and knowledge—requires birth. Because the child lacked one, he never achieved the second."

"I know for myself, sir." I spoke with an urgency I didn't quite understand myself. "My own mother died giving birth to me. I have no memory of her. None. Yet I am certain she loved me."

He frowned. "That does not seem possible, Mary. Perhaps you instead recall the affection of your father, and mistake it for the love of your mother."

"That is not possible, sir." I swallowed, for I'd never told him the circumstances of my birth, but now—now it seemed as if I must. "My father was a British soldier who raped my mother."

"Ahh." He drew back a fraction and released my hand. "If that is so, then I cannot imagine how your mother could have felt any fondness for a child whose very presence would be a constant reminder of such a reprehensible crime of war."

I hadn't expected that from him. But then, given the comfortable luxury of his own family and birth, how could I have expected anything else?

"Because she was my mother, sir," I said. "That is the truth I have always believed. There is no logic to love. I know she loved me, just as your son would have known that he was loved as well."

He didn't reply, and carefully set the now-empty cup on the table. But his head dropped forward with sorrow, and his shoulders bowed beneath the weight of it.

The silence of his grief seemed far more terrible to me than Mistress's wracking sobs and laments. I could not help myself. I rose, and went to him, and bent to wrap my arms around his shoulders and rested my cheek against his temple. I'd never touched him first like this, never touched him except in response to how he'd touched me.

This was different. I held him close to share his pain and offer my solace, without words. I'll admit that I drew comfort in this embrace, too, and in the closeness that came with it. There'd been precious little of either in my life, and I wouldn't question it now.

I'm not sure how long we remained like that. At last he sighed, and as he did I stepped away. But he took my hand again to keep me close, and once he'd stood, he drew me into his arms and held me, just held me.

"Thank you, Mary," he said against my ear. "You're every bit as wise and kind as you are beautiful."

He kissed me lightly on the lips, his mouth barely brushing over mine, then kissed my forehead. As he left, his steps were slow and heavy on the stairs.

Poor man, I thought sadly. *Poor, grieving man.*

And I realized that, for the first time, I'd thought of him as more than Mistress's husband.

As soon as Mistress recovered sufficiently for travel, she took her two daughters, Ginny, me, Mr. Partridge (the tutor for Miss Burr), and another woman recommended for her nursing skills for a prolonged stay with her sister. The announced purpose was to remove Mistress to a healthier location, away from the foul air and racketing of New York, where she could recover both her health, and her peace. Mrs. Browne's husband was a physician, and trusted by the Colonel, and he, too, promised to watch carefully over her, and make certain she dined properly and took exercise, as had been prescribed.

But though no one would say so beyond the family, Mistress's health was not the only concern. Little Sally, who had reached but two years in June, was not flourishing as she should. Although Sally was in spirit as merry and quick as her older sister, she had begun to be plagued by a myriad of ailments, most often a seemingly endless complaint of the bowels that left her exhausted and weak and small for her years.

I sensed the shared anxiety during this time from the number of letters written back and forth between Mistress and the Colonel, often sent and arriving with every stage. Mistress read aloud the cheerful parts to Miss Burr and to Miss Sally, too, but I could tell from how her expression changed that she'd skip over parts when she'd reach yet another worried inquiry after Sally's health.

At her husband's urging, Mistress and the rest of us remained in the country and away from town through the summer to avoid fevers. These were a yearly curse in New York, and could easily have carried away Mistress and her daughters alike. With the frost and the end of the contagion, we finally returned to the city.

I was glad of it. I was now accustomed to having more responsibility in the household than simply looking after Mistress. I'd grown restless while we'd been away, and I hadn't liked taking orders from Mistress's sister, Mrs. Browne, either, who set me to tedious tasks such as sewing sheets simply because she believed me to be idle and impudent. I'd also missed my own acquaintances among other servants in our neighborhood, people who'd greet me by name and not only as belonging to Mistress.

We returned by the stage, and were met at the inn by the Colonel and Mistress's sons. Their reunion was joyous, with none of them caring about who else at the inn witnessed all the kisses and embraces and exclamations. I'd no one to meet me, nor had I expected there to be, and thus busied myself by making sure none of Mistress's baggage was stolen.

But while the Colonel was all happy smiles at our return, I didn't miss the shock on the faces of the two boys—less skilled at masking their reactions—when they first saw Miss Sally again as, with a squeal of delight, she was plucked from the carriage by her father. We who were with her each day were not as aware of her decline as they would be. The Colonel must have seen it as well, for he held her close, and insisted on carrying her home himself in the crook of his arm, with Miss Burr hopping along beside him and hanging on his other hand.

The happiest reunion, however, was between Mistress and the Colonel. Throughout the evening, he praised and petted her at every opportunity while she blushed as if she were sixteen instead of forty-one. They presented each other with journals they'd kept while apart, and the Colonel had increased the sweetness of that gift not with a jewel, as most fond husbands would, but with a stack of the latest books that he'd ordered for her from his bookseller in London. She cried out with delight and wept as well, and could not have been happier. They could scarcely wait for the children to be taken to bed before they, too, retired to their bedchamber, and did not call for breakfast until nearly noon the following day.

Beyond the simplest of greetings, the Colonel had no time to spare upon me. A blessing, that. I began to set to rights everything that had been allowed to grow slipshod in the house while I'd been away.

This became more toil than I'd expected since, while I'd been away with Mistress, the Colonel had seen fit to sell Celia. I was shocked, but not surprised, if that makes sense. Not surprised, for Celia, who had been brought to New York direct on a ship from Gambia, had struggled to learn both English and Mistress's ways. Shortly before we'd left for Mistress's sojourn in the country, Celia had dropped and broken a Chinese porcelain jar, edged with gold—worth far more than poor Celia herself—that had belonged to Mistress's grandmother.

Still, I'd never expected the Colonel to act upon Mistress's discontent with such suddenness. From the swiftness of this action, Celia might never have dwelled within the house at all. She was not mentioned again, not by any of us servants, almost as if her sale and disappearance were a disease that could pass from one of us to another. Nor did I ever see her again, in the streets or markets or at church, which likely meant she'd been sold far from New York, perhaps even to work the fields of a Virginia plantation. It could happen to any of us, at any time, and that sobering knowledge hovered over us all like a cloud—which was, perhaps, exactly what Mistress had wanted.

At the end of the year, the house was filled with the customary share of guests and family for the holiday season, work and more work for me. There were twenty to dine at the grandest of the dinners, with many dishes of rich food and wine, port, and brandy. After the last of the plates were cleared away, the Colonel rose at the head of the table to lead the first toast of the night.

"*À mon Theo,*" he said, his glass held high. "*Au plus parfait des femmes, et mon cher ami.*"

A murmur of agreement followed as the guests emptied their glasses in Mistress's honor, and then waited while Tom and I filled them once again.

Now it was Mistress's turn. For Christmas the Colonel had given her a magnificent necklace, a ring of golden topaz stones to match the earrings and brooch that had been earlier gifts of his. She glittered and sparkled in the candlelight, her eyes bright and her dark hair frizzed and puffed into the latest French fashion, with small white plumes tucked into the curls. She raised her glass and held it high, smiling as she saw the anticipation in the faces around the table.

"*Pour mon Aaron,*" she said, and then switched to English so everyone would understand her. "My love, my husband, the father of my daughters, and, God willing by summer, our son as well."

At once she was overwhelmed by a noisy clamor of good wishes. Her announcement was, of course, not news to me. I'd known—as had the Colonel—that she was again with child weeks ago. Given her age, her uncertain health, and the sorrowful outcome of her last pregnancy, a less jubilant announcement might have seemed more appropriate. But then I had tended her through her last unhappy confinement, while these others cheering her at the table had not, and if the Colonel himself, beaming now with male pride, was happy with her announcement, then why should I be otherwise?

"Now surely you and the girls must come visit me as you're always promising, Theo, and bring Frederick and Bartow, too," said Mrs. Williamson, one of Mistress's innumerable cousins. "This would be the perfect time, before you grow too unwieldy, and you know how all children thrive at Williamson Hall."

"How dare you make such an invitation, Juliana?" the Colonel asked, his smile taking any sting from his words. "To send her traipsing about in the snow in her condition, to wait upon your whims!"

"She wouldn't be traipsing anywhere, Aaron, as you know perfectly, perfectly well," said Mrs. Williamson. "I'd send my own coachman in the sleigh, with orders that your three ladies be swathed in furs and arranged with coals at their feet. There's no smoother way to travel than by sleigh, and the entire journey would be complete in less than an hour's time."

"He'll agree, Juliana, because he knows how much it would please me," Mistress said, smiling not at her cousin, but at the Colonel, and knowingly at that. She'd placed her hand over the barely perceptible swelling of her silk-covered belly, all maternal protection. "Is that not so, *mon cher seigneur?*"

He chuckled, holding his hand upraised in surrender.

"Absolutely so," he said as he added a slight bow. "I am helpless before your wishes, for all I desire is the happiness of my Theo."

Charmed beyond reason, the ladies at the table sighed and applauded his nonsense, as did Mistress, which made the Colonel preen and smile more in the glow of their approval. For all that he liked to claim he was a plain and honest speaker, he relished the company of women too much to be completely free of gallantry. I suspected it was all part of the familiar game of pursuit and amusement to him—a game that, like everything else he did, he always played to win.

But however foolish his words had sounded to me, the visit had been agreed upon, and late the next morning Mistress called me back to the breakfast table in the parlor so that she could tell me my part in her plans. The Colonel still sat at the table, too, paying little attention to his wife's words as he finished his coffee and read the newspaper.

"I will be leaving tomorrow, Mary, directly after breakfast," Mistress said, glancing down at the sheets of notes she'd made so that nothing would be forgotten. "I will expect everything in readiness so that we might depart as soon as Mrs. Williamson's sleigh arrives. I don't wish to tax her team by making them stand about in the cold while we dawdle."

"Yes, Mistress," I said; she traveled often enough that I knew what was expected of me. "Have you a list of which clothes you wish me to pack for you and the Misses Burr?"

"You'll find there's nothing unusual," she said as she handed the papers to me. "We shall only be away a fortnight at the most, so I believe two trunks will suffice. The red one for me, and the small green for the girls. I'll also be packing the small calf-hair trunk with my books, but you needn't concern yourself with that. Oh, and the round hatbox, too. This new fashion for large hats is such an inconvenience!"

"You needn't follow the fashion if it displeases you, Theo," the Colonel said dryly, without looking up, but proving he had in fact been listening. "I know I would not object to be rid of the millinery account from Mrs. Henshaw."

"You'd be the first to complain if I ceased to be fashionable,

Aaron," she said, tipping her empty teacup toward me to show that she wished me to refill it. "What you'd say if I dressed myself like a dull dowd to accompany you!"

He glanced up over the edge of the paper. "I'd congratulate myself on having a financially prudent wife rather than one who was a lady of fashion."

"You would not," Mistress said, adding sugar to her tea. "You'd say I was a shabby advertisement for your services, and that people would wonder what had become of the fortunes of poor Colonel Aaron Burr, Esquire, to let his wife go about in such a disreputable condition."

"Then pray take a dozen hatboxes with you, my dear, so as to preserve my professional reputation." He tossed the paper aside with open disgust. "There is nothing to read this morning but more of Hamilton's ravings in favor of the Constitution. Which people are you taking with you, Theo? You know there's always a crowd at Williamson Hall."

"I do know we shall all be packed together in those old-fashioned rooms," Mistress said, "and that is part of the amusement in visiting there. Of course I'll take Ginny to look after the girls. Frederick and Bartow can tend to themselves. For two weeks, I can look to Theo's lessons myself, so there's no need of asking Mr. Partridge to join us. Of course I'll bring Mary for—"

"I don't see the purpose in taking Mary," the Colonel interrupted. "You've said yourself that when you went to your sister's house it would have been far more useful if you'd left Mary behind here."

Mistress sighed deeply. "Yes, but Mary can dress me more quickly than any other woman I've ever had."

"Which would be perhaps an hour from her day at most," the Colonel said. "Surely Juliana has a woman who can help with your hair and clothes."

I listened as they discussed me as freely as if I weren't standing there beside Mistress's chair. I'd no particular desire to return to Williamson Hall, a rambling old house with fireplaces that smoked and rooms and stairs that stank from Mr. Williamson's pack of spotted hunting dogs, permitted to roam wherever they pleased.

But what good could come of remaining here in this house for two weeks—fourteen days, fourteen nights—with the Colonel and no one else? He might continue to leave me alone, and remain faithful to Mistress. He might spend every night out late at taverns with friends. He might not even be here in New York himself, but attending to a case at a court elsewhere in the state.

Or he might do none of those things, but other things instead, other things that involved me.

I realized I was holding my breath, and forced myself to let it out. The two of them would make their decision, and I'd have no say in any of it.

"You are right that Mary is the only one who can truly see to the house when I am away," Mistress was saying, thinking out loud, "and be certain that the others do their tasks. I could not believe the woeful state of the housekeeping when we returned last week."

"That is true," the Colonel agreed. "All true."

"And Mary would be sure that you ate properly while I was away," she said. "None of those dreadful, greasy meals with pipes and bad liquor and Governor Clinton's rascals that make you groan and beg for the cream of tartar the next morning."

For the first time he glanced at me, and smiled a conspirator's smile that he should not have made.

"Mary can prepare as fine a decoction of cream of tartar and barley water as any apothecary," he said. "I can myself vouch for its efficacy. Isn't that so, Mary?"

I should have simply nodded, but some demon of truth possessed me instead.

"No, sir," I said. "It was cream of tartar with vinegar, not barley water. The vinegar makes it stronger."

He chuckled, more pleased than he should have been. "There now, Theo, what did I tell you?"

"You've won your case, counselor," she said. "I'll leave Mary to look after you."

She smiled over her tea at him, believing his smile had been intended for her, not me. Perhaps it was. Perhaps everything he'd said here had been for her benefit alone.

But I'd only to let my gaze meet his to know otherwise, and the truth as well.

The next morning was sparkling bright with fresh, fine snow

that had fallen overnight. Mrs. Williamson's driver appeared with her sleigh as promptly as she'd promised, the team stomping with impatience to be off and the brass bells on their harnesses jingling. Frederick and Bartow were standing with their horses, too, ready to ride alongside the sleigh. The trunks were quickly lashed to the back, Mistress and the girls were bundled snugly beneath so many fur robes that their faces scarcely showed, and with final kisses and farewells from the Colonel they were off, the runners of the sleigh squeaking over the new snow.

We'd barely returned to the hall before the Colonel stopped me.

"I've a request for you, Mary," he said, fishing in his pocket for money. "Long ago you promised to make me a true Indian curry, and tonight I want you to do exactly that. Purchase whatever you require. If you can't buy it on my account, then pay cash, and have it ready by the time I return this evening."

"Yes, sir," I murmured, already remembering the spices I'd need. "I'll do that, sir."

"Thank you, Mary." He nodded, and worse, he winked. "You've no notion of how much I've anticipated this night."

That morning I did as he'd bidden, and tried to think only of the curry and no further. I went to a grocer near to the docks who sold the less common spices, beyond the usual cinnamon and black peppercorns. He was an old Scotsman who'd served in the East India Company, and he liked me because I'd listen to his sorry attempts at Hindi. But he let me choose my spices carefully, sniffing and tasting and insisting that Colonel Burr would accept only the best. They wouldn't be fresh, of course—they'd come clear around the world by sea, just as I had—yet I knew how to coax their flavor to bloom.

All afternoon I let the kettle simmer on the hearth, watching the color deepen and the fragrance grow richer until the whole kitchen was filled with it. Cumin and cardamom, coriander and turmeric, with grated gingerroot and plenty of onion besides. Given how early it was in the new year, I'd paid dearly for lamb, but the Colonel wouldn't care. He never asked the price of things, and besides, I was certain he'd forget everything else after his first taste.

Others, however, were not so appreciative.

"What is that mess?" demanded Carlos, peering suspiciously over my shoulder. "The whole yard stinks of it."

"Curry," I said, a single, succinct word that, to me, said everything.

It meant nothing to Carlos. "You're going to serve that to Colonel Burr?"

"I am," I retorted. "Don't worry. I wouldn't waste any of it on you."

Each time I lifted the lid to stir it again, I breathed deeply, closing my eyes to savor the aromas. I've always believed that smell and taste are the senses that memory loves best. Sight and hearing are like pretty baubles, easy to admire, but smell and taste are the ones that can call back the past in an instant. From the scent alone, I could once again be in Pondicherry, watching Ammatti standing over the fire as she stirred the pot and sang to herself. The memory was so clear, so distinct, that I wanted to weep. Let the Colonel believe I was doing this for him. I knew it was much more for myself, and I'd not a single regret.

But too soon the short winter day was done, and before long the Colonel would return from his office. I laid a single lonely place for him in the dining room, the way Mistress had specifically told me to do; she believed he should dine as the master of the house, even if there was no one else to see him.

I heard Carlos open the door to the Colonel when he arrived, and take his cloak and hat with a murmur of conversation. I also heard the Colonel continue upstairs, and when Carlos came back to the kitchen he'd an odd look on his face.

"The Colonel says he wants to dine in his room," he said. "He says the little gateleg table will suffice for him. And—and he says he wants you to dine with him, too, Mary, on account of you making this dish special."

I nodded, but didn't explain, avoiding the question in Carlos's eyes. Hadn't he noticed the Colonel's attentions toward me before? Or was I the only one, being the only one who'd had to bear them?

I sent Carlos to arrange the little table upstairs, and carry the Colonel's wine upstairs to him as well as tend the fire. Because Mistress was so often unwell and this house was sufficiently large, the Colonel kept a small bedchamber of his own apart from hers. Here he'd room for not only his bed, but also a comfortable cushioned armchair, a shelf of books, his dressing stand, and the table, which he most usually employed for writing letters when he didn't care to go to his library.

I knew I couldn't avoid it any longer. I ladled the curry into one of Mistress's best porcelain serving bowls and the rice in a second, smaller one, and put them both on a tray. I smoothed my skirts and cap, and climbed the stairs with the tray in my hands.

He'd left the door to his room open for me. He was standing before the fire, and he turned as soon as I entered.

"Good evening, Mary," he said, smiling. "I'm glad you're joining me."

He made it sound as if I'd a choice. He had replaced his dark coat with the quilted blue silk banyan, a garment that was painfully familiar to me.

"Yes, sir," I said, setting the tray down on the table, where the room's two chairs now stood cozily facing each other. "Shall I serve?"

"Be sure to serve yourself, too," he said, closing the door after me. He sat, watching as I filled his plate. I hesitated, then put a small spoonful on the second plate for myself, taking care to choose only onions and none of the meat.

"That's not enough, Mary," he said. "Be more generous with yourself."

"That's all I want, sir," I said. In truth, my stomach was twisting into such knots that I wondered if I could eat even this much.

"Then sit," he ordered, pouring wine into the two glasses. "I don't like to dine alone."

Slowly I did sit, on the very edge of the chair.

He'd plunged his fork into the curry, holding a large forkful now poised before his mouth, the lamb and the onions steaming and glistening.

"Eat, Mary," he said. "I told you, I don't like to dine alone."

I'd washed and polished Mistress's silver forks more times than I could count, but I'd never held one in my hand for eating. I tried to balance the fork between my fingers, the way the white people did, but it felt heavy and precarious, and instead I held it more firmly against my palm and hoped the Colonel wouldn't remark upon my awkwardness.

But he was already grunting with pleasure over his first bite of my curry.

"You were right, Mary, more right than I can ever explain," he said. "This is as unlike that other curry—what did you call it? An English curry?—as night is to day, and the most wondrous thing I've ever eaten. If you don't try it for yourself, I'll begin to think you've poisoned me."

I dipped my fork into the little mound on my plate, raised it, tasted it.

"It's good, sir, yes," I said, disappointed in myself. "But I should've done better."

"I cannot fathom how," he said, eating with unabashed relish. "It is perfection to me, and all the more so because you made it."

I flushed and looked down, wondering if he was thinking the same as I. This curry was different from every other dish I'd set before him, but not just because of the ingredients. My *ammatti* would have understood, and so would Orianne. There was part of me mixed into these spices, of who I'd been and who I was and likely who I'd become. No wonder I'd never be satisfied with it.

"Perfection," he repeated, and smiled. "Now drink your wine."

I shook my head. "Thank you, sir, but no," I said. "Where I was born, women like me don't drink wine, except as medicine."

"You mean as slaves?" he asked curiously, already refilling his own glass. "Is it prohibited by your rulers?"

"Not by the state, sir, but by my people, and my religion," I said. "I was born a free Tamil. I wasn't always a slave."

"Free, you say," he repeated, marveling. "It would seem that I know very little of you, Mary Emmons. You make me feel exceptionally ignorant."

I smiled at that. I knew how much he prized his knowledge and intellect, to the point of arrogance. I doubted he'd ever believed himself to be ignorant of anything, even in his cradle.

"There now, that's better," he said. "You don't smile nearly enough."

How fortunate he couldn't know my thoughts! "I haven't much reason for smiling, sir."

"Then it shall be my special challenge to change that." He

reached across the table, gently nudging the wineglass toward me with his fingertips. "Drink. You're not in India any longer, and I know my wife has made a Christian of you. Here in New York, women may drink as they please. Try it, and then tell me more of yourself and your history."

I didn't know why this mattered so much to him. I'd only once before drunk wine, that one night with Lucas, and never since. From what I'd seen, wine and strong drink did little to improve anyone. But if he insisted, a small sip might be enough to satisfy him.

The sweet sharpness startled me, but it wasn't unpleasing. It seemed to give me courage, too, courage to speak things I'd always wished to say.

"Mistress always says I'm from the city of Calcutta, sir," I said. "But she is wrong, and I am not. I was born in the south, in Pondicherry. My family wove cotton muslins."

I said it proudly, for it had been a skill and a trade to be proud of. I raised my glass again, and drank more of the wine.

"How fascinating," he said, his voice low and encouraging. "Did women take part in the trade as well?"

"Oh, yes, sir," I said. In nearly twenty years, only Lucas had ever asked me any of this. "We were spinners. I began spinning when I was only five."

I drank again, until I realized to my embarrassment I'd emptied my glass. Quickly he poured more, and from nervousness I drank that, too.

"Yet you were, and are, a slave," he said. "Were you captured by slave traders?"

I shook my head. I chose my words with care, speaking slowly so he'd understand them all.

"My uncle found me a nuisance and a disgrace upon our family." Even now, the truth—that I'd been entirely unwanted—remained so blunt and painful that tears welled in my eyes. "When I was eight, he sold me to a Frenchwoman."

"Oh, Mary," he said softly. His eyes were filled with kindness and understanding, a lure I could never resist. "You didn't deserve that fate. Come here."

He pushed his chair back from the table and held his hand out to me. Because of the wine, I saw his gesture as offering only comfort and succor, and I went to him freely. He kissed me, and this time I slipped my hands over his shoulders and kissed him in return.

I do not like recalling what came next, though it must be easy enough to guess. Before long, he'd coaxed me free of my clothes, the better, he claimed, to admire my beauty. I let him see the scars upon my back, again a privilege I'd shared only with my husband. One by one he pulled the pins from my hair, so that it fell around my bare shoulders and breasts.

From there he laid me on his bed, and shed his own clothes before he joined me. It is true that I'd coupled with him before, but it had always been in haste, with our clothes awry, and intended only to satisfy his immediate lust. It had never been by my choice, and in that small way I'd been able to keep my distance, and withhold at least a small part of me from him.

But for whatever reason, he had now resolved to make a true wanton of me, and he'd all night to do so. He wooed me with the most skillful caresses, and by his touch and tender words made me believe for that moment that I was most dear in the world to him. He built my passions as if he were building a fire, with practiced experience, until I'd no choice but to burst into the same greedy flames that soon consumed him as well.

Yet when that was done, he still was not content. Twice more that night he claimed me, in twisting, diverse ways that I'd never imagined, and together we took such pleasure in each other that afterward I was left sobbing and shuddering and weak from the force of it.

I stayed with him throughout the night, sleeping curled against him. I had never slept in a bed: raised from the floor, upon a mattress stuffed with downy feathers, between fine linen sheets, and beneath a soft coverlet, with the warm glow of the fading coals in the grate.

Nor had I ever slept with a man: his skin warm against mine, our arms and legs tangled together as if we were one, his measured breath against my back, and his heady animal scent mingled with my own.

But when I awoke, the fire had burned out and the room was cold. The first light of the new day was gray in the windows, meaning that it was long past the time I should have been in the kitchen. The dirty plates and glasses still sat on the table along with the guttered candles, and what remained of the curry in the serving bowl had settled with a dull skim over it.

The Colonel's possessive arm was heavy across my waist, holding me close to him, and the rough stubble of his beard grated against my shoulder. My head ached abominably and my mouth was dry and foul. My limbs were sore from the contortions of the night, my lips raw, and my thighs sticky with our spendings. Yet all of it together was nothing compared with the weight of my conscience, and the shame I felt to my very core.

Somehow I eased free without waking him, and found my scattered clothes. I shivered as I dressed, making a sorry mess of repinning my hair, and tucked my shoes into the crook of my arm so as to make no noise upon the floor. With great care, I opened the door only far enough to escape, and finally, too late, I left him.

CHAPTER 18

City of New York
State of New York
January 1788

"Mary, my dear," the Colonel said. "There is something I want you to do for me tomorrow night. I trust you won't object."

Drowsy, I opened my eyes. He was lying on his side next to me, his head propped on his hand as he gazed down at me. His hair was loose about his bare shoulders, the dark strands still dusted gray from having been powdered for an appearance in court yesterday. During these last nights, there had been a great many things he'd wanted me to do for him, and he hadn't bothered to ask if I'd object.

"What is it, sir?" I asked, unable to keep the wariness from my voice.

He chuckled. "Nothing too demanding, I assure you," he said, idly trailing his fingers along my ribs to my breast. "You might even find it amusing. Why won't you trust me?"

I didn't reply. The truth was obvious, at least to me. I didn't trust him because he'd yet to give me reason to do so.

To be sure, I was not without blame in this, either. When I had first come here to his bedchamber two nights earlier, I had made the mistake of drinking the wine he'd offered me. It had been sufficient to soften both my conscience and my resistance to the point that I'd submitted to him with shameful ease, even eagerness. I'd scuttled away the next morning, and had carried my guilt with me throughout the day, certain that every person I encountered could read what I'd done written boldly across my countenance.

But the following night I had gone to him again when he'd summoned me, and there hadn't been any wine in my glass to dull my wits, either. I could say that I'd joined him only because I'd no choice, as any other woman in my position would have done and understood, but I couldn't entirely claim that defense. It was more complicated than that. Between us, it always was.

"Tonight I have invited several men here to dine," he continued. "You will note that I have not called them gentlemen, for they do not deserve that designation. I wouldn't inflict them upon Mrs. Burr, but while she is away, she need not know."

I didn't believe he kept much of anything from Mrs. Burr (except, of course, his connection to me). I was intrigued. I also decided that, lying here beside him, I'd earned the daring right to ask a question.

"If they are not gentlemen, sir," I asked, "then why entertain them within your house?"

"Because I want them to see that I *am* a gentleman," he said easily, and not in the least perturbed that I'd questioned him. "I wish them to be impressed as much by what I represent as by who I am. That will be the surest way to make them desire to be my associates, and oblige me however they can."

This was curious, and made no sense. "Forgive me, sir, but I don't understand why, as a lawyer, you should wish to impress these men."

He smiled. "Oh, this has nothing to do with my legal career," he said. "The law pays me respectably well, but there is little challenge to it, and traipsing from court to court is tedious, low labor for a gentleman. I win my judgments, and I receive my fees. It is all very dry and dull."

Now I understood. The country had been foundering about like a rudderless boat since the end of the war, but at last a constitution had been written that would provide laws and reason—and that rudder—to the federal government. This new constitution required the approval of a majority of states for it to become the rule, and while this seemed to be taking more time than it should (doubtless because it was men who voted), it likewise seemed destined to happen. The papers had been full of it, and so had the conversations at the Burrs' table. Once the Constitution was passed, there would be all kinds of fresh opportunities in the new government for gentlemen like the Colonel.

I smiled, more pleased with myself for deciphering his explanation than with him. "Do you mean to return to politics, sir?"

"My wise little sphinx." He agreed without admitting it, a particular habit of his. "These men are aligned with that old rogue Governor Clinton, and they may in time support me as well. Tonight I intend to keep their glasses full—though mind you, not the best brandy—and listen to what they say. That is what I wish you to do, Mary."

"I, sir?" I said, surprised.

"You, my dear," he said. "I know you are a consummate eavesdropper. Every servant is. At some point in the evening, I shall excuse myself. You and Tom shall remain in the room to see to my guests' needs. They will continue to talk, and doubtless speak of me. I want you to listen, Mary, and remember all, and tell it to me later."

I settled against the pillow and tipped my head to one side, regarding him with sidelong skepticism. "What if their remarks are critical, sir?"

"Especially if they are critical," he said without hesitation. "It's always more useful to know enemies than friends."

I smiled. I much preferred the Colonel when he spoke like this, plain and direct, rather than the flowery nonsense and flattery he'd employ when he and Mistress were with company. I liked his truth, and it also meant he felt sufficiently at ease with me to share it with me.

"You wish me then to be a spy among your guests, sir?" I asked.

"Yes," he said. He took a strand of my hair and idly began to twist it around his fingers. "A spy, an agent, an intelligencer. Whatever word pleases you."

I watched him, thinking how he never seemed to weary of toying with my hair. I suspected this was because I usually kept it knotted and pinned and covered by my cap; having it loose like this must seem somehow like one more exotic, forbidden thing about me that he could relish.

"There is a risk to me, sir, in doing this," I said. "If these men realize that I am listening, they will not take it well. A servant caught listening to betters is always punished. Will you put me at that risk, sir?"

"What, the risk that I would punish you for doing what I asked?" he said, making a jest of it.

But I wasn't jesting, not entirely. Men who'd been encouraged to drink so freely that they'd be unguarded in their speech were also men who'd likewise be free with women.

"A female servant is always at risk from men, sir," I said. "Or do you expect me to be agreeable in that way, too?"

From his expression it was clear that the notion hadn't crossed his thoughts, even though he himself had expected exactly the same of me.

"I would never want you to do that," he said, his surprise genuine. "You should know that of me by now."

I didn't answer beyond a low hum in the back of my throat. Sometimes it was better not to trust to words.

"Not you, Mary, not that," he said as he leaned forward to kiss me, and slide upon me as well. "I'd never want to share you with any other man."

As we kissed, I tried not to think of how he'd turned my question around to be his worry, and not my risk. I knew I shouldn't expect more. He was a white gentleman, and like most every other gentleman, he believed the sun and the moon rose and set on his bidding.

But that night I did as he'd asked, carrying dishes to the table, then standing beside the sideboard to anticipate any need that a guest might have. I was also the Colonel's conspirator. Even if he hadn't told me, I would have known at once that these were not gentlemen; serving Mistress as long as I had, I'd learned to tell the difference.

These men wore clothes that were rougher, not the usual silk worn for evening dress. Their linen wasn't as tidily pressed, their hair wasn't powdered, and they didn't have a small cluster of elegant gold toys and seals hanging from the fobs of gold watch chains, if they'd watches at all. They spoke with the broader accents of Albany and Saratoga to the north, some even tinged with a memory of Dutch, rather than the quick, clipped speech of Manhattan Island.

They stared at the prints and paintings on the wallpapered walls, and took their seats in Mistress's silk-covered mahogany dining chairs gingerly, as if fearing the chairs might break beneath them.

Yet I couldn't dislike them for that. From their conversation, it was clear that they'd all fought in the war, some of them for many years. This was the one thing that they had in common with the Colonel. I listened as he skillfully kept the conversation on old battles and generals and why the British had deserved to lose, and saw how that—combined with the second-rate wine, and whiskey for those who preferred it—made the men slowly relax and become more jovial and at ease.

By the time that the Colonel excused himself to reply to an urgent message that I'd pretended had just been delivered (a message that was in fact an old apothecary's bill that he'd plucked from his desk earlier, part of the ruse we'd planned together), the six men had nothing but the best things to say of their host.

To them, the Colonel was a fine, right gentleman, sharp as a whip, and the sort of clever officer they'd wished they'd served with in battle. With no grounds except what the whiskey had supplied to their imaginings, they also declared him to be brave and honorable and likely a good shot with a pistol. In short, they said that he was exactly the kind of gentleman that Governor Clinton should bring to the capital to help look after the concerns of honest men like themselves, and they agreed that they'd do whatever was necessary to bring that to pass.

"That is all they said?" the Colonel asked when I told him later, after the others had left and we were alone in his bedchamber. He hadn't sent for Carlos to come undress him, but was shedding his clothes willy-nilly as he paced about the room, tossing his coat over the back of his armchair, letting his waistcoat fall to the floor when he'd shrugged it from his shoulders, yanking the silk bow from his queue like a crushed black butterfly. "That is *all?*"

"That is all, sir," I said, echoing him. I followed after him to gather up the discarded garments, and smoothing and setting them aside as best I could. "They'd only compliments for you."

"How the devil can I tell their true nature if that's all they say?" he demanded, cross and disappointed both.

"Why should what they say matter, sir?" I asked, hoping to

soothe him. "They were pleasant enough men, but I cannot see them being of much importance to you for politics."

He wheeled to face me.

"But they are, Mary, they are," he said. "Despite their shambling appearances, they're wealthy men with more acres of land and timber, rich farms, and trading schooners and barges among them than you'd ever imagine. Blast these buttons!"

He was twisting and fumbling with the buttons on the cuffs of his shirt, venting his irritation on them so forcefully that I feared he'd soon rip the fabric.

"They have influence in their own counties," he continued, "and their opinions will be heeded by their neighbors. Hamilton and Livingston can keep courting the gentlemen like themselves, chasing around and around like dogs after their own tails, but there are far more men like the ones here tonight who'll vote for the future of New York. Unfasten this damnable button for me."

He thrust his wrist out to me, upturned and oddly vulnerable.

"Forgive me, sir," I said, my fingers slipping first one button, then the next, free of their buttonholes. "But didn't you find the terms you served in the Assembly to be disagreeable?"

"It *was* disagreeable, and a blathering waste of time," he said impatiently, though whether at me or the cuffs I could not tell. "I gained nothing and achieved nothing from the experience. That whining little Congress in Philadelphia is much the same. But soon there will be power, real power, to be had in government."

I finished the last button, and at once he pulled the shirt up over his head and off in a cloud of white linen, tossing that aside as well. He remained as lean as when he'd been a soldier, without an ounce of fat or softness to him.

"Is that what you want, sir?" I asked. I remembered how he'd once introduced a bill for the statewide abolition of slavery, and I thought of all the good he could do in such a setting. "More power so that you might achieve more, and better serve those who you represent?"

He stopped and stared at me. I couldn't tell his thoughts, or his mood, either, and I felt my cheeks warm from his scrutiny. When he still did not answer, I wondered if it were my question, and I decided to repeat it in a different manner.

"What more would you do if you'd the power, sir?" I began again. "How could you help—"

"Don't make me into what I'm not, Mary," he said sharply. "I'm not one of those stargazing idealists like Hamilton or Adams or Washington—*Washington,* for God's sake!—dreaming of some fantasy Rome or Athens that never existed. I've no delusions regarding this world, nor the men who inhabit it."

He could have added my husband's name to that list, and mine as well: a noble, proud list, or so I believed.

"Yet you fought in the war, sir," I insisted. "You served as a gentleman officer. You must have believed you were fighting for something worthy, didn't you?"

"Oh, the war, the war, the endless war," he said, all weary scorn. "When I volunteered, I was only nineteen and fresh from college, and the sum of my knowledge had come from histories and prayer books. It took only one campaign to see of how little use any of that was, and how often the grandest of ideals are employed by the lowest of men to justify their deeds."

I shouldn't have been shocked. I remembered how disillusioned he'd been after the Battle of Morristown, and how he'd never made any effort to hide his contempt for General Washington. Nor, since then, had he ever taken the kind of noble and high-minded court cases that had become Colonel Hamilton's specialty.

I shouldn't have been shocked, but I was, and that shock gave more heat to my indignation than was likely wise.

"Then what *would* you do with more power, sir?" I demanded. "You convinced these men this evening to support you, but for what cause? What purpose?"

He turned his head to one side to regard me sideways.

"Do not step too far, Mary Emmons," he said, his voice low. "What I choose to do is not your affair."

"Yes, sir," I said, not heeding his warning. "Yet if you—"

But before I could finish, he seized my jaw in his hand, holding me so I could neither speak, nor look away from him.

"You ask too many questions, Mary," he said, "and questions are not what I want from you."

He kissed me then, hard, still holding my jaw. He didn't wait for me to undress, but pushed me back onto the bed and took me that way, with my petticoat shoved up around my waist and no care for me. As soon as he was done, he rolled away from me and sat with his legs over the far edge of the bed. His back was like a wall against me, a broad, dark silhouette against the candlelight. I watched as he used that same candle to light one of his prized cigars, drawing deep to make the tobacco catch the spark, and with more interest in it than in me.

I hadn't wronged him, and I hated that he'd taken out whatever had vexed him upon me. The abrupt change in his manner left me both furious and hurt, and in that moment I forgot the circumstances of who—and what—I was to him.

Without a word, I rose from the bed and went to the door. I'd sleep on my own pallet in the attic tonight. I turned the latch as quietly as I could, not wishing to disturb him.

He heard it anyway.

"Stop," he said sharply. "I didn't give you leave to go."

I turned. He'd turned, too, and now we faced each other over the rumpled bed.

"Stay," he said, the sharpness lessening a fraction. "You know I do not like to sleep alone."

As he'd ordered, I didn't leave, but I didn't move any closer to him, either, my hand still on the latch, and I purposefully kept my expression as empty and blank as I could. I'd years of experience at little things like that.

"What you did this evening by listening to my guests," he said finally. "That was useful to me. That was good. I appreciated it."

I let my silence stretch longer.

"I am a practical man, Mary," he said. "What I said earlier may have the ring of a cynic, but for the sake of those I care for most, I prefer to address the world as it is, not how I wish it to be."

The fire popped in the grate, and somewhere in the street a horse whinnied.

"Please, Mary," he said at last. "Please."

I knew this was more of an apology than I'd any right to receive from him. I sighed, and lifted my hand from the door's latch.

He crushed out the cigar, rose, and finished undressing. I slowly undressed, too, and joined him in the bed. For most of the night, all he did was hold me close, though around the first dawn he woke me. He took his time to give me pleasure, too, his way, I suppose, of showing he regretted how he'd treated me earlier.

"I should go down to make breakfast, sir," I said finally as the little clock on the mantel chimed the hour.

"Peg can do that," he said, his breath warm and close against my ear. "You don't need to go yet."

"But don't you have court today, sir?" I asked, even as I stretched languorously against him.

"There's time." Lightly he stroked his fingers along my throat. "How did you come by this scar? Were you punished?"

At once I stiffened. Because I'd been a child when I'd been forced to wear Madame's collar, the scars on my neck had faded with time, and were now so faint—a zigzagging line left by the jagged edges—that most people took no notice. But the Colonel did.

"I ran away, sir, and I was punished for it," I said softly. "A collar was fastened around my neck."

"To make you recognized, and more easily captured?" he asked, tracing the pattern of the scars.

I wished he weren't so curious. He'd accepted the ragged scars from the whip across my back for what they were, but these other ones seemed to fascinate him.

"So I couldn't run away again, sir," I repeated. "I was a child, and I foolishly believed I could find my way back to my old home. I ran away several times, and was always caught. At last they put the collar on me. Each night I was chained to one of the posts of Madame's bed. Only she had the key."

"Cruel," he said, but without much emphasis. I wondered how he'd feel if one of his own daughters had been treated in such a fashion. "You wouldn't run away now, would you?"

In truth, I had never really considered it, in either New Jersey or New York. Perhaps I was too cowardly, or perhaps I realized the dangers too well to take the risk. Here in the city, and with Mistress's trust, I'd certainly have had my opportunities to flee. I could take all the small money I'd saved, buy myself new clothes, and find a captain who'd give me passage on a ship bound to another place. But the Colonel had already said he'd hunt me down if I fled, and I didn't doubt that he would. Without friends to help me find a sanctuary, I'd more likely be captured and sold again, and into a much worse situation than I had at present. I wanted to be free, but without the papers to prove it I would spend the rest of my life on guard and on the run.

"Tell me, Mary," he said again; his voice was rough with need, and his hand now cupping my breast. "Would you ever try to run away from me?"

So that was what he'd really meant. Once again my freedom was only part of the game to him. I wasn't his property; I belonged to Mistress. Yet he didn't want me to run away from *him*. Had he even realized he'd said it?

By my best reckoning, I was twenty-eight years of age. My knowledge of men was slight, and based more on my observations of others than my own experience. Yet in these last days and nights, I'd soon realized that when the Colonel was alone with me he wanted me more than anything else in the world, and with a ferocity that I hadn't before encountered. My husband, Lucas, had been the most gentle of men, and I had loved him for his purity and tenderness. The Colonel offered me neither, nor did I wish him to. But his desperate need to possess me ironically gave me a kind of power over him that I'd hoped to have, as if our lots in life were reversed so long as we were in this room.

This power was largely an illusion, of course, as insubstantial as a shadow by the firelight. I was not so great a fool as to believe otherwise. In this city, he was an important gentleman with wealth and power, while I was only his wife's chattel, without so much as a name that was truly mine.

Yet I dared to hope that in some fashion I would be able to turn his desire for me to my favor, and coax my long-promised manumission from him. If he pursued me as a kind of game, a hunt, then I would do the same to him.

I twisted sinuously to face him, and slid my hand lower between our bodies. He grunted with satisfaction, pressing against my palm.

"I would never leave you, sir," I whispered. "Never."

As can be imagined, everything changed when Mistress and her children returned. There were no more private suppers with the Colonel, no more long nights and late mornings spent in his bed.

He again assumed his role as a devoted husband and father, so completely that I marveled to see the ease with which he did it.

The time away from the city had done Mistress good. Her belly was beginning to show more fully beneath her clothes, with her lying-in calculated to be in the late summer. Both she and the girls appeared cheerful, happy, and in as good health as could be expected. Even little Sally appeared to be improving, too, and her parents dared to hope that perhaps their prayers for her were finally to be answered.

Mistress suspected nothing, and greeted me warmly as well. She'd even told me how glad she was to return to my care, and how badly run the household was at Williamson Hall in comparison to my management. I smiled, and nodded, and thanked her, but in my heart lay a different truth.

Although Mistress would likely be stunned to learn it, I'd no great affection for her, and never had. I knew she believed herself to be a fine Christian lady, good and generous toward me and the other people she owned. I was given clothes and food and a place to sleep, and she'd never raised her hand against me herself. But she had refused me the chance to become Lucas's legal wife. This selfish decision had deprived me of being declared his widow, and receiving the soldier's benefits that Lucas had wanted for me, as well my chance at freedom with them. I couldn't forgive her that.

Especially not now. If I had captured even a small part of her husband's attention, then for once, Fate had smiled at me, and I smiled, too.

I returned to my own responsibilities, and to sleeping upstairs with the others. No one said anything to me of why I'd returned, or where I'd been sleeping before. I'm sure they all knew. A master showing interest in a servant was so old and sad a story that no one found it remarkable. I suspected the rest of the servants in our neighborhood were aware of it, too, from the silent commiseration I received from other women when I saw them in the street or at the market. What had happened to me could happen to any of them. The only difference was that I was the housekeeper and cook, not some cowering scullery maid who spoke no English, which made the Colonel's actions even more noteworthy. All the whispers were directed toward him, for his lasciviousness, his hypocrisy, even his daring, and none for me—though in some ways I knew I was equally deserving.

My friendship with the Colonel didn't cease with Mistress's return. Our assignations were not so frequent, to be sure, but if the Colonel was at home while Mistress was out for a length of time, calling on friends or visiting shops, he'd summon me to his library or his bedchamber, or seek me out himself within the house. I believe the intrigue even increased his ardor and his interest. If anything, he seemed more devoted to me than before, all of which I tried to turn to my advantage.

But I knew it could not last.

The first month I missed my courses, I thought nothing of it. I'd often missed a moon or two. Besides, I wasn't retching and feeling poorly the way Mistress had always been with her pregnancies. But when a second month had passed, and then the third, I could no longer deny the truth. I felt different, changed in a way that I could not define. I'd new life sprouting within me, and I was not as I'd been before.

One morning on my way to the market, I stopped at the home of Mrs. Conger, a free woman who served as midwife to other black women, both free and not, in this part of the city. Her rooms were clean and scrubbed, and she herself was brisk and tidy and worthy of trust, with her head wrapped with a brilliant striped silk that made me think of Pondicherry. She put me at ease with a cup of cider, examined me, asked me the questions I'd expected, and then affirmed what in my heart I'd already known: that I was three months gone with the Colonel's child.

"Do you know the child's father, Mrs. Emmons?" she asked as she helped me dress. It would sadly be a common question among her clients.

"I do," I said, "though I have not shared my suspicions with him."

She looked at me closely. "Will you?"

I hesitated, then nodded. "Yes," I said. "It will become a difficult secret to keep to myself."

"Babies usually are," she agreed, then leaned closer, and lowered her voice. "Do you wish to contrive an accident? You are still early enough. I can guarantee nothing, of course, but there are ways that often—"

"No," I said quickly, and from instinct I placed my hand over my belly. As terrible as my own conception had been, my mother had not sought to do away with me, but had given me life, even as I'd taken her own. I could not do otherwise for this babe. "That is, I wish to bear the child."

She nodded. "Have you any notion of how Mrs. Burr will take this news? I've yet to tend another birth in that house."

"I—I do not know," I said. I did, though. Long ago Mistress had told me she'd give away any bastards born to her servants, something she'd every right by law to do. I wanted to believe that the Colonel would not permit this to happen with any child of his, though that would mean he must confess to Mistress its parentage.

But I also believed he would not let his child—our child—be born into slavery. He'd need to grant me my freedom before the birth. Before this, I'd blithely told myself that this would be the surest card I'd have to play with him. Now that this child was real, however, I was stunned by how much more intense my sentiments were. Already I felt the fierceness of mother-love, and the willingness to do whatever I must for its sake.

I'd ten days to fret and plan what I'd say and how I'd counter the Colonel's arguments, ten days while he was away at court elsewhere in the state. When he returned, another two days passed before I had my opportunity to find him alone, writing at his desk in his library. I didn't squander my chance, either, but told him directly, while he'd the warm smile of desire for me.

That smile froze in place, the pen still in his hand.

"You surprise me, Mary," he said. "You are certain of this?"

"I am, sir," I said as calmly as I could. "From the fortnight in February when Mistress was—"

"There is no need to mention my wife's name in connection with this," he said quickly, his smile now gone. "She must never learn of it, especially not in her present condition."

I'd always known that he loved Mistress, not me, but it hurt to hear her and her own unborn child so bluntly put ahead of me and mine.

"In time she will know, sir," I said, unwilling to stray from my purpose. "Unless you choose to send me away, then she soon will see for herself."

His gaze flicked to my waist, calculating. "November?"

I nodded.

He sighed deeply. "She would suspect more if I sent you away," he said. "Let me consider what will be the best course, and I'll proceed from there."

"No, sir," I said, raising my chin. "I am bearing *our* child, and I won't let you decide what is best without me."

"Brave words, my dear, brave words indeed." He leaned back in his chair, finally tossing the pen on top of the unfinished letter. "But considering the circumstances of our, ah, friendship, I am the one with the greater responsibility for the child's future."

I knew I was fortunate that he neither denied that the child was his, nor refused to provide for it. Many other gentlemen would have not been so agreeable.

I wished for still more.

"I don't doubt that you'll be generous, sir," I said, "and I am most grateful. But as the mother, sir, I must beg that the child not be taken from me, but remain mine to raise."

He frowned, and looked down at the unfinished letter before him. It was not a favorable sign that he couldn't meet my eye. For all I knew, he'd sired a score of other unwanted children and they were no more than inconveniences to him.

"Then you already are aware of my wife's mandate on the subject of bastards," he said, absently rubbing his finger along the barb of his pen. "Though as far as I know, it has never been tested within her household."

"No, sir," I said, more sorrowfully than I'd intended. "This would be the first time. But I would ask you to consider the future of our child. This will not be a—a common bastard. Consider how your son or daughter will be blessed with a measure of your intelligence, your wit, your resolve, the bravery you showed in battle."

"Your bravery as well, Mary, in coming here to me," he said, glancing up at me again. "That's a substantial heritage for any child."

His expression had softened as I'd spoken, and the hint of a smile again played upon his lips. He was imagining the child that I described, exactly as I'd hoped. As a young child, he'd been left an orphan himself, and he often spoke of how lost he'd felt without the guidance of a loving parent in his life. I could see he was remember-ing that again as he listened to me, and blending his own childhood with that of this son or daughter. His eyes, so large and luminous, could betray him at times like this, and I'd often thought of how much effort it must take for him to remain impassive in court.

I wondered, too, if our child would have those same eyes, and for the first time I felt the tremor of tears rising in my throat.

"How could I give our child away to be raised by strangers, sir?" I asked with a catch to my voice. "Our child, sent away like some unwanted mongrel?"

"That will not happen," he said slowly, firmly, leaving no doubt. "I do not want to lose you, Mary, and I will do my best for you, and for the child. You have my word on it."

I nodded, speechless with relief, and my tears spilled over. My knees began to sway beneath me, and I grabbed for the edge of the desk to steady myself.

He noticed, and hurried forward to catch me, his arms around my waist. I hadn't yet asked for our child's freedom—or mine—but these were the first steps toward it.

All I could do now was pray that he'd keep his word.

Through that spring and into the summer, I was surprised by how easy it was to keep my pregnancy a secret. I tired more easily, and was also more hungry, but beyond that I wasn't ill, as many women were. I continued my tasks as usual. Undressed, my grow-ing belly and fuller breasts were evident enough to me—and to the Colonel—but hidden beneath the layers of my clothes they scarcely showed. I worried that this might mean some sort of defect in the child, but Mrs. Conger assured me that there was no danger. Rather, because this was my first pregnancy, and because my form was by nature more rounded, the changes were less noticeable. I also took to wearing an extra petticoat as well as a larger apron, both to help mask my increasing girth.

In contrast Mistress grew more and more unwell as her time approached. Again she took to her bed, and slept fitfully for more hours than she was awake. The Colonel sat beside her as much as he could spare from his work, often with Sally and Theodosia on her bed to cheer her. As before, one of the midwife's women stayed in the house for the last weeks, and I was grateful to be in Mistress's company so little lest she take notice of my own state. She was forty-one, and it was understood that this child—her eighth—would likely be her last. Once again, she desperately longed to give the Colonel a son, and she kept a hand pressed to her belly at all times to reassure herself that the child moved and prospered.

On a sweltering night in early July, only days after Independence Day, her travail began. Both the midwife and physician were summoned, and all signs pointed to a happy delivery. But alas, the much-wanted son she delivered that evening was without life, perfectly formed yet stillborn like his brother had been the winter before. Again the house was swallowed in grief for a child, the worst grief imaginable. When at last I was able to retreat to my pallet, I curled on my side, my hands protectively cradling my own belly, praying the same grim fate would not befall my own little one.

Haunted by these fears, I didn't sleep well, and before dawn I'd already crept down the back stairs toward the kitchen. On my way, I saw the door ajar to the Colonel's library, and the light from candles. I found him within, asleep at his desk with his head pillowed on his arms and two of the three candles guttered out.

"Sir," I said softly, resting my hand on his shoulder to wake him. "Sir, you should go to bed."

He jerked awake, blinking at me in sleepy confusion before he remembered his grief.

"Ah, Mary," he said, his voice low with anguish. "How could this have happened again?"

"I am sorry, sir," I said, and I was. No one deserved such a grievous misfortune. "For you and for Mistress both."

"I do not know how she will bear this loss," he said wearily. "My poor wife! To come so close on the heels of last year is insuperable, even for a Christian."

"I'm sorry, sir," I whispered, the words so insufficient. "I'm sorry."

He turned as I stood beside him and placed his hands over my apron, over our child. Through my clothes, I knew he wouldn't feel anything. I'd only sensed the first quickening myself in these last weeks, the tiniest of fluttering kicks.

"You are well, Mary?" he asked. He was, I suspect, desperate for some reassurance that there was more than grieving in the world. "You and this little one together? You are well?"

When I saw his fingers spread over that worn blue linen, gently outlining the rounded swell where our child lay curled within me, a rare happiness spread and warmed me from within. Perhaps every mother shares these moments with the father of their child, no matter the circumstances. Perhaps the sorrows of that day and the keenness of his loss had served to heighten my own appreciation for what I had.

Of course I knew that it was but a pretty dream of happiness and no more. There'd be no future for us as a family. The Colonel was not my husband, nor was I his wife, and it was more likely than not that he'd forbid me to tell our child that he was his or her father. But for this moment, I'd turn my back to reason and truth.

For this moment, I'd be happy.

"I'm well, sir," I said. "The babe and I are both prospering."

"I am glad of it." He nodded, reassured. Then he rose from the chair, and left me to join his grieving wife.

No matter how much unhappiness besets a house and the people within it, outside its walls the world continues at its usual pace. The City of New York in the summer of 1788 was alive with excitement and fresh promise on account of the country's new constitution. As the Colonel had predicted, the Constitution had in fact been confirmed and established when New Hampshire became the ninth state (and the last necessary for a majority) to vote for ratification, and New York soon followed before the end of July. Since the war, New York had been the bastion of those in favor of both the Constitution and the strong federal government that went with it.

These supporters had styled themselves Federalists. Led by Colonel Hamilton, who had also personally fought the hardest for ratification, other New York Federalists included Colonel Hamilton's father-in-law, General Philip Schuyler, Colonel Troup, Gouverneur Morris, and John Jay. But the Federalist Party was embraced by many other prominent gentlemen from elsewhere in the country, too, including General Washington, Colonel James Madison, Benjamin Franklin, and John Adams.

Now you will wonder if Colonel Burr included himself within this illustrious group. By education, prominence, wealth, service in the war, and inclination, there should have been little doubt of it, and in fact he did align himself publicly with these gentlemen.

But to anyone who paid close attention, it was obvious that the Colonel's support was lukewarm at best. He had been considered for the state's ratification convention in Poughkeepsie, and had withdrawn his name. He hadn't once lobbied on behalf of the Constitution, or written any of the opinionated letters that were cleverly published behind false names in the newspapers in its support. Instead, he'd waited until ratification was inevitable before he'd spoken in its favor.

I recalled how Carlos had long ago observed that because the Colonel hated losing so much he'd never take a case that he wasn't sure to win. It was this way with the Colonel and the Federalists, with him waiting until they were clearly the leading party before he joined their number. His actions were the very essence of being the practical man he claimed to be. I didn't question him. It all made sense to me.

I could also understand how others who'd been loyal to the cause for years would find his hesitation disingenuous, even falsehearted. It was also exactly the kind of misunderstanding that would plague the Colonel for the rest of his public life.

It was on account of the Federalists that on a Wednesday morning in late July I found myself watching a grand procession in honor of the Constitution. Standing on the balcony of a neighboring house on Broadway, I'd the Colonel to my right, and Miss Burr to my left, whose hand I held tightly in mine, and a group of the Colonel's friends and acquaintances crowded around us. Mistress was still too despondent from her unfortunate lying-in to join us, and Miss Sally, too, had been determined insufficiently strong to watch the procession in its entirety, and had remained at home with Ginny to watch her.

Still, the Colonel and Miss Burr were merry enough, and the procession was a splendid sight, the grandest parade I ever witnessed. I've heard that there were five thousand men who marched behind brightly painted banners that morning, before crowds so large that they must have included most of the city. The various divisions of the procession represented every kind of trade, profession, and artisan to be found in the city, from coopers to engineers, shipwrights to the gentlemen of the bar, physicians to students to distillers. There were also bands playing music, and ceremonial guns being fired, and even an actor on horseback as Columbus in ancient dress.

The Colonel was determined to turn the procession into a lesson for Miss Burr, as he did for most things with her, and lectured her upon each of the useful occupations whose representatives were marching by. He was a doting but strict father, and if an event was neither educational nor edifying, then it had no place in his daughter's young life. While he was distracted by greeting acquaintances, I was the one who crouched down beside Miss Burr to point out the ponies with the red and blue ribbons woven into their manes, or the sly little dog that was stealing food from the carts along the way. In my opinion, these were the things that truly interested a five-year-old girl, and no lasting harm came of it, either.

But when the Seventh Division of the procession appeared, even the Colonel was left speechless. An enormous wood and canvas replica of a ship, mounted on a hidden wagon and drawn by drays, sailed down Broadway with numerous "crew" on board waving to the crowds on either side of the street. Only when the canvas ship passed by us could we see the ship's name painted on her stern: the Federal Ship *Hamilton*.

"That's Philip's name," Miss Burr said, proud of being able to read it for herself. Tipping back the wide, flat brim of her Milanese straw hat, she squinted up into the hazy sun at her father. "Is the boat named for Philip's father, Papa?"

"It's a ship, not a boat, Theo," the Colonel said, "and yes, I suppose it is indeed in honor of Colonel Hamilton, and all he has done to promote the ratification."

He said it mildly enough for the sake of his daughter, but I could tell he was chagrined to see Colonel Hamilton singled out with such gaudy honor and drawing the most cheers, too. To a gentleman like the Colonel, winning the favor of a handful of farmers and merchants from Saratoga in private wouldn't compare with a cheering crowd on Broadway, no matter how much hard work Colonel Hamilton had done to earn it. I knew Colonel Burr well enough by now to sense that he found the adulation of Colonel Hamilton somehow vaguely unfair—not that he'd dare say it aloud.

But his daughter did. "I don't know why Philip's father should have a boat—I mean a ship—with his name, Papa," she said. "He doesn't deserve it, because New York hasn't ratified anything yet."

"True enough, sweet." The Colonel chuckled, pleased beyond measure by both her logic and the sentiment. "I've heard the Assembly will vote this week for ratification. But you are right that it's much wiser not to claim the reward before the accomplishment is complete, nor should politics be ruled by emotional displays such as this."

"Yes, Papa," Miss Burr said, equally pleased that she'd earned her father's approval. "At least Colonel Hamilton didn't get to *see* the ship. He didn't have his reward. Philip told me his father is not at home, but still in Poughkeepsie, and won't be back until next week."

"Well, then, I suppose that absolves Philip's father from any charges of unseemly vainglory, doesn't it?" the Colonel said. "Though it might be wise of you not to make that point with your friend Philip."

"Yes, Papa," she said solemnly. "Most likely he already knows, anyway."

"Most likely his father does as well." The Colonel's smile widened as he gazed fondly down upon his daughter. They truly were so much alike. Not only did she resemble him more each day in her face and expressions, but in her thoughts as well. I do not know if this was a natural inclination between them, or if it came as a result of how closely he oversaw her studies. No matter: the result was the same. Even at this age, they were exceptionally close, and whenever I saw them together I longed for him to be able to share even a fraction of that devotion with our child as well.

But as precocious as Miss Burr could be, there were also times when she was very much her tender age. As the three of us walked home after the procession, a welcome light breeze swept up from the water. The breeze caught beneath the wide brim of the little girl's hat, threatening to carry it away from her head as the silk ribbons on the crown danced and fluttered around her face. Miss Burr wrinkled her nose and giggled at the sensation, and I swiftly placed my palm atop her head to keep the hat from blowing free.

"Mind your hat, Theo," her father said mildly. "It's not Mary's responsibility to stop your carelessness, and I don't want to hear you weeping if it's lost."

But Miss Burr had forgotten entirely about the hat. Instead, she was staring at me, and how that same mischievous breeze had whipped the soft, worn linen of my apron and petticoats close against my body.

"You've gotten fat, Mary, like Mama was," she observed. "Are you going to have a baby, too?"

"That's a rude inquiry to make, Theo," the Colonel said quickly. "No lady makes common observations of another person's appearance. Pray apologize to Mary at once."

At once the girl's face grew solemn, for she hated any rebuke from her father.

"Please forgive me, Mary," she said dutifully. "I misspoke, and I was wrong."

"You're forgiven," I said. "But come, we must hurry home now, Miss Burr. Your mother and sister will be wanting their tea."

She nodded, and quickened her steps as I'd asked.

But the damage had been done, and the glance that the Colonel and I exchanged over his daughter's head showed we both knew it. The secret that I'd so carefully kept this long could not be kept much longer, and decisions we'd both postponed must soon be made.

CHAPTER 19

City of New York
State of New York
August 1788

I never learned if it was Miss Burr's unthinking chatter that finally betrayed me to Mistress. Perhaps it was the midwife who still came to tend to Mistress, and who might have observed me with a professional eye. And perhaps it could simply have been Mistress herself who'd at last seen what I'd been hiding in plain sight.

I'd been reading to her in the back parlor, as she still asked me to do on occasion. She lay on the sofa in her dressing gown, propped with pillows so she could see the flowers blooming in the small garden behind the house. Although the physician and midwife both agreed that her body was healing well enough from her last sorrowful lying-in, her soul had not, and she remained despondent and low in spirits. She declined all invitations from friends, and refused to see them when they called upon her. The Colonel and her surviving children did all they could to cheer her, but only time would ease the grief she felt over this last, and likely final, loss of an infant at birth. As a wife, she'd been brought to bed eight times, with only four of those children surviving; it was clear that with each loss the sorrow had become more difficult for her to bear rather than easier.

"Close the window, Mary, please," she said, waving weakly toward it. "There is a draft that is making me chill."

I didn't know how she could feel a draft on so warm an August afternoon, but I was happy enough to put down the grim collection of sermons that I'd been reading to her. In these last two years, Mistress had turned more to religion for solace than to the ancient philosophers who had once been her constant companions. I couldn't fault her, poor lady, though I'd have thought a happier book of humorous stories or poems would have been a better choice to cheer her.

I crossed the room and stretched my arms up high to reach the open casement, pulling it down with a thump. When I turned back toward her, her expression was strangely fixed.

"Mary," she said slowly. "Is there something you need to tell me?"

"No, Mistress," I said, feigning surprise. I should have known better than to stand as I had before the window, or perhaps part of me had done it on purpose so I might stop the pretending. Either way, my growing belly must finally have been impossible to ignore. "I've nothing to tell."

"Mary, don't lie to me, please," she said with a sadness I hadn't expected. "You have been with me far too long for that. Can you reckon when the child will be due?"

I took a deep breath. "November, Mistress."

There, that was my admission. She seemed to wilt a bit beneath it, sinking back against the cushions.

"November," she repeated. "Oh, Mary. Did you come to harm through some violence, or is the man known to you?"

"Yes, Mistress, I know him," I said. "Or I did know him."

She sighed. "You either know him, or you don't," she said in the too-patient voice she used when reasoning with her children. "Evidently you knew him well enough to—to engage with him."

"Yes, Mistress," I said. "I did know him then. But he is a mariner, an Englishman. He has left New York, and I do not know when, if ever, he shall return."

The lie had come readily to my lips, well polished and well practiced, as the best lies always were. Lies had often been a part of my life, not from choice, but in self-defense. My words had never meant anything to those who'd owned me. Why shouldn't I have learned how to twist them to protect myself as best I could?

I met her eye, and did not flinch. She was the one who was uncomfortable, not I. Everything I said now, everything I did, was for the sake of my child, and that was what gave me this courage to stand so straight before her. But telling Mistress the truth wouldn't have been possible, even if I'd wished to do so. She wouldn't have believed me and the Colonel would have denied it, and I would have soon found myself on the trading block at the end of Wall Street, an inconvenience to be swept away and sold.

"Oh, Mary, a *sailor*," she said with dismay. "How could you have let this happen?"

"I met him walking in the park, Mistress, while you were at Williamson Hall," I said. "I was lonely, Mistress, and he was kind to me."

That was all I'd say, letting her imagine the rest. A good lie was short.

"I don't care how lonely you were, Mary," she said, her voice growing more upset with each word. "I have trusted you for years to behave in a certain way that reflects well on me and my family, and now you have cast that trust aside as if it were nothing. You have betrayed me, simply because you believed yourself to be *lonely*."

"I am sorry, Mistress," I said, though I knew that would never be sufficient for her.

It wasn't. "I am sorry, too, Mary," she said, "sorry that you couldn't conduct yourself like the respectable woman I'd believed you to be. I suppose it cannot be helped, considering, but still."

Absently she picked up the book of sermons from the table where I'd left it, smoothing her fingers over and over across the leather binding. I couldn't tell whether this was to draw comfort from what was written on the pages within, or to wipe away my touch from the cover.

"I told you when Colonel Prevost first brought you into my house what would be expected of you in a Christian household," she continued. "I warned you then that there would be consequences if you didn't obey. I will not permit you to keep this bastard under my roof."

I gasped. I'd told myself that she wouldn't truly follow that threat to give away my child, and that the Colonel wouldn't permit it, but to hear her now say it again made dread run chill within me.

"Please, Mistress, no," I pleaded. "Please don't do that."

Her mouth grew tighter. "Don't argue with me, Mary, or I shall—Is that Colonel Burr?"

She twisted around on the sofa to look toward the front hall. The Colonel could not have chosen a better—or was it worse?—time to return home earlier than usual from his office. Mistress struggled to free herself from the coverlet, her thin legs tangled in the quilted silk.

"I'll fetch him, Mistress," I said, offering as I would have done countless times before.

But now she looked at me not with gratitude, but with unhappiness, and a certain resentment as well. For years I'd made her household run smoothly for her, so that her attention could be directed in other ways more agreeable to her. Now, suddenly, I wasn't making things easier for her, but more difficult.

"Tell Colonel Burr I wish to see him at once," she said. "Return here with him, Mary. He'll know best what needs to be done to address this situation of yours."

I hurried into the hall, where the Colonel was shrugging free of his coat for Carlos to take. He must have walked home from his office. His face was flushed and gleamed with sweat, and he'd soaked through the white linen of the sleeves of his shirt.

"Good afternoon, Mary," he said pleasantly. "Though it is warm today, isn't it?"

"Mistress wishes to see you in the back parlor, sir," I said. My words were unremarkable, but he knew at once from my expression what had happened.

"How is she?" he asked quickly, his heels brisk across the marble floor.

"Unhappy, sir," I said, following after him.

He nodded, visibly bracing himself.

It did not take long for Mistress to repeat my story. The Colonel sat beside her on the sofa, his arm around her shoulders and her hand upon his knee, turned inward toward each other and linked together as husband and wife. I stood alone before them with my hands clasped over my child, cast in the role of the sinner awaiting judgment.

"A common sailor, Mary," he said, frowning at me. "Did you learn the man's ship? The name of his vessel's owner, or its master?"

"No, sir," I said meekly. I'd told him before what I'd intended to say, of course, but this was exactly why I hadn't left it to him to devise my story. He would have made it too long, too complicated, just as he was doing now. The name of the vessel's owner! I knew he didn't like me lying to his wife, but he'd like confessing to her even less, and so my lie now must serve for us both. It didn't need more details.

Yet still it was my heart that raced, my mouth that was dry. Not from the lie, but from fear that I'd been wrong to trust him.

"It doesn't matter, Aaron," Mistress said. "The rogue has clearly fled, with no intention of returning. It's left for us to determine what's to be done with Mary and her—her issue. Of course as she is, she cannot be permitted to remain in this house."

"I do not see why not," the Colonel said evenly. "Mary is the most efficient woman at her position in the entire city. You know you would be lost without her. We all would."

Bright pink patches showed on Mistress's pale cheeks.

"Be serious, Aaron," she said curtly. "After Mary has demonstrated this laxity in her morals, you would wish her about our daughters?"

"The girls will model themselves after you, Theo, not a servant," he said. "You know that. You're the very best model a daughter could possibly have. Come now, calm yourself. It's not good for you to become this distraught."

But Mistress only shook her head, quick little shakes that made the ruffles on her cap twitch. "If you wish me to be calm, Aaron, then I would prefer you not take her side against me."

"I am taking the side of reason, expediency, and Christian compassion," he said. "Upon reflection, I'm certain you will do the same."

She continued to shake her head, refusing his arguments and his attempts to soothe her as well. More ominously, she withdrew her hand from his knee.

He glanced up at me, his eyes for once impossible for me to read.

"Mary, go to the library," he said, "and wait for me there. I wish to speak to my wife alone."

"Yes, sir," I murmured as I curtseyed. "Mistress."

I held my head high as I left the room, reminding myself that in all of this I'd done nothing wrong. Yet as soon as I was alone in the library, my show of confidence shattered, and I pressed my hand over my mouth to keep from sobbing aloud. All around me in this room were reminders of the first time the Colonel had taken me, there against that wall and beneath the print of the view of the harbor, and I remembered how demanding he had been and how I'd been helpless to refuse him. I told myself yet again that I wasn't the one at fault and never had been, yet still I couldn't help from thinking that if only I'd somehow been more adept at avoiding him, or been able to say something that would have made him stop, then I wouldn't be here now.

I closed my eyes, fighting both my fear and panic as I tried not to imagine what fate was being decided for me in the other room. Ah, they'd so many genteel ways to describe what had befallen me, didn't they? Because the Colonel had wanted a friendship with me, a friendship filled with assignations, I'd now found myself with what Mistress called a situation.

My poor child kicked and twisted within me, doubtless sensing my fears, and for his or her sake I took a deep breath and another, striving to calm myself. Weeping would achieve nothing; it never did. I went to stand at the window, and with my hand on my belly I forced myself to focus upon what I saw, not what I feared. I counted the paving stones on the curb, and the panes of glass in the windows of the house across the street. Then I looked up, and began to count the shingles on the roof as well.

I turned about quickly when the door behind me opened. I'd expected Carlos or Peg to have come to summon me back to the parlor. Instead, it was the Colonel himself.

"Sit, Mary," he said as he closed the door. He wasn't smiling, and my heart plummeted. "Please. I won't have you standing before me like some woeful penitent."

I sat on the very edge of the chair he'd indicated, one of a pair of straight-backed chairs that stood before his desk for visitors. To my surprise, he took the other, sitting near to me instead of in the armchair behind the desk.

"Mary Emmons," he said gently, so gently that I wanted to weep again. "I regret that you suffered through that. I'm sure it was difficult for both you and my wife."

"It was difficult, sir," I said, biting back my bitterness. "But necessary."

"Yes." He cleared his throat, never good. "Once you left the room, Mrs. Burr grew calmer, and was able to see matters in a more rational light. I believe you will be pleased with her final decision. It will be best for you, and I know it's what you've always wanted. First of all, you will be permitted to keep your child. I've persuaded her of that."

"*Our* child, sir," I said, insisting he remember. "Ours."

"Yes," he said, another of his answers that wasn't an answer. "The small pantry off the kitchen will become your room, for you and your child, as soon as I can have the men clear it out. Tell me what you'd like to furnish it, and I'll see that you get it. A comfortable bed, of course, a washstand, a chair, a small table. Whatever you wish."

"The pantry, sir?"

"Yes, I thought that would suit you," he said, clearly pleased with himself. "After all the years you've served Mrs. Burr, and the responsibilities you have, it seemed that it was time you should be rewarded. What do you make of that?"

"What do I make of it, sir?" I looked down at my clasped hands, resting on my belly. "That I will be permitted to sleep in the cellar rather than the attic?"

"The room will be your own, with privacy to go with it, and a latch to the door if you wish it," he said, striving to make me understand his notion of generosity. "A little gratitude would not be amiss, Mary, considering."

It wasn't difficult to understand that the privacy and the latch would benefit him as well, and that the only reason I would be given a comfortable bed instead of my customary pallet would be so that he could visit me there. That privacy was for him, not me.

Abruptly I rose and went to stand at the window again, heedless of how my back was turned toward him.

"Then I thank you, sir," I said to the window, but loudly enough that I was sure he'd hear my bitterness.

I heard the scrape of the chair as he rose to join me. I stiffened as he slipped his hands around my thickened waist, and then higher, to cup my heavy breasts. My pregnancy hadn't deterred him at all. He relished the ripeness of my body, and took cocksure pleasure in knowing it was his doing. Mistress must have gone upstairs for him to be so free with me.

"Mary, my Mary," he whispered against the side of my throat. "I'd never deny that you have dreams."

"No, sir?" I twisted around to face him, pointedly pressing my belly between us. "You know what I wanted. I wanted—I *want*—for this child to be born free. You always promise me in time, in time, in time. That time is almost done, sir. I've only three months left. Three months, sir, else your son or daughter will be only one more piece of your wife's property."

I was glad to see him flinch. "This was not the time to raise the issue with Mrs. Burr," he said. "You saw today how she remains low and unwell."

"What I saw, sir, is that she was ready to give away our child like the last whelp in a mongrel's litter," I said bitterly. "If any ill came to you, then I would be left upon her mercy, a place I never wish to be."

"That won't happen, Mary," he said firmly. "I swear to you it won't."

I gave a small cry of frustration, and shoved my hands hard against his chest. "I've lived too long in your house not to know the power of the law. I know that without a paper that's been sworn and signed and witnessed, your oath will mean nothing beyond this room."

"Then you must trust me, Mary, that it will be done at the proper time." Gently he lifted one of my hands from his chest and turned it in his, kissing my palm. "That's all I ask. Trust me."

If I was good at lies, then he was every bit my match. He was a lawyer, and accustomed to telling tales that swayed the truth as easily as wind blows through a field of corn. I searched his face, hunting for some reason to believe that he'd keep this promise where he'd failed before.

I did not find it.

If Miss Burr was her father in miniature, then Miss Sally was twin to her mother. With tilting dark eyes, glossy ringlets, and a dainty little chin that mirrored Mistress's, she was as fair and delicate as a doll made of French porcelain.

Because of that same delicacy, Miss Sally had been spared most of the rigorous education and long hours of study that her older sister had endured. While at the same age Miss Burr had been able to read any passage presented to her and to write a pretty hand as well, Miss Sally still preferred books with pictures, and printed her letters rather than wrote them. The Colonel might be concerned that his younger daughter was being spoiled, but little Sally was well content to spend most of her days in her mother's company, the two of them telling stories with dolls and other toys to play the roles. In turn Mistress had come to rely upon the little girl to help ease her own sorrows after the recent deaths of her two infant sons, and she'd found much comfort in Miss Sally's innocent charm and laughter.

It had become the custom in the last months of summer for Mistress and her daughters to leave the city for a country retreat, and avoid the fevers that often rose with the season. This year, however, it was determined that neither Mistress nor Sally could withstand the rigorous journey, and the Colonel also wished them near to the care of their physician.

He and Mistress both were concerned for Sally, and with good reason, too. Since the beginning of the summer, she had suffered from some form of wasting that no doctor could diagnose, let alone cure. She had grown so thin that her breastbone showed through her skin above the neckline of her gown, and her eyes were ringed with bluish shadows. By the end of September, she had become so enervated and weak that she was content to spend much of the day lying within her mother's arms and venturing no farther.

If ever a mother's determined love should have saved a child, then Mistress should have had that power with Miss Sally, and not even the cruelest Fate should have chosen her to suffer further.

Yet Fate has never been known to be fair, and one morning as little Sally lay curled beside her mother she closed her eyes as if to sleep, and slipped away. It was for her a painless death, as easy as if an angel had come from Heaven itself to carry her off in his arms, but the anguish and suffering this death left within the family cannot be imagined. Three children lost in less than two years was a fearsome blow by anyone's standards, but there was no doubt to anyone who knew Mistress that this death was easily the most painful to her, and the most difficult for her to bear.

It also made for a peculiarly melancholy atmosphere for me.

As can be imagined, there was no further talk of my freedom, not when Mistress was shattered with grief. Nor could I accuse the Colonel of breaking his promise to me yet again, for he, too, mourned deeply for Miss Sally. As was the custom, Mistress and Miss Burr did not attend the funeral, leaving it to the Colonel, Mr. Prevost, and Master Bartow to follow the little white-painted coffin on its final journey, and freely water the grave with their tears.

I was in the final weeks of my pregnancy, and like most women approaching motherhood, I thought often of my own mortality. It was at this time that I began to more thoroughly consider myself a Christian and a true child of God, and I found comfort in a small congregation of local servants and tradespeople, some free, some not, who gathered together on the Sabbath to read the Scriptures. This wasn't the chilly, vengeful faith of Mistress and the Colonel, but one that gave me hope and peace when I was most in need. Childbirth was a perilous time for mothers and babes alike, and death was always a possibility for one, the other, or both. Not only had I witnessed Mistress's sorrows, but my own mother's death remained a constant warning, as it had been ever since I was old enough to learn of it.

My child was lively in my womb, yet still I worried endlessly. What would become of my little one if I were to die? Would he or she have a haven in this house, or be cast off to perish?

I'd another worry, too, one that I'd little choice but to keep locked tight within me. In New York I was carelessly considered a mulatto, for most people here hadn't heard of Pondicherry, let alone of Tamils. Because of my English father, I was myself fair enough to be called yellow, or bright, in America. My child would only be a quarter Tamil, and might in time prove to be so light skinned as to be mistaken for white by strangers.

But what if this child strongly favored the Colonel, or even Miss Burr? What if my well-told lie of the lonely English sailor was proved false in the most obvious way possible? If Mistress were to see her husband's face in my child, she'd realize at once the deception that had occurred, and continued still, beneath her roof. There wouldn't be anything that the Colonel could say that would change it, either.

My pains began in the afternoon of the last Tuesday in November. The Colonel and Mistress were having a small supper for close friends that same evening. My midwife, Mrs. Conger, had warned me that since this was my first labor, I could expect it to be lengthy, and that the best way to make it progress was to continue as usual for as long as I could.

This I did, preparing the meal and overseeing service, though I kept to the kitchen and didn't show myself, bent over and groaning, at the dining table. None of the company upstairs knew that my travail had begun. I was proud of my brave persistence, yes, but also grateful that I'd something to keep my thoughts busy as my pains progressed. I waited until the table had been cleared and the last dishes brought downstairs for washing before I finally sent for Mrs. Conger.

By the time she arrived, my pains were sharp and close together, and soon after midnight in my room near the kitchen I was delivered of a beautiful girl. I wept when I first held her, still covered with the blood that we shared: tears of joy and wonder, as every new mother sheds, but also of melancholy regret, that I had brought this poor child into the same captive condition as I suffered myself. She was my daughter, my most precious love, but she was also Mistress's property, and it fair broke my heart to think it.

For many months, I'd thought long over my daughter's name, an important decision that I was determined to make before Mistress did. I'd been forced to give up my birth name when I'd been sold into bondage, and the two I'd been called by since then had been chosen for the simple convenience of others. I couldn't give my daughter much, but I could give her this: Louisa Charlotte, an elegant New York name that was as perfect as she was herself, and worthy of the free woman I was determined that she'd become.

Being all too aware of the power of legal records, I had her baptized quickly, the morning she was born, to make certain her name was recorded. Mrs. Conger's brother, who led our little congregation, came to me and saw to it that my daughter was welcomed as another lamb into his fold.

I didn't send word to the Colonel, preferring to keep my daughter to myself a little longer. But Carlos never could keep a secret, and let the news slip when he took the morning coffee to his master. The Colonel hurried to my room with flattering haste, his jaw unshaven, a red silk dressing gown tossed over his nightshirt, and his bare feet in slippers.

"I came as soon as I heard," he said as he closed the door. "You should have called me last night, Mary. How do you fare?"

"Well enough, sir," I said with a weary smile. His surprising solicitude touched me.

"I'm thankful you are." He bent and kissed me gently. "Carlos said the child is a girl."

I nodded. I was exhausted and my entire body seemed stretched and torn, yet in that moment I felt nothing but contented pride as I unfolded the corner of the blanket so he could see our daughter's face.

His smile was true and full of wonder, enough to make fresh tears well up in my eyes. After he had seen his last two sons stillborn, this baby must truly seem a miracle.

"What a pretty child," he marveled softly. She *was* pretty, with full cheeks, a rosebud of a pout, and thick, feathery lashes. "She is healthy?"

"She is, sir," I said, with more pride. "The midwife swore she was as strong and fine as any babe could be."

"So she is," he said. "Like you, Mary."

I smiled, choosing to take that as a compliment. I'd never been a delicate lady, not like Mistress. True, I was not tall, and could be overlooked among a crowd, but I was sturdy and strong and stubborn. I'd survived where others twice my size had not, through wars and disease and perils at sea, and now childbirth, too. I prayed my daughter would, too.

Lightly he touched a finger to her velvety cheek, and instinctively she turned toward it, her tiny lips rooting even in her sleep. He chuckled with delight, and so did I.

"She suckled from the first," I said. "The midwife said that being hungry like that's a sure sign she'll prosper."

"Oh, it is, it is," he said softly. "Isn't that so, little girl?"

That was what he'd called both Miss Burr and Miss Sally, and once again tears stung my eyes. I wept whenever he showered fond endearments upon me, too. But by now I understood that no matter how sweet his words might be, the affection behind them was always destined to be empty and false. I didn't want my daughter to learn that same bittersweet disappointment, or the pain that came with it, either.

"You can't call her that, sir," I said, drawing her more closely into the crook of my arm. "If you do, people will know the truth."

"No, they won't," he said, his gaze still intent on the sleeping baby. "People only see what they expect to see."

"You shouldn't be here now at all, sir," I said. I glanced up at the single small window in one corner of the room, judging the hour by the first weak November sunlight. "Mr. Prevost and Master Bartow will be awake soon, if they're not already."

He ignored me as if I hadn't spoken.

"She'll need a name, then," he said. "What shall we call her?"

"She's already been named and baptized, sir," I said. "Reverend Sampson obliged me, directly before you came. Mrs. Conger served as the godmother and witness."

"That was hastily done, Mary," he said, not hiding his disappointment with my decision. "Something more seemly could have been arranged."

"Waiting has never benefited me, sir, nor would it have done so for my daughter," I said firmly, refusing to let him try to persuade me otherwise. "Her name is Louisa Charlotte Emmons."

He looked up sharply, not merely surprised, but shocked.

"Louisa Charlotte, sir," I repeated proudly. No doubt he thought it too grand for her, or for me, but I didn't care. It was what I wanted for my daughter.

"You are certain?" That first shock I'd glimpsed had disappeared, or leastways been hidden away. He was good at that.

"I am, sir," I said, as determined as I could be in the circumstances. "Besides, the name cannot be changed now."

"Everything can be changed in court, Mary," he said, too thoughtful by half for my liking. "Nothing is permanent. You should know that."

But even as I grew uneasy, the moment seemed to pass for him. He looked back to the baby, and smiled.

"Louisa Charlotte," he said softly, gently. "It's a fine name for her. You did well, Mary."

I smiled, too, even as I fought my foolish tears. Mrs. Conger had warned me I might feel unsettled and weepy, and that it was all part of childbirth. But I was glad that the Colonel left soon after that, and because he'd court cases in other counties I didn't see him again for the next two weeks.

Within three days, I was back at my usual responsibilities. Mistress considered herself generous to allow me that much time to myself. I suppose she believed as most white people did, that my body would heal much more quickly than hers on account of having darker skin; she'd taken at least a month to recover after each of her confinements. Still, I'd heard of other bondwomen who'd been expected to return to their toil the following day, and that included those who worked in open fields, too, so I was more fortunate than that.

As it was, I crept up and down the stairs like a bent old woman. I bled, and my breasts were heavy and ached with the unfamiliar weight of mother's milk. Worst of all, however, was having to leave my sweet babe alone as I went about the rest of the house.

Louisa slept in a basket, on a mattress I'd made for her of old flannel stuffed with rushes, and I put the basket atop my bedstead so she'd be raised from the chill and drafts of the bare floor. Peg, Mina (whom Mistress had bought earlier in the year), and even Carlos had promised to listen and go to Louisa if she cried, but if they, too, were not in the kitchen my poor little mite was left to wail, piteous and alone. As her mother, I fretted for her, but I also worried that Mistress would be irritated by her cries. Although the Colonel had prevailed on Mistress to let me keep Louisa, I didn't wish to give her any reason to change her mind.

I would sooner end my own life than have my daughter taken from me. Each day I grew more in love with her, with every tiny feature of her face and form becoming more dear to me. I never tired of holding her or rocking her gently in my arms as I sang to her, sometimes in French, sometimes in English, and sometimes even in Tamil. All she cared for was my voice, my touch, and the nurture of my breast. To give my daughter what I'd never received from my own mother was the sweetest joy imaginable, and every moment I was apart from her I thought of nothing beyond how soon we could be reunited.

Mistress did not come downstairs to congratulate me, though to be fair, I could not recall her ever coming down to the kitchen in that house. But she did ask me how the baby and I did the first time I saw her after the birth. It was a formality, no more, that I answered in as few words as possible, and I believe we both were relieved to have it done.

Thus I was doubly surprised when several days later she and Miss Burr came downstairs together with the express purpose of viewing my daughter. I had just finished suckling Louisa, so while I was daubed with spit-up milk, Louisa was full and content and sleepy, which is the most agreeable way to present a new infant.

"We've brought you some of my old baby clothes, Mary," Miss Burr said importantly, setting the bundle she carried on the table. "Mama said you could use them now."

"Thank you, Mistress," I said. I recognized the clothes as things that had been worn first by Miss Burr, and then by Miss Sally. I'd stitched many of them myself, so it pleased me that my daughter should wear them, too.

"Your baby is very pretty, Mary," Miss Burr said, wide-eyed with interest as I placed Louisa into her basket. "Her fingers are so tiny."

"Thank you, Miss," I said as I swiftly put my bodice to rights. "She's a good baby, and scarcely cries at all."

"Might I hold her, Mary?" asked Mistress. Her expression was both doting and inexpressibly sad.

I couldn't refuse her. I nodded, and gently lifted my daughter from her basket to place her within Mistress's arms. My daughter was still so young that she was content in most any embrace, but Mistress held her with the well-practiced confidence of a mother many times over, swaying gently from side to side in a rhythm that soon lulled the baby to sleep.

"I've missed this," she said softly. "There is nothing on earth more precious than a new baby."

"No, Mistress." For once we agreed completely. "There isn't."

"Have you named her yet?" she asked. "To me she is as sweet

as a spring blossom. You could call her Rose, or Tulip, perhaps, or Daisy."

No, I thought: *no.* Flower names were slave names, given to girls who'd never have more value to their masters than a wildflower to be admired for their beauty, and then trod under foot.

"I've named her Louisa, Mistress," I said instead. "Louisa Charlotte Emmons."

Mistress stopped swaying, stricken. It wasn't so very different from how the Colonel had reacted when I'd told him.

"Louisa," she repeated, gazing down at the baby in her arms.

"I like that name," Miss Burr said. "It's the same as the French king's name, only for a woman. May I please hold Louisa Charlotte, too?"

"Of course. You must be very careful, Theo," Mistress continued, "and you may hold her only for a moment. Here, sit in this chair, so I might place her into your arms and lap."

While I hovered and held my breath, ready to rush in and preserve my child if necessary, Mistress did as she'd said. Once Miss Burr had climbed into the old armchair and carefully arranged her petticoats to form a welcoming lap, her mother set Louisa across Miss Burr's legs. At once the little girl circled her arms around my daughter and smiled happily down upon her, and I was reminded of how she, too, had lost a sister and brothers just as Mistress had lost a daughter and two sons.

Yet when I saw Miss Burr and my Louisa together, I also thought of how they were half sisters. Did they sense that bond, I wondered, even if they were both too young to recognize it? Would there ever be a sympathy between them from the common blood of their father, or would the gap between their stations be too great ever to be bridged?

When the Colonel returned home several days later, he, too, brought me gifts, but of a different nature: a pale blue coverlet of the softest wool I'd ever touched for Louisa, and for me small gold hoop earrings with tiny coral drops.

"These are too fine for me, sir," I said as I held the earrings in my palm. "Mistress would take notice at once, and ask how I'd come by them."

"Oh, I doubt she will," he said. He'd come to my room early, before Mistress was awake, to see both me and Louisa. He was already dressed for work in his customary black suit and with his dark hair clubbed and powdered.

"Besides," he continued, "the earrings will be hidden by your cap, where only you will know they're there."

"And you," I said, still disturbed by the lavishness of his gift. The only ornament I'd owned was the small heart-shaped token that Lucas had wrought for me long ago, and even that I'd ceased to wear. These earrings from the Colonel seemed a very different kind of gift, both in their value, and in their intent.

Not that the Colonel cared. "Come, Mary, let me see how they look on you."

Reluctantly I slipped them into my ears, into the old piercings that Ammatti had made when I'd been a baby. I hadn't worn earrings of any kind since I'd been brought to New Jersey, and I'd forgotten how they felt, dancing lightly against the sides of my neck as I turned my head from side to side.

He nodded with approval. "They suit you," he said. "Wear them always, and think of me."

I kissed him in thanks as he expected, and gathered Louisa up from her basket to put her to my breast. I didn't need gold earrings to be reminded of him, not when I'd his daughter.

"Theodosia is very taken with Louisa," he said, smiling fondly at his daughter. "I'd wanted to hear what she'd been studying in her lessons, but Louisa was the sum of her conversation with me last night. She's lonely for company her own age, poor child."

I thought again of how the two girls were half sisters, and how sad it was that they'd likely never know it.

"She liked Louisa's name, too, sir," I said. "But Mrs. Burr thought I should have called her Rose or Tulip."

"'Tulip'?" he repeated with dismay. "I'm glad you didn't. What she really wishes is that you hadn't chosen the name that you did. You didn't know any better, of course. You couldn't have."

"Known what, sir?" I asked uneasily.

"Oh, it's old, sad history now." He shook his head. "Long ago, before the war, she bore two daughters to Prevost. Neither of them were strong, and both died, much to my wife's considerable sorrow. Their names were Anne Louisa, and Mary Louisa."

I gasped, horrified that I'd accidentally given Mistress one more reason to dislike me.

"Why didn't you tell me, sir?" I exclaimed, holding my daughter—my Louisa—more tightly. "Oh, if she thinks I chose the name from spite, or to be cruel, or—"

"She doesn't," he said, unconcerned, even callous. "She hasn't mentioned it at all to me. But her thoughts were clear enough when Theodosia prattled on about your child's name. I said nothing to you because you were already determined upon the name. As I said, it's old history."

But this wasn't old history to Mistress, and all the more poignant to me now that I'd become a mother myself. I didn't doubt for an instant that she could recall those little girls as clearly as if they'd been lost to her last week, not twenty years before, and I remembered her wistful expression as she'd held my daughter.

The Colonel drew his watch from his pocket to check the hour and sighed.

"I must go," he said, clicking the watch shut. "I predict a veritable mountain of rubbish waiting on my desk for my attention. Having the Constitution settled with a president soon to be elected is necessary, but the courtrooms have become as clamorous as Bedlam itself with everyone racing about to file this or that before the new government has its way. If it were up to me, I'd toss it all into the river and begin again, instead of piling old laws and decisions atop one another."

"That is true, sir," I agreed. As fine as this new constitution was in many ways, as a woman and a slave I'd no rights under it at all. I, too, wished the congressmen had begun fresh, with more freedoms for more people, as had been promised at the beginning of the war. "Perhaps more changes will come in time."

He made a *harrumph* of disdain. "Not until they choose a president who isn't a stolid donkey from Virginia."

"Oh, sir, you shouldn't speak so of General Washington," I said, chiding mildly. I'd always enjoyed how he'd speak of politics to me and it was a relief to hear it again now, even if I didn't agree. It interested me, yes, but it also made me feel as if he considered me worthy of such conversation. The best compliment he ever paid me was calling me clever, and I'd preferred that first gift of the little notebook for writing that he'd given me a hundred times more than the earrings he'd insisted I have today. "Especially since the Federalists will see that he is the first president."

"The Federalists aren't obligated to see to anything," he said as he rose from the single chair, preparing to take his leave. "No sane gentleman would run against the almighty Washington, though I've heard of a few who might throw themselves upon their swords like that simply for sport, and to be contrary."

Sated, Louisa began to shift and fuss in my arms and I quickly put her to my shoulder, rubbing her back to calm her. For once, I didn't want her to distract him.

"But the General is the only natural leader who can bring the states together, sir," I reasoned. "No other gentleman is as respected, nor as capable of uniting men."

He smiled, and wagged his finger at me.

"Oh, Mary, sweet Mary," he said. "You've been reading Hamilton's ramblings in the papers again, haven't you?"

I flushed, but in truth I liked when he teased me for reading.

"I have, sir," I said, "and I'll continue to read them so long as they make sense to me. Colonel Hamilton can be powerfully persuasive."

"Like a little Scots terrier," he agreed. "But then, you've that kind of determination, too. No wonder you agree with him."

"I agree with his sentiments regarding General Washington, sir," I said. "That is not the same as agreeing with him in everything."

He laughed. "One day I should bring you to court with me as my counsel, Mary, and let you parse words with him before a jury and judge."

I laughed softly with him, trying to imagine so preposterous a scene.

"If I'd the chance, I would, sir," I said wistfully. "You know I would."

"I do indeed." His smile faded, but his eyes were filled with affectionate regard as he reached out to cradle my cheek in the palm of his hand.

"You're a treasure to me, Mary Emmons," he said. "Have you any notion of how much I value our friendship?"

"Oh, sir," I said, my eagerness instantly deflated, and replaced by guarded disappointment at his mention of friendship, a word that would for me now always have another meaning. "It is too soon after Louisa for an assignation. I am not well yet, and I—I would not please you."

He frowned. "I didn't intend to lie with you, Mary," he said bluntly. "I'd hurt you, and there'd be no pleasure in that for either of us. I'm not that kind of brute. I pray you don't believe I am."

I looked down, avoiding his gaze. He was playing the pad of his thumb over my lower lip, a seductive little gesture that contradicted everything he was saying.

"No," he said, answering himself when I didn't reply. "What I meant, Mary, is that these last months—this entire year—has been a difficult one for me, and yet through it your peace has been a constant comfort to me. And now this child, our daughter. What a gift you have given me amidst so much sorrow!"

From the kitchen on the other side of the door came the sounds of voices—Peg, Mina, Tom, and Carlos—and clatter of pots and pans for breakfast. They all knew of the Colonel's attentions to me, but still it shamed me when he so blatantly left my room in their presence.

"You must go, sir," I said softly. "You'll be late to your office."

He nodded, and bent to press his lips upon our daughter's forehead, gently, sweetly, as a father should. There was no sweetness when he kissed me next, but instead such sufficient possessiveness that he grunted with satisfaction when he finally broke away. It hadn't mattered to him that I'd held our daughter between us, or perhaps it had.

After he left me, I continued to stand there, my eyes squeezed shut as I struggled to compose myself before I joined the others. I thought of all he'd said and what he'd done, and I thought of Mistress, and I thought most of all of Louisa.

He could promise me again and again that in time (how I'd come to hate those two meaningless words!) he'd see that Louisa and I were freed. Now I was sure he wouldn't do it, not so long as he could keep both his unknowing wife and me beneath a single roof. More risk, more daring, a dangerous spark to his male passions, and the excitement he craved to counter the daily tedium of his legal work.

It was all the same for the Colonel. Not so long ago, I'd hoped to turn his games around to my own advantage. Now I knew better, and with my daughter's birth the stakes had become too high. I unhooked the gold earrings from my ears and stuffed them into my pocket. This life he'd created was far too precarious for me and now for my daughter, too, and I could see no good nor happiness coming from any of it.

CHAPTER 20

City of New York
State of New York
September 1789

The long line of carriages crept along Cherry Street, along the East River shimmering in the early-evening sun. To pass the time, the idle passengers in those carriages could calculate their progress in several ways. The easiest was to count each cross street as it was passed: Roosevelt, James, Oliver, Catherine, George. Another was to spot the various wharves that jutted into the river, much like water-bound streets themselves: Beekman's, Rutger's, Bedloe's, Ackerley's, with each shipowner's distinctive pennant fluttering from the masts of his vessels. For those who had no patience with such man-made markers, however, the setting sun offered the truest measure, slipping slowly downward toward the green hills to the west as the day's end approached, and with it the single goal for every one of the carriages.

Lady Washington's Friday night levee began promptly at seven o'clock. Only ladies were invited to these levees, the acquaintances, friends, and would-be friends of the new president's wife, and no lady wished to be early, and made to dawdle and wait in her carriage until the appointed hour. Nor did any wish to be caught so far toward the end of the line of carriages that they arrived late, and were perceived as uncaring, or even disrespectful.

Tonight Mistress's arrival would be safely in the middle. I could tell from the set of his feathered hat that Jem, Mistress's driver, was pleased with our place in the line. It reflected honorably on Mistress, and therefore on him, too. I suppose I could claim my share of the credit as well for having Mistress dressed and ready at the precise moment that Jem had drawn up before the front door. The more successful the Colonel became, the more effort it took by me and the others to present that success to the world.

For now, however, I was simply thankful to be sitting where I was. Louisa was cutting teeth, and we'd both spent several miserable, sleepless nights because of it. But where she could sleep during the day, I'd no choice but to work as usual, and I welcomed this rare chance to sit and do nothing. I rode high on the box beside Jem, where we'd enjoy the breezes from the river at the end of this warm September day, while Mistress likely sweltered below in her splendid closed solitude. The sleek little chaise and the two horses that drew it had been one of the Colonel's latest purchases, for while he was content to travel about the state on his business by way of public stages and sloops, he wanted his wife to be driven about the city in the most elegant style.

At last our turn came to stop before the President's House, a stately brick house three stories tall and five windows wide. Swiftly I clambered down from the box as the footman opened Mistress's door and handed her down. She paused expectantly, waiting for me to step behind her to adjust her peacock-blue silk skirts so they trailed behind her in the short train that had become the fashion. Then she glided up the white marble steps and into the house while I followed at a proper distance.

To most eyes, I was no more than another sign of the Colonel's prosperity, like the chaise or the jewels around Mistress's throat. My very person was an enviable luxury. When the Washingtons had brought a dozen or so of their slaves with them from Mount Vernon to New York as house and body servants, they'd set one more fashion in the new capital. Now when I accompanied Mistress, I also wore a silk gown, chestnut brown and plainly cut much like the dress worn by Lady Washington's girl, who was also light skinned. It was our form of the livery worn by the men, calculated to impress others rather than to flatter us.

Only I knew that my presence was much more than that.

Even in Lady Washington's large drawing room I remained close to Mistress like a respectful shadow. I handed her her fan when she grew too warm, and I fetched her tea prepared as she preferred, with an abundance of sugar. I saw that her cup was kept filled, and though I knew she'd no taste for the ice cream that was served later, I brought her the smallest possible serving so that she could pretend to have enjoyed the indulgent treat along with the other ladies.

But I also watched her closely for any sign that she might be faltering, or that the crush of the crowded room was too much for her. As long as I'd served her, she'd suffered from bouts of random illnesses, and her spirit had always been stronger than her mortal body. But since Miss Sally's death last autumn, these various maladies had increased. Sometimes it was a pain in her breast and side, and on another day it might be an unbearable gripping of her bowels and belly. She tried to brush it all aside as nothing, jesting that her ailments derived only from the trial of living in a city filled with Federalists.

But the Colonel's concern grew, and one physician after another was called to tend to her. None could find a reason for her complaints, let alone a cure. Though no one in the household would dare say it aloud, her condition seemed a painful echo of Miss Sally's final affliction, and the Colonel instructed us all to do whatever we could to ease her every discomfort, and coax her toward recovering her strength.

We all obeyed. It was Mistress herself who refused to take any additional care, especially when the Colonel was away from town. I'd only to watch her here tonight to see the proof.

The weekly levees at the President's House were one of the ways that she sought to help forward the Colonel's political aspirations. When General Washington had been sworn in as president and the offices, positions, and other favors for the new government were distributed, the Colonel had been optimistic. Given his military record, his legal accomplishments and other merits, and his ever-growing political standing, there seemed few other men in the country who would be more useful or more deserving.

Yet when all the plum posts had been announced, the Colonel was left with nothing. He had not seemed surprised, and professed to be untroubled by it. I knew he cared, but hid his disappointment well, even as I silently recalled all the times he'd spoken disdainfully of the new president. Only Mistress was openly outraged, convinced that the Colonel's enemies had succeeded in denying what should have been his.

That outrage gave her the strength to engage however she could on her husband's behalf. The Colonel respected her efforts as he did her judgment; he always had. While he was away at court, she held small gatherings and dinners to help smooth over misconceptions and win him more support among those in power. She never missed services on Sundays (something the Colonel himself could not claim), since all the most influential families also belonged to Trinity Church's congregation. Even when she was confined to her bed by illness, she still wrote letter after letter, many to her husband that were, I suspected, filled with observations and advice based on what she'd seen while he was away.

Most noticeable of all, she attended these levees at the President's House. She understood the power of petticoat politics, as she wryly called them, and did her best to coax and charm Mrs. Hamilton, Mrs. Livingston, Mrs. Adams, and all the other wives whose husbands she suspected of undermining the Colonel. Most of all she tried to woo Lady Washington, an older lady with a cloud of white-powdered hair, a plump chin, and a gracious manner. She was much admired among the white populace. Among us servants, however, it was said that she was an unkind owner with a sharp tongue and an overseer who believed in whipping. I'd heard the Washingtons also forbid their people the simple privilege of reading and writing, and it was little wonder that they were closely watched from the constant fear they'd run.

Mistress was as skillful at this kind of diplomacy as anyone, and as I watched her I thought of how fortunate the Colonel was to have her toiling on his behalf, and not against him. But all that smiling and scraping and clever conversation was hard work, and by nine o'clock I saw that Mistress was tiring, her shoulders sagging and her cheeks pale.

"Forgive me, Mistress," I whispered, coming beside her. "Should I send for the carriage?"

Without turning, she nodded quickly. Within a quarter hour she'd made a final curtsey to Lady Washington, said her other farewells, and been bundled back into her chaise. Yet as I undressed her for the night, she unburdened herself, too.

"I cannot believe what a pack of deceitful old cats those women are," she said. "Smile and nod, smile and nod, as if I don't know their husbands were quick enough to call my Aaron a traitor to their ridiculous Federalist cause!"

"I'm sorry, Mistress," I murmured, too tired to do more than half-listen as I eased the pins from her hair. In the past year she'd begun to turn gray, the white hairs stark against her dark, and she'd continued to powder her head to help mask them.

"It's an out-and-out disgrace, Mary, and an appalling betrayal as well," she said, her voice taut with irritation. "The president and his toadies expect complete obeisance. To them a man who thinks for himself is a hazard, not a prize. How readily they can turn even the tiniest whisper into a scandal!"

As weary as I was, I heard that word "scandal" and my heart quickened with uneasiness. It was a word that white people used to hide all kinds of unpleasantness, all kinds of things they'd been forced to see against their wishes. I would be considered a scandal, and so would my daughter.

"It's all because my husband took poor Greenleaf's civil suit over their ridiculous procession last summer," she continued, talking to my reflection over her shoulder in her looking glass. "My Aaron did what was right, but what he did pricked the puffed-up pride of Hamilton and Livingston, who went crying to Washington. Oh, it's clear enough, isn't it?"

"Yes, Mistress," I said. This was old news, and had nothing to do with me or my daughter. For now we were safe.

Besides, none of what Mistress was saying seemed to me to be much of a scandal at all. Soon after the Federalist-sponsored parade in support of the Constitution that I'd attended along with both the Colonel and Miss Burr, the editor of an Anti-Federalist newspaper had dared to print a satire mocking the procession. I'd recalled reading it myself, just as I recalled the Colonel remarking that the piece had only said what needed saying about the infernal procession, anyway.

But Federalists in the city had taken grave offense, and had stormed the newspaper's office and destroyed the press. The leader of the attack had been no drunken apprentice, but the parade's own grand marshal, Colonel William Smith Livingston, an old acquaintance of Colonel Burr's from the war and from the College of New Jersey. When the editor filed suit for damages, Colonel Burr had chosen to represent the editor as being in the right, not his Federalist friend who wasn't, and the fact that he'd been successful in court had only increased the insult in Federalist eyes.

I'd now witnessed enough to understand that mixing politics and lawyers seemed always to lead to heated tempers, empty accusations, and wounded manly pride. The patriotic good humor that had followed President Washington's inauguration had all but vanished in the city, replaced instead by a constant display of acrimony and accusations between Federalists and Anti-Federalists. The Federalists seemed the more prone to declaring they were absolutely, even violently, in the right, and I recalled how Colonel Burr had wisely explained to his daughter at the parade that emotional displays and politics should never be mixed.

I also thought of how, while all this was occurring, Colonel and Mrs. Hamilton had ceased to accept Mistress's invitations to dine. Clearly there were different lessons being taught in the Hamiltons' house than in the Burrs'.

Even Miss Burr was aware of the change. The Washingtons' grandchildren, Miss Nelly Custis, who was ten, and her brother, Master George Custis, who was eight, lived in the President's House. Small gatherings with dancing were arranged for them with other suitable children, and Miss Burr was invited. I was often her companion when her mother was unwell, and I could see for myself how much more accomplished and well-spoken Miss Burr was at age six than the other, older girls. Doubtless this was on account of her father's insistence on rigorous education, but I suspected it was also in large part because she spent much more time among adults than children her own age.

For her own part, Miss Burr was unimpressed by the young Virginians.

"I don't know why Mama says I must attend them, Mary," she said after one such gathering. Because of her youth, I was sent to ride with her in her father's chaise. She sat beside me in her white linen dress with a wide salmon-colored silk sash and a matching pelisse. Her feet in red slippers didn't reach the carriage floor, and instead swung back and forth with the motion of the carriage.

"Nelly Custis is a perfect fool," she continued. "Her entire conversation is about her wardrobe, and nothing else. She says she's just now begun lessons on the harpsichord, and that practicing makes her *cry*. If that is what she has learned at Mrs. Graham's school, then I'm most grateful that Papa insists I have tutors instead."

"Colonel Burr does what he believes is best for you, Miss Burr," I said mildly, though I knew that, in her heart, she would like nothing better than to be with the other girls at Mrs. Graham's. "He and your mama both take special care with everything you learn."

"Yes, they do." She smiled and slanted her gaze up toward me, exactly as her father did. "Do you know that the girls at Mrs. Graham's are taught filigree, fancywork embroidery, and japanning? Papa will laugh aloud when I tell him. Could there be more idle occupations than that, fitting them for nothing of usefulness? I read Herodotus, while they learn *japanning*."

"I'm sure that's what their parents wish for them, miss," I said. Doubtless those other parents would be equally horrified by Miss Burr's curriculum, which the Colonel had proudly designed to be identical to a boy's.

"That's because they are all Federalists, unable to think for themselves," she said, "which makes them as idle and foolish as their daughters."

I raised my brows. "I do not believe your parents would wish you to speak so plainly of your friends, miss."

"Oh, indeed not," she said promptly, sniffling and rubbing at her nose. "Papa says a person of breeding must always strive to be agreeable and at ease, and ignore what others might say or do to vex them."

I handed her a fresh handkerchief to replace the one she had inevitably mislaid at the President's House. "That is wise advice, miss."

She blew her nose with noisy exuberance that betrayed her age rather than her breeding.

"That's because my papa *is* a wise man," she said with a final sniff, rolling the handkerchief into a tight little ball in her palm. "I think he's the wisest in all New York. Mama says so, too. That is why I hate it when those girls call him names, and say he's two-faced and false, and other things besides."

"They are mistaken, miss," I said firmly. "You know they are. Politics brings out the worst in people, miss, and makes them say all kinds of foolishness, even about people like your father who do not deserve it."

She nodded solemnly. "That's what Papa says, too. He says I must ignore them, and be better than they are."

But though she tried to be resolute, as the Colonel would surely have expected of her, I couldn't help but see how she seemed to droop beneath those same expectations. I placed my arm lightly across her shoulders, and at once she slid across the bench. With a little sigh, she snuggled close to my side, silently seeking relief from the adult foolishness of politics.

She was still a child, and there were many grown women and men who wilted before the slanders and sharp tongues of others. Surely the Colonel understood the power of words, and the damage they could do as well, especially to those he loved most.

It was a thought that I often considered over the next days, worrying and fussing at it like a dog with a bone. I'd every reason, too, and I was still afire by the time the Colonel returned home a fortnight later, after a lengthy court case in Poughkeepsie.

Mistress had gone out in the carriage, and had carried her daughter with her. I was taking advantage of their absence and Louisa's napping to finish some mending. Earlier in the day, Miss Burr had caught her heel in the hem of one of her dresses, and with Mistress away I'd dared to sit on the cushioned window seat here at the top of the stairs, where the sunlight would be brightest for stitching the delicate white linen.

I started when I heard the front door open in the hall below; I hadn't expected Mistress to return so soon. Quickly I bundled away my sewing, and rose before I could be caught where I didn't belong. But it wasn't Mistress and Miss Burr who'd returned. It was the Colonel, already at the foot of the stairs.

"Good day, Mary," he said, his smile wide and warm as he climbed the steps to join me. "I'm glad to see you. Where are my wife and daughter? I'd expected more of a welcome home."

"Good day, sir," I said, dropping a curtsey to him with my mending in my hands. I wondered why Carlos had not appeared to take his hat and coat, and carry his bags to his room; I'd have to speak to him about that. "They've taken the carriage to drive along the river, sir. Mistress wished for a change of air."

"Ah." He paused on the stair, drumming his fingers lightly on the banister. Whenever the Colonel had been away, his return always took me by surprise, as if I were seeing him for the first time. I don't mean his mere arrival, either. Somehow while we were apart, I forgot the intensity of his very presence, and how it affected me. It was a condition, almost an affliction, that is not easy to describe without sounding foolish. Yet every time he came back, it was like this for me: how the air is charged and changed before a rising storm, with rumbling dark clouds that race across the sky, fair crackling with both anticipation and dread of what was to come.

"How long have they been gone?" he asked.

"They've only just left, sir," I said as evenly as I could. "I do not expect them back for some time."

He nodded, and resumed climbing the stairs. "Then you shall be the one to welcome me home, Mary. Come with me."

I waited until he'd passed me on the landing, then followed him.

"It appears the weather has improved in New York while I was away," he said, shrugging his arms free of his coat as he entered his bedchamber. "Poughkeepsie was a veritable swamp of rain and flies."

"Here the skies have been fair, sir," I said, from habit taking his coat and folding it. "Forgive me, sir, but we must speak."

"Yes, Mary, we must, though from pleasure, not obligation." He turned to face me and reclaimed his coat, tossing it carelessly over a chair. Gently he took me by the shoulders to draw me closer. "You know how I miss you when we're apart. Tell me how our little Louisa does."

"She flourishes, sir," I said, smiling a little at the mention of my daughter as I always did. "But it is for Miss Burr that I worry."

Instantly his bantering manner vanished. "Is she ill? I'd a letter two days ago from my wife, and she said nothing of any mishap."

"She's perfectly well, sir," I said quickly. "You needn't worry for that."

"Thank God for that," he said fervently. Poor man, he'd already had so much stolen from him that even the hint of losing this cherished daughter must have been unbearable, and I placed my hand lightly on his chest.

"It's a different kind of distress that plagues her, sir," I said softly. "When she attends gatherings with other children, for dancing and such, she has begun to hear gossip that they repeat from their parents."

"That's easily resolved," he said, his hands sliding back and forth across my shoulders and slipping beneath my kerchief to find my bare skin. "She shall remain here at home, where she won't be distracted by the prattling of other children."

"Forgive me, sir, but that is not the answer," I said. "She needs friends."

"They're hardly friends if they're unkind to her," he reasoned. "They won't be missed. Besides, Theodosia scarcely has time for her lessons as it is."

I shook my head. It was a strange coincidence that Miss Burr, with love and luxury lavished upon her, was in much the same lonely predicament that I had suffered at her age so long ago in Madame's Pondicherry household: locked away from other children and set to tasks that seemed endless, with only adults for company.

"You cannot keep her apart from the world, sir," I said, wanting to forget my old memories of loneliness. "She will hear the gossip when she attends church or the playhouse. Everyone in New York speaks of politics."

He sighed, more resigned than impatient. He traced his finger along the side of my throat to touch the tip of my earlobe beneath the edge of my cap. "You're not wearing the earrings I gave you."

"Forgive me, sir," I said, prepared to tell him a half-truth, or perhaps it was a half lie. "But they're too grand for me."

"Nothing is too grand for you, Mary," he said, his voice low.

It was an empty compliment, yet still I smiled, tipping my chin a fraction toward him.

"I don't know what Theodosia has told you to gain your sympathy, the little minx." He now stood so close to me that I smelled the scent of the oiled leather reins and the horse that he'd ridden still clinging to him, and mingled with his sweat on his linen and the hint of the lemon soap he preferred for shaving. "But she understands the difference between Federalists and Anti-Federalists, and why her papa didn't receive an appointment in the new government. I've explained it all to her."

"You explained it to her too well, sir." If he wished to continue this conversation like this, then I would, too. There was a strange allure to discussing Federalists and Anti-Federalists even while his hand was upon my breast. I also knew from experience that he'd be more likely to agree to whatever I asked of him now, more so than if I spoke in other circumstances. "She knows your ambitions, sir. When others speak ill of you, she fears your hopes will be denied, and shares your unhappiness. Mistress does as well, though she hides it better."

He chuckled, and nipped his teeth at my lower lip. "Words alone can't hurt me, unless I let them."

"They will, sir, if the scandal is sufficient." I drew back, forcing him to meet my eye. "What Mistress calls a scandal is petty and small, like you taking Mr. Greenleaf's case against the wish of your rivals. But a true scandal could ruin you."

He was irritated that I'd pulled away from him; he never liked to be denied in anything. This was exactly my argument, if he'd only listen.

But perhaps I'd pushed him too far. I slipped my hands around the back of his waist and leaned my body into his. Even through our clothing, we fit together with a sensual tidiness, both of a size to please the other. He always claimed I tempted him, but he tempted me as well, tempting and tempting until I gave way.

He knew it, too, the curve of a smile flickering upon his lips.

"I worry for you, sir," I said, more sadly than I'd intended. "If your Federalist enemies were to—"

"They are not my enemies, Mary," he said with maddening logic. "How many times must I tell you?"

"I know you don't believe that, sir, no matter how many times you say it aloud," I countered. "Everyone has enemies."

"Mary, please," he said. "I refuse to view my life like some ancient vengeance-mad tragedy. I'll leave the histrionics to Hamilton and Livingston and the rest. Some Federalists are my friends, and some Anti-Federalists are not. Some hold beliefs that I share, and others will always be in disagreement with me. None of that will make them my enemies."

"But *they* think otherwise, sir," I insisted. "What if they sought to ruin your honor and good name? What if they were to learn of me and Louisa, and tried to use that knowledge to discredit you?"

His frown returned, a deep furrow across his brow. "We have spoken of this before, Mary. So long as we are discreet, no one will know of our friendship. It is between us alone, and the world shall not learn of it."

I shook my head. "I am not so convinced, sir," I said, my words now coming in a desperate rush. "I fear that one day someone will see me with my daughter, and note a resemblance to you."

"You trouble yourself over nothing, Mary," he said, as if simply by speaking the words firmly he would make them true. "I have certain aspirations, yes, but I am far more devoted to those who live beneath my roof than I am to any reckless fantasy of power. Anyone who gazes into Louisa's face shall only see her sweetness, her beauty, and unless they are told otherwise they'll see nothing more."

He paused, his expression turning oddly fixed.

"Unless you yourself were to tell someone, Mary," he said slowly, his fingers tightening ever so slightly into my shoulders. "You wouldn't do that to me, would you? Turn Judas, and spin a sordid tale of lies to a newspaper or pamphlet writer in exchange for a handful of silver?"

I gasped, shocked he'd think me capable of such a disgraceful act.

"No, sir, never!" I blurted out. "Surely you must know that I could never betray you like that, not when—not when—"

My words stumbled, with me unsure of where they would go next.

"When you care for me as you do?" he said, smoothly finishing my sentence for me. "That's what you meant to say, isn't it? That your heart is too tender for such an unwomanly action?"

I looked away in confusion. Was that in fact what I'd begun to say? That I'd come to feel a genuine tenderness for the man who'd forced his child upon me, whose wife owned me as her property, who had used me as the Colonel had done for years?

With a tenderness of his own that I hadn't expected, he turned my face back toward his and kissed me.

"My own dear Mary," he whispered, his voice low and confidential and seductively sweet. "You know of my considerable affection for you, and the joy I find in your company. That you would worry so about my happiness, my honor, pleases me beyond measure."

I wanted to explain that I'd no choice but worry for his happiness, because his prosperity and success were bound so tightly with my own. But he kissed me again before I could, and took me to lie upon his bed, and then it was too late for me to speak, as it so often was.

But not for him. "Since you have shown such concern for me, Mary, you shall be the first in New York to hear my news," he said afterward as he rebuttoned his breeches. "Governor Clinton has asked me to be the new Attorney General of the State of New York."

"Governor Clinton?" I asked, more surprised by the governor's name than the appointment itself. "He has rewarded you, even though you publicly supported Mr. Yates against him in the last election?"

"But you see how little that matters, Mary, exactly as I told you earlier," he said with a confidence that was very close to smugness as he poured himself a glass of wine. "Clinton chose me for my knowledge of the law and my connections, not because I'm a Federalist or Anti-Federalist or any other nonsense."

"Congratulations, sir," I said as I retied my apron more tightly about my waist. I glanced from the window to the street, thinking I'd heard the carriage. I was uneasy about Mistress's return, even if he didn't seem to be, and I went to restore the mussed coverlet on the bed. "It sounds to be a very grand position for you."

"What it sounds to be is a damnable amount of trouble and work, and endless nights in bad inns and country taverns with wretched meals," he said with far more good humor than his words merited. "The salary is an absolute embarrassment to a gentleman, as it is for all state posts. I'd earn more as a wandering tinker, peddling pans and pots. I'll also have to contend with that rough old rogue Clinton. But I shall do some good in the state, and that makes it a worthy endeavor."

I paused, my hands resting at my hips. I knew him far too well to let that bit of foolishness pass unchallenged.

"This post is but a means to an end, sir, isn't it?" I asked suspiciously. "You'll only linger long enough to make yourself known throughout the state in all those country taverns. Then you'll jump to something better, won't you?"

He laughed, and set down the now-empty glass.

"Mary, my Mary," he said, hooking his arm around my waist to dance me in a small circle. "Could there be a more clever woman in all this city?"

I scoffed and rolled my eyes toward the ceiling, but I also followed his steps through the little dance that he was humming, my petticoats swinging about my ankles and me smiling in spite of myself.

And later, of course, I realized that once again he hadn't answered what I'd asked.

The Colonel's prediction of how the attorney generalship would be a thankless post proved correct. He was in fact paid next to nothing, or at least that was how Mistress described the four hundred pounds he received each year, a fraction of what he ordinarily earned through his private practice. His hours were long, his work tedious, and I suspect his fellows were often dull and provincial. He was away from his New York home and from us for weeks at a time: in court, speaking before the State Assembly, serving on commissions, and in those bad inns and country taverns.

He wrote almost daily to Mistress and Miss Burr, and to his Prevost stepsons as well. His letters were greeted with great fanfare and arranged along the mantel when they arrived until they were read aloud after supper. Whenever these readings took place, I tried to linger in the parlor on some pretext or another—clearing away the cloth after the meal, trimming the candles on the table, sweeping up the crumbs that had fallen—so that I, too, might hear news of the Colonel, and what he was achieving, or not.

His letters were like he was himself, filled with witty observations and descriptions of the people he met in the course of his days. Knowing the letters would be shared within his family, he clearly wrote for his audience, and I do believe that, had he wished it, he might have pursued another career as a writer of tales and fancies. He could wring amusement from even the driest of courtroom debates, nor was he above turning his pen against himself, either, and wryly making himself a hapless character in the comedy that Albany law and politics seemed to be.

Now I understood why the Colonel could not write directly to me, nor I to him. Like any good lawyer, he was by training loath to put anything into writing that could be misconstrued or maliciously used by others. I understood that I was not his wife. Still I yearned to hear from him myself, a reassurance that Louisa and I had not been forgotten, and that we'd still a place in his thoughts. I wished for a letter, however brief, that was meant only for me.

I knew he wrote them to Mistress. It was clear enough when she'd come to the parts of his letters that were intended for her eyes alone. She'd break off into silence, and smile fondly as she continued reading to herself. Often she'd trace the letters he'd penned with her fingertips, as if by touching the dried ink she could likewise touch their author.

When the Colonel did at last return to the house on Broadway, he was greeted like a hero, and swept away not only into his family, but also by friends and other acquaintances eager for political news and gossip. To the howling displeasure of most New Yorkers, Colonel Hamilton and Mr. Jefferson, the Secretary of State, had made a devil's bargain to move the federal capital from the City of New York to Philadelphia for the span of ten years, and then to a new capital city to be constructed to the south on the Potomac River. While it appeared that much of the political excitement had departed with President Washington, Congress, and the rest of the federal government, New York's state and city politics once again surged upward to supply their own peculiar drama.

As attorney general, the Colonel was positioned to know most everyone and everything in the state, and there was rarely a night when he was not out in a tavern with other politically minded men, sharing information and favors. Unlike most Federalists, he didn't keep the exclusive company of gentlemen like himself, but mingled freely with mechanics, lower merchants, tradesmen, and old soldiers who were veterans of the war. He held the then-unpopular belief that these men had as much a right to be heard within government as did the city's fine gentlemen, and in many quarters the Colonel's name and popularity grew. Now whenever I was sent to the market or a shop, I saw that as soon as it was known I'd come from Colonel Burr's house I received a better cut of beef and an extra dozen eggs, and wide smiles with it.

But with so much to occupy his attentions, there was little time left for the Colonel to spend on me. Our assignations were few and infrequent, most usually long past midnight. He'd come to my little room from one of his public house meetings, smelling of tobacco and liquor. Without lighting a candle, he'd slip into my bed in the dark, and often not even bothering to undress more than halfway. Sometimes he woke Louisa, but most nights she slept through his visits, and when I awoke again in the morning I often wondered if I'd dreamed them myself.

If during this time the Colonel had simply ceased coming to me, I believe I could have forgotten him, and even found myself another man who cared for me as I deserved. I'd my opportunities, too. I was only thirty, and still sufficiently handsome that men were drawn to me whenever I went in public. I might even have found another man I liked well enough to wed.

But the Colonel's hold remained too strong for me to shake. I do not know why this was so, nor could I explain the reason for it. When he was with me, he was as eager and passionate as ever, and as full of compliments and promises, too, more than enough to fill my thoughts until the next time he appeared.

Did I wish for more of his time and companionship? Did I wish he could be a true father to my daughter, as he was to Miss Burr? Did I wish that he did not have a wife, and that I was a free woman, with the power of choice? Of course; I would not be a woman with a beating heart if it were otherwise. But I tried not to think of what I was missing, and thought instead only of what I did have from him, and nothing beyond that.

Then, finally, after two years of serving dutifully as attorney general, the Colonel received the reward that he'd been seeking all along.

In those days, the senators sent to represent each state in Congress were not elected directly by the people, but were chosen by each state's assembly and senate. This was perhaps an efficient system, given how difficult a general election was to conduct; nearly four months had been required to tally the votes for President Washington's election. But it was also a system that was ripe for corruption and manipulation, and Governor Clinton was well experienced in both.

As the Colonel later explained to me, the governor and the rest of his supporters had had enough of Colonel Hamilton's arrogance. The governor determined that Colonel Burr would be elected as the next senator from New York, replacing the current senator, General Philip Schuyler, who happened to be Colonel Hamilton's father-in-law. The Colonel won handily over the General, and Mistress held a succession of celebrations in honor of the newest senator from New York.

By all reports, Colonel Hamilton and General Schuyler both were livid. Colonel Burr did not gloat or glory in his triumph, but simply noted that there would be certain persons who would find his election displeasing. In the autumn of 1791, he headed south to Philadelphia to become part of the Second Congress. There he secured lodgings in a respectable house run by a Quaker widow, and cast himself into his new employment. Once again, the women of his life—Mistress, Miss Burr, me, and Louisa—were left behind in New York.

As always, he wrote letters home, describing the splendid city of Philadelphia in great detail, as well as his less-than-splendid fellow senators and the speeches he'd already had to endure. He jeered at the wealthy Federalist hostesses who wished to emulate the royal courts of Europe with their showy displays of silver, jewels, rich dress, and exaggerated manners. He listed the invitations he'd had to dine, and claimed he'd decline them all for lack of the properly opulent clothing.

But there was an undercurrent to these letters that hadn't been in the ones he'd written while he'd been the attorney general. To me it was clear that while he was a man of importance in New York, he was scarcely noticed in the larger city. He'd few old friends in Philadelphia that he trusted. He resolved to balance the time spent in the Senate chambers with more activity, and went skating upon the river, on which he fell, and thanked the hardness of his head for its preservation. His lodgings were lacking, and he could not sleep. He missed his home and his family.

He was, in short, homesick.

Nor was I the only one who realized it.

"It appears your father is lacking agreeable company, Theodosia," Mistress announced one evening in March, crisply refolding his latest letter. "I believe he'd be pleased by a visit from us."

Miss Burr's eyes widened with delight. "When, Mama? When might we leave?"

"As soon as it can be arranged, pet," Mistress said, smiling. "True, it's not the most agreeable season of the year for a journey, but a passage by water should take only a few days at the most. Mary, you will come with us."

"I, Mistress?" I asked, surprised.

"Yes, yes," Mistress said. "You can tend both Theodosia and me. From what the Colonel says, his quarters are too confined for me to bring more than a single servant. The others here can look after the house perfectly well."

"But my daughter, Mistress," I said plaintively, though I already knew the answer. Louisa was now three, a lively, quick, and beautiful little girl, and my dearest joy. We'd never been parted since her birth.

"Peg can mind her while you're away," Mistress said. When I didn't answer, she glanced back at me, her brows raised incredulously. "Come now, Mary. You didn't believe you could bring your child with us, did you?"

"No, Mistress," I said softly, already dreading the separation that Louisa would not understand. "I shall begin our preparations tomorrow."

And yet it was for the best that I would see the Colonel again in person. I'd news for him that could not wait, and that I didn't dare write to him, from fear my letter might fall into malicious hands. When he'd left New York in the fall, he'd also left me again in an unfortunate condition. I'd taken care to count the weeks until I was sure, but my body had told me long before my reckoning did. It had been the same with Louisa. My breasts were full, my waist was thickening, and I was so weary that I could scarcely complete my tasks each day.

Yet I did, because I'd no choice, and I didn't complain, either. It wouldn't be long before I'd have to contrive and confess another passing indiscretion to Mistress. I already knew that, whatever story I told her, she would not be happy with my news.

I was less certain of what the Colonel's reaction might be.

I'd no doubt that he loved Louisa, and that he'd keep his word to see that she'd never be in want. I hoped he'd feel that way about this babe, too. But a second child would only be more difficult to explain, not just to Mistress, but to anyone else who might be too inquisitive. A trail of mulatto bastards would not be a benefit to a United States senator, and an easy target for his enemies.

Within the week, I found myself in Philadelphia, a place I'd never before visited. Unlike New York, Philadelphia had not suffered much during the war, and its streets were lined with imposing brick houses, churches, and public buildings. Also unlike New York, whose streets wandered willy-nilly from following the shape of the island as well as old Dutch boundaries, Philadelphia had been planned by Quakers in a straight and orderly fashion that made it both pleasant and convenient, a modern city in every sense.

That convenience, however, did not include the Colonel's lodgings. He wryly called it his Spartan quarters, a half-hearted jest with too much truth. All the congressmen in the city were suffering from the same plight, with a great many gentlemen and not enough rooms. The Colonel had only a small room that faced an alley, with a disagreeable privy in the yard outside. A low field bed with a blue-checked canopy, a washstand, a ladder-back chair of pine, and a table for writing were the sum of the furnishings. He and Mistress would share the bed, while Theodosia and I would have pallets on the bare floor. She thought it a great adventure, but I found it a grim reminder of where I'd been, and where I and my daughter could easily find ourselves again if circumstances turned against me.

I also doubted that I would be alone with the Colonel for any time during our stay. He and Mistress attended as many of the gaudy dinners and balls as they could, even though they ridiculed them and their hostesses' pretensions afterward. On several afternoons, Mistress also instructed me to take Miss Burr to walk along

High Street to a confectioner's shop, and to show no haste returning. She'd been almost giddy, her cheeks pink with anticipation, while the Colonel pretended to attend to business at his makeshift desk. I didn't want to think of what they did together while I was banished to the confectioner's shop.

The days of our visit slipped by and dwindled in number. I'd tried to tell the Colonel I needed to speak with him alone, but there'd never been a proper time, and my desperation grew. Finally, three days before Mistress was to sail on the packet back to New York, the Colonel asked me to come out with him under some pretext or another while Mistress was resting and their daughter was at her lessons.

At first we didn't speak at all, with me following a half step behind him, as was to be expected. The air was sharp and crisp, yet the sun was warm enough on my face that I pushed the hood of my cloak back against my shoulders. I stole a glance at the Colonel, his black cocked hat pulled low over his brow as he stared steadfastly ahead. There were many people on Chestnut Street on so bright a day, and often he'd touch the front of his hat and smile in greeting to someone we passed.

I knew we were playing our usual roles of Colonel Burr and his wife's girl. I knew that was what the world must see, and yet I longed to be able to reach out and slip my fingers into his, even if only for a moment. I wanted him to look directly at me and smile, and call me his own Mary. Most of all I wanted to tell him the secret I carried within my belly.

"Please, sir," I said at last as we paused at a cross street for a wagon to pass. "I must speak to you."

"Soon," he said curtly, as a master would. "I haven't forgotten."

He walked on without looking at me, and I lowered my head and followed, taking no comfort in his brusqueness. There was a small hole on the back of his left stocking, large enough that the pale skin of his calf showed through it. I'd have to mend that, I thought absently, or at least see that he had a proper new stocking. It wasn't right for the senator from New York to be so shabby.

"This way, Mary," he said, and we turned down a narrow street that was lined on either side by tall brick walls that hid the gardens and yards behind them. There were no other people in this street, and at last he slowed his pace to match mine, so we were side by side.

"Mary Emmons," he said softly. "I've missed you. You wished to speak, and here we are. How is our Louisa?"

"Oh, she is very well, sir," I said, breathless not from walking, but from being in his company. "When I left, she'd just discovered how to run, back and forth as fast as can be along the path in the backyard, like a tiny pony. And her smile, sir . . . she's so many teeth now, as white as little pearls, and when she smiles, she shows a dimple in each cheek, and she's—"

I barely caught myself before I erred. I was going to say that her smile was exactly like Miss Burr's had been at the same age. Like her, too, my daughter had her father's eyes, large and dark and full of life. But I'd learned that such remarks made the Colonel uneasy. He might love my daughter, but he still wouldn't think it proper to liken her to Miss Burr.

"She's a beautiful child, sir," I said instead. "Happy and beautiful."

"How I wish you'd brought her with you," he said impulsively. "I miss her merry little face."

"I couldn't, sir," I said sadly. "I had to leave her behind with Peg and the others to look after her. Mistress wouldn't—"

"Oh, I know, it wasn't possible," he said, "and with good reason, too."

The only good reason was that Mistress didn't wish to be troubled by my daughter on our journey, or to have less than all my constant care for herself. To me, neither were acceptable reasons to separate a mother from her child. But I also knew better than to say that to the Colonel.

And now I must tell him that he'd fathered a second child with me.

"How do you like Congress, sir?" I asked, stalling. "I overhear what you write when Mistress and Miss Burr read your letters aloud, but you make so many jests for their amusement that I cannot tell for certain. Is being a senator all you wished?"

He smiled wryly. "Nothing is *all* that I wish," he said. "But while the company is often fatuous, the actual labor of the Congress is not. The most useful of my committees addresses the woes of the widows and orphans left destitute by men who served in the war. Their petitions would break the hardest heart, and I am glad to help ease their suffering."

"That is most admirable, sir." How curious the twists of life could be, that he'd be called to this particular task on behalf of soldier's widows, when his own wife had stolen this same benefit from me.

"It is," he said. "But there is so much else that is discussed and addressed. The violent troubles in France, the unrest among the native peoples along the western frontiers, new laws and regulations and tariffs at every corner: little wonder that each day brings its own challenges and satisfactions with it."

"How fine it must be to do such good work, sir," I said absently, paying little heed to his words. "Does Congress ever speak of abolition?"

He grunted. "You would ask me that, Mary."

"I would, sir," I said, "because it affects my life and that of my daughter far more than what the French will do with their king and queen."

"Then I regret to tell you that abolition is not discussed as a federal issue, and likely never will be," he said frankly. "Too much of the wealth and economy of the southern states are bound to the labor of slaves for them to abandon it. When the country's Virginian president and his wife hold over a hundred slaves of their own—"

"You and Mistress own slaves, too, sir," I said with more sorrow than anger.

He pretended not to have heard me, exactly as I'd expected.

"It's as I've always believed," he said. "Abolition will eventually come through the states, in a manner that suits the people and economy of each particular place."

It was what he always said, a convenient explanation and a ready excuse, though I'd never been able to tell whether or not he truly believed it.

Perhaps that was what made me say what I did. "I've heard from other servants, sir, that if Mistress kept me here in Philadelphia for six months, I'd become a free woman by the laws of this city."

He stopped walking, and I stopped, too. He scowled down at

me, his eyes as penetrating as a hawk's, and though my cheeks grew warm beneath his gaze, I did not retreat.

"Is that truly the law, sir?" I asked, though I already knew it was: a tantalizing possibility, there for the taking. "I ask, because you of all gentlemen would know if it was so."

"It is," he said at last. "Any slave that resides in Philadelphia for a period of six months can claim his freedom without fear of retribution, and also without any financial recompense made to his owner for the loss of his property. But this does not pertain to you, because my wife has no intention of remaining here for such a considerable length of time."

"But if Mistress did, sir, then—"

"You would not abandon our daughter," he said bluntly.

I gasped with shock, reeling from it. "You would keep Louisa from me?"

"You and she are both my wife's property," he said. "You seem to know the law as well as I."

"But, sir," I said. "You would make a hostage of Louisa? You would use my child like that?"

"Would you leave me?"

I had no words for an answer, at least none that he'd wish to hear.

"I'm with child again, sir," I said.

He went very still. "So that is why you asked about the laws of this place," he said slowly. "You'd abandon one child in New York to assure the freedom of the second here in Philadelphia."

"No, sir, never!" I exclaimed, stunned he'd consider me capable of such a coldhearted action. "But I would be dishonest if I said I didn't want this child born into freedom, just as I'd wanted for Louisa."

"What is your reckoning?"

I still could not judge his reaction. "Summer," I said. "July."

He nodded, the first sign of possible acceptance. "You've said nothing to my wife?"

"No, sir," I said. "I thought it best to tell you first."

He glanced down from my face, judging my figure. "There is no need to tell her yet."

"I won't, sir," I said, disappointed in spite of myself. He'd been so kind, even playful to me earlier, and now he'd become cold and hard and unfeeling.

"You'll return to New York this week, and give birth there," he said brusquely. "I'll be in New York by then on recess. But remember, Mary. If you ever try to run from me with our children, I will hunt you down, and find you, and bring you back. Remember, and do not forget."

I was fighting tears as I edged away from him. Nothing I could say would make any of this right.

Words were not what he wanted. He pulled me into his arms and kissed me roughly, there in the street, and heedless now of who might see. I struggled at first, and then did not, my hands hanging limp inside my cloak. Possession, not passion: with him I'd learned to understand the difference.

Two days later, I sailed from Philadelphia for New York in the company of Mistress and Miss Burr. Over those two days, I do not believe the Colonel spoke directly to me again. He'd no need to, for there was nothing left to say. I thought often of the beckoning temptation of freedom that the laws of Philadelphia had so briefly offered to me, and the child I carried in my belly.

But in the end, it had been a mirage, shimmering and unattainable, and gone as swiftly as it had appeared.

Mrs. Emmans

CHAPTER 21

City of New York
State of New York
July 1792

I did not wait for Mistress to ask me about this child. Instead, I told her outright, in April, before the Colonel returned from the session of Congress. Unlike last time, when I'd been made to feel like a guilty sinner, I addressed her as directly as I could one afternoon while she sat writing at her desk. I stated my impending confinement as a fact, rather than the confession of a disreputable wanton, and I offered nothing of my child's father.

She sighed, and gazed at me, her expression filled with sad regret, and perhaps resignation as well. She'd long ago abandoned her habit of sitting so that sunlight would not fall over the scar on her forehead, and now it stood in stark prominence, a jagged line over one weary eye.

She set down her pen, and folded her hands before the letter she'd been writing. "Do you intend to keep this second bastard as you did Louisa?"

"Yes, Mistress," I said, determination clear in my voice. "I'd be a poor mother otherwise."

"I'd be a poor mistress to let you do so," she countered, "and give myself another hungry mouth among my servants to feed and clothe."

"Please, Mistress," I said softly. "Louisa has never brought you a moment's care or interruption."

"A child is not a stray dog to be brought into my home on a whim, Mary," she said, and for one dreadful moment I thought she'd tell me she intended to sell my child. Then she sighed again, and picked up her pen to dip it freshly into the well. "Fortunately for you, the Lord God advises us to be merciful, and you have managed well enough with Louisa. All I ask is that you look after yourself as well, Mary. You are too valuable to me to risk losing. Now go, and finish ironing those white-work ruffles. You are the only one I'll trust not to scorch them."

Now I have always wondered why, when she'd been so distraught when she'd learned of Louisa, she raised so little fuss over this second child. Had I earned that trust from her? Had she turned so much to her faith that she could be this benevolent toward me? Had the wasting succession of her illnesses made the effort of outrage simply too great?

Or had she finally come to realize what I was to the Colonel, and that my children had been sired by her adulterous husband— the husband she still loved beyond measure, even enough to forgive him?

I didn't know then, and now I never will. I simply curtseyed, and left her, and returned to my ironing.

My son was born soon after dawn on a fiery-hot morning in July 1792. My travail was easy, and he was the one who cried in loud amazement and irritation at the undignified process of his birth. Again I'd Mrs. Conger to support me, there in my room in the house on Partition Street.

Louisa instantly took to her place as an older sister, content to gaze at her brother and rock his cradle by the hour, though Miss Burr, too, found the little man to be a source of enchantment. I'd no trouble understanding their fascination, either. My son was a handsome fellow from his birth, with golden-brown skin and curling black hair, and his father's same eyes.

The Colonel was away in Albany when my son was born, engaging in his legal practice during the recess to augment the miserly sum paid to senators. This time, I waited to name and christen my child until his father had had the opportunity to make his acquaintance.

As he'd done when Louisa had been born, the Colonel came directly to me when he returned, his boots dusty and his clothing grimed from travel. All that seemed forgotten the moment he saw our child in his cradle, waving his tiny fists impotently in the air.

"My son," he said softly, marveling again as I suppose every father does. "What a beautiful boy he is, Mary."

In that instant, all the animosity and uncertainty between us in the last months fell away. What mattered was that we had made this child between us, and like Louisa he bound us together in ways that neither of us could deny.

Quickly the Colonel shed his coat, and carefully lifted our baby from the cradle, neatly tucking him into the crook of his arm. At once the child's fussing stopped, and he gazed upward, solemn and unfocused, into his father's eyes. My own eyes—and my heart—filled with tears at so tender a sight.

"What have you called him, Mary?" the Colonel asked without looking away from his son, nestled so happily against the white linen of his sleeve.

"Miss Burr began calling him *mon petit homme*—my little man—and we've all followed," I said. "I waited for you for something more proper."

He smiled, clearly pleased. "What should you like to be called, *mon petit homme?*"

"By rights it should be Aaron, sir," I said wistfully. "But I do not think that would be wise."

He glanced at me, his smile briefly fading. "I wish that it could be so, too," he said. "My own son! But as you say, I fear my name is too distinctive."

I nodded. "George Washington is a popular choice these days, sir," I teased. "George Washington Emmons."

"I think not," he said, chuckling. "We can do better than that. I believe Theodosia had the proper notion. A French name perhaps?"

"French names are both elegant and honorable," I said, liking the idea. "What of Jean? That's close enough to John that he could be called that as well. Jean Emmons."

"Jean-Pierre Emmons," the Colonel declared in his best courtroom voice. "No French baby enters this world without at least two Romish saints to bless him."

"Jean-Pierre, Jean-Pierre," I repeated, smiling as I tried the sound of it.

"Then Jean-Pierre he shall be," he said, and bowed to press his lips to his son's forehead.

At the Colonel's insistence, Jean-Pierre was baptized later that autumn at Trinity Church. Because of the humbleness of my son's parentage, the ceremony was done on a weekday afternoon, with only the Burrs, Louisa, and me present. It was a curious ceremony, too: Mistress had insisted on standing as Jean-Pierre's godmother, as was often the custom of owners and their slaves, with the Colonel naturally his godfather.

As can be imagined, I wasn't easy with this decision, but there was no possibility to object without causing more attention than I should. I pretended not to notice how the registrar had delicately drawn a line through the space reserved for "father," and left space only for my signature. What would they all have done, I wondered, had they known that the true father's name was already on the same registry page? Yet in this way my children and I had now been grafted onto the Burrs' mighty family tree, as sizable and noble as any other New England oak. The significance was not lost upon me.

As I stood in the church's dappled light with my newly christened son in my arms, I'd no notion that this would be among the last occasions for happy celebration that the Burrs would share together. Birth and death too often came closely together in that family, and that would not change now.

"You should feel some relief within the next several hours, ma'am," Dr. Bard said. "As I have explained previously, a general course of depletion helps relieve the convulsive action of the blood vessels, and hence lessen the pain."

He briskly wrapped a narrow strip of linen around Mistress's arm, over the inside of her elbow whence he'd drawn her blood. It was the third time he'd bled her this week, and her pale skin was mottled and bruised around the cuts that he'd made with the blade of his lancet. Solemnly his assistant took away the small pewter cup, nearly filled with the blood he'd caught from her arm, and passed it to the nurse to empty into the washbowl like a swirling crimson blossom in the water. I didn't want to consider how much of Mistress's blood had been drained from her veins over the years.

"I am glad to hear that you concur with Dr. Rush," the Colonel said as he stood beside the bed. "I've always suspected that an imbalance of humors was at the cause of my wife's suffering."

At Mistress's wish, there was a small crowd of us gathered about her: Dr. Bard, his assistant, and the nurse he'd suggested, the Colonel, Miss Burr, and me. The bedchamber was warm with the windows closed, the curtains drawn, and a fire in the grate, as the doctor had also recommended. If I'd been Mistress, I would have much preferred the sweet scents of a June afternoon through my window, but then she'd sadly had far more experience with illness than I, and always followed whatever physicians prescribed.

"You shouldn't tell one doctor to follow another, Aaron," Mistress said. She lay pale and wan against the propped pillows, her face pinched with suffering. "They do not like comparison within their trade any more than you do in yours."

Dr. Bard smiled and nodded as he wiped spatters of her blood from his hands with his handkerchief. I stepped forward, and gently laid a handkerchief dipped in lavender water across her brow, and she sighed her gratitude.

"I take no offense from the senator, ma'am," the doctor said in the falsely jovial manner that was calculated to encourage his patients. "Dr. Rush is arguably the most esteemed physician in our entire country, even if he is from Philadelphia, not New York."

"Nor are Dr. Rush's theories new ones in themselves," the Colonel said. "Tell me, Theo: who was the first to discover the four humors?"

"Galen of Pergamum," his daughter answered promptly. "He was the first to declare that blood was the most dominant of the humors, and bloodletting the surest of cures."

Dr. Bard's brows rose. "Well, well, Senator," he said. "It would seem you have a scholar of medicine in the family."

"My daughter aspires to scholarship," the Colonel said proudly, resting his hand on Theo's shoulder. "If she continues to be assiduous in her studies, she may one day merit that distinction."

I could not agree. It seemed strangely cruel to turn Mistress's suffering into one more lesson for Miss Burr.

This was not the first time, either. When Mistress was too ill to write to the Colonel directly, he expected his daughter to provide full medical accountings to him of her mother's condition. I'd seen her labor carefully over these, perfecting her spelling of the difficult terms used by Dr. Bard and others, just as I'd witnessed her dismay when the Colonel returned her letters with her misspelled words corrected, as he customarily did for her own improvement.

But at heart Miss Burr was still a young girl, not a learned scholar, and a daughter with concern for her mother, too. She leaned across the bed to take her mother's hand in her own, striving to offer as much comfort as she likely received.

"I hope you will be better soon, Mama," she said softly, stroking her fingers over the back of her mother's hand. "Perhaps then we can visit the new house."

"Oh, dearest, I didn't intend to spoil your excursion today," Mistress said with regret. "I'd rather you and Papa went without me. You know I always sleep after Dr. Bard visits, and Mrs. Johnson will watch over me. The house will still be there another day, when I'll be able to appreciate its charms."

"Are you certain, dearest?" the Colonel said, unconvinced. "There's no harm in waiting another day for you to join us."

"There is, because this day is beautiful, and should not be wasted," she said wistfully. She turned her face as best she could toward the window, and the sun that glowed through the curtain. "I wish for you and Theo to enjoy it. Take Mary with you, too. She has always been skilled at noting particulars of the rooms and conveniences, so I can begin to plan where everything shall be arranged."

Thus I believed it to be decided, but when I met the Colonel and Miss Burr in the front hall Miss Burr had an additional suggestion.

"We wish you to bring Louisa with us, Mary," she declared. "Jean-Pierre is too little, but not Louisa. Since she will also come to live with us to Richmond Hill, she should see it, too."

"Oh, miss, I do not know if that's wise," I said at once. "Louisa is working with Peg in the kitchen."

It wasn't that my daughter wouldn't enjoy both the ride and the lawns and gardens that the Colonel had told me surrounded his new house. Louisa was nearly five now. She adored Miss Burr, who in turn petted and indulged her as if she were a doll come to life. But I was always hesitant for the half sisters to appear together before others, from fear that their resemblance would be remarked. The Colonel always scoffed, and said only I saw the likeness because I sought it. He was doubtless right—Louisa was of a darker complexion, darker than I, while Miss Burr was exceptionally fair—yet still I fretted.

I also worried that someone might notice how the Colonel tended to treat the two girls as equals. He ignored my efforts to raise my daughter as she was and what she would be, a chattel slave. I wanted her to be industrious and skilled and accepting of her lot, for that would make her life easier. But if the Colonel bought sugared strawberries for Miss Burr from a vendor in the park, he'd buy another for Louisa as well. My daughter was still too young to take special notice of these little favors, nor did she think that a lack of a father was remarkable, because many servants' children among her acquaintance had a similar lack. One day she would, however, and I wondered how much longer I could preserve the myth of her conception.

None of this mattered to the Colonel.

"Bring Louisa, Mary," he said indulgently. "Who wouldn't prefer a ride in the country to spending the day in the kitchen?"

I thought of how that was a choice that few people like Louisa and I ever could make for ourselves, but dutifully I hurried her into her best dress, a flower-printed linen that I'd cut down from an old one of Miss Burr's, with a straw hat over her cap. I quickly suckled Jean-Pierre so he'd sleep, and then we went to join the others.

The Colonel kept a full coach now, painted a glossy dark red with his arms painted on the doors. The carriage could be drawn by a team of either four, or two, depending on the length of the journey. Today two would suffice, since we'd only be traveling three miles or so beyond town. Better yet, the Colonel let us ride together inside, an indulgence that Mistress never permitted.

I'd heard the Colonel speak with admiration of his new property, but even knowing his love of occupying grander and grander residences hadn't prepared me for his latest prize, a property and house called Richmond Hill. The property consisted of many acres of gardens, greenery, and even a large pond in addition to the house, with so much land that no neighbors were visible. The house itself stood high upon a hill with views of the North River in the distance. Three stories tall and painted white, this house was far larger than any other we'd lived within, even larger and finer than the President's House had been. A two-story porch with a filigree railing ornamented the front, along with five bays of tall windows, and a long flight of steps that led to the front door. There were also several outbuildings, including a barn, stables, and a house for carriages.

Once we'd stopped at the crest of the drive before the house's steps, we set the girls down to go across the lawn with the warning that they must remain within sight. The Colonel and I stood on the steps to watch them, an opportunity to speak alone that I hadn't expected.

"I've always admired this house," he said, glancing back at the house over his shoulder with satisfaction. "When it was Washington's headquarters during the war and I was his lowly aide-de-camp, I dreamed of living here. The place will require repairs and improvement, of course, considering it's at least thirty years old. John Adams lived here while he was vice president, though he and his wife did nothing to maintain it."

Dutifully I looked back as well. This close, it was clear the house needed a fresh coat of paint at the very least, but that sounded as if it would be only the beginning of what he intended. "How fortunate that the house has now come to you, sir."

"Oh, more than fortunate," he said lightly. "I represented the heirs of an old deed who claimed the war had made this land belong again to them and not to Trinity Church, who now possess it. The court did not agree, and though I lost the case, in gratitude the kind gentlemen from Trinity offered me the property at a most favorable rate."

He smiled, the disingenuous smile that meant he'd done something that he realized wasn't entirely right, but didn't particularly care.

I looked back to the girls on the lawn, thinking of how all this land now belonged to the Colonel. It hadn't been so very long ago that we'd all lived crowded together in the first miserable lodgings in Albany. He also intended to keep the sizable brick town house we currently occupied on Partition Street, just west of Broadway and not far from the North River. He and Mistress could rail on all they wished about the vulgarity of the Federalists. The Burrs were no better, not with his house, the glossy red carriage, the matched team of horses, the imported wines and spirits that accompanied every dinner, the paintings and prints in gilded frames that hung on the walls, and the silver tea service that gleamed on its own special table.

"Being a senator must pay handsomely, sir," I said dryly.

He watched the girls, not meeting my eye. "Six dollars per diem, Mary. That's what the position pays. No one grows rich on that."

"It appears you have, sir," I said. "You are a far better manager than ever I credited."

He chuckled. "I've been able to continue to shepherd a few choice cases through the courts," he said, "coupled with several wise investments and a modicum of luck. I'll make no apologies, Mary."

"It's not my place to ask you to, sir."

"Not out loud, no," he said, his gaze shifting back toward me. "But I know you so well that I can sense your disapproval without you speaking a single word. Wealth that is not enjoyed and put to good use only serves to make a man a miser."

I didn't answer, though perhaps according to him, I didn't need to. Despite his merry aphorisms, I suspected there was much more behind his rise. Last year there had been talk of the Colonel running for governor of New York. While he hadn't seriously entertained the idea, he'd enough supporters who wished him to do so that he was considered a true candidate, along with General Clinton and the jurist and diplomat John Jay. Finally he withdrew his name from consideration, claiming he'd more to accomplish in Congress.

Nonetheless, the newspapers had found much to say about him, both good and bad. For every line of praise, there'd been more hints of dubious land speculations, gifts from wealthy merchants who sought favors in return, and out-and-out bribery. To be sure, he was not alone in this. Most every New York gentleman believed in taking whatever opportunities presented themselves, and turning a blind eye to any improprieties. The Colonel had brushed the stories aside, claiming they were all empty rumors produced by Colonel Hamilton and his followers with the purpose of discrediting him.

Still, I could not help but think of another aphorism: where there is smoke, there is fire, and there was often more smoke puffing about the Colonel than from a chimney in December. Who could look at Richmond Hill and think otherwise?

We called the girls to us, and began to survey the house's interior. I'd brought a small commonplace book with me, and industriously made the notes that Mistress had requested: the number of windows in each room, the condition of the floors and stairs, and if there were signs of mice, birds, or dampness having made their way within.

For their part, the two girls enjoyed the echoes of their own voices and footfalls in the empty rooms. But the Colonel's mood grew increasingly more somber as we walked through the house, and by the time we had returned to the front steps he'd nearly ceased to speak at all. He sent the girls to pick flowers for Mistress, and then stood in silence for another few minutes beside me.

"Do you think my wife will like this house, Mary?" he asked at last.

"Oh, sir," I said. "How could she not?"

He pulled off his hat and blotted his brow with his handkerchief, but then kept his hat lowered in his hand as if he'd forgotten it was there.

"She has always been content wherever we've lived," he said. "All she's ever desired for happiness was her family and her books."

"This house will have much room for both, sir," I said. "The country air will be better for her than the city, too."

He fell silent again, absorbed in his thoughts with his hat still in hand and the breeze fluttering the black bow on his queue.

"I'm losing her, Mary," he said at last, so quietly I nearly didn't hear him. "Her constitution has been fragile from the first, but now she's slipping from me. I can tell from her eyes, by how hard she must labor to hide her pain from me."

"I am sorry, sir," I said. There was no use in denying what was so sadly evident. "For you, and for her."

He looked down. "I asked her yesterday if she wished me to resign my seat in Congress to be with her. She would not hear of it."

He reached blindly for my hand, but I stepped back, away from him. Tears stung my eyes. I didn't wish to be cruel to him, not now, but I'd no choice.

"Forgive me, sir," I whispered. "But you cannot hold my hand, not before Miss Burr and Louisa."

He nodded, and still looking ahead and not at me, he settled his hat back upon his head.

"Then call me by name, Mary," he said. "This once, let me not be sir, but Aaron."

"Oh, sir," I said. "Is that wise?"

"I do not know," he said, "but today I believe it is . . . necessary."

I sighed, a small breath of acceptance. "Very well, Aaron."

"Thank you, Mary," he said as Miss Burr and Louisa came bounding toward us with a basket filled with wildflowers. "Thank you."

The Colonel's household moved to Richmond Hill in late autumn, shortly before Congress resumed in November. Although there was still much work to be done about the house, the rooms were freshly painted and many of the walls covered with bright-patterned papers from France. Some of the furnishings had been shifted from the house in Partition Street, but most were new, featuring carved and polished woods and rich silk upholstery.

I was pleased by my new quarters as well. At first the Colonel had offered me the use of a small cottage on the property. But while the little house and the privacy it offered was tempting, I decided for Louisa's sake it was better to be in the main house, where there were more eyes to watch over her when I couldn't. I was given quarters in the cellar near the kitchen, much as I'd had both in the Broadway house and on Partition Street, but larger, with more room for Louisa.

Mistress declared it to be the most beautiful home in creation, and vowed she'd never leave it for another. Her words proved tragically accurate. Although the air at Richmond Hill was sweet and free of the coal smoke and seagoing stench from the docks, it was not enough to cure her. Her mother and her sisters and their families came to visit during the Christmas holiday, as they'd often done before, but this time the celebrations were subdued, and more tearful farewells than any rejoicing. After they'd all departed, Mistress seemed to grow weaker by the day. She was seldom able to leave her bed, but instead lay curled on her side as if surrounding the pain that ate at her belly.

Miss Burr and I took turns reading aloud to her from the new books ordered from the Colonel's London bookseller and from her old favorites, well-worn volumes that I recalled first seeing on her shelves at the Hermitage. We read in French—Rousseau, Voltaire, La Fontaine—as well as English, the better to divert her. The laudanum that Dr. Bard prescribed often made her stuporous as well, and some days I doubted she even heard our voices, let alone the authors' words.

Still we read on, as much for our own comfort as for her own. Unwilling to leave her mother's side, Miss Burr took to writing her daily lessons from her tutor Mr. Leshlie at the table in Mistress's room. Here, too, the girl dutifully wrote the letters that the Colonel expected, describing her mother's condition and treatment in great detail. It was the grimmest of tasks for a young lady of her age, and one that was too often completed through a haze of tears.

Because Congress had resumed later than usual on account of the yellow fever in Philadelphia, the Colonel was forced to remain there over the Christmas holidays, and into the spring as well. For Christmas he sent books, the gifts he knew were most desired within his family. As a special remembrance for Mistress, the Colonel sat for the artist Mr. Gilbert Stuart, whose studio was not far from Congress Hall. She wept when the portrait was delivered and taken from its crate, and ordered it hung immediately opposite her bed, where she would see it day and night.

The Colonel had obviously ordered the picture as an intimate gift meant for her, not posterity, for it showed him informally dressed against an unadorned black background, with his shirt collar open and his hair unpowdered. Considering that he was in his prime, only thirty-seven, the Colonel hadn't even asked the artist for the vanity of hiding how his dark hair had begun to thin away from his forehead. But Mr. Stuart had perfectly captured the intelligence in the Colonel's dark eyes and the sensuousness of his full mouth, so much so that whenever Mistress was asleep and unaware I would stand before it, and marvel at how it seemed as if the man himself were with me once again.

Yet books and a portrait were not all the Colonel sent to Richmond Hill. Even from afar he sought cures for his ailing wife. His friend Dr. Rush first advised hemlock, in a dose of a tenth of a grain, and when that brought no relief prescribed the dose to be increased to two whole grains, fresh and pure. Because Mistress could keep nothing in her stomach, he suggested attempting a spoonful of milk at a time, mixed with molasses or porter, to provide some nourishment. When that failed (as had everything else), Dr. Rush recommended Peruvian bark, and then, as a final resort, a tincture of mercury, which even the Colonel balked at employing. To me it seemed as if in desperation Dr. Rush was suggesting every remedy he knew, and every one was equally seized upon by the Colonel.

In early May, Mistress showed a slight improvement. She was able to sit up in bed, and she listened to Miss Burr recite her lessons again, as she'd once always done. Because everyone had expected the worst, the change in her condition seemed so remarkable that Dr. Bard himself sent an optimistic letter to the Colonel in Philadelphia with the good news.

A week later, I sat alone by Mistress's bed, knitting a stocking by the light of the fire while she slept. By Dr. Bard's orders, she was never now left alone, but I was here in place of Mrs. Johnson, who had gone down to the kitchen for tea. The hour was early, sometime before dawn. I'd heard the case clock downstairs chime four times, and the rest of the house was quiet. On the table beside Mistress's bed was a large Chinese vase filled with yellow and white Dutch tulips, proudly gathered by Miss Burr from the bulbs that she and her father had purchased together last fall.

I was so accustomed to the raspy rhythm of Mistress's breathing that I took no notice of it. Because she'd felt better, she lay on her back tonight, her painfully thin arms and hands resting over the coverlet with the long plaits of her hair—mostly gray now— arranged beside them. Since the flesh had shriveled from her fingers, she wore her wedding ring on a gold chain around her neck, and the little gold circle had also been carefully centered on her chest. Mrs. Johnson must have done that, too, in her constant desire to tidy things, and shaking my head, I returned to the needles in my hands.

It was the little sigh that caught my ear, a sharp intake of breath that was almost a cry, and then silence.

Silence.

Swiftly I rose and hurried to the bed. Mistress's eyes were open and staring, her head slipped awkwardly to one side and a half smile on her parted lips.

Once again, I'd been death's companion.

I should have gone directly to raise the rest of the house. Instead, I stood there beside Mistress for the last time, just the two of us. I pressed my hands over my mouth to keep from crying, overwhelmed in a way I didn't understand, and made little sense. She would be mourned as a good woman, a fine mother, a loving wife and daughter and sister.

But she had owned me. I had come to her as a girl and now I was a woman with children of my own, and her actions and decisions regarding me had altered my life in more ways than I would ever know. Even now in death, she'd determine not only my future, but those of my son and daughter, too. By the terms of her will, we would be disposed of like the rest of her property.

Yet I lived, while Mistress was dead.

I closed her eyes and mouth, and gently settled her head into the pillow. Mrs. Johnson was not the only one who liked order.

Then I left her, and went to tell the others.

The Colonel came home from Philadelphia for his wife's burial. Through a terrible coincidence, he'd received Dr. Bard's first letter informing him that Mistress had improved, and then, only an hour later, a second letter by an express courier that told him she was dead.

The first shock of his loss had passed by the time he reached Richmond Hill. The house was filled with Mistress's family, Brownes and Prevosts and Bartows and Stillwells. I was kept busy making sure that we servants looked after them, fifteen more people who required food and drink and beds and laundry done, so that they might have the luxury of their grief and tears. I suppose the Colonel found consolation among them, just as he in turn did his best to comfort Miss Burr and Mistress's grown sons.

Mistress's family all remarked on how fine the funeral was, on how the Colonel had arranged for Mistress's casket to be carried in a white hearse, drawn by white horses. Dr. Miles made elegant remarks, and there was an impressive group of gentleman mourners, from the most distinguished families in New York, to accompany her to her grave.

Finally they all left, a rumbling process of carriages returning to the city and beyond. Dr. Bard and Mrs. Johnson and all the others were gone, too, their absence from the house more noticeable than I'd expected.

It wasn't until late that afternoon that the Colonel sent for me to join him in his study. As I stood outside the door, my heart was racing so fast that I feared I'd be ill. This would be the first time I'd seen him alone since Mistress's death. I didn't know if this had been by his choice, or by circumstance in the crowded house. But his summons now could mean only one thing: as the executor of his wife's will, he knew my fate, and that of my—of *our*—daughter and son.

"Mary Emmons," he said as I entered the room. He hadn't called me that for a long time now, and I couldn't tell if it meant good, or ill. He looked exhausted and impossibly sad, the black of his new mourning stiff and heavy on his shoulders. Everything had changed. His desk was uncharacteristically clear, with only a single portfolio in the center of it. He motioned toward the nearest chair for me to sit, and I perched on the very edge, too anxious to do otherwise.

"This will not take long," he said in his lawyer's voice. "In accordance with my late wife's status as a *feme covert*, her estate is quite small, and limited to several personal bequests that were read to the others earlier today. I judged it best to spare you being party to that, and—"

"Tell me, sir, I beg you." I had never before interrupted him, but I could bear it no longer. "Tell me."

He sighed deeply. He opened the envelope, took three bundles of folded pages from it, and slid them across the desk to me.

"You're free, Mary," he said quietly. "Those are your manumission papers, for you and your children. It was the wish of my late wife, in return for your service to her."

My eyes swam with tears as I stared down at the papers that sat between us. As foolish as it sounds, I didn't dare touch them from fear they'd somehow vanish, and my freedom with it. After all Mistress had done to me, I could not believe she'd done this as well.

"You knew of this," I whispered. "Through everything, you always knew."

"I did," he said with a catch to his voice that betrayed his pain. "But I also knew that your freedom could only come at the cost of her life."

"I am sorry, sir," I said. "I am sorry."

"Don't be." He pushed the papers closer to me, then stood abruptly to leave. "I also knew this day would arrive. It's what you said you always wanted, Mary. You're a free woman. What you do next is for you to decide."

A free woman. When I'd imagined this moment, I was sure I'd be elated and joyful, my freedom as light as the wings of birds in the sky.

But with these papers now finally before me, instead I felt bewildered and confused and strangely lost.

I was free, and yet I wasn't. He'd made sure of that. In ways I could not explain, not even to myself, he'd bound me as closely as Mistress had done through the law.

I twisted around in my chair. "Please, sir, don't—don't go."

He pretended not to hear, his hand on the doorknob, and I quickly crossed the room to him.

"Please, sir," I said, and my voice broke. I'd no idea of what I wanted, or what I expected. All I knew was that I didn't want him to leave me like this.

"You were with her when she died," he said, his back still to me. "I wasn't."

"You couldn't help it." I was weeping now, heavy, confused tears. "She didn't suffer, not at the end."

He groaned, and turned, and I could see that he wept, too. At once I wrapped my arms around his shoulders, drawing him close. I held him as tightly as I could, and he held me. I do not know how long we stood together like that, but I knew then that I hadn't the strength to leave him.

I was finally free, but I wasn't.

CHAPTER 22

Philadelphia
State of Pennsylvania
June 1794

"Do you think Papa will be much longer, Mrs. Emmons?" Theo asked, more hopeful than plaintive. Taking advantage of the warm early-summer evening, she and I were walking in the small park behind Congress Hall in Philadelphia, where we'd agreed to meet the Colonel once his committee's meetings had ended for the day. "He promised we'd dine together."

"You know he'll come as soon as he can," I said. "He'd much prefer your company to any committee."

She smiled, a rarity these days since her mother had died. Dressed in black muslin for mourning, she seemed bundled in grief. I could scarcely fault her for it. She'd just celebrated her eleventh birthday, yet she had already endured the deaths of her three siblings and now her mother. It was no wonder that in these last months she'd become even more devoted to her father, for he was all she had left.

Her father, too, had been unable to leave her behind when he'd returned to Congress. With only a short time remaining before the summer recess, the Colonel declared that a change of scene would do her well, and had brought her, and me, to Philadelphia with him.

But then, there'd been many changes since his wife's death. In light of my new status as a free woman, I was no longer Mary, but Mrs. Emmons. I'd long been the highest-ranking servant in the household, and now I was also the only one who wasn't in bondage. I was paid wages for the first time in my life: twelve pounds per annum, a most handsome sum to me. When black mourning ribbons to wear on sleeves and around caps and hats were supplied for the other servants to wear, I'd been given a black gown, as if I were part of the family.

Now there will be some who'll say I should have taken my children and fled the Colonel as soon as I had my manumission papers. I say that my departure would not have been so easy as it might seem.

I was a widow thirty-four years of age with a young daughter and an infant son. At Richmond Hill, I was over a mile away from the city, without any family or other free people to guide my next steps. True, I possessed considerable skills and experience, but I'd also no knowledge of how I'd find an employer. The money I'd managed to put aside over the years would be pitifully small against the costs of starting a new life on my own.

It was also a cold fact of those times that the world did not look kindly upon unattached women, especially those with children. My situation would have been made worse on account of being considered a mulatto or Negro. I would have been regarded with suspicion, and judged to be licentious, dishonest, lazy, and a bad risk all around. I knew what desperation had forced many women to do, and I didn't want to subject my daughter to that.

Yet despite these impediments, I was determined to remain in the Colonel's employ only until I'd saved sufficient money to leave, and could find myself another place. I'd decided upon Philadelphia, a city that seemed more hospitable to free men and women than New York, and one that I'd come to know when I visited with the Colonel.

To this end, I took in as much sewing as I could, often working far into the night. I paid one of the boys for the wild rabbits he snared in the gardens, and, late on Saturday night, I'd bake raised game pies. On Sundays, the one day when my time was my own as a servant, I'd pack these into a basket, walk with Louisa into the city for worship, and then sell the pies to a tavern keeper who paid me well, well enough that the three-mile walk was as nothing. Because

I wanted to be thorough and prepared, I began to take extra notice of the workings of things, such as the dock for the sloop to Philadelphia, and the cost of the passage.

I was careful about these preparations. I didn't hide them from the Colonel, but I didn't mention them, either, and I doubt he took any notice on his own. I was sure that it would be only a matter of a few months, a year at most, and then I'd be able to make an honorable escape with my children into true independence.

I thought of it as honorable, because despite my new wages and the respect of my title, there was much in my position that wasn't honorable at all.

The Colonel continued to use me as his concubine, and I still went to his bed when he summoned me. I believed that he cared for me, beyond simply being a partner to his desire, and in turn I found my own comfort in lying with him, his caresses and his embrace. I knew I should have felt shame and I should have felt regret, yet I didn't.

With all this in my thoughts, I'd tried to look cheerfully upon this journey to Philadelphia, so soon after Mistress's death. The Colonel had brought me here as a companion and servant to his daughter, but also for his own convenience. By his orders, both Louisa and Jean-Pierre had been left behind with the others at Richmond Hill. I understood the main reason behind this—that he did not wish his illegitimate children to be paraded about the capital—though it grieved me mightily not to have them with me. The Colonel had urged me to wean our son, and I knew that physical separation was the easiest way to accomplish this. But I wasn't happy. My bound breasts ached with my milk, and my heart was just as sore to be apart from my babies.

And it was in Philadelphia that I realized exactly how many rivals the Colonel had acquired. He'd always maintained he had no enemies. Not even he could deny that he had enemies now. The notion that the government was run by gentlemanly politicians engaging in civil discussions and consensus had been proved to be the fool's world that no longer existed, if it ever had. Instead, the factions in Congress were crystallizing into two distinct groups, or parties, and their dislike of each other was like an open, suppurating wound for all the world to see.

The Federalists tended to attract men who'd wished they'd been born English noblemen, with all the rank, show, and arrogance that went with it. They were merchants, landowners, men of wealth and conservative beliefs from the more northern states who believed they truly were better than those less fortunate, and continued to cling closely to British ways. They also favored a powerful central government that would benefit their investments and interests. The most noteworthy Federalists were President Washington and his vice president, John Adams, but the most vocal Federalist was surely Alexander Hamilton, the Secretary of the Treasury.

The Democratic-Republicans were different. Most of their supporters were laborers, tradesmen, farmers, and old soldiers, and they were a noisy group who liked to make their beliefs publicly known. They favored the common man, plain speaking, and plain living. Many of the wealthy Virginian Federalists had become Democratic-Republicans, including the Secretary of State, Thomas Jefferson, and Congressmen James Madison and James Monroe.

Knowing the Colonel as well as I did, I wasn't surprised that he'd become increasingly identified with the Democratic-Republicans. His supporters were the ones who now were forming the Democratic societies, organizations that seemed to me to be descendants from the old Sons of Liberty. These men appreciated the Colonel's forthright manner and independence in politics. Despite his grand home at Richmond Hill, he'd never been one to hold himself aloof from those he represented, and he freely sought the opinions of his constituents wherever he was within New York.

He also shared the Democratic-Republican stance on the greatest international topic of the day. In 1793, the French revolutionaries had taken their rebellion to the most shocking extreme, and murdered their king and queen by way of a gruesome machine called a guillotine. This was all the Federalists could see, and to me they began to sound like royalists themselves, lamenting over the dead king. In the process, they also denounced everything else about the French Revolution, and everything and everyone who was French with it. They conveniently forgot how the French were but emulating our own American Revolution, and how without their aid fifteen years before we surely would have lost to Britain.

Needless to say, the Democratic-Republicans sided with their fellow revolutionaries in France, whether by wearing tricolor emblems, writing fierce articles for the newspapers, or parading in the streets. Of course the Colonel supported the French. He'd always been fond of the French way of thinking, regarding them as the most civilized and intellectual of peoples. He ate French food and drank French wines, purchased French paintings and books, and enjoyed French music. He and Mistress had often spoken French to each other, and he'd insisted that Miss Burr learn the language, too. My ability to speak the language was one of the things he'd always found most beguiling about me as well, and he'd even given our son a French name.

The Federalists were so determined against anything with the taint of the French that they tried to deny a French-speaking congressman from Pennsylvania, Albert Gallatin, from taking his seat. Born in Switzerland, Mr. Gallatin had immigrated many years ago, and had already served in several other political posts. He'd become a good friend of the Colonel, who found him intelligent, educated, and agreeable company. But because his native language was French—and because more importantly he objected to Colonel Hamilton's financial designs for the country—the Federalists in Congress had declared him to have been in the country for an insufficient time to be considered a true citizen, and that he was therefore ineligible for his elected office.

The Colonel was rightly furious on his friend's behalf, pointing out that Colonel Hamilton himself had been born on a foreign isle in the Caribbean. He led the Democratic-Republicans defending Mr. Gallatin in congressional debates, his speech being praised for its elegance and logic, but to no avail. In the majority, the Federalists voted against Mr. Gallatin, and stripped him of his seat, thereby violating the rights of the voters who had elected him.

But the entire affair did have the effect of making the Colonel better known, both among those who judged him a champion, a wise and eloquent gentleman, and those who decried him as a deceitful, conniving rogue. His name now appeared often in the newspapers, and in the anonymous broadsides that appeared from nowhere, like mushrooms in the grass after a rainy night.

While I had been in New York tending his dying wife, he had been here, becoming a leader in his party and growing more powerful by the day. I often thought back to the first time I'd met him during the war, when he'd appeared at the Hermitage fresh from an ambush and still spattered with Redcoat blood. He'd been supremely confident and supremely male, his aggression apparent but contained.

Honed and refined and intensified beneath a veneer of refinement, those same qualities remained within him now. I was certain he would be merciless with anyone who crossed him. No wonder he made the Federalists anxious.

I would not wish to be his enemy.

"There is Papa!" cried Miss Burr, her face alight as she spotted the Colonel on the steps of Congress Hall.

"Don't run," I said quickly. "You know your father doesn't wish you to be bold in your manners."

Visibly she controlled herself, straightening her shoulders and raising her chin, and tamping her excitement into a genteel smile worthy of a lady. It was a remarkable demonstration of restraint for a girl her age, and exactly what her father expected of her.

"Good day, Papa," she said with a small curtsey. "I trust your day was a pleasant one?"

"Good day to you, Theo," he said, taking her hand to bow over it. "And to you as well, Mrs. Emmons."

He smiled warmly at me, as much a greeting as was wise in so public a place, before he turned back to his daughter.

"My day was as pleasant as can be expected, Theo," he said as we three began to walk slowly toward the City Tavern, where they would dine, while I would return to our lodgings to eat alone; some things had grown more familiar between us, and others had not. "But I commend the progress in your manners, my dear. Agreeable moderation, with spirits neither too high, nor too low, always makes for pleasurable company. Did you complete the translation Mr. Leshlie set for you?"

She nodded, always eager to please him. "The passage from Terence's *Heauton Timorumenos*. I writ a fair copy especially for you, Papa."

"'Nothing is so difficult but that it may be found out by seeking,'" I said, repeating the translated line that she'd labored to perfect through much of the afternoon.

He glanced up at me and grinned with delight. "'*Nil tam difficile est quin quaerendo investigari possit.*'"

"Exactly so, sir," I said, and smiled, too. To be sure, that was the sum of my Latin. I knew that the Colonel had a special weakness for learning in women, and I'd been hoping all afternoon that I'd find a way to repeat that scrap of Miss Burr's lesson to surprise him.

"Did you bid farewell to Colonel Monroe today, Papa?" Miss Burr asked.

"I did," her father said. "He sends you his regards, and Mrs. Monroe said she would be sure to bring you a special remembrance from Paris."

President Washington had recently appointed Colonel Monroe the new Ambassador to France, and he and Mrs. Monroe were leaving Philadelphia to take their passage across the ocean from New York. The Monroes had long been acquaintances of the Burrs. Colonel Monroe had been another of the young officers among Mistress's admirers at the Hermitage during the war, and although he was a Virginian, his wife was from the City of New York. More recently the two gentlemen had been drawn closer together as political allies in Congress.

"Bartow said he would bring me a dozen French novels," Miss Burr said. Her stepbrother Bartow Prevost, now twenty-six, was joining Colonel Monroe as his private secretary, a post arranged by his stepfather and an enviable adventure for any young gentleman.

"Only after I've read the books first," the Colonel warned. "There's a wide assortment of French novels, and I'm not certain that Bartow will know which are suitable for you as a lady."

"He would. He knows my tastes." She sighed with obvious longing. "How I wished you'd been named ambassador instead, Papa, so we could all go to Paris together."

"If I had, you would not be joining Bartow and me," he said. "Paris is too dangerous at present for little girls such as yourself. But I am certain that before long the French will return to their senses, and then I promise you I shall take you myself."

She nodded with excitement, then caught herself. "I thank you, Papa. I shall be honored to accompany you."

"One day, my dear," he repeated his promise. "For now I'll have my hands full with everything that Colonel Monroe has left behind for me in Congress."

"I'm sure you'll be equal to it, sir," I said. "Either you possess twice the energy of Colonel Monroe, else he has but half of yours."

He smiled, but didn't laugh as I'd expected. "Oh, Monroe shall find it easier to contend with Jacobins than Federalists," he said with a forced lightness, and a quick glance to me before he returned the conversation to his daughter. "This evening truly does put me into mind of summer. Tell me, Theo, do you think the roses we planted last summer at Richmond Hill will have blossomed by now?"

I understood. There was more he'd tell me later, once Miss Burr was asleep and we were alone.

He did, too, in the narrow bed of his lodgings.

"I expect to be reviled for my convictions, Mary." He lay beside me, his head pillowed beneath his clasped hands, a posture I'd learned he often took when making declarations. "It is part of the game of politics. I always presume that my friends will treat as false everything that is said of me, which ought not to be true. The darts aimed at my appearance, my history, my morality, and my acuity are of no consequence to me. The larger my role becomes on this particular stage, the larger a target I must appear as well."

I curled beside him, my cheek resting on my palm and my hair loose around me. These kinds of conversations reminded me of how we'd first talked together long ago in Mistress's kitchen, of how he'd encourage me to speak my thoughts and then listen to what I'd said. If the Colonel chose to entrust me with his confidences, what more private place could there be than here in his bed?

"You shouldn't be called a traitor on account of supporting the French, sir," I said, thinking of a recent tirade I'd read in the Philadelphia newspaper supported by the Federalists. "You're not a Jacobin."

"Oh, that's all carefully calculated to increase the public fears," he said. "If they can raise enough of a racket about godless Jacobins ready to swarm like locusts into every port, ready to murder, rape, and steal, then they hope the people won't take notice of how they're letting the British destroy our shipping and kidnap our sailors. But the people are not fools, Mary. The people know lies when they hear them."

"I fear there are plenty who do not, sir," I said. "I heard from a cook at the market that her master had forbidden her to serve any French dishes at his table because it was treasonous to do so, and another woman told me that her landlord now refuses to grant lodgings to any French refugees, from fear that they will burn down his establishment."

The Colonel grunted with disgust. "What ridiculous rubbish," he said. "Fearmongering and bigotry should have no place in this country. I expect you to bring French dishes to table as often as you please."

I laughed softly. "I will not do so because of politics, sir, but because the French dishes please you."

"Ah, Mary, you do know what pleases me, don't you?" Gently he pulled me down to kiss, my hair falling around us both. Afterward I rested familiarly upon his chest, a place that it pleased me to be.

"You know you frighten them, sir," I said. "Otherwise they wouldn't bother to attack you as much as they do."

"They may do that as much as they wish," he said. "My skin is as tough as it comes. But they've no right attacking my daughter with me."

I frowned. "I didn't see that," I said. "Where? When? Oh, sir, how dare they say a word against Miss Burr!"

"But they did," he said grimly. "At least one of them did, in doggerel verse. They slandered my Theo on account of her learning and called her unnatural for it, knowing full well that her education is by my design. To challenge the author or even acknowledge his venom would be exactly what the villains wish, but we must make sure Theo never sees it."

"Of course, sir," I said. "But who would dare write such cruelty?"

He sighed, stroking my hair back from my face with his fingers. "Oh, I've an idea of who was behind it, because he's behind most of these attacks in the press. It's Hamilton."

I should have been surprised, but I wasn't. As Secretary of the

Treasury, he should have been above such mischief, yet he seemed to be unable to resist.

"Who else could it be?" the Colonel continued. "He's been doing it for years, slyly planting all manner of lies and tales about me. My old friend Bob Troup has sunk much in his ways, and often acts as his toady. I'm sure Hamilton has convinced himself that he possesses a score of reasons to assault me in print. The one he won't admit, of course, is that he fears I have become far too popular for his liking in New York, and that I'm a threat to his own power. That's an unpleasant truth for him."

"I told you that you frightened the Federalists, sir," I said. "Or at least him."

"Wise Mary," he said, his hand sliding familiarly up and down my bare back. "I once heard that he'd claimed his railing against me was a religious obligation, as if I were some devil who must be destroyed for the good of the country."

"He's a fine one to talk, sir," I said, indignant on his behalf. "I don't recall often seeing him in Sunday attendance at Trinity. His wife and children, yes, but not Colonel Hamilton himself."

"I can only imagine the pleas that poor, pious Eliza must make to her husband about the state of his errant soul." He smiled, doubtless picturing exactly that. "Likely the man was too busy at home composing another scurrilous account of me to spread through his network."

But all this talk of Colonel Hamilton and his whispered slanders made me feel uneasy and vulnerable. It was one thing for the Colonel to dismiss the rumors about him as beyond his notice, but another entirely for me and my children, who could well find ourselves at the very heart of similar attacks.

"You say that Colonel Hamilton has slandered you for your morality, too," I asked carefully. "What if he were to learn of our—our friendship?"

"Not again, Mary," he said, more teasing than perturbed. "How many times must I tell you not to worry? The rumors that have fluttered about me have been the usual concoctions, linking me to a French dancer here or a brothel keeper there, and every one of them lies. Not once have they hinted at you."

I was taken aback by that. I had never considered that there might be other women besides me in his life and his bed. There was no doubt that he was a man of fierce appetites, and the longer I thought, the more likely it seemed. He'd denied it, of course, as he denied most everything. But why else would he mention it now if there wasn't some grain of truth to the rumors?

"You and I have been beyond discretion," he continued, "and always have been. I do not want you fretting over nothing."

"I wish I shared your conviction, sir," I said, tracing little circles with my fingers through the hair upon his chest. I must try not to fret over those other mysterious women, either. I'd no right to be jealous, especially since, as he said, they might not even exist. "I do not want to be the reason your career is ruined."

"Even if Hamilton were to learn of us, I doubt he'd ever make use of the knowledge," he said. "Do you recall me handling the divorce of a young woman named Mrs. Reynolds?"

I shook my head. "You handle so many divorces, sir, that I cannot begin to keep them straight. You've never been able to resist a lady in legal distress."

He chuckled. "The ones who come to me are often in need of a knight to save them," he said. "Mariah Reynolds was among those in the very deepest distress. She'd a worthless, faithless husband who beat her, refused to support her, and acted as her pimp in a clumsy blackmailing scheme. Madison was the first to tell me of the whole sordid affair, and Mrs. Reynolds supplied the details."

"Poor Mrs. Reynolds." This did in fact sound more sordid than his usual divorce cases, and I could not think of another where the husband had treated his wife so ill. "Did you ever learn the name of the gentleman her husband blackmailed?"

"He's the point of this entire tale," he said. "It's Hamilton."

I caught my breath. I couldn't have predicted that, not at all. "Yet he dares to lecture you upon morality?"

"Exactly so," he said. "It seems that Mr. Secretary was eager enough to go rutting with Mrs. Reynolds while his family was away in Albany. The payments he made to Reynolds to keep quiet about it were discovered and brought to the attention of Monroe and several others. They believed the payments indicated financial impropriety. Hamilton assured them that he was only being blackmailed by the husband of his inamorata, his political reputation apparently more dear to him than his poor wife's love and trust."

I remembered Mrs. Hamilton well, not only from the early dinners that she'd attended as guests of the Burrs, but also from various gatherings that her children had attended with Miss Burr in New York, when they'd all been neighbors. She'd always been kind to Miss Burr and to me as well, recalling my name and asking me how I did, a rarity among fine women.

It saddened me to think of such a pleasant lady betrayed by her husband, but then I'd also pitied Mrs. Reynolds, who'd been forced into the affair by her own husband. Behind the smirking scandal were two women who'd suffered grievously because of the base desires of men.

"Hamilton should have thanked me for closing that particular door for him," the Colonel continued. "The former Mrs. Reynolds is now divorced and safely removed from his sphere and living with another man, in Virginia, I believe. At least her daughter was spared. Perhaps now the girl has an opportunity for the virtuous life denied her mother."

"Mrs. Reynolds has a daughter, sir?" I was sorry to hear that there was a child caught in the intrigues of her parents; the Hamiltons also had a half dozen children, and the ones who were old enough to comprehend the scandal were doubtless suffering along with their mother.

He nodded. "The Reynolds girl is a sweet-faced child named Susan, about Theo's age," he said. "I persuaded her mother to give her over to me as her ward. It was an easy decision to place the girl in the care of a family in Boston, where she will attend school and learn a trade. I determined it would be for the best, given the general slatternly ways of her mother."

To me this didn't sound as if it were for the best, and it troubled me as well. The Colonel knew how to arrange the law to follow his purposes. No man was more adroit in a courtroom, which was why he'd always more cases than he could handle. If he'd been the one to determine that Mrs. Reynolds's daughter must be separated from her mother and sent far away, then he would also have made sure legally that her "slatternly" mother would have no further contact with her daughter.

Uneasily I thought of Louisa and Jean-Pierre in New York. Now that we'd all been given our freedom, I'd always believed the Colonel would have no further power over them. They were my children, in my care. There existed no document to prove that he was their father. He'd always been careful about that, given how wary he was about committing anything to paper and pen.

But what if the time came when he decided that he knew better than I what was right for my children? I could never rival him in a courtroom, nor could I find another attorney in New York who'd dare go against him. In a way, I was no more secure than when I'd still belonged to Mistress and she'd had the power to keep or sell my children as it pleased her. The sooner I could take us all from New York and from his influence, the better.

"But to separate a mother from her daughter, sir," I protested. "How can that ever be in their best interests?"

"In this case it was," he said, "and the judge and court agreed with me. But that's quite enough of the woes of the unfortunate Mrs. Reynolds. I'm far more interested in the excellent Mrs. Emmons."

He growled against my ear and rolled over atop me, and there'd be no more talk of any kind, not that night. But I could not put the story of Mrs. Reynolds from my head, and I prayed it wasn't meant to be a lesson against my own uncertain future.

We returned to Richmond Hill as soon as Congress was dismissed for the summer recess. I was overjoyed to be reunited with my children, though saddened to see how much they'd grown in the two months we'd been apart. I hated missing so much as a single day of their lives. For now, I'd no choice. As long as I remained in the Colonel's service, I must do as he bid. But my heart had wept to hear Peg describe Jean-Pierre's first shaky steps while holding to the bench in the kitchen, taken while I hadn't been there to see them.

For the Colonel and Miss Burr, the return to their country estate was more bittersweet. The attributes of Mistress's sickroom—the basins for bleeding, the row of medicinal bottles, the discreetly draped clyster—had all been cleared from her bedchamber. At the Colonel's order, everything else remained as it had been, from her neatly arranged books to the brush and combs on her dressing table, and each day Miss Burr continued to pick flowers for the vase beside her mother's bed. On occasion I'd observe him in there, too, sitting in the chair near the window as if they were conversing still while she wrote at her little desk, and I'd always steal away and leave him to his sorrow.

Every person's grief is different from another's, and mourning can take many forms. I respected that. I was relieved, however, that the Colonel had not decided to take his wife's former bedchamber for his own. There was much in our friendship that was not right, but that would have been too far, even for him.

I do not mean to say that he'd adopted the sentimental pose of the gently grieving widower, withdrawn from society. Far from it. He continued to handle cases at a feverish pace, likely in part to pay for the improvements and furnishings that he was constantly making to Richmond Hill. His entertainments here, in the city, and in taverns when he traveled about the state were known for their prodigious but elegant scale, with guests that included not only friends and acquaintances, but also fellow politicians, high and low, whom he wished to cultivate to further his aspirations.

More and more these politicians were exclusively Democratic-Republicans, and by the end of that summer I don't believe he'd invited more than a handful of the old New York Federalists to dine at Richmond Hill. Once Mr. Jefferson had resigned his post as Secretary of State and retired to his own country estate of Monticello, the Colonel was now considered one of their leaders in Congress, the one who made the most important speeches.

Encouraged by President Washington's Proclamation of Neutrality, a wishy-washy and cowardly attempt to keep America from supporting the French in a war against Britain, Federalists had continued to reject and berate anything with a French taint.

Not the Colonel. Since we'd returned from Philadelphia, he had given sanctuary to a French governess named Madame Senat, a refugee from the Terror. Madame Senat was accustomed to teaching only the most nobly born of young French ladies, and she had escaped from Paris with one of her charges, Natalie Marie Louise Stephanie Beatrix Delage de Volude, the daughter of a marquis. This young lady was the exact age as Miss Burr, and the two of them instantly became fast friends. The Colonel saw only the benefits of this acquaintance, and gave over half of his Partition Street house to Madame Senat for the teaching of these young ladies and several others besides. In addition to her usual studies in Greek, Latin, and mathematics, Miss Burr was now expected to perfect her French and her manners under Madame Senat, as well as playing upon the fortepiano and harp. I do not believe I have ever seen her more content, living there in the company of her new friend.

If Miss Burr was happy to be living in the city among Madame Senat's other students, I was even more so, because I was able to spend more time with my own daughter. Louisa was nearly six, and I'd already taught her to read and write, much as Miss Burr had at that age. One of Mistress's favorite books that I'd read aloud to her when she'd been ill had been written by an Englishwoman named Mrs. Wollstonecraft, who believed that learning gave women both strength and contentment, and many other wise things besides. I'd want nothing less for Louisa, and thus encouraged her as best I could to persevere.

On this particular afternoon, we sat together out of doors at a table I'd had removed from the kitchen to beneath a tree. Peg and I were peeling peaches, the first true crop of the orchard that the Colonel had had planted when he'd first acquired Richmond Hill. Little Jean-Pierre, now two years of age, was curled like a puppy on a coverlet on the grass, while I had Louisa reading a recent copy of the newspaper aloud to us. The paper was spread flat before her, weighted down on the four corners by stones she'd gathered for the purpose. I had placed her on a stool that made her level with the table, but it was so tall that her little bare feet dangled beneath her petticoat, her toes pointing inward toward one another.

"'The . . . birth of . . . such a *monster* . . . in the shape . . . of a *calf* was . . . remarked by all . . . and-and . . . feared by some as an omen of coming *haz-zards,*'" she read slowly, swinging her feet in rhythm with every word as she sounded it out.

"Very good, Louisa," I said, striving to be encouraging. I knew she was sufficiently clever for this task. It was the desire she lacked. "What follows?"

She looked up at me without raising her small dimpled chin, her eyes huge and doleful. "That's all there is, Mama," she said. "That's the end. The calf was born in Rye with two heads, and then it died."

"But there's another story below that one, sweet, isn't there?" I coaxed. "You needn't stop there."

She sighed mightily. "But that's the *end,* Mama."

"Oh, let the child be, missus," Peg said. "She's read more than enough for today. Here, Louisa, take these peaches inside away from the flies, and be sure you put a cloth over them, too."

"Yes, Peg." Obediently she scrambled down from the stool, took the bowl of peaches that Peg handed her, and hurried back toward the house before I could say otherwise.

Silently I watched her go, the too-long strings of her apron bouncing against her legs.

My words were better reserved for Peg.

"She was supposed to read to the bottom of the page, Peg," I said, not hiding my unhappiness. I hated how my children turned more often to Peg than to me, almost as if she were their true mother. "That was the lesson I'd set. She needs practice."

"Begging pardon, missus, but that poor girl reads enough for all of us," Peg said, undeterred. The blade of the knife in her hand sliced deep into the yellow fruit, the juice sliding over her thumb. "She's not Miss Burr, and never will be."

"I didn't claim she was, Peg," I said defensively. "But Louisa is free, and being able to read and write and cipher will help her better herself. She could learn a trade. She could be apprenticed to a mantua-maker, or a pastry-maker, or a cook, or become a house-keeper."

Peg's expression didn't change, her mouth pursed and her round, sleepy eyes unflinching as the knife in her hand kept circling beneath the skin of the peach in her hand.

"You keep telling Louisa she's better than she is, missus," she said, "and that little girl'll end up just like you."

A short gust of breeze rustled through the leaves overhead like laughter.

"What do you mean to say, Peg?" I asked sharply, even though we both knew the answer. As a bondwoman and only a maidservant at that, Peg was supposed to answer to me, but she seldom did, from jealousy and disregard. She knew too much of me and the Colonel. No matter what I did, I'd never be respected until I left this household for another.

"Whatever you please, missus," Peg said. "You got your freedom. Colonel Burr don't own you. Why don't you leave? Why do you stay and be his whore when—"

"No more, Peg," I said sharply, standing so I'd be taller. "No more of that talk."

We both heard the sound of a rider's horse on the road before the house, and we both turned toward it.

"Look at that," said Peg, standing, too. "The devil himself comes a-riding."

She didn't wait for my permission to leave, but thrust her knife into another peach and sauntered back toward the kitchen before the Colonel could see us.

I was standing there still beneath the tree, my hands knotted in frustration, when he joined me.

"Good day, my dear Mary," he said as he kissed me in greeting. "What a pleasant place you have for yourself here, with the breeze coming from the river."

"It's much more agreeable than inside the house, sir," I said, still discomfited by Peg. "I didn't believe we'd see you from Albany until tomorrow."

"I was eager to be home," he said. "I'll wash and change my clothes here before presenting myself at Partition Street. How much I'd prefer to stay here, and never be troubled again with Albany or Philadelphia! Though if Schuyler has his wish, I suppose that may happen soon enough."

"Does he truly believe he can take your seat from you, sir?" I said, surprised. He could jest all he wished, but I knew how much he relished being a senator and all that came with it. He would be unhappy—very unhappy—to lose his seat. But from all I'd heard and read, the Colonel seemed as secure as any senator, while even with the support of his son-in-law Colonel Hamilton, General Schuyler appeared no more than a disgruntled old gentleman in uncertain health, whining for what he'd lost.

"Oh, Schuyler has believed that since the day I was first elected, but his indignity is loudest in Albany." He spotted Jean-Pierre asleep on the grass, smiled, and bent to gather him up into his arms. "Come here, my own little man. Where's Louisa?"

"She's in the kitchen with Peg," I said, even as my son snuggled more closely against the Colonel's chest, drooling over his sleeve. "You shouldn't say such things to him, sir, not if you don't wish it known that you're his father."

"I don't see anyone else within hearing," he said mildly, his voice low. He slung one booted leg over the bench to sit with his son, the silver spurs at his heels jingling. "I also believe Jean-Pierre himself isn't overly inclined to pay me any attention whatsoever."

"He listens, and he talks," I said. "Louisa already asks about her father."

"Then I trust you've told her what we agreed," he said, too absorbed in Jean-Pierre to be truly listening to me. "That her father is dead."

"I have told her that, yes," I said. I'd done it, but my conscience had not been easy with giving the Colonel's bastard my husband's name. Lucas's memory didn't deserve that. "But, sir, if someone else were to tell her otherwise—"

"Then we shall confront that if it occurs," he said, fondly stroking the velvety curve of his son's cheek, as sweet as the peaches piled on the table. "How much my boy has grown in only three weeks!"

My worries were not so easily assuaged, but I couldn't help but smile at how tender he was with Jean-Pierre. I had to remind myself that Jean-Pierre was his son, too, his only son. I'd never had a father, and likely because of that I hated to imagine depriving my children of theirs. Already there was no denying that a wordless bond existed between the Colonel and Jean-Pierre, even if it was a bond that could never be acknowledged.

This was also why I didn't leave, I thought, watching them together. This was why I often feared I couldn't.

He smiled, and patted the bench. "Sit with me, Mary," he said. "You can't know how much I've missed you, and the pleasure it gives me to know you've been waiting here for me."

That voice, that voice. He'd the power to persuade the sternest judges, and to make entire juries weep. When it was known he would address Congress, every chair and bench was filled to hear him. Even if he'd said nothing but gibberish, his voice alone had that same power over me. When he spoke of how he'd missed me or how he desired me, I was as helpless as a new lamb, and I'd only grown more susceptible since Mistress had died. That a gentleman as powerful and as wealthy as the Colonel would miss me—me, who had been bought and sold and cast away as worthless—was a lure I never seemed able to resist.

I'd been peeling peaches, not waiting for him, yet still I sat on the bench beside him exactly as he'd asked. Immediately he reached for me, slipping his hand beneath the hem of my petticoat to lightly caress the inside of my knee. I caught my breath: not from surprise, not from dismay, but from pleasure. I won't deny it. I'd missed him, too.

I slid closer to him and our son, and slipped my hand inside his coat and around his waist.

"My entire journey home, I could think of nothing else but you, Mary," he said. "You've been my pillar these last months. I cannot imagine my life now without you in it."

"Oh, sir," I said softly, and I rested my head against his shoulder. Such sweet words overwhelmed me. How could they not?

"I'll need you with me more than ever when Congress convenes," he said. "It's not too early to begin planning what you and Theo must bring with us to Philadelphia."

I felt as if I'd just stumbled into a trap of my own making. Swiftly I sat upright, the better to see his face.

"But what of Louisa and Jean-Pierre?" I asked, my heart already knotting in my chest. "Won't they be coming with us this time as well?"

"Mary, please," he said evenly, meeting my gaze without hesitation. "You know how much I'd also wish to have them with us, but lodgings in Philadelphia are always crowded, and far too small for children. Nor will you have time to watch over them, not and accomplish all I'll need you to do."

"But sir—"

"It's decided," he said, more firmly this time. "The children will remain here. Besides, Philadelphia is a dangerous city for fevers in this season of the year. I love them too well to put them at that risk."

I was a free woman. I could have refused. I could have said that

Philadelphia's fever season ended with the first frost, before we were due to arrive. I could have asked how he could love our children so well that he'd leave them behind, yet still take Miss Burr with him to endure an equal risk. I could have told him that if he refused me my children, then I would leave his employ, and take myself, and them, elsewhere.

I could have been strong, and left him then.

Instead, I bowed my head and fought back my tears, and as I watched him cradle our son in the crook of his arm I forced myself to think, the way Mrs. Wollstonecraft might have wished me to do.

"You're right, sir," I said, striving to sound as confident as I could. "If you're to gather the Democratic-Republicans in Congress around you to help preserve your seat, you will scarcely rest a moment this session. You must host dinners and suppers and general meetings, and perhaps even a small ball. Your table must be excellent, to inspire confidence, though not so luxurious that you're mistaken for a Federalist. You should keep a conveyance, a small chaise at the very least, with Thomas to drive and Alexis as your footman."

He nodded, and smiled, clearly pleased that I could anticipate so many of his wishes.

"Exactly, Mary," he said. "How glad I am to see that you understand what will be necessary."

"Oh, I do, sir," I said. "Beginning at the Hermitage, Mrs. Burr trained me well in these matters."

In the way of young children, Jean-Pierre woke abruptly, in a disagreeable mood and with a two-year-old's temper. He blinked and scowled up at the Colonel, then twisted around to shove against him with both his chubby small feet before letting out a grumpy yowl. Startled, the Colonel looked to me for assistance. I stood, and I leaned across to take Jean-Pierre from him. Deftly I put our son to my shoulder, rubbing his back and murmuring wordlessly to calm him. Soon he'd be too old and too large for me to hold like this, but for now he was still my baby boy.

"How fortunate I am to have you at my side, Mary," the Colonel said with good-natured relief. "You'll be indispensable during this next session, when I shall require your talents."

I smiled as I swayed back and forth with the baby in my arms, the best ally I could have at that moment.

"You know I always do my best for you, sir," I said softly, gently, for I'd already made my point. "But in return, I believe I should also receive a greater recompense for my services."

He narrowed his eyes, suddenly wary. "I pay you twelve pounds per annum with lodgings for you and your children as my house-keeper now, don't I?"

"*Our* children," I said. "They are not to be included in this, Aaron."

I dickered over every price I paid in shops and markets. I told myself this would be no different with the Colonel, though of course it was.

"Our children," he repeated. His expression didn't change.

"Given all you expect of me," I said, "I do not believe that twenty pounds per annum would be amiss."

I knew how much he paid his tailor, his bookseller, his cabinet-maker, and his physician, as well as Miss Burr's tutor, her dancing master, and her harp teacher. What I asked was little enough in comparison.

I knew how much I was worth to him.

And for the first time, I believe he was realizing it as well, and not just as a pretty compliment.

"Twenty pounds, then," he said finally. "Now take the boy to Peg, and join me upstairs. I've only a half an hour before I must leave for Partition Street."

Without waiting for my response, he turned and left me with our son. I knew what he intended to do in that half hour, and what would be required of me. I had won in one way, but he'd win in another. I suppose that had been my choice, too.

I shifted Jean-Pierre to my hip, and slowly began to walk toward the kitchen.

CHAPTER 23

Philadelphia
State of Pennsylvania
December 1794

"All you must do, Miss Burr, is sit as still as can be," Mr. Stuart said, squinting critically at the Colonel's daughter as he began to sketch, quick flicks of his chalk across the page. "I can already tell you will prove to be a splendid model."

"I've never sat for my portrait before," Miss Burr said, taking care to move her lips as little as possible. She was seated on a chair on a small, raised platform, her white dress carefully arranged and her hair neatly feathered and combed across her forehead and over her shoulders. "Papa says you are very patient for an artist, on account of having painted many grand people in London."

"Your papa is most kind," Mr. Stuart said. I'd never seen an artist before, but to my disappointment he looked much like any other gentleman, with a long, thin nose, pale skin, and gray eyes that seemed to take in every detail around him. "I enjoyed painting him, and I'm honored that he has brought you to my little studio as well."

The "little studio" was in his home, across the street from the statehouse. It was one of my duties to bring Miss Burr to her sittings each morning when Mr. Stuart declared the sunlight to be most fortuitous for his inspiration.

"Papa says that you should strive for a likeness that captures my intellectual endeavors," she said. "He doesn't want me painted like an empty beauty."

"But you are beautiful, Miss Burr," the painter protested mildly. "I cannot deny what I see before me."

"Papa said you'd flatter me like that, too," she said. "But you are to make certain to include books, instead of a basket of flowers arranged in my lap or other foolishness. Papa says you must stress my intellect rather than my fecundity."

Mr. Stuart gulped, and seemed to concentrate more fully on his sketch. He might have painted the Colonel previously, but it was clear he wasn't prepared for Miss Burr's frankness, another quality suggested by Mrs. Wollstonecraft and much encouraged by her father. There was a reason why the Colonel had hung a portrait of that wise lady in his gallery at Richmond Hill. As a result, however, the directness of Miss Burr's conversation could take some—like this poor artist—by surprise.

In the end, Mr. Stuart did follow the Colonel's wishes. Unlike all the other portraits of young ladies that I'd seen in their families' homes, pictures that presented them sitting against blue skies with pets and flowers, Miss Burr was shown alone against a plain and windowless wall, her gaze direct and her chair surrounded by thick books, which was often the truth of her scholarly life.

At least in the capital city of Philadelphia there were more amusements that her father judged suitable, plays and musical performances and displays of fireworks. Mr. Peale's new museum offered curiosities gathered from around the world, including the giant bones of fearsome ancient beasts. The entertainment provided by Ricketts Circus might not be as edifying with clowns, dancers, and daring equestrienne feats, but even the Colonel would occasionally relent and take his daughter to a performance. There was also Congress itself. With great fanfare, we went once to hear President Washington's address, and disappointing it was, too. The president seemed much aged and sadly diminished, and for a general who'd been so commanding in battle, his voice as an orator could scarcely be heard.

Most of my days and evenings, however, were devoted to my duties for the Colonel. While we lived in lodgings, I still had much to do to manage our small transient household, from making sure that the laundry was sent out and brought back to arranging elegant suppers for the Colonel's guests. He trusted me to make nearly all decisions on my own, from choosing which purveyors and tradespeople to patronize to hiring the extra servants to selecting the dishes and wines to be served when he dined.

I knew his tastes that well. Not only was my knowledge based upon our private friendship, but I'd already been occupying this role for him for many years on account of Mistress's long illness. In fact, in many ways I did act as much as his wife as his housekeeper, short of sitting at the head of his table. The greatest compliment to me was to be invisible, and my goal was to be able to create the impression of elegant ease and hospitality, without any signs of effort, the way the Colonel preferred. I liked pleasing him, and earning his approval: that was what made me proud. I never wished to call attention to myself in any fashion.

In most ways, I didn't. The Colonel's closest friends knew me, of course, and in time I became recognized in the city as Mrs. Emmons, Colonel Burr's woman, but that was all. I preferred to dress in somber colors and unadorned styles, which also suited my small stature and rounded form. My only visible ornament was not really an ornament at all, but the plain steel chatelaine with the household keys that I wore at the waist of my apron. It was now almost impossible to recall how as a child in slavery I'd worn gaudy silks and spangles and glass jewels. The Colonel teased me by calling me his Quakeress, and I did in fact more resemble those admirable Friends, so prevalent in Philadelphia, than any lady of fashion.

But in the next breath the Colonel would tell me how much he relished being the one man to know my most intimate charms, hidden away from the gaze of all other men like the favorite of some Indian prince kept in purdah. This was foolish and disrespectful in many ways, and I told him so, too. He'd only laugh and kiss me, as if that were enough to make me lose both my wits and common sense.

Perhaps it was. Although keeping our secret was more challenging while living in lodgings, I continued to come to the Colonel's bed at night whenever I could, to curve my body around his and take him in whatever way delighted us both. Together we found considerable satisfaction in this intimacy, and if there were times when he was more demanding than I would have wished, he always took care to see to my pleasure, too. While I was no longer in my first flower—I was thirty-four, and the Colonel was thirty-eight—our passions were still ripely well matched.

If only there had been a way to have my children with me! I knew the Colonel would not relent, just as I understood the reasons why he shouldn't. But I couldn't help but think of them while we were apart, and my heart ached to imagine them both without the benefit of a parent's love. When the Colonel went to New York for a case in early 1795, to my joy I returned there with him and Miss Burr.

Yet those two weeks at Richmond Hill passed far too swiftly and, instead of relieving my longing, seemed only to magnify it.

"Couldn't we bring Louisa and Jean-Pierre with us to Philadelphia in the spring?" I asked as the Colonel and I lay side by side in bed soon after we'd returned. It was a cold night, with frost on the insides of the windows and ice in the washbowl, and even with the curtains drawn around the bed, we relied upon each other for warmth beneath the coverlets. "Couldn't you consider that, sir?"

"I could consider it from now until June, Mary, but I'm not going to change my mind," he said. "We've spoken of this many times, and my answer must always be the same."

"I know, sir, I know," I said wistfully. "But this last time, Jean-Pierre didn't recognize me, and clung to Peg's petticoat. I've been away so much that he's come to believe Peg is his mother, and . . . and she's not."

"Of course she isn't," he answered patiently, drawing me closer. "You are, my dear, and a fine mother at that. I've often been parted from my Theo, and the separation never grows any easier to bear, whether a day or a half year."

"But you've been able to leave her in the care and education of those you trust, sir." I couldn't keep the quavery little catch from my voice. "I do not have that same confidence in Peg, especially with Louisa."

"You must remember the complete span of our daughter's life, Mary," he said, that initial patience changing to mild irritation, "and how small a part this separation will seem to Louisa as she grows older. This will not be forever."

It seemed like forever to me. I thought of all the things I wished my daughter to know, the things I wished to teach her myself, that were not valued by Peg. There was no reason she should, of course. Born into bondage, Peg was without ambition for betterment, content to scratch out her mark, and nothing more.

"Louisa is your daughter, too, sir, as much as Theo is," I pleaded. "She has your cleverness, a quickness that is being squandered the longer she remains—"

"Mary, no," he said, sharp and terse. "I agree that this separation from your daughter is unfortunate, but for now it cannot be changed. Louisa and Jean-Pierre are perfectly well at Richmond Hill. Let that be an end to it. You know I've other more serious matters to occupy me at present, and I'll thank you not to worry at me again on this subject."

That silenced me, but not my fears, and I was grateful that in the darkness of the curtained bed he couldn't see the tears of frustration that surely gleamed in my eyes.

The Colonel never did anything without a reason. I couldn't decide if he kept us apart so that I would be more attached to him, or because he wished to retain our children. I'd always believed that this would become simpler once I'd my freedom. But it hadn't, not at all. He still seemed to control my life, and our children's as well.

Nor could I claim that all of it was his doing. I was at fault as well. Remaining with him was by far the easiest path for me, and I couldn't deny that he offered security. He loved my children, and I believe in some fashion he cared for me as well. But that affection and security and habit, and my own uncertain sentiments, were all so woven together that I could not easily untangle them; even to attempt to do so made me feel foolish. I'd been with the Colonel for so long now that it had become increasingly difficult to imagine parting with him.

Soon after this, however, I was given a glimpse of what my life might be if I dared to break with him.

I'd arranged a small supper for the Colonel and several of his closer friends in Philadelphia. Several wives were included in the party; this was unusual, since most congressmen left their wives at home to oversee their affairs and estates while they were away, and also because of the limited lodgings available in Philadelphia.

One of the ladies in attendance was Mrs. Madison, wife to Representative James Madison of Virginia. The Colonel had known Mrs. Madison when she'd been the widowed Mrs. Todd, and he had been a resident of her mother's Philadelphia boardinghouse. It was the Colonel who had introduced Mrs. Todd to Mr. Madison, an old acquaintance from college, and when they'd recently wed he'd jovially claimed all the credit for the match.

Mrs. Madison had been raised a Friend, and perhaps that was why she was more direct than many other ladies. She'd taken care to learn my name, and greeted me by it. After this particular supper, however, she drew me aside at the bottom of the stairs as the farewells were being made by the door.

"A word, Mrs. Emmons, if you please." She was a tall woman, much taller than her husband, with full cheeks and a small, merry mouth, and she lowered her voice in confidence as she addressed me. "Between us alone."

I drew myself a little straighter, preparing myself to be told of some flaw with the supper: that the soup hadn't been sufficiently warm, or a footman had been clumsy.

"I've observed how well you look after the Colonel," Mrs. Madison continued. "Poor man, he needs looking after, too, since his wife's death. But tonight was exceptional. Everything was arranged exactly as it should be, with the precise degree of French influence in each course, and I vow the Colonel keeps the best table in Congress. That is entirely to your credit, Mrs. Emmons. I know how difficult it can be to make a good showing in lodgings, with everything and everyone hired."

I flushed with pleasure. I never heard compliments like this. Happy guests praised the Colonel, not me, as was to be expected.

"Thank you, Mrs. Madison," I murmured. "I'm glad to learn that you enjoyed Colonel Burr's supper."

"Oh, I more than enjoyed it," she said, "and so did everyone else. Now I know you are loyal to the Colonel, and loyalty is a fine, fine thing. But if you should ever wish to find a more permanent position within a larger household here in Philadelphia, I hope you shall come to me first. I know of at least half a dozen ladies who would give their eyeteeth for a housekeeper who manages as well as you. I should like to recommend you to them, if you'll but say the word."

I nodded, stunned. I had always been puzzled as to how I'd find a position in a household here in Philadelphia, and here Mrs. Madison was offering assistance to me. It surprised me that a woman whose husband kept scores of women and men in bondage on his Virginian plantations would volunteer such assistance to me. Perhaps she didn't know what I was; because of my dress, there were on occasion people who mistook my light color, and didn't realize I was mulatto. As the Colonel often said, people saw what they expected.

"I am a free woman, ma'am, and a widow with two young children," I said, thinking quickly. "Would that change the opinion of these ladies?"

"Given your skill, Mrs. Emmons," Mrs. Madison said, "you might have a dozen children in tow, and if they don't hinder your duties, you'd find a new place within a day."

I noticed that she continued to overlook the color of my skin, so perhaps it truly didn't matter to her. But to keep house for a family without all the complications of the Colonel, to have my children with me, to be regarded as a respectable widow here in Philadelphia, where there were so many other free men and women like us—what a heady dream that would be!

"Thank you, Mrs. Madison," I said, my thoughts spinning fast. "Thank you for your—your kindness."

I made a small curtsey to her from gratitude, and caught the Colonel's curious expression over Mrs. Madison's silk-covered shoulder.

"What was that about with Dolley, Mary?" he asked later, when we were alone and he was having a final cigar as he reviewed some letters delivered earlier in the evening. "What conspiracy were you two brewing, eh?"

"You see conspiracies everywhere, sir," I scoffed, employing his own useful habit of deflecting difficult questions without answers. "Mrs. Madison was merely praising the quality of your dinner."

He smiled through the smoke, the cigar clenched tight in the side of his mouth.

"As it was, and as you knew, since I'd already praised you to the skies," he said. "I'm still not discounting a conspiracy among you women. I'll have to be sure to warn Jemmy to guard himself at home."

"Hush, sir," I said mildly. "I'd think that you have enough to battle with Colonel Hamilton and the rest without taking on all the women in Philadelphia, too."

He sighed wearily, no longer teasing. "You can't begin to conceive of all I must battle, Mary."

But I could, because each night I listened to him recount the events of his day. Those events often were battles, too; he was not exaggerating. The conflict between the Federalists and the Democratic-Republicans had continued to grow wider and more vicious, with accusations and slanders both in the press and in person. It seemed impossible to believe most of these same gentlemen had been of the same accord less than twenty years before, unified for the sake of the new country born from the war, and the people who were its citizens. That spirit was entirely gone, and not even the noble figure of President Washington appeared able to heal the ruptures.

With their support of merchants, bankers, and other wealthy gentlemen, the Federalists held the balance of power in Congress, and appeared determined to push through policies and laws that benefited only these same individuals. Representing most everyone else, the Republicans attempted to push back against the Federalists as best they could, and still with little success. Yet still the Colonel remained their leader in Congress, always speaking so eloquently and logically that the Federalists were made anxious, even as they continued to vote as a bloc.

It was clear that support among the more common people for the Republicans was growing, and growing loudly. One of the least popular policies that Colonel Hamilton had concocted as Secretary of Treasury to support his federal banking schemes was a series of taxes upon the people, including a tax upon whiskey. Even I knew that no man likes to have his spirits threatened, whether that spirit is a costly imported port or canary wine, or whiskey distilled by the drinker in his barn. Most whiskey drinkers resided to the west, far from the cities along the coast, and when Colonel Hamilton's tax collectors appeared at their farms and small towns they were not welcomed, some being tarred and feathered and lashed to a rail before being forcibly banished. Liberty Poles—those familiar signs of defiance from the Revolution—began to sprout from various village greens. There were even rumors of some towns importing French-made guillotines, with the intention of removing the head of any Federalist politician who dared come poke his nose in their affairs.

In private, the Colonel and his associates found this more than a little entertaining. Nor were they above inflaming these frontier passions to suit their own purposes, and to increase the popularity of the Republicans. But the Federalists were not so amused. Encouraged by Colonel Hamilton, President Washington called out a large force of militia, once again put on his uniform, and rode out to put down the rebellion, with Colonel Hamilton preening and puffing at his side.

As the Colonel said, this was a sad picture all around, with the federal government forcing the citizen-soldiers of the militia to confront other citizens for the sake of taxes. The whole affair leaned disastrously close to a civil war. To the relief of sensible people, the resistance melted away at the sight of the militia, and there were no casualties because there were no battles. Everyone came trooping back home to Philadelphia again, including the poor old president, so infirm that he returned not on his familiar white steed, but huddled in a carriage. It was scarcely the victory that the Federalists tried to claim.

More shocking, however, was the news that came at the end of the year. Colonel Hamilton resigned from his post at the Treasury, and was leaving the government and Philadelphia to return to New York with his family. Many Republicans rejoiced to see this most powerful of Federalists gone from Philadelphia. The Colonel didn't, especially once the reason became known. Mrs. Hamilton had suffered a miscarriage, and the Colonel had himself endured too much similar sorrow himself to gloat at their loss. Nor did he believe that Colonel Hamilton was truly removed from politics, but would instead likely still continue to maneuver from behind the scenes, especially in the state politics of New York.

One evening before we returned to New York for the winter recess, the Colonel told me to fetch my cloak to walk with him. I was surprised, because I knew he'd plans to dine with other gentlemen. The evening was crisp and wintery enough to keep most people in their houses, yet the Colonel walked with such purpose that I knew this was not simply a pleasant stroll. At last he stopped, and pointed to a handsome brick house on the corner, across Fourth Street.

"I wanted to bring you here before we left, Mary," he said. "I'll wager you'd no notion that I lived in Philadelphia before, there in that corner house."

"Truly, sir?" I asked uncertainly, not sure whether to believe him or not. It seemed odd that he'd never mentioned this before.

He nodded, gazing up at the house. "It remains the residence of Dr. William Shippen, and for a time it was mine as well. I do not recall much of my tenure, however, for I was only two years old at the time."

"Were your parents with you, too, sir?" He'd told me before that he and his sister had been orphaned as young children, but little else beyond that.

He shook his head, still looking at the house. "My parents had both died by then. My father first, then my mother, in swift succession. Sally and I were next sent to our mother's people, but then my grandmother died, and my grandfather as well. Without anyone else, Dr. Shippen became our guardian."

"I'm sorry, sir." He'd never told me this before. "How cruel for two young children to be left so alone!"

"It was," he said, and finally I heard a note of regret to his voice. "After Dr. Shippen, we were given over to my uncle's care. We did not see eye to eye, my uncle and I. He judged me willful, and believed a sound beating was the only cure. You were not the only one who ran away, Mary."

"Truly, sir?"

He nodded, an odd half smile on his face. "I was determined to escape and become a cabin boy, and sail the seas far from my uncle and my tutors," he said. "I'd actually signed the master's papers and was aboard the vessel when my uncle found me. I scampered to the top of the mast and refused to come down until he promised not to thrash me again."

"Did he keep his promise, sir?" I already knew the answer.

"Not at all," he said wryly. "He might not have put a dog's collar around my neck as was done to you, but I was closely watched so I wouldn't flee again."

I thought of how fascinated he'd always been by the faint scars around my throat. Now I understood.

"I was so young when my parents died that my grandmother is the only one I can recall," he said, again looking up at the house before us. "It's only the faintest memory at that, of her holding me as she sat in a rocking chair near a window."

"I remember my grandmother, too," I said impulsively. "Ammatti was the only one who did not despise me. She sang to me when she held me, and called me her little pigeon, and taught me first of spices and cooking."

He turned to look at me. "You never speak of India, Mary."

"It was a long time ago," I said. "And I wasn't Mary then. I was Veeya."

"Veeya, sweet Veeya," he repeated, relishing the foreignness of my first name. "Perhaps I should call you that again."

"No, sir." I drew my cloak more closely about my shoulders, as if that worn wool could protect me from all my old sorrows. "It—it has no place here. Ammatti died when I was seven. Once she was gone, there was no one left who loved me. Like you."

"Like me," he said quietly. "We've both of us our sad beginnings, haven't we?"

I nodded, thinking of how the tragedies had continued through our lives. He'd lost his wife and I'd lost my husband, and he'd also seen three of his four children with Mistress die as well. So much sorrow, so many losses of those we'd held dear. Though it was wrong of me in so public a place, I couldn't help but slip my hand into his as we stood side by side, there on the corner in the dusk.

He didn't rebuff me, but tightened his fingers more closely into mine.

"I saw Mrs. Madison today in passing," he said, in the same quiet manner. "She asked me if you remained in my service, or had found another place here in Philadelphia."

"You told her the truth, didn't you?" I said quickly. "That I was still in your household?"

"I did, Mary," he said. "I did. Come, let's return to the inn."

We walked on in silence, and he said nothing more that evening of either his childhood or Mrs. Madison. But it did not take much for me to decipher his meaning, whether he'd intended it to be so or not.

He'd shown me the place where he'd been taken as an orphan. He'd told me of his mother, father, grandmother, grandfather, all of whom had died and left him behind, to later be followed by his wife and three of their four children. He'd been the survivor, the one who remained.

Surviving often means being left alone, however, as I knew all too well myself. We shared that, yes. It was also clear that when he'd mentioned Mrs. Madison, it was his way of telling me he didn't wish me to be the next to abandon him.

But I understood his meaning, for I felt some of it myself. *A little while longer,* I'd told myself. In the spring, when I had more money saved, when the weather was warmer, when we returned to Philadelphia. A score of reasons and excuses, anything but the truth.

I stayed because of him.

What I didn't realize then was that the Colonel was making plans of his own. At the same time that he'd been fighting his several battles on behalf of the Republicans in Congress, he'd also been preparing for a heady future in New York that could change all our lives.

He told me when we were again at Richmond Hill, the evening after Twelfth Night. Rather, he did not tell me. He mentioned it in passing, as if it were already common knowledge, and of little consequence—which it decidedly was not.

The big house had been filled with guests for the holiday who'd all now departed, and even Miss Burr and Mademoiselle Delage had returned to Madame Senat's care. The Colonel, the servants Thomas and Alexis, and I were ourselves to leave for Philadelphia the following morning. Nearly everything was packed in readiness.

I'd said good night to Louisa and Jean-Pierre, my heart already aching at the prospect of leaving them in the morning, and I'd come here to the dining room to pack a few large serving salvers that the Colonel had decided to bring with him to Philadelphia. I didn't trust any of the other servants to do this. The salvers had belonged to Mistress and her mother before that, and could not be replaced.

"Here you are," the Colonel said, standing in the doorway. He was still dressed as he'd been when the last guests had left earlier in the day, in black silk smallclothes and a black coat over a dark gray vest, a serious silhouette against the dining room's bright French wallpaper. "The house is quiet, isn't it? We're rattling around in this place like two lost souls."

"That's a cheerful way to consider it, sir," I said, bending to close the lid on the trunk and clicking the latches shut. "But that's what comes of having a large house."

"The house in Albany will be smaller." Absently he tapped the folded letter in his hand across his palm; he always had a letter in his hands these days. "But it will suffice for the present."

I straightened, my hands at my waist. "What house in Albany will suffice?"

"For the election," he said, as if this were perfectly obvious. "Instead of sitting high and mighty on Mount Olympus while others conduct my campaign, I believe more can be achieved by engaging with the people directly."

"What people, sir?" He'd still two years remaining in his term as a senator. "What campaign?"

"Why, for governor, Mary," he said, and smiled. "Governor of New York. Clinton is finally stepping down, and the seat is begging for a new leader. The other two running are Chancellor Livingston and Robert Yates. I shouldn't have much trouble from either of them."

"You would step down from the Senate if elected, sir?" I asked, incredulous. To be sure, the governorship of New York was a noteworthy position, and given the size and importance of the state, it likely held more water among politicians than did a mere senator's seat. I also knew the rumors that drifted about Governor Clinton, of how he'd grown rich on the patronage that came with the post, a benefit lacking in the Senate. That, too, would appeal to the Colonel. "You would abandon the Republicans in Congress for Albany?"

"I would," he said evenly. "You needn't be distraught over this, Mary. I intend to take you with me."

"But I have no wish to go to Albany, sir," I said. "None. Albany . . . Albany was not a welcoming place to me."

When I'd first lived there with him and Mistress, I hadn't understood. But now that I'd seen both New York and Philadelphia, I realized why I hadn't liked Albany. I wanted to be in a city where

I saw other free people like me, where my children and I would be at ease and not curiosities, and that was not the case in Albany.

"If I'm elected, I'll need you there, to do all the things you do so splendidly in Philadelphia," he said, frowning.

"But it will be Albany, not Philadelphia," I said. "I'm sorry, sir, but if you become governor and remove to Albany, then I regret that you must find another housekeeper for yourself there."

He stared at me, clearly shocked. I will admit that I'd shocked myself as well, and if the coming separation from my children weren't so heavy upon me, I likely wouldn't have dared speak so honestly. But sometimes the heart will find words that the head cannot, and once I'd spoken, I realized how every word was true.

The Colonel, however, realized nothing except that, for the first time since I had known him, I was refusing to do what he asked. His eyes were filled with disbelief, and he took a step toward me, and another.

"No other woman will suit me as well as you do."

I'd said "housekeeper," not "woman." Didn't he realize the difference?

"I am sorry, sir," I said again. "But I am a free woman now."

"But there's more between us, Mary, isn't there?" He moved quickly, taking me by the arm. "You're no ordinary housekeeper, and you cannot be replaced. You know that as well as I."

I tried to pull free, but he held my arm fast. He'd always been bigger and stronger than I, and he always would be.

"You do not own me," I said. "It is my right to leave your employ if it is no longer agreeable to me."

He curled his other arm around the back of my waist and pushed me backward until I felt the edge of the dining table pressing against the backs of my thighs. He wasn't rough, and there was gentleness in that arm around my waist, but it still wasn't my choice. He leaned closer, and though I tried to turn my face away, he followed, and kissed me against my will.

This was the way things had begun between us. I would not let it be the way it ended.

I knew the moment he relaxed, the only advantage I'd have. As quickly as I could, I slipped free of him. He lost his balance for a moment, stumbling forward against the table without me to break his fall, and as he did I darted across the room and into the hall. He called my name, but I didn't stop. With my skirts bunched high in one hand, I ran down the stairs to the cellar and into the now-empty kitchen, the fires banked for the night. I grabbed the nearest cloak hanging beside the door, threw the bolt, and hurried outside.

The January night air was so sharply cold that it hurt to breathe it. I covered my nose and mouth with the edge of the cloak and ran through the kitchen gardens, past the tall hedges, and into the formal gardens that, in summer, were the Colonel's pride. Old snow and ice crunched beneath my shoes, and I slipped and scrambled as best I could until, at last, I reached the little six-sided garden folly. I brushed the bench clear of snow and sat, breathing hard.

The folly had arched windows on all six sides, the better to let in breezes in the warmer months. From one side, I could see the river, a silvery stripe dotted with the dark shadows of boats. If I looked to the other side, I saw the white house with its columns, porch, and balustrades, ghostly in the moonlight. Everything was silent, and nothing stirred. I'd wanted to be alone, and I was. Now I huddled in the oversized cloak that must belong to one of the men, and tried to think.

To *think*. I was shaking. I told myself that I'd finally spoken from the freedom that Mistress had given me last year. I told myself that I'd done what was right for my children, and that they should always come first.

Yet in the middle of all that clear thinking was the Colonel himself, where he always was, and the memory of his expression would not leave me. I'd glimpsed sorrow and suffering and regret in his eyes, all things I'd never wanted to cause him. I must put my children first, but he was their father, while I was—oh, who knew what I was?

I do not know how long I remained there, gazing out across the shining river. Long enough that my fingers and toes grew numb and my cheeks burned from the cold, but still not enough to settle my thoughts.

The sound of the door echoed across the snow-covered fields, and I turned back toward the house. Two figures and a dog walked along the house's road, one carrying a lantern, their shadows stretched long in the lantern's light across the snow. I was sure one was the Colonel. I watched them walk back and forth, doubtless searching for my footsteps. I could've called to them, but I didn't.

Finally they came to the back of the house, and at once the dog found my trail. Soon the lantern, held high by Alexis, discovered me in the folly.

"Mary." The Colonel stood on the steps of the folly, now holding the lantern, as Alexis and the dog trudged back toward the house. "Are you unharmed?"

I nodded, silent.

He stepped inside, but didn't sit. "I thought you'd run away."

I doubted he believed that. In the snow, in the cold, at night, without money or belongings, and, most of all, without my children? No.

He sighed, his face lit oddly from beneath by the lantern.

"You were right, Mary," he said. "I cannot demand that you join me in Albany, and I'm sorry I did. I'm sorry for the rest, too. You're free, exactly as you said. You may do whatever you please, including wish me heartily to the devil."

"Don't make jests like that, sir," I said.

"I was speaking the truth, albeit with considerable clumsiness." He set the lantern on the floor, and sat beside me. "Had I shown more care with my words, I would have told you how indispensable you have become to me. Not only by making certain there are sufficient spoons and forks on my table, but as my . . . as my friend. I cannot imagine embarking on the governorship without you, even if it must lead to the benighted city of Albany."

I let him speak, and I listened. The truth was that despite everything else, I thought of him as my friend, too. Ah, what a twisting of that humble word!

I leaned my head against his shoulder, and tucked my cloak-wrapped hand beneath his arm. "Albany *is* benighted."

"I agree," he said. "But my intention would be to remain there for only a term or two."

I turned to look him squarely in the eye. "You have further ambitions, don't you?"

He shrugged. "Most men do."

"You are not most men, sir."

"Be grateful that I am not." He stood, and held his hand out to me. "Come. It's far too cold to linger out here, and I know of at least one room in the house that still has a decent fire."

I took his hand, and let him lead me back to the house, and the fire, too. He deflected what I'd said about his ambition, but I knew him well enough to understand what he hadn't said.

He'd no great desire to be governor of New York. It would be the means to a greater end, nothing more.

What he wished instead was to be president.

As it turned out, neither the Colonel nor I went to Albany. The Colonel had told me he'd two rivals for the governor's seat—New York State Supreme Court Justice Robert Yates and Chancellor Robert Livingston—and that neither of them, although worthy gentlemen, would offer much competition to him in the election. This wasn't merely his vanity, but truth.

But as soon as Colonel Hamilton and his father-in-law, General Schuyler, learned that the odious Colonel Burr was likely to become the next governor, they and their supporters quickly declared former Chief Justice John Jay as their candidate. It didn't matter that Justice Jay did not place a single step within the state of New York during the entire election process (having been sent to London to negotiate the new treaty with Britain), or that the Colonel campaigned relentlessly. The Schuyler-Hamilton Federalists used their considerable power to see that Justice Jay was elected, with his inauguration postponed until his return from abroad in July 1795.

The Colonel had seen this coming, and withdrew from the race in March. He was philosophical about this, and not as disappointed as I'd expected him to be. But then, I'd learned that he saw such matters on a much grander scale than most gentlemen, and that his thwarted run had many larger benefits toward the future. He was the first and only candidate to go among the people, to shake hands and listen and collect his votes one by one. Electioneering, it was called, and while he was faulted for it as being a vulgar opportunist, the men he'd met this way appreciated it, and liked him. His popularity continued to grow within the democratic societies, those increasingly popular groups denounced by Federalists as "demonic societies." He was mentioned more and more in the newspapers, not only in Philadelphia and New York, but in other cities as well, praised for his independence in politics.

But while he'd conceded to Justice Jay in the election, he was not so forgiving in regards to the treaty the other New Yorker had negotiated, and with good reason, too. The Colonel had first objected strongly to John Jay's appointment as a special envoy to the British the year before. The Federalists had had their way, and although the treaty that Justice Jay negotiated with the British was completed in the fall of 1794, the president and the Federalists kept the details of the treaty as well as their own villainy secret from Congress until the spring of 1795.

When at last it was shared with Congress, the Colonel, the Republicans, and many Federalists were appalled by what Justice Jay had conceded to the British, giving up nearly all the trade advantages won by the Revolution and sidling closer to the British against the French. It made no mention of protecting the American sailors who had been routinely kidnapped from their ships and forced to serve the British, or negotiating compensation to those who'd lost property during the war. Now known as Jay's Treaty, so there was no mistaking who was to blame, it was an obvious affront to the French, but also, by its very secrecy, an insult to the American people.

The Colonel tried his best to stop the treaty as it stood, urging for a renegotiation. He met with every Federalist who might waver in his vote, spending so many hours in these discussions that there were days that it seemed he returned to his lodgings only to be shaved, wash, and change his linen. He scarcely slept and he made speech after speech. He broke the secrecy surrounding the treaty's details, and shared it with newspapers and his constituents in New York. He even appealed directly to the president, who didn't deign to reply.

As everyone now knows, Jay's Treaty was passed, as it most likely was destined to be from the beginning. But because of the Colonel's considerable efforts, he was hailed as the leader of the "Patriotic Ten," meaning the ten senators who had gone against the Federalist majority and the president in their voting.

It made him a hero. Jay's Treaty was even more wildly unpopular than the whiskey taxes had been, and there were public protests in every city with bonfires, marches, and pictures of Justice Jay being defiled and burned. To no surprise, some of the most violent gatherings were in New York. In the middle of one such "meeting" during the city's Fourth of July celebrations, Colonel Hamilton himself tried to defend the treaty, and was showered with stones and catcalls for his trouble. Instead of withdrawing, his temper flared brighter, and he not only jumped into the rabble to battle them, but also ended his day issuing two challenges for two separate duels.

"The man has lost his wits," the Colonel declared when he told me of this. "No gentleman brawls with drunken apprentices and sailors in the streets."

"But consider poor Mrs. Hamilton, sir," I said, pausing in my sweeping. "Colonel Hamilton is fortunate he wasn't killed."

"They say he was struck with a rock in the forehead," the Colonel said, glancing back down at the letter that had brought the news. "A shame that the rock didn't relieve some of the pressure upon his brains, or what's left of them."

"Colonel Hamilton can't bear to be without power, sir," I observed. I'd seen my share of white gentlemen, and how important it was to them to control their affairs and those of everyone else as well. "For nearly twenty years he had President Washington's ear, and it clearly grieves him that he no longer does."

"Oh, I suspect he's still busily scribbling his endless missives to Washington," the Colonel said. "Only death will stop that pen."

"Don't wish that upon him, sir," I chided uneasily. His humor could often turn dark like this, and I didn't like him tempting fate by speaking so lightly of death and dying.

"I don't wish Hamilton any bodily harm," the Colonel said, comfortably stretching his legs before the fire. "Nor need I do so, when he appears to be so determined to plunge toward disaster on his own. I expect his seconds will smooth the waters again so there'll be no satisfaction demanded. This is far from the first challenges issued by that little gamecock."

There was nothing to be gained by pointing out that he and Colonel Hamilton were of similar height, though through his more measured and confident demeanor Colonel Burr did appear to be the larger and more substantial of the two men. He'd always been richly somber in his dress, and had recently adopted the new style of a white waistcoat with his habitual black coat, breeches, and stockings, all contributing to his confidently elegant presence. By comparison, Colonel Hamilton preferred bright colors in his dress, and combined with his often-agitated movements and rapid speech, he did give the impression of a small, gaudy parrot—or a game-cock, as the Colonel called him.

"You know he's jealous of you, sir," I said. "Your star is rising, while his has tumbled clear from the sky."

The Colonel didn't deny it. "It's Hamilton's own doing," he said. "That, and the other Federalists'. They've already decided that Adams will be their next man after Washington, not Hamilton."

"And you, sir, are second only to Mr. Jefferson among the Republicans," I said, being both loyal and truthful. "Perhaps your star may be even brighter than Mr. Jefferson's, given that you appear on every horizon, while he has retreated to hide like a hermit to Monticello. Colonel Hamilton has every reason to be jealous of you."

"Oh, Mary," he said, smiling. "No one should be jealous of anyone until old man Washington finally expires. The presidency is as good as a throne so long as he's in office. No one will ever dare run against him."

I didn't for a moment think that he believed that. I know there are many who believe ambition to be a cursed fault, and that the humble folk in this life are to be praised and admired over those who are driven to improve themselves and their fortunes. Certainly, ambition was often the greatest criticism that the Federalists leveled at the Colonel. I myself could never fathom how this could be considered such a grievous flaw. Where, indeed, would the world be without men who'd the ambition to better it?

No matter. Throughout the remainder of 1795 and into the summer of 1796, there was no denying that the Colonel acted like an ambitious gentleman. This might have been because he knew he'd lose his Senate seat at the end of the term, with Governor Clinton and the Hamiltonian Federalists deciding to swing back to support General Schuyler against the Colonel. He'd need a new challenge, and he didn't like retreats.

He made journeys throughout New England, listening with special care to grievances regarding Jay's Treaty, and then progressed southward, lingering for a full three months in Virginia. Because of Mr. Jefferson, as well as Mr. Madison and Colonel Monroe, Virginia had been the very heart of the Democratic-Republicans, and the Virginians gave the Colonel the warmest of welcomes. He met with Mr. Jefferson at Monticello, and he also visited another southern ally in his old friend Colonel Monroe, who had been ignominiously called home from France by the president for failing to persuade the French that Jay's Treaty was a wondrous thing—which it wasn't.

For me this time was bittersweet. There was no purpose to me accompanying the Colonel on his journeys, and only possible harm in us being observed together. I missed him while he was away, most keenly at night. As much as I longed to write to him, or have a letter of his for my own, the risk of discovery still made it impossible, as it always had. The only news of him came secondhand, from letters he wrote to Miss Burr or through the New York newspapers reporting his travels.

And yet there was a certain relief in being away from the attention that always followed the Colonel, and the constant fear of discovery that likewise shadowed me. If our friendship became known, my very presence would delight his political enemies, who wouldn't hesitate to use me and our children as a weapon against him.

Thus while the Colonel traveled, I remained in New York, going back and forth between Richmond Hill and Partition Street, wherever I was most useful. The fact that the Colonel was away did not mean that entertaining at Richmond Hill had ceased. Far from it. If friends or associates of his were visiting New York, he continued to extend invitations to visit and dine, with his daughter acting as his hostess. Miss Burr was now thirteen, and due to her rigorous education, she was poised and confident as a hostess, even with guests that ranged from American politicians to French philosophers to Joseph Brant, a Mohawk military leader from the Iroquois League. Just as I did for her father, I helped Miss Burr with her menus, oversaw the proper arrangement of her table, and made sure the service was as it should be, leaving it to her to charm her father's guests.

But best of all, this time in New York meant that I'd be with my children. This was the longest the three of us had been together since Jean-Pierre had been an infant, and I intended to savor every moment.

Louisa was now eight, and though she continued to be a pretty child, she no longer much resembled her half sister, Miss Burr, for which I was grateful. I was less happy about another way the two differed. Despite my hopes, Louisa continued to show little interest in learning. She could read, and compose simple sentences in a serviceable hand, and cipher well enough, but that was the end of it. She preferred the kitchen to any books, and was already showing skill at baking and other cookery.

With a mother's guilt, I blamed this on Peg's care in place of my own while I'd been with the Colonel. Soon, however, I realized that this was my daughter's true nature, and that Louisa was instead only following after me in cooking and housekeeping. I'd hoped she'd become a tradeswoman, but that had been my dream, not hers. I loved her as much as I ever did, and came to accept that this was where her future would lie, and to guide her gently in the direction that would make her happiest.

Jean-Pierre was entirely different. At four, he'd already learned to read, and would patiently work his way through whatever text I set before him. He was learning to speak French with the same ease as he did English. He was fearless and bold, both traits that delighted the Colonel. With Jean-Pierre held safely on the saddle before him, the Colonel would ride by the hour across the fields at Richmond Hill, and I couldn't say whether father or son enjoyed it the more.

Yet I worried that my son would grow too attached to this father who wasn't his. I saw how Jean-Pierre's round-cheeked little face brightened whenever the Colonel appeared, just as I saw the tenderness and affection in his father's eyes. To me, the likeness between the two was too strong to be ignored, and growing stronger as Jean-Pierre became less a baby and more a boy.

One Sunday afternoon in late August, my children and I sat on the low stone wall in the kitchen garden. I'd washed some old clay pipes that I'd come across in a cupboard, and made a dish of soapy water so that we could blow bubbles. As was to be expected, Louisa and I did all the blowing, while Jean-Pierre darted after the iridescent bubbles as they drifted over the lawn. As he ran over the grass, my son's shock of unruly dark curls pulled free of the ribbon and queue I always tried to make of his hair, bouncing around his face like a lion's mane.

It was a pretty game with much laughter and foolishness, and as I watched my two in the dappled sun I realized how happy and at peace I was. There were no secrets here, no demands, no expectations. I felt as light and unencumbered as the soap bubbles, and I laughed with purest joy. For the first time in my memory, I felt truly free, and it had little to do with the deeds of manumission that I kept in the locked box beneath my bed.

"Mrs. Emmons?"

I twisted around on the wall, shading my eyes with my hand. The young blond man in the wide straw hat smiling at me was Mr. Vanderlyn, another of the Colonel's random guests. He was an artist, a former apprentice of Mr. Stuart's, and the Colonel had granted him the use of one of the outbuildings as a studio for the summer. He generally kept to himself and his paints, and I'd seen little of him until now.

"I heard the children," he said, glancing again at them.

"I'm sorry," I said, sliding off the wall. "I didn't mean for them to disturb you at your work. Louisa, Jean-Pierre—"

"No, no, please," he said quickly. "Let them play. They didn't disturb me. They inspired me. Here, permit me to show you."

He opened the portfolio he had tucked beneath his arm, and spread the drawings he'd made out on the wall for me to see. He'd perfectly captured my children at play, and I covered my mouth, overwhelmed by my sentiments.

"This is my favorite of your son," he said, handing me another sheet. "What spirit he has! The resemblance is quite remarkable, isn't it?"

I glanced at him sharply, reminding myself in the last moment not to show my alarm. "The resemblance, sir?"

His smile faded into uncertainty. "Ah, yes," he said. "To his, ah, father."

"Yes, he is very much like my late husband," I said, determined to protect my son however I could. "Mr. Emmons was a handsome man, and I'm thankful my boy so favors him."

He gave me the drawing to keep, and the next time that the Colonel returned to Richmond Hill, at the end of September, I showed it to him.

He smiled. "Hah, that's my Jean-Pierre, no doubt," he said. "I believe Vanderlyn will one day surpass Stuart."

"Do you know what your Mr. Vanderlyn told me, sir?" My voice shook with the anxiety that I'd been keeping back. "He said that the resemblance between Jean-Pierre and his father was remarkable. He said that, sir, and he drew it that way, too. A blind man could see that this picture shows your son."

"No one cares, Mary," he said, still looking at the picture. "I've told you that before, and I'll tell you again. You worry unnecessarily."

I shook my head. "Once I worried what your enemies would say and write of you in the papers if they learned about us," I said. "But now I look at Jean-Pierre—*my* son, sir—and I fear for him. Do you think his innocence would matter to Colonel Hamilton, and the poisonous slanders he orders written for the papers? Do you think he'd pause even for a moment about how his words could forever ruin the reputations of me and my children?"

"Mary, my Mary." He tossed the drawing onto his desk, and took me gently by the shoulders. "Listen to me. Now that Washington's officially withdrawn his name for a third term, this has become a real election, with real issues. Adams, Jefferson, and me. That's the choice, and men will cast their votes based on what affects them, like taxes, tariffs, and whether they can claim stake in a homestead to the west. No one will care if there's a young boy in New York that bears a passing resemblance to me."

He kissed me then, as he always did when he judged a conversation was done to his satisfaction. I let him, too: not because I'd accepted his argument, but because I knew he'd refuse to accept mine.

Less than a month later, and only weeks before the election, I'd all the sickening proof I required.

There on the fourth page of the *Gazette of the United States,* the most popular of the Federalist newspapers, was yet another editorial about the election and the Republican candidates by Phocion. When the first editorial had been published, the Colonel had explained to me that Phocion had been a statesman in ancient Greece, reputed to be the most honest man in Athens. The irony, of course, was that the writer now hiding behind this name for his despicable, name-calling editorials was Colonel Hamilton, whom no one considered honest in the least.

This week as Phocion he'd chosen to skewer Mr. Jefferson, calling him a coward, a feckless philosopher, and a score of other things besides. But he saved his most venomous attack for last: how Mr. Jefferson's life at Monticello was one lascivious, illicit pleasure after another, and how he lolled in the arms of his dusky Negro mistress, Sally, surrounded by their grinning little bastard quadroons.

What assurance did I have that my children and I wouldn't be next? I sank to my knees, and buried my head in my hands in despair.

I could postpone it no longer. It was time for me to make my preparations to leave in earnest.

CHAPTER 24

Philadelphia
State of Pennsylvania
March 1797

Nothing about the presidential election of 1796 went as anyone expected.

According to the laws of that time, every candidate was running for president. Whoever received the most votes would become president, and whoever received the second-most votes would serve as vice president. After President Washington declined to serve again, three gentlemen stepped forward to run: Mr. Jefferson and the Colonel, both Democratic-Republicans, and Mr. Adams of Massachusetts, a Federalist.

The Federalists believed that Mr. Adams, having served as President Washington's vice president, would handily win the presidency. The leaders among the Democratic-Republicans, however, were eager to secure both positions, believing that Mr. Jefferson and the Colonel would support each other in securing the majority. Later in the campaign, however, Colonel Hamilton feared that Colonel Burr might actually win the presidency itself, which would have been unbearable to him and other New York Federalists. To keep this from happening, he introduced a second Federalist candidate, Mr. Thomas Pinckney of South Carolina, with the hope of both bolstering Mr. Adams and blocking Colonel Burr.

That is the simplest version of the election. In reality, it was filled with intrigue and guile, promises made and broken, name-calling and accusations, and more shameful deceit than can ever be imagined now.

Yet somehow throughout that ugly autumn, my children and I escaped the Federalists' notice. I do not know how this was possible, but it was, and I thanked Heaven that we'd been spared. I'd understood the danger, and the consequences, too. If I'd been publicly denounced as the Colonel's concubine and my children revealed as his bastards, then no white lady would ever consider me for her housekeeper. Had I still been in bondage (like Sally, who belonged to Mr. Jefferson), then the assumption would be that I'd had no choice, and those ladies wouldn't have cared. But the fact that I'd remained with the Colonel after I'd been freed—and continued to do so—would make it seem as if I truly were a wanton, and no lady would wish me in her home, temptation to her husband and sons.

It was during this time that I did something I'd never before done: I wrote a letter. To be sure, I knew how this was done, and I'd even written them on behalf of Mistress, when she'd been too ill to hold a pen herself. But this was the first I'd written for myself, in my own words. My letter was addressed to Mrs. Madison, and in it I inquired if she did in fact know of a Philadelphia lady looking for a housekeeper with my skills. It took me many attempts before I had the wording to my satisfaction and could take it to be sent with the general post from the city, rather than with the Colonel's mail. Although he'd no right to keep me, I judged it better not to alarm him in advance of my hopes. To be doubly sure, I asked Mrs. Madison to reply to me not at Richmond Hill, but in care of the tavern keeper who bought raised rabbit pies from me.

To my disappointment but not my surprise, I never received a reply. I did not know if this were due to the color of my skin, or if her promise had been simply an empty one, like that of so many ladies in her position. I also worried that somehow the Colonel had learned of my letter, and interfered.

The Colonel, however, had much more to consider than me. Instead of the election going the way that the two factions had hoped, most men voted according to their regions, not beliefs. When the final votes were tallied, the new president was John Adams, with

Thomas Jefferson as vice president. Thomas Pinckney came in third, with a dozen or so other additional men claiming a few more straggling votes.

And despite all his canvassing, meetings, travels, speeches, and dinners, Colonel Burr only managed to be fourth.

It was a staggering blow to his pride. For the last decade, he'd served the public in one position or another, and now that same public had rejected him. To his credit, he didn't rage or grieve. Intemperate displays were never his way. Yet as I oversaw the packing of his belongings from his Philadelphia lodgings in March, the sense of defeat and humiliation was unavoidable—not only for his own political ambitions, but for the Democratic-Republicans as well. Their leader Mr. Jefferson would now serve as vice president and be in constant conflict both with President Adams and with the Federalist-dominated Congress.

As if all this were not sufficient, true sorrow came at the end of the month, when the Colonel received word that his sister, Sally, had died. Though she had been an invalid for much of her life, her death was still a shock to him. Mrs. Reeve had been his only sibling, the sister who'd been his constant comfort since they'd been children, and a close friend of Mistress's as well. Now she, too, was gone.

During this last, brief sojourn in Philadelphia, I'd made a few desultory inquiries regarding new places. But even if something had come of my queries, at this time I knew I hadn't the heart to leave the Colonel, not when he'd lost so much. Some might say this was weakness on my part, that after how he had used me in the past he deserved no kindness from me. I won't deny that perhaps it was.

"What next, sir?" I asked as we stood together on the deck of the ferry, the first part of our journey from Philadelphia to New York. While the others went with our belongings on the cart, he and I would return together by stage.

It was a question I hadn't dared to ask before, but one I knew he'd considered long and hard. It took him only a moment to reply.

"What next, Mary?" he repeated, looking out over the murky water of the Delaware River. "Why, to move forward, of course."

"That is wisest," I said carefully, not certain of his meaning.

His smile was melancholy. "You needn't be so gentle with me,

Mary. I am resilient, and I am philosophical. As are you. We've always been alike that way."

I smiled, too, for he was right. Compared to what we'd each seen in our lives, the loss of an election was insignificant indeed. "You see, sir, I've always said that you were wise."

"Philosophical, not wise." If there hadn't been others on the deck, I am certain we would have embraced. "Nothing is gained by looking backward, Mary. Only forward, and toward the future."

Once again in New York, he did exactly that. While his enemies surely wished otherwise, he did not withdraw into private life at Richmond Hill. Instead, he remained engaged in politics, determined to learn from what he now saw as his mistakes. He ran for the New York state legislature as an assemblyman, and won with ease. A lesser gentleman would have seen this as a terrible fall from his exalted seat in the Senate, but he did not, relishing the challenge of politics so well that he saw only the opportunities.

He remained thick among the Democratic-Republicans, and now–vice president Jefferson continued to seek his advice and opinions. He would travel back to Philadelphia whenever his voice was needed, and think nothing of the journey.

When James Madison—another whose fortunes had seemingly fallen—returned from France after his abrupt dismissal, the Colonel was there to greet him along with Mr. Jefferson and Mr. Gallatin. Dinners at Richmond Hill often seemed more like a political caucus than a genteel gathering. As had always been the case, men with influence, men who could persuade others with money and favors, were also welcome.

He also resumed his legal career, and only in part for the income. More important to him was choosing cases that would increase his prominence around the state and in the city, and continue to bring him in contact with men who were powerful in their regions, as well as the individual voters whose favor he would need for another race in the future.

In short, he carried himself not in defeat, but as a gentleman vigorous and eager to fight fresh battles for the good of the country. He was only forty-one, and as he noted more than once, General Washington had been nearly sixty when he'd become president.

But while I was glad of all this for the Colonel's sake, his return to New York politics as well as to Richmond Hill was not easy for me. Keeping my children from the inquisitive and often cruel gaze of others had been simpler while the Colonel had been in the capital. Louisa was content to remain belowstairs when there were guests, but Jean-Pierre wanted nothing more than to be in the Colonel's company as much as possible. At five, he was still too young to understand that his presence in turn might not always be desired, nor, for that matter, did the Colonel send him away, as I often begged him to do. I knew it would be kinder in the end and, after the incident with Mr. Vanderlyn, the more cautious course as well.

"Where's the harm in it, Mary?" the Colonel asked when I confronted him again as he sat at his desk in his library. Jean-Pierre had been with him there for most of the afternoon before I'd come to send him back to the kitchen. The blocks that had once been the toys of Miss Burr were still scattered on the carpet, a fortress that Jean-Pierre had left half knocked down. "Why can't my son be with me?"

"Because to the rest of the world, he's not your son," I insisted.

The Colonel sighed, looking up from whatever letter he'd been writing. "I still don't see the harm in it."

"Because you do not wish to see it," I said as firmly as I could. "No other man can compare to you in Jean-Pierre's eyes. You are his hero in every possible way. But someday he'll realize that while you truly *are* his father, you'll never be able to acknowledge him as your son. It will fall to me to console him as best I can, and explain to him what will be impossible to explain without making him suffer more."

"You underestimate the boy, Mary," he said with maddening composure. "I'll tell him the truth at the proper time. You'll see. It will all settle itself."

I'd left then, before my frustration spilled over. I could not comprehend his stubbornness, even as I knew how unlikely he was to change. It was not laziness on his part, or determined inaction, but his constant belief that things would fall into place without any help. Years before in Albany, when Carlos was still his servant and eager to relay to me everything that the Colonel said or did in the course of his workday, there had been one story that I'd never forgotten.

Another attorney had urged the Colonel to make more preparations in a defense than the Colonel had believed necessary, quoting the old maxim of never putting off for tomorrow what could be done today. The Colonel had merely smiled, and told him that he preferred never to do today what could as well be done tomorrow, because something might occur before then that could make one regret one's premature action. Carlos had found this wonderfully clever, especially since in the Colonel's ever-changing legal affairs its wisdom had been proved again and again.

But my son's little heart was neither a legal brief nor a scrap of diplomatic intrigue, and I did not want to see him hurt by his father's selfishness.

Later that July, I witnessed exactly that.

The Colonel had planned a large supper for the evening, and because the day was already warm, I'd risen before dawn to begin the preparations, leaving my children asleep. The Colonel had especially requested mille-feuille pastries to astonish his guests and make a statement about French loyalty. The many layers of pastry would be a special challenge in the day's heat, and I went to work in the stone springhouse near the pond, where I could keep the flour and butter chilled.

By the time I'd returned, the sun had risen and Peg, Louisa, and the others were gathered at the table at their breakfasts. Jean-Pierre, however, was nowhere to be seen.

"Colonel Burr came and took him," Peg said when I asked. "Said they'd plans together, out in the north field."

I frowned, and still wearing my flour-dusted apron, I quickly crossed the formal gardens and orchards. I saw them at a distance against the green, one large figure and one small, but I heard them, too. Not their voices, not at first, but the repeated crack of the pistol through the heavy morning air.

I hurried toward them, practically running. I'd always considered the Colonel to not be much given to shooting, as some men were. Oh, I remembered overhearing at the Hermitage during the war that he was regarded as an excellent shot, but though he'd take a rifle hunting if another gentleman invited him, I'd never seen him choose the pastime on his own. I hadn't known he even possessed a pistol. Yet obviously he did, and knew how to use it with ease and skill, too.

Jean-Pierre saw me first, his curls bobbing in the sun as he danced with excitement. With his back toward me and his arm steady, the Colonel fired another shot. Fear for my son's safety clutched in my chest as I rushed forward, terrified that my unpredictable child would run across the grass and into the path of his father's gun.

"Mama, Mama!" Jean-Pierre called. "Come see what the Colonel is doing!"

"I can see from here, darling." I grabbed him by the wrist and pulled him close, though he tried to wriggle free. The Colonel joined us, his boots cutting a path across the dewy grass.

"Good day, Mrs. Emmons," he called cheerfully through the acrid clouds of gunpowder smoke, as if he weren't holding a pistol in his hand with studied nonchalance. "A fine summer morning, isn't it?"

"We were dueling, Mama," Jean-Pierre said proudly. "Like gentlemen. Those apples were supposed to be *heads*."

Now I noticed that the pistol the Colonel held was designed for that deadly practice, the barrel longer than usual and a curving spur on the trigger guard, and that the row of green apples set along the tall fence at the height of a man's head and exactly twenty paces in the distance. I also saw that the space where other apples must previously have stood was now empty, having been shot clean away.

"Why?" My single word was as sharp as the gunshots had been.

The Colonel smiled, unperturbed. "Monroe and Hamilton exchanged words the other night about that old business with Mrs. Reynolds and the bribes to her husband," he said. "I shall tell you the particulars later."

He glanced pointedly down at Jean-Pierre, though it struck me as a bit late to be protecting him.

"I intend to do my best to mitigate the disagreement," he continued. "But you know what a hotspur Hamilton can be."

I didn't need further explanation. Colonel Hamilton and Colonel Monroe were on the verge of a duel, an affair of honor where one or both of them could be killed over impulsive words and stubbornness. Somehow Colonel Burr had been drawn into it, likely as Colonel Monroe's second, which had brought him here to practice, pistol in hand.

Oh, I understood, and the risk and the danger and the foolishness of it made me sick.

"Then tell me, sir," I said. "Why did you bring my son here for this?"

"The boy's old enough to learn the importance of marksmanship," he said with a studied blandness. "Familiarity with weapons and an ease around them is important to a man. It's also a useful lesson in the potential cost of honor to a gentleman."

"Colonel Burr said the apples were heads," Jean-Pierre said, jerking on my hand with excitement. "Before you came, Mama, he'd shot every one of them *dead!*"

"Are you happy, sir?" I demanded. "Are you content? Is that what you wished to hear? He's a *child*. What if he'd run forward into your path? What if you were distracted, and your aim had been off?"

He took a step toward me. "Dear Mary, please—"

I took a step back, pulling my son with me. "I'll thank you not to call me that, sir, and I'll also thank you not to fill my son's head with your talk of honor. I thank God he's not a gentleman and never will be, if your variety of *honor* is the price he'd have to pay."

I grabbed Jean-Pierre and swung him onto my hip, and went striding off back across the field. I ignored how Jean-Pierre wailed in protest and how heavy he was bouncing in my arms, and I also ignored the Colonel. I do not know if he continued his shooting practice, or if he called after me. I was too angry to hear either.

I didn't see the Colonel again until much later that evening, when he was surrounded with his guests. These were important gentlemen with loud voices and louder laughter. Their ladies were all dressed in fashionable white muslin, their painted fans moving briskly before their flushed faces despite the Colonel having ordered every tall window in the dining room open to the air. The Colonel laughed with the gentlemen and flirted with the women, as he always did. But whenever he tried to catch my eye as I glided through the room at my tasks, I pretended I didn't see him. I was still too angry.

Because Colonel Hamilton had confronted Colonel Monroe while he was dining with his wife at their lodgings, the entire affair had swiftly become public knowledge. Everyone in the room knew of it, and the conversations were filled with what exactly had been said, who was in the right and who wasn't and what Colonel Burr could do about it, and even the costly dueling pistols from London—bespoke from the legendary Wogdon himself!—that Hamilton's brother-in-law and noted duelist John Barker Church was sure to provide.

As always, that night I was the last one awake in the kitchen, and as I closed and latched the windows the Colonel appeared. After today, I would have been surprised if he hadn't.

"That was a splendid dinner, Mary," he said. He'd shed his coat, and the white linen of his shirt and waistcoat seemed very white by the muted light of the banked fire, while the gold chain, watch, and toys of his fob glittered at his waist.

"Thank you, sir," I said curtly, with no hint of forgiveness. He didn't deserve it.

"Are you still angry about this morning?" he asked behind me.

I continued putting things to rights for the night, and not looking his way.

"I'm angry about this morning, yes," I said. "I'm angry that you would dare introduce my son to such dangerous idiocy, and put him at risk by doing so, and I'm also angry that you would tangle yourself in the middle of Hamilton's madness."

"The boy is mine, too, Mary," he said. "You often seem to forget that."

I turned about quickly to face him.

"I never forget it, sir, not for a moment," I said. "Every time I look into Jean-Pierre's face, I see yours. Yet you treat him like a pet, not a son, to be your plaything when it amuses you, and forgotten while you're away."

"That's hardly fair, Mary," he began, but I cut him off.

"It's fair, sir, because it's the truth," I said. "Why do you protest? You have no responsibility, no obligations, and no rights to either Louisa or Jean-Pierre. You'll never even have to admit that they're yours. That's the law, isn't it? Your precious law?"

"Is that how you mean to leave here, and take them from me?" he asked abruptly. "Don't look at me like that, Mary. I know what Mrs. Madison told you. Dolley herself asked me last month if you'd left my employment now that I was no longer a senator."

Sharply I drew in my breath. I hadn't expected that, not at all, and I crossed my arms over my chest, marshaling my anger into a defense.

"If I leave, sir, that wouldn't be the reason," I said. "I'd leave because I wished to provide a better life for my children."

"Better than you have here?" He flung his hands out as if to encompass all the richness of Richmond Hill, as if that alone were enough.

"Better for us, sir," I said. "Better for the people my children will become. Today you took my son to play with pistols, and pretended to shoot other men in the head for the sake of an affair of honor. You conveniently forgot that he will never be a gentleman, and that he has no need to learn of such things, ever."

The Colonel grumbled with frustration that likely matched my own.

"Very well, then," he said. "I was wrong to take Jean-Pierre to shoot with me. I am sorry, and ask your forgiveness. But I'm not Hamilton, Mary. I've never been involved in a duel in my life, not even in the army."

I didn't believe him, not after what I'd seen this morning.

"Besides," he continued, "I'm not one of the principals. Seconds are almost never called upon to fire."

I shook my head. "That brings me no comfort, sir."

For a long moment, he was silent, and so was I. He knew how to use silence as powerfully as his words, and he'd always possessed the uncanny ability to stand very still. He was doing both now, knowing how it unsettled me.

Finally he took a step—only one—toward me. "You said that you were angry that I'd put myself in the way of Hamilton."

"I said Hamilton's madness, sir." I sighed deeply, still hugging my arms against my body. Of a sudden my anger seemed spent, and now that it had gone, I felt close to tears. "He hates you beyond reason. In some way, he *is* mad, sir, and you must be as well, to agree to this."

He held his hand out to me. "I'm many things, Mary, but I'm not mad."

I looked at his offered hand, and shook my head.

"Is it any wonder that I fear for you, sir?" I asked. "If you were brought home having been killed for the sake of honor—I couldn't bear that, sir, nor would I wish that sight upon my children. *Our* children. I couldn't bear that at all, and I would rather leave here than be forced to see it."

He still held his hand outstretched to me, and still I refused to take it.

"You care that much?"

"For you?" I asked, incredulous that he would ask. "Yes, I care for you, sir, and the greater fool I am for doing so."

He nodded, and slowly lowered his hand back to his side.

"What must I do to make you stay?" he asked quietly.

I bowed my head, avoiding his eyes. I didn't want to weep before him, and yet I would if I tried to answer.

When I opened my eyes, he was gone.

As the Colonel had told me, the confrontation and challenges between Colonel Hamilton and Colonel Monroe had all come from Colonel Hamilton's infidelity with Mrs. Reynolds, and his subsequent blackmailing by that wretched woman's husband six years before. At that time, Colonel Monroe had believed the blackmailing related to Colonel Hamilton's position as Secretary of the Treasury, and had headed an investigation into the matter. When he learned the truth, he'd dismissed the investigation, and the shameful matter was considered closed, as was the way between gentlemen.

Somehow, however, the papers related to the investigation had lately found their way into the hands of an unscrupulous publisher, who had printed them. This had resulted in the would-be duel. At least Colonel Burr appeared to be successfully dismantling it, easing the tensions so that the entire affair would dissipate honorably, and without bloodshed.

But Colonel Hamilton's anger—and his madness—remained unchecked. To prove that he was innocent of the rumors of financial impropriety, he wrote and published himself a pamphlet describing his seduction by Mrs. Reynolds in lurid detail, a confession that must have broken the heart of poor Mrs. Hamilton.

"What would possess him to do such a thing, sir?" I exclaimed after I'd read the pamphlet, which of course the Colonel had bought and brought home.

The Colonel barely glanced up from the book he was reading. "What possessed him was Mrs. Reynolds, a most alluring if empty-headed creature. Like a sugary pink-and-white confection that only brings regrets after consumption."

"I meant how he could treat his wife so, sir."

"Reticence has never been one of Hamilton's strengths," he said. "You know that as well as I. His mouth runs on like the flux."

Not for the first time, I thought of how different the two men were in this regard, with the Colonel always so reluctant to commit anything to paper. No wonder that he and I together had safely kept our own secret for so many years.

"I've heard his wife has left him," the Colonel continued, "and that she has taken the younger children with her to stay with her parents in Albany. Who can blame her? Imagine having to listen to his blather day and night."

I rose and went to kneel beside his chair, so he could not avoid me or what I said.

"Listen to me, sir, I beg you," I said, my words soft but urgent. "If Colonel Hamilton would willingly injure his own wife like this to preserve his reputation, what would he do to someone he despised, someone he saw as his enemy?"

He closed his book, and began instead to caress my shoulder, likely intending to distract me.

"My dear Mary," he said. "I can already see the twisting path you wish to lead me along, and like a recalcitrant nag, I am going to refuse to follow. I have known Hamilton since we were both fresh from school. I know both his qualities and his flaws, and his hazards with them. But I also know how not to let him vex me, or draw me into his imagined intrigues and schemes."

"Then why did you let him involve you into his duel, sir?"

"I didn't, sweet," he said mildly. "That was by Monroe's invitation, and I agreed because he, too, is my friend."

"I am your friend as well, sir," I said, daring, for the word applied to Colonel Monroe was not at all the same as to me. "Might I likewise ask a favor of you? Swear to me there'll be no more affairs of honor, not with Colonel Hamilton or anyone else."

He frowned indulgently. "When will you ever trust me, Mary?"

"Your word, sir," I insisted. "I do not want to see you dead."

"You won't," he said, leaning forward to kiss me. "Be assured that I am safe, you are safe, and our children are safe, and that should be an end to it where you are concerned."

Even as Colonel Hamilton's follies were paraded through the press, I soon learned there were other ways, equally painful, to be humiliated in the public eye.

While I myself remained the Colonel's greatest single secret, he'd many others besides. He'd always had a love for rich living and fine things, and a dangerous attraction for speculations in land and finance. In a way, I think he believed himself equal to any great English aristocrat in taste and refinement, and entitled to all the trappings that accompanied that refinement, no matter the cost.

There was no doubt that he possessed a brilliant mind, educated and precise. Yet like too many other men before him and since, he believed that brilliance in one area—in his case, politics and the law—meant that he was equally wise in others. It was a special kind of arrogance, and a terrible flaw as well, as all New York soon came to understand.

He listened to most any rascal who presented himself as a gentleman, and who invited him to invest in a tract of land that was certain to be increased tenfold in value in no time at all. He craved the easy reward without the unpleasant bother of toil. He trusted where he shouldn't trust, and let himself be dazzled and seduced by false promises like the most foolish of maidens. To make it worse, like all gentlemen, he believed in standing by his friends, and signed as surety for their investments just as they signed for his, until their financial affairs were so tangled that if one of them were to fail, they all would be drawn down into disaster together.

It wasn't entirely the Colonel's fault. There were at that time certain upheavals in the country's finances that I myself couldn't begin to comprehend, but enough that made for great unease among both bankers and amateur investors like the Colonel. Regardless of the causes, the results soon became painfully apparent.

"There's men with wagons out front, missus," Alexis said one morning, finding me. "The Colonel's with them now, but he says you should come, too."

"Are they come with a delivery?" I asked. I was accustomed to that, a new marble-topped sideboard for the dining room or another Italian painting for the Colonel's gallery in the upstairs hall.

Alexis shook his head. "No, missus," he said. "Looks like they've come instead to take away."

I hurried up the stairs. The Colonel was standing in the center of the back parlor, his expression grim, while several rough-looking men were beginning to carry away the suite of Roman-style mahogany chairs covered in French silk.

"Mrs. Emmons," he said, speaking loudly in a fashion that I realized was meant for the carters' men to overhear. "I am making some, ah, adjustments to several of the rooms. Once these men have finished, I wish the room well swept and cleaned, and then closed for the present."

"Yes, sir," I said, agreeing for the sake of our audience. "As you wish, sir."

"Papa, what is happening?" Miss Burr appeared in the doorway to the parlor, her eyes wide at the sight of the familiar room being torn apart by strangers. "Who are these men? What are they doing?"

At once her father went to her side. "I've decided to sell a few things, Theo, that is all," he said, too heartily to fool anyone. "A change will benefit us all."

"But that man has Mama's looking glass!" she protested with distress. "Papa, you can't mean to let them take that away!"

As we soon learned, the Colonel had no choice. He tried to put the best light upon it for his daughter's sake, but even so the reality was unavoidable. He'd become so deeply in debt—"embarrassed" was the term he used—that he was forced to sell many of the furnishings to be able to keep the house itself. Most of the horses in his stable went to auction, as did the carriage. He'd sold other properties at a loss, mortgaged Richmond Hill itself, and leased a portion of the acreage to farmers. He'd even drawn his grown stepsons, Bartow and Frederick, into co-signing on one of his schemes, and now Frederick had likewise been forced to sell his own house and farm to make good on the bonds.

The Colonel's debts struck the lower household, too. One morning, Mr. Strong arrived at the house and asked for the two newest servants, Bet and Anny, to fetch their belongings and join him in the yard. We all wept as the two women were taken away to be sold, and never seen by us again.

To be sure, the Colonel was not the only New York gentleman in this predicament. There were some prominent families who lost everything they owned. But because of who he was, the Colonel's situation was widely reported in the papers, and gloated over by his political enemies, who held him up as an example of Democratic-Republican finances. He was called impecunious, a wastrel, a spendthrift, a debtor who could never be entrusted with the public good after so shamefully endangering his own family's estate.

Most painful to the Colonel, however, was the effect his losses had upon Miss Burr. Now a young woman, she didn't mourn the end of dancing lessons and new dresses from the mantua-maker, as some girls would. Instead, she thought only of the sorrows that had befallen her father and brothers, and lamented that she'd no fortune of her own to help relieve their suffering.

I understood, for I felt much the same way. I'd carefully saved both my wages and anything extra I'd been able to earn through sewing and cooking for others. Though I'd worked for years to save it, my own little security, I knew it was a pittance compared to his debts. Even one of those dining chairs would have been worth five times my savings. Still, one night I offered it to him. The gesture reduced him to near tears, shaking his head, as he'd held the small, battered tin box in his hands as if it contained the ransom of a king. As warmly and nobly as any gentleman in his situation could, he'd pressed the box back into my hands, and called me the most generous woman in Christendom.

In spite of all these woes, by late summer he'd thrown himself wholeheartedly into campaigning for a seat in the State Assembly. It was, fortunately, one election that had never been in doubt, and once he'd been declared the victor, he returned to Richmond Hill, and me, for the last few weeks before he'd take his new seat in Albany.

There were no merry celebrations at Richmond Hill that January, no rich dinners or fine wines or sprigs of mistletoe hanging in the doorways. Instead, the house was cold and ghostly quiet, the now-empty rooms echoing with the winter and the sounds of ice and snow rattling against the glass panes behind the latched shutters.

With Miss Burr visiting her cousins, the Colonel was living entirely in his old bedchamber upstairs, the only room that still kept a fire. He jested that he was in hibernation, and indeed he did put me to mind of some great bear waiting out the snows in his lair, gathering his own strength from the force of the winter.

There was no doubt he'd been bowed, but he still wasn't beaten. He'd never been a man to make a public show of either his disappointments or his triumphs, preferring to keep such things to himself as a gentleman should, and he didn't now, either, no matter how diminished his circumstances had become.

The cherrywood bedstead with silk hangings had long ago been sold, as had his desk, the tall chest of drawers, the washstand inspired by Pompeii, and all the rest of the furnishings. All that he'd kept were books—his as well as Mistress's—stacked in neat towers along the walls, and a few trunks and chests on the floor that contained personal belongings. To read and write his correspondence, he sat upon an old rush-bottomed chair with a portable desk balanced on his knees, and he slept in an old camp bed that must have dated back to Queen Anne's War.

I often lay there in that narrow bed with him during these last weeks, the two of us neatly curled together as we always had. He spoke to me about what he hoped to accomplish in the Assembly, whose support he meant to attract, and what influence he planned to wield. To him the empty house was not a reminder of what he'd lost, but a challenge for what he intended to regain. The loss of the actual paintings and furnishings hadn't meant nearly as much to him as the power and prestige that they'd represented.

Over and over again I heard of how he meant to take it all back and more besides, and with each telling his determination seemed to grow. He didn't intend to remain in the Assembly for long. He was considering running for governor again, and higher. He believed that President Adams was vulnerable, and that Vice President Jefferson's support was growing stronger by the day. If Mr. Jefferson became president, then he'd need another Democratic-Republican to run with him for the vice presidency.

As the Colonel lay beside me, his eyes were fierce as a hawk's with their intensity, and I didn't doubt that his ambition burned brighter than it ever had. When he vowed that he'd do whatever he found necessary to succeed, I believed him. It also made me uneasy, because I'd seen it before. This was the kind of talk that led him to the deepest of intrigues, and made him believe that no risk was too great to be taken. It was dangerous talk, because he believed it himself.

Yet I listened as I always had, with my palm resting upon his chest and his arm around my waist. I listened, and while I hoped he'd achieve all he desired, I prayed that no harm would come to him from it.

On the last day before he was to meet Miss Burr in the city, the sky was clear and blue and the air not as cold as it had been. The Colonel had bought Dutch-style skates with curving steel blades for Louisa and Jean-Pierre to use on the frozen pond at the bottom of the hill, and during the time he'd been here he'd patiently held each of them in turn as they'd learned to find their balance on the ice. Now I watched from the bank, as proud as any mother hen, as they darted about with the other children from the area who came to the pond.

I watched the Colonel skate, too. I'd been surprised to see that he had owned skates himself, and further, that he was an accomplished skater, cutting swift, graceful curves over the ice and around anyone else who was slower or less skilled—much, I realized, as he navigated through his life.

At last he sat on one of the rocks beside the pond and unbuckled his skates to come and stand by me.

"Thank you again for bringing the skates," I said. "Jean-Pierre in particular has wanted them ever since he could walk."

"He does well," the Colonel said with approval. "He's as fearless with this as in everything else."

"Sometimes a little fear would not be amiss, sir," I said ruefully. "There's a fine line between being fearless, and reckless."

"That's a line every man must decide for himself," he said, and though he was watching his son, I wondered if he was thinking of himself as well.

I drew my cloak more tightly around my shoulders. "For his sake, sir, I hope he decides soon."

The Colonel smiled, still intent on the skating children. "Mary, I cannot take you with me to Albany."

"No?" I asked, instantly disappointed. I'd never wanted to return to Albany. Yet as much as I enjoyed being here at Richmond Hill with my children, I'd little to do with the house closed up, and I'd missed the challenges and excitement of arranging his entertainments. Most of all, if I'd admit it, I missed being with him. "But I'd thought you need me—"

"I'm taking Theo with me instead," he said. "She's old enough now for the responsibility of greeting my guests, if I should have any."

I didn't tell him that if Miss Burr was ready for this responsibility, it was because I'd always been at her side, guiding and teaching her in place of her mother.

"Albany's a smaller place," I said instead, striving to find another reason. "There's a greater chance we'd be noticed."

"No, that's not it," he said, taking away the excuse that I could have believed. "I can scarcely afford decent lodgings for Theo and me. Albany's become every bit as dear as Philadelphia. You'll fare much better here with the children."

I nodded, numb, saying nothing, the both of us still staring forward at the children and not each other.

"I'll continue to send you an allowance for their care, of course," he said. "That will never change. They're my responsibility."

"Is this how it's to end, sir?" I asked, at last saying it aloud.

He turned quickly to face me.

"Nothing is ending," he said. "How did you come by such a notion?"

I nodded, accepting his explanation. But I understood. If he was making grand plans for a future that did not include me, I must begin in earnest to do the same.

That night, after everyone else was abed, I spread the latest newspaper from Philadelphia on the kitchen table, and wrote my first letter in reply to an advertisement for a housekeeper.

CHAPTER 25

City of New York
July 1799

There was not much I recalled of my grandmother. I had been very young when Ammatti had died, and more than thirty years, three oceans, and several continents now separated me from my memories of Pondicherry. But I hadn't forgotten how she'd warned me and my cousins that everything we did, both bad and good, would lead to the next like links in a chain we could never escape. As a child, I'd pictured the enormous anchor chains that I'd seen on the English ships in the harbor, with each massive link as large as I was tall, and my youthful imagination had imagined such a chain wrapping around me, an iron serpent of my misdeeds to drag me to the bottom of the sea.

Now, however, I saw only the wisdom in what my grandmother said. Everything that had happened in my life was one link after another, impossible to separate.

If I hadn't slipped in the puddle in Pondicherry and fallen into the light of Madame's carriage, she wouldn't have bought me from my uncle.

If I hadn't defended myself at Belle Vallée, then Major Prevost wouldn't have bought me for his wife.

If I hadn't been taken to New Jersey on the eve of the war, then I wouldn't have been noticed by Colonel Burr.

If I hadn't been used by him, I wouldn't have given birth to Louisa or Jean-Pierre.

The newer links were bright with my children. Now eleven, my daughter was already sufficiently skilled at cookery to be hired in even the largest of households. I'd even taught her what I knew of curries, so that that part of me, and of Ammatti, and of Orianne, who'd taught me on board the *Céleste,* would be part of her as well, another link in our shared chain. Yet still I held Louisa back, keeping her safe and close to me for a bit longer, remembering too well the perils to a girl at work where all around her were older.

Jean-Pierre was now seven. At Richmond Hill we were too far from the city for him to attend the free Negroes' school as I wished, and instead I taught him as best I could myself. I took books from the Colonel's room that would link Jean-Pierre to his father and his half sister both and together we read and learned of history, government, great men, and great thoughts. He'd been blessed with his father's intelligence, and the more he learned, the more he wished to know.

It grieved me that my son would never be permitted the education that his father had received. Because of me and my blood, there'd be no tutors, no schools for young gentlemen, no university. Already he showed the abilities that would have made him an admirable attorney like the Colonel, or a clergyman like his grandfather and great-grandfather, or even a physician, all fields that were sadly forbidden to him. While his eventual employment would be compelled to be more modest, I did want a good apprenticeship for him, so he could become a skilled tradesman with his own establishment, whatever that proved to be.

For now I made sure that he worked about Richmond Hill, weeding, cleaning the stable, fetching water to the kitchen, wherever a boy would be of use. I wanted him to understand that he'd never have the life of an idle gentleman, but must work for his living. I was sure he would somehow one day accomplish great things, and I wanted him to be prepared.

It was one more reason I wished to take him to Philadelphia, where there would be more opportunities for him. Alas, I'd no prospects there myself, nor had I heard further from Mrs. Madison. Although I answered every advertisement I found in the Philadelphia newspapers, I never received a single reply. I do not know if this was on account of my letters going awry, or that I currently resided in New York, or that, more directly, I was not found suitable.

Still I persevered, and put aside more coins in my little box, which was easier to do with the Colonel now so often away. From afar, through the newspapers that were still brought each week to Richmond Hill and set aside for the Colonel to read later, I followed all he continued to achieve, both in the Assembly and in the wider world as well.

While President Adams and the Federalists continued to contrive a war against France, the Colonel likewise continued to speak against it, and the outrageous measures instituted against the French people. The army that had lain dormant since the Revolution was revived, with President Washington as commander in chief, and Colonel Hamilton—now raised to be Major General Hamilton—second-in-command. The Colonel's reaction to this can well be imagined, yet for the good of the country he served with General Hamilton on the military committee in charge of improving New York's defenses. There was even talk of the Colonel being made a brigadier general, though in the end, nothing came of that, or of the nonexistent war, either.

The Colonel was also vocal against Federalist legislation that aimed to stifle the free press and criticism of the government, and prohibit foreign-born citizens from holding office. While aimed at prominent Republicans such as the Colonel's old friend in Congress Mr. Gallatin, the irony of these laws was the now-general Hamilton had himself been born on an island in the Caribbean. The Colonel spoke often, and he spoke eloquently, and while he was addressing the New York Assembly, his speeches were printed in Republican newspapers throughout the country.

But he was also involved in more local affairs. Because of its location so near to the sea, one of the greatest problems facing the city of New York was supplying drinkable water to its ever-increasing citizenry. A particularly deadly course of yellow fever in 1796 had led to demands for a privately run water company to bring clean water through a system of pipes to the city. The Colonel was a member of the group that was ultimately selected, called the Manhattan Company, and he personally shepherded the Company's charter through the Assembly to acceptance. The Company was unique in that it counted both Federalists and Republicans on its board of directors, a feature that the Colonel had insisted upon; one of the most prominent Federalists was General Hamilton's brother-in-law John Barker Church.

Nor was that the only part of the charter that was noteworthy. As the Colonel himself explained to me, the city of New York had only two banks, both controlled by Federalists. Anyone known to be a Republican had no recourse for loans or other banking needs. But the Colonel wisely added a small and overlooked amendment to the Manhattan Company's charter that permitted them to open a bank that would serve all New Yorkers, and not just wealthy Federalists.

The Federalists howled when this was discovered, but to me at that time it seemed both clever and fair, creating services that would benefit many rather than a few. I was proud of the Colonel for his perseverance. Others, of course, did not agree with the high esteem in which I held the Colonel, as I soon learned. To my sorrow, the Manhattan Company and what it stood for would lead to the next link in the chain of my life that could never be undone, no matter how I might wish it.

It was a fine September morning, already warm, with the trees just beginning to change color. Louisa and I were sitting in the folly on the hill, seaming long strips of linen for bedsheets. While the Colonel was slowly beginning to furnish the house again, the grounds were still neglected. The folly was in sorry need of fresh paint and repair, and long, curling strips of old white paint on the arches trembled in the breeze from the river. But the spot was a good place for sewing, shaded yet with plenty of light, and we sat on the benches with the lengths of linen billowing around us like clouds.

My humor matched the sunny day. The Colonel had spent much of last week in our company, and his presence had made all of us happy. He'd continued to come to Richmond Hill whenever he came down to the city from Albany, and during his recesses, too. The once-grand house remained largely unfurnished and neglected. There were no other guests when he visited, either, which, in a way, I preferred, because it meant that my children and I needn't share him with anyone else. He taught Jean-Pierre to ride and quizzed him on his studies, and he praised Louisa's pies and showed her how he always carried the fine linen handkerchief she'd worked for him. With me, he was as he'd always been, charming and ardent and demanding, too.

But this time was different. In my pocket was a secret. To my amazement, I'd finally received a reply to a letter I'd sent regarding a newspaper advertisement. It had come from a woman named Mrs. Tyler, a member of an abolitionist society in Philadelphia, who was particularly interested in speaking further with me. I'd read it first in disbelief, and since then I'd read it over and over with growing excitement and pleasure. This could be the opportunity I'd sought, that I'd always told myself I desired above all else.

Yet this same letter also changed everything about the Colonel's visit. When I watched him with my children, I thought of how fine a memory of him this would be for them. When he looked at me and smiled, I thought of how dull my life would be without that smile to brighten it. And when I lay with him, I considered how this could be the final time we were together like this. It now would be my decision when I left, my choice, and the power of that knowledge was exhilarating and daunting at the same time.

He had spent the last few days at Partition Street, there for the opening of the Manhattan Company for business on Wall Street. I'd wished I'd been with him for the inevitable dinners and other celebrations, but he'd told me that others who could afford it better than he would be the hosts, and that he'd only be a guest.

"Is that the Colonel?" Louisa asked when we heard a rider in the distance, and at once she jumped up to look through one of the arched windows to the road below. "He said he'd come back if he could."

"I'd be surprised if he returned this soon," I said, but joined her at the window. It was in fact the Colonel, greeted at once by Jean-Pierre, who'd been raking leaves before the house. The Colonel pulled the boy up before him on the saddle, and together they trotted back to the stable to water the horse.

"We'll finish here, Louisa," I said, beginning to bundle up the strips of linen, "and then join them in the house."

With the seams finished a short time later, we carried the bas-

kets with the linen back to the house, and then went up the stairs to
the Colonel's bedchamber. I could hear the Colonel talking to Jean-
Pierre, his voice calm and measured as he explained something. I
smiled, for I loved to hear them together. The door was ajar, and
not wanting to interrupt whatever lesson he was imparting, I gently
pushed it the rest of the way open myself.

The windows were open wide, and sunlight filled the room.
The Colonel stood in his shirtsleeves behind Jean-Pierre, bending
slightly over his son's back, their profiles nearly identical.

With his arm outstretched and taking aim through the open
window, my son held one of his father's dueling pistols.

"Oh, sir, no!" I cried, appalled. I shielded Louisa behind me in
the doorway, determined to keep at least one of my children safe.
"What are you doing with my son?"

Startled, Jean-Pierre looked to me, and let the heavy pistol wob-
ble in his hand. At once the Colonel reached down and took the
gun from him, pushing back the safety on the gunlock.

The gun had been loaded. He'd given my son a loaded pistol—
a loaded *dueling* pistol—to fire.

"No harm," the Colonel said mildly.

"No harm?" I repeated, all I could do in my fury. "No *harm?*"

"You shouldn't have interrupted us, Mama," Jean-Pierre said,
disappointed and resentful. "The Colonel said I'd the aim exactly
right, and all I had left to do was to squeeze the trigger."

The Colonel smiled proudly. "It *was* exactly right," he said.
"Level and true. I couldn't do better myself."

"You will tomorrow in Weehawken, sir," Jean-Pierre said, his
eyes filled with adoration. "Mr. Church won't have a chance against
you."

The Colonel chuckled. "Now, now, don't say that. The goal is
to redeem lost honor, not to murder the other gentleman where he
stands."

"What are you talking about, sir?" I demanded, though they'd
already told me enough that I knew. "Tell me. Have you planned a
duel with Mr. Church?"

"Mr. Church said Colonel Burr's guilty of bribery in the Assembly," Jean-Pierre said, delighted to have this knowledge that I
didn't. "Colonel Burr had to challenge him to make him apologize."

I stared at the Colonel, my heart racing so fast that I could scarcely breathe.

"Is this true, sir?" I demanded. "That you have challenged John Barker Church to a duel?"

He tipped his head to one side, and smiled. "It will amount to nothing, Mary, I promise you. I wouldn't have troubled you about it at all, except that I'd left my pistols here. Church has no more wish to harm me than I do him, but he cannot be allowed to speak of me in that fashion."

He smiled, trying to coax me into agreement. On this day, it didn't work. I'd seen too many deaths that could not be helped, too much agony and suffering and sorrow, and I couldn't bear to watch him now taunt death as if it were one more gamble, one more game. All I could imagine was the breast of his white shirt and waistcoat splattered with a great, growing blotch of his blood as the ball from this gun tore through him and I could do nothing as his life spilled away, one agonizing drop after another.

Even worse, I imagined my son, my beautiful, innocent son, trained by his father to do this same dreadful act. To imagine Jean-Pierre holding this gun as he aimed at some other woman's beautiful son, and the moment he squeezed the trigger . . .

I was crying now, hot tears sliding down my cheeks unchecked, because I knew what I must do. In a matter as important as this, the Colonel hadn't cared what I believed or wanted. As always, he'd put his own desires before mine, and I couldn't deny it any longer.

With Mrs. Tyler's letter in my pocket, he'd left me no choice.

"No more, sir," I said, my voice breaking and my heart with it. "You've gone too far, and—and no more."

Before he could change my mind, before he could make me forgive him one more time, I turned away and ran down the stairs.

Having found the pistols he'd come for, the Colonel departed for the city later that afternoon. I didn't see him again, though both Jean-Pierre and Louisa said he'd been very sorry he'd upset me. "Upset": I suspected that was their word, not his, and pathetically insufficient for all that I felt toward him.

We all were quiet at dinner in the kitchen, wondering what would happen the next evening on that flat stretch of ground in

Weehawken, on the far side of the North River in New Jersey where New York gentlemen went to do their foolishness. After my children had eaten, I told them to pack their clothes and belongings, one trunk for each. I could see the question in their eyes, questions that they didn't dare ask of me.

They learned soon enough. I woke them early, before dawn, and bid them climb sleepily into the wagon, using their trunks as benches. I paid Jem to drive us into the city and to the docks, where I quickly found us passage on a sloop bound for Philadelphia.

The tides and winds were with us, and within three days we'd found our way to a lodging house on Dock Street that I recalled as welcoming to free people. The following morning, I presented myself at Mrs. Tyler's door with her letter in my hands. She knew I'd been last employed by Colonel Burr, but she was much more concerned with my abilities in the kitchen than my history. She agreed to take me on trial with Louisa as my scullery maid. Included in my employment were two large rooms behind the kitchen, more than enough for the three of us. I could not believe my good fortune, and at once resolved to prove my worth to my new mistress through industry and skill.

As soon as I could, I enrolled Jean-Pierre in the Negro school, and I made sure we began to attend the Christian services held by the Free African Society every Sunday. My children had lived too long apart from others at Richmond Hill, and I wanted them to have friends who were free like them, among people they could grow to trust and respect.

It took twenty-two days for the Colonel to find us. I knew because I kept track, counting off each day I'd been away from him before I slept. I had left him no letter of farewell or explanation, in part because of my anger when we'd left, but also because I hadn't wanted to give him any clues as to our whereabouts.

He came himself to Philadelphia and the Tylers' house, and called not upon me, but Mrs. Tyler. She'd recognized him at once. Senators were celebrated in the capital city, and the Colonel had been one of the most memorable. Mrs. Tyler had impressed me from the first as being a practical lady, and I suspect she'd quickly guessed both my past and the role of the Colonel in it. She'd shown him to her front parlor and given him tea, and then had a maidservant summon me to meet her in the smaller back parlor, where the family dined.

"Mrs. Emmons," she said. "Senator Burr has called, and wishes to see you."

I stood before her, my hands tightly clasped over my apron. I resolved to be strong, yet to think that he was here, waiting in the next room for me, was almost too much for me.

"Thank you, ma'am," I said. "But I do not wish to see him."

"He predicted you'd say that," Mrs. Tyler said. "He told me that if you did, then I was to give you this."

She held a letter out to me. I recognized the creamy white stock he ordered from London, and the crimson wafer stamped by the gold seal he habitually wore on his watch chain. Only two words were written on the face, in his familiar slanting hand: *Mrs. Emmons.*

How it tempted me, that letter! In all the years I'd known him, he'd never once written to me. With his dread of committing things to paper, the fact that he'd done this was proof of how much he wished me back. I knew what would happen if I took that letter, cracked the seal, and read what he'd written.

I kept my hands clasped tight, so tight my knuckles ached, and shook my head.

"If you please, ma'am," I said. "I'll ask you to return the letter to him. And—and to thank him for his trouble."

She nodded. "He also asked to see your children. I told him that was your decision."

"No!" I cried, forgetting myself. I'd left Louisa and Jean-Pierre in our quarters, and I wanted to rush to them now to make certain they were safe. "That is, I do not wish him to see them, not at all."

Again Mrs. Tyler nodded, her approval clear, and I thought of how fortunate I'd been to land in her household. Most other white ladies would have taken the Colonel's side against me.

"You are certain of this, Mrs. Emmons?" she asked. "That you wish me to send him away?"

I took a deep breath. "Yes," I said. "I am certain."

And I was.

Mrs. Burr

CHAPTER 26

Philadelphia
July 1, 1804

I took one last look around the kitchen to make sure everything was as it should be before I closed and bolted the door for the night. It was well past midnight now, with the moon sliding lower into the summer night sky. I was always the last one awake in the house, the last one to my bed. That never changed. No matter how weary I was, I found my own peace in this time, when the house was still and quiet and one more day was done.

Five years had passed since I'd left the Colonel. In truth, I still thought of him far more than I should, especially at night. This had been the hour when he'd most often sought my company, not only from what he'd called friendship, but also to share with me all his plans for his future.

From a distance, I had followed the Colonel's career through the newspapers. He'd climbed to the very top of the glory he'd always craved, but his fall had been precipitous. In 1800, he had indeed run for the presidency, tying Mr. Jefferson for that great prize. Only a lengthy process through Congress had finally granted the presidency to Mr. Jefferson, and by a single vote the Colonel was made vice president. Because of the acrimony of that election, however, it had become increasingly clear that he would not be endorsed again by the Democratic-Republicans for the next election. Earlier this year, he had tried one more attempt to recoup his political power, running for governor of New York, only to be roundly defeated there as well.

Yet it wasn't just the disenchantment of the voters that filled the newspapers. At only seventeen, Miss Burr had married a gentleman named Mr. Joseph Alston, who had taken her far away from New York to his home in South Carolina. I could imagine how lonely the Colonel must be without her, left behind and alone in his great echoing house. Perhaps that loneliness was why his name had been linked to charges of influence and bribery and every other kind of political intrigue, financial misdoings, and personal immorality. He was said to host debauched balls with prostitutes at Richmond Hill. There were even rumors that he was, at last, bankrupt.

I reminded myself that this was what had finally forced me to leave him. Desperation can drive men to acts they'd not ordinarily consider, and the Colonel had clearly become a desperate man. I'd done what was right for myself and my children, and I'd been fortunate to escape when I had. He'd always promised to support my children. He hadn't. Perhaps because of how I'd left, he'd never sent them or me so much as a single dollar, and now I doubted he could even if he wished to.

Yet there was some small, shameful part of me that remembered other things: how tenderly he'd held Louisa when she'd been newly born, how we'd turned to each other for comfort in bad times and good, how his desire for me could make me overlook everything else that was wrong.

One evening, I paused on the kitchen's doorstep, gazing out at the small garden between the Tylers' house and the next. A man's shadow moved at the garden's brick wall, and the gate squeaked open. Despite the July heat, the man was wearing a dark hat and long dark cloak that shrouded him into the night. Whoever he might be, he'd no business here at this hour, and I quickly began to retreat inside the house.

"Mary, wait, please." The man pulled off his hat and stepped into the moonlight, and I gasped aloud as the Colonel came toward me.

I was shocked to see the toll his life had taken upon him during these last years. Though his eyes seemed as keen as ever, his once-handsome face was weary and drawn, with deep lines of melancholy carved on either side of his mouth. His hair was now more gray than black, receding higher upon his head. As if to balance that he now wore full side-whiskers nearly to his jaw, their stylishness in sharp contrast to his old-fashioned ribbon-tied queue.

"You look well, Mary Emmons," he said, his voice as deep and seductive as I remembered. "Clearly fate has treated you far better than it has treated me."

"Please, sir, you shouldn't be here, not now," I pleaded, keeping my voice low from fear I'd wake the rest of the household or, worse, Jean-Pierre and Louisa. "I have my position to consider. I cannot let Mrs. Tyler find me here with you."

"It's not as easy as that," he said. "You see, we must talk, you and I."

I knew too well where that could lead, and I drew back and into the house. He began to reach for me, to grab my arm or person the way he would have done without thinking in the past. But to my surprise, he stopped, his hand paused for a long moment in midair before he finally lowered it.

"Please, Mary," he said in a weary, urgent whisper. "I don't have much time."

I should have closed the door against him then, but I didn't.

"What is it, sir?" I asked. "Are you in some difficulty?"

He smiled. "How well you know me, Mary," he said. "Perhaps better than anyone else alive."

That gave me a small anxious chill. "You haven't answered me, sir. Are you in distress, or trouble?"

"Nothing worth remark." He made a slight, dismissive shrug that was, to me, the greatest of lies. "The uncertain wheel of fate has spun away from me at present, but it will come back. It always has before, hasn't it?"

"It has, sir," I agreed softly. How could I do otherwise, when I saw the desperation so clearly in his eyes? Through his ambition and determination, he had always been able to push back against whatever ill fortune had stood in his path. But there was a melancholy about him now, a resignation that I had never before sensed in him.

"You see why I return to you, Mary," he said softly. "There is no artifice to you, no deceit. Even when you compel yourself to lie to me—as you so obviously have just now done—it is only from the most selfless kindness. Yet what have I done for you in return?"

"Oh, sir, don't," I said, my eyes filling with tears.

"No, Mary, you must listen," he said. "Regard this as my pitiful confession. I've come to an unavoidable time of reckoning in my life. It's all my own doing. I cannot fault, or credit, anyone other than myself. It grieved me mightily when you took our children and left me. I understood, of course. I'd given you every reason to go, and few to remain. Yet I've never blamed you, not for so much as an instant."

I listened in silence as his words pulled up old memories, old pain, and old joys, too. The first tear spilled from my eye and down my cheek and others soon followed. I let them fall unchecked, for they, too, were proof of what I'd shared with him, good and bad, and of what he was saying now.

"Do the children ever speak of me?" he asked with a poignancy I'd never expected. "Five years is an eternity in a young person's life."

"They do, sir," I said. "It was hardest on Jean-Pierre."

He smiled again, thinking of our son. "He'll be twelve soon, won't he?"

"This month, sir," I said proudly. "He's growing like a weed, too. Soon he'll be taller than I. And Louisa—Louisa is sixteen, a woman in her own right with a good place in Mrs. Fisher's household."

"I've not been much of a father, have I?" he said, his regret palpable. "Let me give them my name now, if nothing else."

I gasped, the second time tonight. "What are you saying, sir?"

"That is my reason for coming to you tonight, Mary," he said. "I wish for us to be married. Now, tonight, if you'll agree. You've never liked how our children falsely carried your husband's name. Now they will have mine. I'll expect nothing of you. You may continue your life here just as you are. Please, Mary. Let me do this."

"Why, sir?" I asked, stunned. "How could such a thing even be arranged at this hour?"

"I told you," he explained. "My time in Philadelphia is short. I'm due back in New York for some infernal celebration of the Fourth of July with the Society of Cincinnati. If I do not appear, my absence will be noticed."

"You've never cared before what others thought, sir," I said. "You *are* in trouble, aren't you?"

"Not yet," he admitted. "If—when—my fortunes change, I will do my best for our children. All I can offer them now is this."

In the shadows, his eyes were so dark as to be black, yet still I could see the rare truth in them. There was no doubt that our children would benefit by having his name, but this proposal signified more than that to him. He'd called it a reckoning. I saw it for what it was: his way to right past wrongs.

For the briefest of moments, I thought of the love, true love, that every woman desires, and what I'd had long ago with Lucas Emmons. There *was* regard and respect between the Colonel and me. It had grown over the years like a tenacious vine of ivy that twines and increases against every attempt to stop it. I couldn't deny that it remained there still, and I suspect he couldn't, either. But love, such as should exist between a wife and husband, was not, and never had been.

I couldn't forget the attentions—the "friendship"—that he had first forced upon me. I remembered how he'd acted against my wishes and my will, and while his first wife had been dying, too. I remembered how he'd seemed cruel and selfish. I couldn't deny that, either. Being who I was, I'd never had illusions, nor did I want them.

Yet my children had come from this same friendship, the children I loved beyond reason and without any reservation. I'd always put them first in my life. Now I would again.

But my decision wasn't as simple as that. Until the Colonel had come to stand before me again tonight, I hadn't realized how hard I'd tried to forget what he'd done to me. All the fear and pain that he had caused me, all the misery and hurt and resentment and shame, knotted into a burden that I'd carried in guilty silence for twenty years. Leaving him hadn't been enough. I needed the salvation that would come with forgiveness. If this was his final chance, then it was likely mine as well.

We were married by candlelight in the parlor of a house I did not know, by a minister I did not recognize. I signed the record; I have the paper still. As the short service rolled over us, I was the one who took the Colonel's hand, my fingers slipping into his with the old familiarity. He glanced at me, surprised, then smiled.

Oh, that smile.

When it was done and we were man and wife, he smiled again. I didn't. "I forgive you, sir," I said quickly, before I lost my courage. "For everything. You—you have my forgiveness."

I watched his expression shift from bewilderment to comprehension, and finally to a kind of humbled acceptance.

"Thank you, Mrs. Burr," he said softly before he kissed me, the most chaste kiss we'd ever shared.

I was crying again, but from peace, not sorrow. I thought once more of my grandmother's chain, and how she'd claimed it was impossible to break one link free of the one before it. For more than half my life, I'd been bound to Aaron Burr, and now, after a ceremony that should have united us, I wasn't.

There was nothing more beyond that. He returned to New York, and I to our sleeping children. To this day, I have not seen him again.

EPILOGUE

I try to listen to the fine words that my son is saying, words that are leaving all around me in awe and wonder at his eloquence. I hope he hasn't looked my way, as sons do with mothers, and seen from my face how far my thoughts had wandered from him.

But because it is July, my thoughts will always wander back to the Colonel, and what he did on a sunny July morning in 1804. Everyone knows of it, even now. Dressed in black silk, he had himself rowed across the North River to New Jersey, and met General Hamilton on the dueling ground at Weehawken. The Colonel shot the General, and then returned to Richmond Hill to dine with a cousin as if nothing remarkable or untoward had occurred. General Hamilton died the next day, surrounded by his weeping friends and family.

My husband (for so he was, though few ever knew it) was reviled as a villain, a demon, a coldhearted murderer who'd carefully planned to slay his rival. I don't believe that. Instead, I believe he'd thought he'd be the one to die. Why else would he have come to me as he had, only days before the duel? Why else would he have made that one final gesture for our children? Why else would my forgiveness matter to him as it did?

Yet it was the General who had died, and claimed his final revenge. By dying, he'd destroyed the Colonel, and condemned him to a life that is, for him, no life at all. He became an outcast. He was forced to flee New York, where creditors finally claimed his beautiful home at Richmond Hill. There was no further place for him in politics; how could there be?

Still the Colonel tried his best to turn that wheel of fate to his advantage one more time. He went to the western frontier, and caused such mischief there that President Jefferson had the Colonel—his former friend and vice president!—arrested and tried for treason. Of course the Colonel slipped free, as he always did, though now he is called a traitor as well as a murderer.

But the tragedy of his life grew darker still when his only grandson, the child Mrs. Alston had named after him, died of a fever. I grieved for her, poor lady. No mother deserves that sorrow. Soon after, Mrs. Alston herself was lost at sea while sailing to join her father in New York

They say the Colonel refused to believe her dead. They say he stood at the docks, day after day, a lonely figure in black waiting for her ship that never came.

They say he is cursed. They say he has outlived his wife and all his children, that he is alone, bitter, heartbroken, without comfort or solace.

They say he got exactly what he deserved.

I've heard that he has wandered farther still, to England, to France, to Germany. I've heard he has returned to New York, and that he even practices law again. I've heard that his health is poor, and his circumstances are so diminished that he lives in a boarding-house.

He has never written to me, nor do I expect him to. I do not see this as a fault, but rather one last gift, to spare me and our children the taint of his contact.

Jean-Pierre and Louisa are not as generous toward him as I. They are known by his name, as he wished, but their father's later actions have pushed aside whatever gentle memories of him they might possess. They know only part of my story, but enough of it that they resent him for how he treated me. I regret that, for when they were young and we lived together he showed them both much love and kindness.

He would be proud of them, I think, of how they have prospered. Jean-Pierre is a barber by trade, with a shop of his own and a flourishing custom that caters only to white gentlemen, while Louisa is housekeeper to Mrs. Fisher, in one of the finest houses in Philadelphia. Both are married; both have given me grandchildren; both are respected by their friends and associates. I could not ask for more.

Jean-Pierre's voice is rising louder now, drawing me back to this day. He must be close to the end of his speech, and I must pay attention now. If I can recall the ending to be able to praise it to him later, then perhaps he won't realize how much of the middle I didn't hear. Freedom: yes, he always speaks of freedom, and I am proud of him for it.

Because his voice is so much like his father's, I cannot help but think of the Colonel one more time. He was blessed to be born into a family of wealth and prominence, with every gift and grace a gentleman could possess, while I had nothing but myself. For many years, our lives were tied together, and there would have been few who envied me over him. Yet now we are both near the ends of our days, and I am the one who is blessed.

I am the one who is truly free.

AFTERWORD

In the history of her times, Mary Emmons (c. 1760–1835) is only the faintest of whispers. You won't find her (or her other name, Eugénie Beauharnais) included in any of the standard biographies of Aaron Burr. No known eighteenth-century documents, diaries, or letters mention her. No record of their marriage remains, nor of Aaron Burr acknowledging either her or their children, or offering them his financial support. She never sat for a portrait, and her appearance is a mystery.

Yet she survived through her children, and in the memories of her descendants. There are only a handful of facts known of her, and even those are uncertain: that she was born in India, that she was brought from the West Indies to the American colonies by Major Jacques-Marc Prevost, that she had two children, Louisa Charlotte (c. 1788–1878) and Jean-Pierre (1792–1864), with Aaron Burr. At some point after the death of Burr's first wife, Theodosia Prevost, he and Mary were married. She was called "colored" and "East Indian," but both could have meant a variety of things in late-eighteenth-century America. By the 1790s, she was a free woman living in Philadelphia.

And that's it.

Obviously, then, the majority of Mary's story as I've chosen to tell it is my invention. Yet in a way, I didn't just tell Mary's story. Thousands of other women of color like her were brought to this country against their will, and yet despite unspeakable hardship, cruelty, and abuse they survived, and endured. Many of these women also inspired me, and their histories became woven into Mary's narrative.

More is known of Mary's two children, who each went on to lead lives worthy of their own books. Her daughter, Louisa Charlotte Burr (c. 1788–1878), married Francis Webb, a prominent leader in Philadelphia's African American community. They and their children were among the hundreds of free African Americans who relocated to Haiti in 1824 as part of an ambitious but ultimately doomed emigration experiment. They returned to Philadelphia again in 1826.

Respected for her resourcefulness as well as her housekeeping skills, Louisa was employed for most of her life in the socially elite household of Mrs. Elizabeth Powel Francis Fisher. Louisa also served as the nursemaid to Mrs. Fisher's only child, Joshua Francis Fisher, who was so devoted to Louisa that he later provided her with an allowance and an annuity for the remainder of her long life.

Jean-Pierre (or John Pierre, or John) Burr (1792–1864), was not only a successful barber, but also became a nationally respected leader, abolitionist, and activist. He was a founder of the Pennsylvania Anti-Slavery Society, and he and his wife, Hetty, participated in numerous organizations to promote civil rights. He was an active member of the Underground Railroad in Philadelphia, and because of his demeanor and light skin he was able to impersonate a white gentleman to escort runaways toward freedom. Much like his father, John-Pierre was an accomplished and persuasive speaker, and he founded the Demosthenian Institute as a literary society that also helped educate young black men and train them to become public speakers. Shortly before his death, he was among the prominent black men listed on Frederick Douglass's famous "Men of Color, to Arms!" recruitment broadside, printed during the Civil War.

Although Mary died before her grandchildren were grown, their accomplishments were also impressive. Louisa's daughter, Elizabeth Susan Webb (1818–88), was a well-educated amateur poet and a professional dressmaker who owned her own shop. Louisa's youngest child, Frank J. Webb (1828–94), became a newspaper editor and an educator, but he is most remembered today for having written *The Garies and Their Friends* (1857), the second novel to be published by an African American author. As a protégé of Harriet Beecher Stowe, Frank and his wife were feted in London as well as America.

All of Jean-Pierre's children (he is believed to have had at least nine) were involved in the abolitionist movement. Several owned their own businesses, and among them were dressmakers, barbers, and carpenters. Mary would have been intensely proud, and, I suspect, a little in awe at the scope of her legacy.

The Colonel was not nearly as fortunate.

Vice President and Lieutenant Colonel Aaron Burr (1756–1836) was as close to an aristocrat as colonial America produced. He was descended from early New England colonists, and his family on both sides were illustrious, wealthy, and accomplished. His grandfather was the famed theologian, preacher, and philosopher Jonathan Edwards, and his father, also a notable minister and educator, was one of the founders of the College of New Jersey (now Princeton University) and the school's second president.

Although orphaned as a baby, Aaron always seemed destined for great things. He was a precocious scholar, completing his baccalaureate degree by age sixteen. He was a gifted speaker, and he was handsome and charming, if small in stature. He first considered the ministry, then shifted to a career in law, before the outbreak of the American Revolution inspired him, like so many others, to enlist in the Continental Army.

He soon added bravery and determination to his attributes, serving with courage and spirit as part of the ill-fated expedition to Quebec led by General Richard Montgomery and Colonel Benedict Arnold, and in later actions around Manhattan. An appointment to the staff of Commander in Chief George Washington seemed a fitting reward for his heroics, and the sure path to success for a young officer. But for whatever reason, Washington never warmed to Burr, nor Burr to the General, and Burr soon resigned from his post for another field command as a lieutenant colonel. Again he served with notable bravery, and displayed a gift for commanding men.

Yet by 1779, Burr had had enough. Disillusioned by the politics within the army as well as in poor health, he resigned his commission, and returned to his law studies, being admitted to the bar in Albany, New York, in 1782. While still in the army, he had met his intellectual equal in Theodosia Bartow Prevost (1746–94), the wife of an English officer. In time the two became lovers, and when her husband died they wed.

Once the couple and their daughter, also named Theodosia, moved to New York City, Burr's legal career began to rise, and his political career swiftly followed as I've described through Mary's eyes. In an age when American politicians chose to govern at an idealistic distance from their constituents, Burr was the first to be openly ambitious, and reveled in the dirty work of campaigning, dealmaking, and trading favors for power. He was exceptionally good at it, too, and he very nearly did seize the ultimate prize in the presidential election of 1800. He was tied in electoral votes with Thomas Jefferson, and the election was finally decided through the House of Representatives, as was the process at that time. By a single vote, Jefferson was named president, and Burr his vice president and president of the Senate.

Neither man trusted the other, and Jefferson did his best to exclude Burr from taking any serious part in the government. Jefferson also made it clear that Burr would not be endorsed by the Democratic-Republicans in the next presidential election. Burr must have known his political career was sinking fast, and ran instead for governor of New York. He lost there as well, and in the summer of 1804 he found himself in the unenviable position of not only having lost his power and position, but teetering precariously on the edge of financial bankruptcy as well. When he challenged his longtime rival and gadfly Alexander Hamilton to a duel, he seemed to be a man with little left to lose.

What happened on that morning in 1804 is the one thing that's most remembered about Aaron Burr. Burr's shot ripped through Alexander Hamilton's abdomen and lodged against his spine, paralyzing him; he died the following afternoon. Whether by Hamilton's design, or by fate, his shot came nowhere near Burr. While the doctor and Hamilton's friends tended to him, Burr's friends ushered him swiftly away, across the Hudson River, and back to Richmond Hill.

On that first day, Burr believed he'd only wounded Hamilton. He'd no idea the wound would prove fatal, and indeed, there were many conflicting rumors around the city regarding the duel. But once Hamilton died, Burr soon realized that what he'd regarded as an affair of honor between two gentlemen was instead perceived by the horrified public as murder. He quickly fled New York, where charges had already been filed against him, and went south. His creditors immediately claimed everything he'd left behind. Although in time the murder charges were dropped and he continued to finish out his duties as vice president, he was in effect as completely ruined as a gentleman could be. He never publicly expressed any remorse for shooting Hamilton, and spoke dryly of his "old friend Hamilton, whom I shot."

In self-imposed exile, Burr traveled abroad, seeing the sights and conducting love affairs. When he returned to America, he dodged creditors under an assumed name, then headed west on an expedition that included inspiring supporters and raising a private militia, but whose ultimate purpose remains cloudy. Whatever he was doing, however, was sufficient for President Jefferson—who still neither liked nor trusted Burr—to have him hunted down, arrested, and tried for treason. Burr was acquitted, but there would be no further grand adventures. He returned to New York and practiced law, and lived on old memories and friendships.

In one last attempt to recoup the glory of his former life, at age seventy-seven he married Madame Eliza Jumel, a wealthy widow nineteen years his junior, and with a past as checkered and opportunistic as his own. (At this time, Mary Emmons Burr was still alive in Philadelphia, but after more than thirty years apart it's doubtful Burr worried overmuch about being regarded as a bigamist.) Within a few months, however, Madame Jumel had had enough of Burr spending her fortune, and tossed him out. His health had already deteriorated, and a stroke left him paralyzed and unable to speak. He died in a boardinghouse on Staten Island on September 14, 1836—the same day his divorce from Madame Jumel became final.

Burr's final thoughts or regrets, like so many other things about him, remain a mystery. Unlike most of his contemporaries among the Founders who made certain to record their thoughts, actions, and beliefs for posterity, Burr was reluctant to leave a paper trail. His letters often include cautions to the recipient about keeping the contents confidential, or that he had more to share later in person. Some of the papers he did choose to preserve were reportedly lost at sea. He gave another batch for safekeeping to a friend, who in turn prudishly destroyed the ones that he deemed unsavory, immoral, or detrimental to Burr.

Burr also had enemies such as Hamilton, Jefferson, and their supporters who were all too willing to tarnish his reputation however they could. The fact that Burr did little to defend himself makes it a special challenge today to hunt for the man he truly was.

Unlike Alexander Hamilton, Burr did not leave a wife and children eager to promote his reputation for posterity. He outlived his wife Theodosia Bartow Prevost Burr by four decades. It's a tantalizing historical what-if?: would the educated and politically savvy Theodosia have influenced and perhaps preserved Burr's career had she survived? More important for Mary Emmons, would he have remained faithful to his wife had she been healthy?

The life of their only surviving daughter, Theodosia Burr Alston (1783–1813), was even more tragically short. Brilliant, charming, and endlessly devoted to her father, Theo had shocked her New York friends in 1801 by marrying at age seventeen. Joseph Alston (1779–1816) was a wealthy planter from South Carolina, and there were unkind whispers that Theo wed him to ease her father's financial woes. Surviving letters prove that there was genuine affection between Theo and Alston. But soon after the birth of their only son—Aaron Burr Alston—Theo's health rapidly declined, much as her mother's had done. Theo's son died of a fever in 1812. Grieving and ill, she attempted to return to New York to be with her father. She took passage on a ship that was lost at sea in December 1813, and Theo, only twenty-nine, disappeared with it. Her husband died three years later.

And once again, Burr lived on while those dearest to him perished.

I wonder, too, what Theo might have achieved had she survived. At the time of her death, her husband had just been elected governor of South Carolina. Given her own education and her husband's wealth and position, would she have become an advocate for women's rights, or perhaps, in time, even abolition?

For the people enslaved by the Burrs, abolition and manumission remained an empty hope. Although surviving records are sadly incomplete, it appears that a succession of enslaved servants lived and worked in the household. Their exact numbers aren't known, and a handful of single names that appear casually in letters by the Burrs are the only record of their existence. Their presence as characters within this book is, again, my invention. But one thing is for certain: When Burr put his affairs in order before his duel with Hamilton, he could have left instructions for the manumission, or freedom, of his enslaved servants. Instead, he specified that they be sent from New York to his daughter in South Carolina, and deeper into the institution of slavery.

Could there be a more determined contrast between Burr's decision and the path chosen by Mary and her children?

Mary's story has not been an easy one to write, yet often the greatest challenges prove to be the most rewarding. I can only hope that Mary herself would agree.

Susan Holloway Scott
October 2018

ACKNOWLEDGMENTS

Creating and telling Mary Emmons's story was not an undertaking I could have completed alone. I've been endlessly fortunate to have benefited from the assistance and support of many scholars, librarians, curators, interpreters, and other experts, and I'm particularly grateful to those who shared their knowledge and research to help bring Mary and her world to life. I also could not have completed this book without the support and good humor of good friends.

Kimberly Alexander
Laura Auricchio
Anne Bentley
Kelly Bolding
Donna M. Campbell
Mary Hardy Carter
Loretta Chekani
Donah Zack Crawford
Christopher Davalos
Erica A. Dunbar
Linda Eaton
Tiffany Fisk
Sara Georgini
Annette Gordon-Reed
Victoria Harty
Linda Hocking
Neal T. Hurst
Carl Robert Keyes
Timothy Logue
Kathie Ludwig
Michael McCarty
Philip C. Mead
Christopher Moore

Barbara Scherer
Jessie Serfilippi
Matthew Skic
Mariam Touba
Mark Turdo
Michael W. Twitty
Janea Whitacre
Sarah Woodyard
Hope Wright

Additional thanks to the staffs of the following historic sites, libraries, and other institutions:

The African American Museum in Philadelphia
The Colonial Williamsburg Foundation
Columbia University Rare Book & Manuscript Library
The David Library of the American Revolution
The Earl Gregg Swem Library, College of William & Mary
Firestone Library, Princeton University
Fraunces Tavern Museum
The Hermitage
Independence National Historical Park
The John D. Rockefeller Jr. Library, Colonial Williamsburg
The Litchfield Historical Society
Monmouth Battlefield State Park
Morris-Jumel Mansion
The Museum of the American Revolution
The Museum of the City of New York
The National Constitution Center
The National Museum of African American History and
    Culture
National Museum of American History
The New York Public Library
The New-York Historical Society
The Pennsylvania Historical Society
Schuyler Mansion State Historic Site
Valley Forge National Historical Park
Winterthur Museum, Garden, and Library

Connect with Us

Visit us online at
KensingtonBooks.com
to read more from your favorite authors, see books
by series, view reading group guides, and more.

Join us on social media
for sneak peeks, chances to win books and prize packs,
and to share your thoughts with other readers.

facebook.com/kensingtonpublishing
twitter.com/kensingtonbooks

Tell us what you think!

To share your thoughts, submit a review,
or sign up for our eNewsletters, please visit:
KensingtonBooks.com/TellUs.